CRYPTURES

JW GRODT

CRYPTURES

iUniverse books may be ordered through booksellers or by contacting:

iUniverse
1663 Liberty Drive
Bloomington, IN 47403
www.iuniverse.com
1-800-Authors (1-800-288-4677)

Because of the dynamic nature of the Internet, any web addresses or links contained in this book may have changed since publication and may no longer be valid. The views expressed in this work are solely those of the author and do not necessarily reflect the views of the publisher, and the publisher hereby disclaims any responsibility for them.

The cover artwork was created by Derek S. Castro from Brazil, his work is featured on Deviant Art.

Any people depicted in stock imagery provided by Thinkstock are models, and such images are being used for illustrative purposes only. Certain stock imagery © Thinkstock.

ISBN: 978-1-4917-7869-2 (sc)
ISBN: 978-1-4917-7870-8 (hc)
ISBN: 978-1-4917-7868-5 (e)

Library of Congress Control Number: 2015916612

Print information available on the last page.

iUniverse rev. date: 12/24/2016

CONTENTS

CRYPTURE 1

Crazy Pete

CHAPTER 1
THE PLACE

Day One

My name is Clark Masson. Today, June 29, 2015, will be my seventy-fifth birthday, and the doctors told me earlier this month that I have perhaps one—maybe two years, at best—left on this earth. Then, I pray, I will dwell in the house of the Lord with my wife, Sarah. Seems I have a rare form of cancer for which, as of now, there is no known cure. But my current state has nothing to do with the story I'm about to tell you; it only gives me the freedom to tell it.

My strange but true story started when I was a kid—my eighth birthday, to be exact, June 29, 1948. It's a story that took place in Dead Plains, Nevada, a small desert town surrounded by mountains. This was a town that grew up overnight when gold was discovered there, and it disappeared just as quickly. Only it wasn't that the gold ran out.

In 1948, the population of Dead Plains was 1,885. By 1960, this town no longer existed; it was no longer shown on any map, and there were no more buildings of any kind. The two-lane road that once took you there no longer exists. In other words, there is no evidence that anyone ever lived there or that a town ever existed there.

If you weren't born there and never had any reason to drive through there prior to 1960, then you've probably never heard of it.

Even before 1960, most maps didn't show it, because it was such a small, uninviting little place. As I said, nobody officially lives there now, only whatever animals or insects can survive its climate and conditions. Today there's virtually no trace that humankind was ever there; it's as barren as it was in the days before people.

I vowed that one day I would tell this tale for the entire world to hear, to know of it and what happened there on that little dot too insignificant to be on a map that one week in the summer of 1948.

Since I need not fear anyone anymore, I can use what time God has given me to tell my story—or at least the part of the story that has never been told and should be. I mean to set aside the time to see that it's published. I have the plan and the money to see that my story is told. So let me begin.

Right after my diagnosis was confirmed, I flew to the airport nearest to that place that doesn't exist. While there I visited a company that makes headstones. Then I rented a Jeep and drove to the spot where my story took place, to see what remained in that location today. I found nothing but a desert surrounded by mountains. That's today; let me take you back to that summer of 1948.

Most kids who were born in this desolate place left after they reached the age of majority—sooner if they were fortunate enough to have parents who decided enough was enough or if they got good opportunities elsewhere. Many got out, but it seemed just enough stayed to keep the dusty little desert town alive. During those days of the Old West, that precious metal, gold, had been found here in great abundance. The town grew up and looked like many of the towns in the days of the Wild West. I was told that the town had once supported a population of nearly ten thousand folks.

After World War II, people slowly began to return here. My father told me they returned because they had real estate or had been left some real estate, some perhaps because this was where they'd grown up. Some even believed there was still gold to be found. Some came because the land was dirt cheap, and it wasn't far from places where people could find work, like Vegas. Only about a thousand or so came but enough to need a grocery store, a drugstore, a fast-food joint, a gasoline station—barely enough to function as a town. The state provided funds to build a small elementary school and for books and salaries for three teachers who taught first grade through eighth. The second floor of that two-story redbrick building was for ninth through twelfth grades. Folks had to travel to larger cities for all specialty items or anything other than the mere necessities.

In the gold-rush days, it was not uncommon for towns to pop up and then vanish just as quickly when the gold played out. Dead Plains was seemingly no different in that respect. When everyone else had left, one man stayed, the last gold miner. Crazy Pete, one old, unreliable drunk, was the only inhabitant of this old gold town prior to the end of WWII. Crazy Pete knew two important things that nobody believed. One was the gold hadn't played out.

Peter Brill had come to Death Plains in the belly of his mother during late 1850, a few years before the streets, houses, businesses, and mines became silent. Pete would tell me many years later that his dad, who taught him to mine gold, died in 1861 and his mom remarried within a year and died in 1863. He had no other family, so Pete learned to live on his own at the age of thirteen and was alone all his life, except for a time when he lived with an Apache woman. He always spoke fondly of her, and when anyone asked what happened, he would clam up and get drunk. Seems she'd been killed in a most brutal fashion.

In his old age, he still wandered the streets of Dead Plains because no one found him dangerous, just whacked out, crazy, loco, drunken, demented, or any other label you would like to attach. No one paid him much mind but the kids. It seems kids, when they reached the ages of about seven through ten, loved to sit at his feet and hear him tell his crazy tale of what had happened to the town way back when. They would then run home and tell their parents what Pete had told them, and the parents would simply laugh it off. Those parents who were born there and had heard the tale believed it in their youth. But as they got older, they were slowly convinced that it was bunk.

I remember the day I turned eight. That was when it started for me. My best friends, Wally, Larry, and Tommy, wanted to get me something for my birthday, but their family—like most here—was dirt poor, so they decided to surprise me.

That Saturday morning after breakfast, my three pals came by to see me. They brought a package of Hostess chocolate cupcakes, put one candle in each one, lighted them, and sang "Happy Birthday" to me. Then we cut the cupcakes in half and shared them. As I mentioned, we didn't have much money for things like presents, so we used our hands to build them, or we'd find them, or we'd come up with other ideas. The guys had decided that they would take me up to the mines in the hills and listen to old Crazy Pete tell his tale.

We all agreed that it sounded like a fun thing to do, so off we went. We rode our old beat-up bicycles up into the hills near the old Wolford Mine. Crazy Pete lived up there in an old miner's shack. He even had a mule. People said he still mined for gold and silver in the mountains and in some of the smaller mines, staying clear of the larger, deeper ones. He had told all who would listen to steer clear of them. We searched the hills and finally found him napping under an old mesquite tree. He heard us coming and jumped up, swearing at something he was calling a Zetroll and pointing his old rifle at us. We yelled out and told him our names and that we wanted him to tell the tale of the ghost town. Old Pete was reluctant at first but could be bribed with some whiskey, which my friend had stolen from his pop. The town was aware that when he told his tale, a bottle would help make the story much more interesting.

CHAPTER 2
THE TALE

Pete's eyes shone when Wally handed him the pint of bourbon. He grabbed it, ripped off the lid, and took a big, long pull from it. Then he said in his crackly old voice, "Okay, boys, gather round here."

We all found comfortable places to sit as old Pete readied himself to tell his tale, a tale that would lead to an adventure I could never forget—and I doubt you will either!

"Shucks, I tweren't even borned yet when me folks brung me here. I twas knee high ta a grasshopper when I first heerd da strange screams in da night. It twere a busy town, and da folks twas real nice, and everyone twas a gettin' rich from that thar gold and silver. Why, thar twas mines all through them thar hills. But tweren't till they opened da Wolford Mine that things done begun ta happen. Old Jim Wolford started that thar mine, just he and his brother, Ollie. They struck er rich! They told stories of chunks of that stuff perten near da size of my dang fist, and they twas hardly started. They hired on a bunch of men, me included, ta dig in that thar mine, and they done paid good! Shucks, I tweren't nothing but a lil shaver back in them thar days, golly bill! Well, one day a man named Iron Mike went down ta dig, and he twas never seen again. Now, Iron Mike got his name 'cause he twere da biggest ring-tailed varmint round dese here parts, and he could throwed a length of railroad steel on each shoulder and walk a mile with it. Yes sirree, bob, nobody done never messed with Iron Mike. Yep, Iron Mike and me twas good friends. Why shoot, he'd pick me up like I twas a rag doll and carry me perten near everywhere.

"Why, I never furgit da day me stepdaddy tried ta whoop me, and Iron Mike twas thar, and he grabbed that old belt from Stepdaddy's hand and picked him up and damn near shook him ta death. From that thar day on, that old scutter never whooped me again if me pal Iron Mike twas anywheres near. Yeah, twas a big mystery, what happened ta Iron Mike, but after a few weeks, everybody seemed ta furgit about it, septing fer me a course."

"Did they ever find him?" I asked.

"No, never did. Anyway, as I twas a sayin', next thing ya know, another man twas missing, then another, then another, and even me stepdaddy. Finally people twas a startin' ta git scered. So da town held an election ta hire 'em a sheriff and hired Black Jack Roberts fur da job. Well, old Jack, he done searched all da old mines, da hills, and valleys, anywhere—but never did find none of 'em. One day, I twas deep in da mine, and I twas pullin' gold out in chunks da size of goose eggs when I heerd a sound that made me shake clean down ta me boots. I ain't never heerd no sound like that thar in me born days. It twas similar ta that of da puma, only deeper, so I grabbed this here old rifle and took me lantern and went a lookin' around. That's when I seed 'em, them thar bodies. Some twas just bones, some still had flesh on 'em, bloody flesh looked like they twas et by some old puma. That thar is what them Injuns called a mountain lion. I skedaddled out of thar so fast—why it make ya head spin. I done went down ta da town, and I told that thar sheriff what I done seen. He git some men, and I took 'em down and showed 'em da bodies. Why, shucks, he done telled everyone it twere a puma, but I knewed it tweren't. Why, I heerd da scream, and ain't no puma ever made no sound like that thar. But old Jack, he din't believe me. That twas when they all start ta call me Crazy Pete. Why, shoot, I ain't no crazier than anybody else."

"So what was it, Pete? Come on! Tell us!" Wally said.

"Um a gittin' ta it. Hold yar britches on, boys. So things kinda git back ta normal when another man and another and another go missing. All miners, all from da Wolford Mine. Then just about da time that thar sheriff wants ta seal da entrance ta da mine, people start a missin' from other mines and then from town. Then when Sarah Parker went a missin', da town went crazy. This twas da first time a woman went gone. Oh, she twere a pretty thing. Now da sheriff went and swore in a posse ta git that thar puma. I done told 'em again, ain't no puma, but they still don't listen. Fact twas I twas just a young'un, and I guess twas no reason that they should listen ta me, but um a telled 'em ever'thin' anyway. Those men killed every puma they could find, and da skins twas sold ta traders who sent 'em back east, and da money given ta da families that done lost men, 'cause they tain't got no money, ya see.

6

"When they thunk they done killed every puma around, they stopped, yet all da while they twas a huntin' and a killin' them thar pumas, folks twas still a disappearin'. Then one night, I twas a coming home late from da mine, and I seed it. I could not believe my eyes. A huge thing, it walked on hind legs, but it tweren't no man, din't walk like no man nither, and, well, it seemed like it had a short tail."

The boys, myself included, laughed and scoffed at the idea that something like a man was prowling around eating people and it had a tail.

"Now, boys, ya done ask me ta tell ya, and um a tellin' ya, so should I finish?"

"Yeah, yeah, go on—tell us!" we said.

"Okay then. Again I telled that thar sheriff what I seen, but he just laughed; he done laughed just like ya boys did. Da sheriff starts lookin' fur pumas again, and again it killed many more. But still da killin's got worse, not better. So I set out with me ol' Winchester rifle ta bag that thar thing myself. Shoot, I looked in every cave and every ravine, but they just tweren't out thar. So I kinda gived up, ceptin one day, I twas way out away from da town, and I runned inta an Injun feller. We talked best we could with hand signals, and when we finished, he done told me what I twas a lookin' fur twas a Zetroll. He done killed one many moons back after it kilt his Squaw and brother. When he kilt it, they made him da medicine man of da tribe. He showed me da fingers he done cut off from it and had on his lance. They twere long with claws big as a bar, and da skin twas like a lizard. It dried ta da bone, but ain't no rot twas on it. I wanted him ta show it ta da sheriff, but he signaled me no. I tried ta trade fer 'em; he said no. So I figured I gonna have ta kill one me self and take it back ta da sheriff. That Injun done told me where he done kilt it though, so I done headed off in that thar direction.

"I never found one, but I found da one that Injun killed, and I cut off its skull and twas gonna take it ta da sheriff. Then he couldn't call me crazy no more. When I twas puttin' it in me saddlebag, I heerd that thar scream again from inside that thar cave where I done found da body. I took me rifle and started in when, in da shadows, something cut me on da arm, and me rifle felled ta da ground, so I runned and

7

runned as fast as I could. When I reached me horse, dead, cut ta pieces ... he dang shur twas. And that thar skull done disappeared. That made me know that them thar things could think, think kinda like folks does. Golly Bill, I twas scered out of me skin. I runned as fur away from them thar caves as I could. Why I plum near kilt myself gettin' back. Look here, boys." Pete rolled up his sleeve to show us the scars. They were real and deep, and we were shocked in disbelief.

"Now, as I twas a saying, when I finally git back and told that thar sheriff what da Injun told me and even showed him me cuts, he still don't believe me. He said I must have run up agin some animal, maybe a wolverine or such. I knowed it'sa hard ta believe, but dag nab it, I tain't no liar.

"Okay, boys, old Pete needs a nap, so ya'll come back tomorrow, and I'll finish da story. And be sure ta bring old Pete something ta drink."

"Ah, Pete, you can't stop now! We just gotta know how it ends!" Wally said. All the other boys, including me, were "yeahing" it up but to no avail. In fact, he was already falling asleep.

We grumbled and moaned as we rode our bikes back down to town. Then Tommy got an idea. "Let's go up to the mines and see if we can see one of those things."

Wally said, "Why not? It's all bullshit anyway."

That was followed by Larry saying, "Fellows, let's be sure about this. Crazy Pete don't seem so crazy to me!"

I agreed with Larry and added, "If we were to go up there, we would need lights and weapons. Not to mention that the old Wolford Mine was sealed up back in Pete's day."

"Yeah, but there is plenty of other mines still open," Wally added.

By the time we reached town, it was about four in the afternoon and too late to do anything but gather the lights and weapons, some rope and other such things, and some food.

Day Two

Wally spent the night at my house, and we set the alarm for five, or as we laughingly called it, *0 dark thirty*. We gathered up our gear and snuck out the back door. When we got to Tommy's house, we bounced pebbles off his bedroom window until he opened it. He tossed down his gear and climbed down the trellis, and then we headed to Larry's. He was already beside the barn with his dog, Alaska, an old German shepherd, and off we went. It was just getting light when we hit the first gold-mine shaft. We pried the boards off the shaft entrance, enough for us to get in. Once inside, Alaska ran ahead, and Larry had to keep calling him back. We all had flashlights and slowly walked on, jumping at every sound. Tommy was the boldest—or maybe the most reckless. We thought there was nothing he was afraid of, and that gave us a false sense of security, that plus Alaska. We descended deep into the mine shaft and found nothing. It was very damp in there, and the rails of the hand trucks were very rusty. Same for the few carts and other man-made things left behind decades ago. On our way back out, there was a short detour that went about a hundred feet in. We had ignored it on the way in and had to hold Alaska to keep him from going in. Having found nothing out of the ordinary, we agreed we would investigate it. Alaska ran into it, and we followed, but as we neared the end, Alaska went crazy.

My buddies and I ran to where Alaska led us. All of a sudden, she stopped dead in her tracks and stood motionless as though see was listening for something—or maybe smelled something. Chills began to run up my back. Alaska ran a little further and began digging. As we approached him, we saw a large bone. We shoveled away the loose dirt and found another and then more and more. We had no idea how many bodies there were, but we counted seven skulls, so we figured at least seven people.

There was also a miner's hat, several picks, canteens, shovels, two buckets, and three rifles—or what was left of them. Most of the wood on these items was rotten and broken. The rifle metal was rusted to where it couldn't work. Wally got a queer look on his face and whispered, "Do you suppose that these are victims of Crazy Pete's monster?"

Tommy shook his head. "There just can't be any such thing." Then we all started talking at once, I couldn't speak for them, but I was scared, and frankly I was beginning to believe ol' Pete's story.

Wally and Harry seemed nervous but wouldn't fess up. No one was going to say they were afraid. I suggested that we should probably go tell the sheriff. "What's the matter, Clark? You scared?" Tommy was mocking me.

Wally jumped in, saying, "What are we going to do with what we've found here then, Tommy?"

"We'll tell the sheriff when we're done exploring the mines. We might find much more." Tommy's voice seemed to crack a little. Maybe he was a little afraid after all. We had never seen a dead person, much less a stack of bones.

We went on a little further and found more bones. "Guys, I think we need to go to the sheriff." Tommy had seen enough. We all agreed, and I was glad to get out of there.

We marked the mine on our map and left.

"I wonder how so many people came to be stacked and buried like that," I said.

Wally and Larry said almost at the same time, "The Zetrolls, stupid."

"Remember? Pete said they were smart like people!" Tommy reminded us.

"Let's go over to that one over there," Tommy said, pointing to another boarded-up mine entrance. He seemed to have regained his courage and was already running in that direction.

We all looked at each other, hoping someone wood say no, but then Wally shrugged his shoulders and ran after him. Larry and I followed suit.

Once again, we pulled the boards away and slowly walked into the shaft. We all had our slingshots, with no shortage of ammo lying about. We felt if it was good enough for David, it was good enough for us, and it made us feel confident having our slings with us. This shaft appeared to be much larger than the first, with more branches off the main shaft. About three hundred yards in, we stopped to listen to a noise that seemed like wind blowing through the cave. We listened intently for a few minutes. It was hard to tell because of Alaska's continued barking exactly which branch it came from or exactly what it was. Then suddenly we heard it again, much louder and closer.

Larry grabbed Alaska's collar and yelled, "Let's get the hell out of here!"

We ran to the entrance and heard it one last time as we exited the mine. We ran toward Pete's shack, ran all the way. When we reached the shack, Pete was standing there laughing at us.

"What da hell ya boys runnin' from, or did ya just miss old Pete so much?" he said, still laughing at us.

We were all gasping to get our breath, and I was the first who could speak.

"Pete, you were right. The Zetroll—we found him in a mine about half a mile from here!" I said, stopping to catch my breath again.

Tommy took over. "Yeah, we heard its call, and it was approaching us fast, so we ran all the way here."

We were like a relay team; when one ran out of breath, another picked up the story and ran with it until he had to stop.

When we finally finished the story, Pete said, "Well, boys, I don't know if ya heerd a Zetroll or just da wind and your imagination. But if ya brung old, thirsty Pete a bottle, I'll finish da story."

"I got it," I said.

It had been my turn to heist some booze from my dad. I handed Pete the pint of scotch. He rapidly removed the cap and seal and poured it straight down his gullet. We were amazed how this old man could take such a large drink. We had all snuck a sip at one time or another, and we all agreed that it was the nastiest taste and couldn't figure how adults seemed to enjoy it. Course, we all knew adults were weird anyway.

Pete pulled the bottle away from his lips with a big "aaaah," wiped his mouth with the back of his hand, and set the bottle beside him, where it was in easy reach for when he needed or wanted another slug. We had already figured out that if the bottle ran out before the story was through, we'd have to heist another, so we pushed him to finish the story.

"Let's see … where twas we, and where'd I leave off yesterday?"

He put his hand on his chin and looked skyward as though he were trying to recall.

I jumped in quickly and said, "You left off where the Indian told you what it was, and you told the sheriff you got wounded by the Zetroll and showed it to him, and he still didn't believe you."

"Oh yeah, that twas it," Pete agreed and continued. "Well, when that thar sheriff din't believe me, I decided that I would go kilt me one and drag it ta da sheriff. By now, some folk twas thinking it twere a might dangerous livin' here, so they done packed up and moved on. Da one man that sorta believed me twas old Doc Adams. He done looked over some of them thar dead folk, and he twasn't sure, but he tweren't convinced that it twere a puma. Especially since they done kilt so many of 'em and da people twere a disappearin' a might quicker than befur. But then da doc knew I twas smitten with da whiskey, and he don't always believe me nither, 'cause I done seen some animals that tweren't even thar.

"So I packed up me mule and headed back ta da mines. I twas out ta git me that thar Zetroll and redeem me repatation. Golly Bill, I done scoured them hills till I twas plum tuckered out but no luck. Then one night I twas a sleepin' round da fire, and I heerd that thing scream. It made me blood run cold, but I grabbed me shotgun and went out thar toward that thar sound. Da sky it'sa black, but them stars and da near full moon lighted things up fur me, and thar it twas. I could see it good in da moonlight. It twas 'bout nine feet tall, long arms with big six-fingered hands with long claws, claws longer than da grizz! Its body twere covered in scales like a fish, and he twere green and brown in a dull striped-like pattern. It had a short tail, and it just stood thar and looked at me as though it tweren't sur what ta do. But then it raised its head and let out that thar scream. Brother, twas it loud at that thar close a range. It run at me, and I done froze for a second. It twere dang near on top of me when I let both barrels rip. That stopped it cold in 'er tracks, and it fell backward on da ground, and it just lay thar. I poked it, and I prodded it ta be dang sur it twere dead. When I twas sur, I went back and sleeped till morning."

He paused to take another large chug on the pint; it was a little over half empty. Then he walked over by a large rock and took a piss. When he came back, I had to jumpstart his story again.

"Oh, yeah. Well, when I done woked da next mornin', I sat thar fer a time whilst I thinked about how I would be a hero and not just crazy old Pete. I pulled me britches on and me boots and walked out of da tent and where I done left it. Ta me shock, it done disappeared. Yep, thar twere so much of that blue-green blood on da ground fur it ta done walked away. I searched fur weeks and never ever found it, nor did I ever see another. And all these years, um still Crazy Pete almost as if it twere my first name. Dang it! I'll go ta me grave that thar way, lest I can find another. Finally da folks just keept on leavin' till I twas da only one left, and I vowed that I would be here fur da time it takes ta prove I ain't crazy."

"Oh, Pete, we believe you, and we'll help you catch it," Wally said.

"Why, yeah, we even know where one is—in that mine, the one we told you about this morning," Tommy added.

Larry and I agreed we would help too. Old Pete didn't seem crazy to us anymore, especially since we had also heard its cry, and with all that, we thought his story was believable.

"Pete, we could come up in the morning, and we could go get that Zetroll. What do you say?" Tommy asked.

"Ya boys really would help old Pete?"

"Why sure! We want to. You're our friend," I said.

"Well then, we'll do 'er. Ya boys be here in da mornin' round about dawn."

"Okay, Pete, we'll be here then. Bye, Pete," Wally said. And we rode off to get home before dark.

I had a hard time getting to sleep, and then when I finally did fall asleep, I awoke from a horrible nightmare. In my nightmare, I was in the mine with the guys, and the Zetroll came for us as we ran for the entrance. I fell, and the Zetroll swiped me across the back, and as I lay there bleeding, I woke up, covered in sweat, thankful that it was *not* blood. I tossed and turned after that, sleeping only lightly.

Day Three

When the guys showed up, I wondered if they had slept as poorly as I did. We gathered up our stuff and rode off on our bikes to meet up with Pete and kill a Zetroll to prove that Pete was just old but not crazy.

We got to the old shack and no Pete. He had promised to be there at dawn. We called out but couldn't find him. We figured he must have forgotten, so we decided to go back to the mine where we had heard the Zetroll. We made a plan that one of us would go a little way into the mine and make a lot of noise to attract the Zetroll. The others would hide by the entrance, and when we drew him out, we would open fire with all our slingshots. When we killed it, we'd drag it back to Pete's shack and give him credit for the kill. We would draw sticks for the one who would be the bait. Lucky me, I pulled the short stick. Maybe my nightmare wasn't a nightmare but a vision of the future. We got to the entrance, and my blood ran cold.

I'll never forget that. We set up the plan, and Tommy, Wally, and Larry picked good spots. Each gathered a large pile of sharp-edged rocks, checked the bands, and hunkered down for the kill. I slowly walked into the entrance with my flashlight, looking and listening. Then I started making noises, throwing rocks further down the shaft. Then I heard it; it sounded like death calling, just as Pete had described it. It kept making noise, and the sound grew louder and louder until I was so scared I almost pissed my pants, and then I saw it. It was stalking me along the wall. It was huge and looked exactly as ol' Pete described it. Pete wasn't crazy; in fact, in spite of all the booze he consumed, he was quite lucid. My legs froze up momentarily, and I saw its eyes glow in the light of my flashlight. It stopped when the light hit its eyes. We seemed to stare at each other without moving, and then it let out another one of those bone-chilling screams it made. That shook me out of my frozen state. I turned and ran, but I could hear it running too. I couldn't help but fear he would catch me, so I ran till I thought my lungs would burst, and still it was gaining on me. There just ahead, I saw the entrance and the sunlight outside. Just as I thought I would make it, I tripped. I felt the rocky floor of the cave rip into my elbows and knees, but I quickly jumped to my feet and ran again. It was just about on me when I cleared the cave entrance and started yelling.

As it came into the morning light, my pals opened fire with their slingshots. They cut it, but none made a fatal strike. It grabbed Larry, who was the closest one to it. Without thinking, I grabbed a tree limb and ran up to it as it lifted a screaming and kicking Larry. I swung it like a baseball bat at the beast's head and connected. It let out a scream that was damn near deafening. It dropped Larry and turned on me. I tried to run, but it grabbed me and raised me over its head like it was going to smash me to the ground. As I was high in the air, I heard the sound of gunfire twice. The Zetroll dropped to its knees and then fell facedown in the dust. I rolled three or four times and cracked my head on a rock.

Day Four

When I awoke, I was in my bed at home. I sighed with relief; it had been just another nightmare. I started to get out of bed, but then my head felt like someone had just hit me. I grabbed my head and felt the bandages. No, it hadn't been another nightmare; it was real. But who shot a gun, and what happened to the rest of the group? I lay back down slowly and yelled for Mom. She came in with my friends, including old Pete.

Mom checked my head, gave me some water and aspirin, and then left so I could talk to my friends. As she left, she said, "Now, boy, if you need me, I'll be right in the other room."

"Okay, Mom."

Wally was bursting to talk, "Oh, man, we did it; we shot a Zetroll!"

"You mean Pete shot it and saved Clark's life!" Tommy corrected him.

"Thanks for saving me, Pete!"

"Ah, shucks, tweren't nothing. Y'all would a did the same fur me, and, Clark, ya done saved Larry!"

"Yeah, Clark, I owe you one, buddy. Thanks," Larry agreed.

"Well, last thing I remember was two gunshots and falling, and that's all until I woke up here. Where is it? The Zetroll, I mean."

"Clark, we didn't get the body. It lay there for a moment; we all thought it was dead. But Pete poked it a few times with his gun barrel, and it jumped up and ran into the cave. Pete didn't have enough time to reload that shotgun," Larry said.

"Yeah, but it lost a lot of that puke blue-green blood, so it'll die in the cave," said Tommy. "But we couldn't go after it 'cause we had to bring you to the doc."

"It'll die fur sure in that thar cave, and we just gotta go in after ya get well, Clark," Pete said.

We all agreed that once Mom let me out, we would go bring back our quarry. Mom came back and shooed everyone out so I could sleep. That was the last thing I wanted to do, but Mom was strict and very protective, God bless her.

I eventually got free from my mom's protective grip, and the gang and Pete went searching for the Zetroll. We never found it; nor did we ever find another. We concluded maybe it had been the last of its breed.

We lost interest in the Zetroll as time passed. We starting thinking of sports, and we never went to visit old Pete again. Two winters later, Pete died; they said he froze to death one really cold winter night. I think he was too smart for that; I think he just wore out. I mean, he was over a hundred years old. They didn't find him for a month. Some hikers were out near his old shack and found him frozen stiff, sitting on the old chair just outside his home. They said his old mule was frozen too, standing—yes, standing. They buried him in an old pine box in Potters field, an old burial ground from the mining days where they put people who couldn't pay for a burial.

The only people who were there that wet, rainy day they put him in the ground were an old priest, the gravedigger, and our gang. We all cried and felt ashamed that we had neglected our old friend, especially me; he had saved me from that creature. Carved on the wooden grave marker were the words *Crazy Pete Brill, 1850 to 1951*. He was our friend of a summer gone by, a man whom we shall never forget. We swore that one day we would get him a real headstone that showed him respect.

His grave was next to an odd-shaped rock that seemed to point toward the old Wolford Mine, which fortunately I remembered, as the old wooden marker was gone. I had a young man from the stone maker's shop help me lift the new stone marker and plant it securely at the head of Pete's grave. The new stone read:

Peter Brill
1850–1951
Gold miner, hero, and
guardian of the secret
RIP

THE END ... NEVER ENDING.

CRYPTURE 2
Am I Lost?

Day One

I am lost! Where did I go? I went nowhere. Then how am I lost? I went out of sight, sound, touch and smell. In fact, if I were standing right in front of you at this very moment and you looked right at me you would never know I was there. How is that possible? Let me take you back to the beginning.

My name is Stanley Portchec. I live in Hopscotch, New Mexico. I am thirty-seven years old, and I have a wife, Jennie, and a son named Jake. He's fourteen and a good freshman basketball player on his high-school team. Basketball is a sport that he really loves. My wife is a stay-at-home mom, and we love it that way. It was the tenth of January, two years ago. I was on my way home to pick up my wife and take her to my son's ball game. My '59 Pontiac Catalina does not have air-conditioning, and it was hotter than usual that day. So before I left work, I rolled down all four windows. I called home and said, "Honey, I'm on my way home to pick you up. Will you be ready? I'm ten minutes out."

"Yes, I'm ready now. Just sending out a few e-mails. See you in a bit. Bye."

Little did she know I would never arrive. Well, that's not exactly true. I would arrive, but no one would know it. It's like the riddle; if a tree falls in the forest, and no one hears it, does it make a sound?

On my route to and from home and work, there is a straight three-mile stretch of road that runs alongside the Sandstone Nuclear

Electric Plant. The current shift wasn't over, so the road was virtually deserted. All the land on the other side of the road is just woods. It seems they own the land on both sides of the road. As I picked up speed, I saw in the distance a truck sitting alongside the road. As I got closer, it turned out to be from the power plant, and it appeared to be just parked there, as I saw no one around it. I was cruising at about eighty-five or so as I passed the parked truck. Just as I was alongside it, a plume of vapor hit the car and filled the cab. I jammed on the brakes as the white, fog-like spray temporarily blinded me. The car lurched left and then right and spun off into the sand and finally to a stop. My heart was pounding so hard I thought it might explode.

I jumped out, coughing; my eyes were burning and tearing. After I got my head straight and my adrenaline back to normal, I breathed a sigh of relief that I hadn't hit anything or anyone. This vapor, whatever it was, now covered the inside of the car and me like a light mist. It made my skin sparkle and felt cool, and it had no odor; I assumed it was simply water vapor.

I was ten minutes later than I had told my wife I would be, and I knew she would start to worry. I tried to call, but the mist must have damaged my cell phone. I started the car, pulled back onto the road, and continued my trip home. Finally I turned down my street and into my driveway, home at last and none the worse for wear—thank God! As I turned off the car, the vapor completely dried from my clothes, skin, and the car's interior. But as I started to exit the car, I felt a strange tingling sensation on my skin, and when I grabbed the door handle, I felt a strange sensation between my skin and the handle. It wouldn't open. I thought perhaps it was a result of the near mishap, so given the time constraints, I simply climbed out the car window, thinking I could deal with the stuck door after the game. I didn't think too much about it until I saw my wife, who was standing at the kitchen sink with her back to me, "Hi, Jen! I'm here. Ready?"

She ignored me, so I walked closer to see if she had on earphones and was listening to music. I repeated, "Jen, are you ready to go?"

Still she paid me no mind. I thought she was pissed about something, so I went to my room, stripped off my necktie and shirt, and put on a golf shirt. I felt a strange sensation between my skin and

19

whatever it touched. Starting to get concerned, I walked back to the kitchen where my wife was now leaning against the sink, looking right at me. I said, "Hi, babe."

She said not a word but looked at her wristwatch and seemed to be impatiently waiting for something. I walked over to kiss her, and my lips went into her skin. I jumped back in horror. I touched her, and my hands went into her. I ran to the hall mirror; I had no reflection. Taken back by the shock of what I saw—or better stated, didn't see— my mind raced for an explanation, some spark of reason about what was happening to me and why.

Then I heard her say, as she again looked at her watch, "Damn it, Stan, where the hell are you?"

"I'm here! I'm right here!" I yelled. She didn't even flinch.

I was stunned, devastated. What was I to do now? How long would this last? How could it have happened? What caused it? Was I dreaming? I even pinched myself like in the movies to wake myself up, but no—no, I was not dreaming.

My wife walked to the front door, looked outside, and said, "Well, there he is, but what is he doing?" I followed her as she walked outside and over to my car and looked in. No one was in the car. Again she asked aloud, "Where the hell is he? Maybe he's at Bob's." She walked next door and rang the bell. I followed her again.

Alice answered, "Hi, Jen. What's up?"

"Hi, Alice. Is Stan with Bob?"

"No, Bob's not home from work yet. Why?"

"We're supposed to be at Jake's basketball game, and I can't find him. His car is here, so I thought he was with Bob. Hey, Alice, you're not fucking my husband, are you?" Jen said, laughing.

"No, not this week. I had him last week, which was enough!" Alice replied. They laughed together. Funny—my wife never used the F word in front of me.

"Well, I'm concerned. The only thing he's insistent about is being on time for Jake's games, and the game started ten minutes ago. I'll skin that man when I catch up with him!"

I stood there for a moment listening to these two women talk and joke about me without having a clue that I was standing right there, right in front of them, then walking between them waving my hands in front of their eyes, talking to them, trying to get their attention, get them to hear me. Finally, Jen went back into the house. I followed her, crying like a baby. Jen called several of my other buddies, and obviously none of them had seen me. She paced back and forth for a while, looking at her watch every few minutes. "I'm calling the police." She used to laugh at me when she caught me talking to myself, and she did it too. She picked up the phone and dialed the police number off the magnetic card on the fridge.

"Yes, my name is Jennifer Portchec, and I live at 1101 Walnut Street. I want to report a missing person, my husband, Stanley ... Well, he was on his way home an hour ago to pick me up to go to our son's basketball game. He called me from his car and told me he was ten minutes away. That was an hour ago, as I mentioned."

She was quiet for a moment.

"But, Sergeant, you don't understand, he'd *never* be late for one of our son's games, and his car is in the driveway! Forty-eight hours is ridiculous."

Jen slammed down the phone and uttered some more words I had never heard her say. Then she called another number, but I didn't see which one it was. "Oh, hi, Sally. Did Stan say anything about going anywhere other than home and Jake's game?" Sally was my secretary.

"He didn't ... Sally, did he seem okay to you when he left? ... Oh, I don't know. His car is out front, but I can't find him. I talked to his buddies and now you and even the police, but they won't do anything for forty-eight hours ... Thanks, Sally, you're a dear. Bye."

I got the idea that maybe I could open the door and slam it over and over again. I went to grab the handle, and my hand passed through it; I could not open it. Then I tried knocking over a large vase, but I couldn't do that either. How would I get in or out of a room if the door were closed? How could I drink or eat? *That's it!* An idea hit me. I ran to the hall toilet and decided to pee in it and see what happened. Nothing happened; there was no pee. There was none—none whatsoever. Then I thought about food. Funny, I wasn't hungry in the slightest. But surely if I didn't eat or drink, I would die, wouldn't I?

If I died, no one would even know. I'll just be a box in the cold-case files of the police department forever, never found, just gone, gone forever. Then I got a positive thought: maybe this anomaly was temporary, and it would wear off and be just a funny thing that happened and a great story that no one would believe.

Jen had to back her car out of the garage and onto the grass to get around my car. When she got in her car, I freaked. She was going to leave without me, and I would be alone in this weird state. I tried for the door. Same problem, so I jumped on the roof of the car. My toes went into the car, yet the rest of me lay facedown on the roof; how strange. As she drove, going faster and faster, I didn't feel the wind, nor did it blow me off. A million questions shot through my mind all at the same time. One was why did my toes go through and not the rest of me? I pushed my arm into the roof of the car up to my elbow, then to my shoulder, and then I did the same with my left arm. Then I was really scared. Could I stick my head through? What if I got stuck? I pondered the pros and cons for a moment and then held my breath and pushed my head into the car. It worked! I didn't get stuck, so I pulled the rest of me through and sat beside my wife, who had tears rolling down her cheeks. There was nothing I could do; I rode along with her. I suspected she was heading to the high school to get Jake. By the time she got there, parked, and went inside, his game was over. He was still in the dressing room with the coach and the rest of the team. We waited just outside the gym. Lots of people walked by, and no one could see me. I had kind of hoped that if just one person could somehow see me, it would stop my wife from worrying—and soon my son as well. Finally he came out of the dressing room and saw his mom.

"Hi, Mom! We won, and I had a really good game—ten assists, seven steals, and ten points. Did you see it? Where's Dad?" Jake said, looking around to find me.

"Your dad's not here. I don't know where he is. Let's go, and I'll tell you all I know."

I could see the stress and Jen's fidgety way, and now I saw Jake mirroring her expression. She tried to not let it show, but Jake seemed to pick up on it. They were both wearing worried expressions.

When they reached the car, we all got in, and Jen relived all the events since my call to her at three thirty that afternoon. They tried to reassure each other that there must be some logical explanation and that perhaps when they got home, I would probably be there waiting. They stopped and got some fried chicken for dinner and took it home, getting enough for me. I'm far from perfect, but they both know one thing for certain. I would *never* miss one of Jake's games, not even for a huge classic car show. No father could love his son more than I love Jake.

Here I was feeling their pain, yet I was with them, but I was lost to them also. I prayed we would wake tomorrow and this nightmare would be over and I could rejoin my family.

I watched them sit and pick at their food; neither seemed to have much of an appetite. I had not eaten since lunch. Normally by now I would be so hungry, starving. I would eat anything in sight. However, I had no desire for food or drink. Very strange. I sat in my usual chair at the table while they tried to eat and not to cry. It appeared to me that each was trying not to upset the other. "Mom, I'm going up to do my homework. May I be excused?"

"Sure, son, go ahead."

She cleaned up the table, stuck the dishes in the washer, and went to our room. She took a shower, and as I looked at my wife's naked body, I was not aroused. That would never happen normally. In fact, she would never allow me in when she showered if Jake was in the house. I could never resist an opportunity to make love to my beautiful wife.

Here I was, totally invisible to anyone, with no desire to eat, drink, or make love. I could feel remorse and sadness though; wasn't that strange.

She came out, dried herself, put on her sleeping wear, and crawled into bed. She tried to read for a while but then threw the book down and grabbed the remote. She turned on the TV and started surfing the channels, pausing only a few seconds on each channel until she hit one where one woman said to another, "Where is your husband?"

She broke into tears and then shut the TV off and cried herself to sleep. I lay beside her and thought I would sleep also. Wrong again;

sleep was not a requirement in my current state. That was bad, as the night was very, very long. No bodily functions and no desires; what a strange time I was living.

Day Two

I saw the sun come up, and it was beautiful. Then it dawned on me. Had I returned? I ran to the mirror only to have my hopes dashed—no reflection. I tried to pick something up. No way, and my spirits plummeted. My last hope was that someone could somehow see me, so I waited anxiously for someone to wake up. Jake didn't have school because it was Saturday. It was a toss up as to who would awaken first, him or Jen. As it turned out, today it would be Jen. I heard her moving about. I had been wandering about the downstairs, so I went back up to the bedroom to check on her. She was sitting on the edge of the bed sobbing. I spoke to her and held my breath for her response. She looked up, and my heartbeat quickened. I moved toward her, and as I got close to her, she stood up and walked toward me—and then right through me. It was a weird feeling. Like for a split second, I knew all she knew, like we were one entity. I could feel the fear she was experiencing. Once again, my moment of relief was shattered. I was obviously still in this state of whatever ... invisibility. She had walked to the master bath, and she was drying her eyes and presumably trying to compose herself before she left our room in case Jake was up.

She went downstairs and straight to the kitchen. On reaching the doorway, she stopped, hung her head, and said, "Oh, Stan, where are you? What has happened to you?"

She sat at the kitchen table, folded her hands, and bowed her head as if she were praying. She stayed like that for a minute or so and then looked skyward and said, "In Jesus's name, I pray. Amen."

She was praying, so I sat down and prayed as well. I prayed that this terrible curse would be lifted so I could return to my family. When I finished, Jen was making coffee. She went over to the window and looked out at the driveway. She was looking in the direction of my car, which was still sitting where I had left it, and again aloud, she asked, "Stan, where the hell are you? Why have you deserted us?"

For the first time, I realized that the thought that I had just run out on them was a possible thought to her and maybe Jake as well. I had to find a way to communicate with them. I had to make them know I was there. My first thought was, since I seemed to be breathing, I would blow in her face and see if she reacted. I did, she didn't. I tried again to pick something up or even just move it, but no way; my hand just went through it like it wasn't even there. I racked my brain for ideas; nothing was coming. Then I tried to kiss her on the mouth, but my face went into her face. I pulled back quickly; her emotions mixing with mine was too intense. I couldn't stay there. What was I going to do?

I could smell the coffee—it was the butterscotch flavor—but while it smelled good, I had no desire for it. That made me remember food; it had been over eighteen hours, and I still had not the slightest hunger pang. The light above the sink was still on. I tried waving my hand in front of it to see if it showed or blocked the light. Nope.

Jake was coming down the stairs and said, "Hi, Mom. Dad back yet?"

"No, sweetie, not yet. I'm going to call the police again soon and tell them he's been gone for two days so they'll start looking."

"But that's not true, Mom. It's only been a few hours. I've never known you to not tell the truth." Jake recognized this was atypical behavior for his mom.

"I know, honey, but I fear for him, and I'm adjusting to their really stupid rule. I don't want to alarm you, but this could be a life-or-death situation."

That gave Jake an idea. "Let's call the hospital."

"Good idea. Why didn't I think of that before?"

She went to the phone and called the only hospital in our area.

"Yes, my name is Jennifer Portchec, and I was wondering if you had an admission anytime in the last twenty-four hours of a Stanley Portchec or perhaps a man who is unidentified? ... No one, huh. Okay. Thank you. Good-bye."

She hung up.

"That's it. I'm calling the police. No—wait—I'm going down there. Do you want to go with me?" Jen was now visibly shaking and kept taking deep breaths, seemingly trying to calm herself.

"Sure I will!"

"Okay, let's get dressed, and we'll go." She charged up the stairs, and Jake was right behind her. Within twenty minutes, we were out the door.

"Let me move Dad's car into the garage."

"No, Mom!" Jake yelled. "The police may need to take fingerprints or something."

"Oh, you're right, Jake. Thank you. We best not even touch it." Jen had left her car behind mine after the game, so it was easy to just go. I was in the car with them. Seemed I had the ability to pass through any solid object. I was determined to stay with them no matter where they went. I just kept hoping this condition would correct itself soon. I even wondered if I was dead. Was I really a ghost?

Jen pulled up in front of the police station, and in we went. "Jake, I hope whoever is on duty is *not* the same man I talked to yesterday!" They walked through the large double doors and up to the front desk.

"Good morning, folks. How can I help you?" His nametag read Officer Thomas.

"Yes, sir, I want to file a missing-person report."

"How long has the person been missing?"

"Two days."

"Okay, ma'am, let me get someone to help you."

"Sergeant Reynolds or Sergeant Blake report to the front desk," he said into the intercom. There was a look of terror in Jen's eyes when she heard the name Reynolds; he was the one she had talked to yesterday. She looked up and saw a tall man in a dark blue uniform coming down the hall. I ran up to him to read his nametag. It said Blake. I yelled to Jen that it was okay, but no one twitched a muscle. Seemed I was the only person who could hear me. A few seconds later when he introduced himself as Sergeant Blake, Jen exhaled in relief. "Would you mind coming this way?" He led us to a room with a computer and conference table, although it was pretty beat up. He offered them a seat while he readied the computer.

"Okay, ma'am, what is the person's name, relationship to you, and address?"

"Stanley R. Portchec. He is my husband and Jake's father. We live at 1101 Walnut Street, here in Hopscotch."

"And when was the last time you saw him?"

"When he left for work yesterday morning."

"You mean the day before yesterday, don't you, Mom?" Jake is always on his toes. It made me smile.

"Oh, yes, sorry." She blushed a bit.

"That's okay, ma'am. I understand you're upset."

I paced back and forth, helpless as Blake kept up the questions. "Now, Mrs. Portchec. I have to ask some tough questions. Please understand that, okay?" Jen nodded. "Have you and your husband been getting along?"

"Yes, of course, we love each other."

"Is there a possibility that your husband could be having an affair?"

"No, I don't think he has ... no, I'm sure that isn't possible." I was shocked and dismayed that she didn't answer that query with more certainty.

"Does your husband have any vices like drinking excessively, gambling, going off unexpectedly?"

"Absolutely not!"

Blake continued for thirty minutes with a plethora of questions. Jen and Jake answered them, and he logged them into the computer. I knew this was a drill, but I had no way to communicate this to them. Believe me, I was thinking—thinking as hard as I could. Nothing else was coming to me.

Finally, Thomas stopped typing on that bloody computer, "Okay, folks, I think that about does it. We'll put out an all-points bulletin to all our officers to keep a lookout for him. We'll also notify all surrounding jurisdictions as well. We'll notify you of any developments. A squad car will stop by to see the car your husband was driving. Do you have any questions?"

"Yes. Do you think you can find him?"

"Ma'am, if he's around, we will find him. I just can't tell you when. I know you checked the hospital, and we'll notify them of the situation, and they'll report to us if he shows up."

Jen and Jake stood up, shook hands with Blake, and left the station. "Mom, can we stop and eat? I'm really hungry."

"Sure we can. I'm sorry. You must be starved. Where would you like to go?"

"How about there?" Jake said, pointing to an IHOP restaurant.

"Sure, that's fine," Jen said as she wheeled into a parking space.

On a Saturday morning, you would usually have to wait to get seated at IHOP, but they weren't in any hurry.

"You know, this is one of your dad's favorite places."

"I know, Mom. Does it make you sad to eat here? Should we go somewhere else?" Jake sounded a little guilty for picking a place that reminded her of me.

"No, son. It's fine. The police are going to find him. I'm sure of it."

What a strange thing to think about, but I didn't need to relieve my body of any waste. Now I'm as regular as a Timex watch, and that time passed several hours ago. All of this was so bizarre. I thought about the vapor that came from the truck; it had to be the cause of all my current troubles. What else could it have been?

"Vapor! I wonder!" I said aloud, but no one responded. Vapor. The thought of it gave me an idea. I walked toward the kitchen of the restaurant, found the big freezer, and walked through the door into it. I stood there for a moment and noticed that I could not feel the extreme cold within. Then I took a deep breath, held it for several seconds to warm it well, and then slowly let it out in hopes of seeing the vapor from my breath. I was shocked. I saw it. I actually saw my breath in the cold air. I could not believe it; I was so happy I was dancing around the freezer. Then the euphoria abruptly ended. How could I show them? How could I get them in the freezer—or anyone for that matter—to show them? The days were too warm outside, and at night when it did get cold, how could they see it in the dark? But at least I had a way, if I could just get someone to notice. Just as that thought went through my mind, the freezer door opened. A young woman walked in and grabbed a package of hamburger patties. I jumped in front of her and exhaled. She stopped dead in her tracks and looked around. I did it a second time; she stopped again, looked around, and then bolted for the door and slammed it behind her. I walked through the door again, and I followed her to see if she would tell anyone. She handed the box of patties to one of the cooks, who said, "What's with you, Shelly? You look like you've seen a ghost."

I thought, *At last*, but my hopes were quickly dashed as she replied, "Oh, nothing, nothing at all."

Once again, my great idea, which this time worked, got no traction at all. Now I would have to figure out how to get beyond this hurdle. Then it came to me; at home, we had a side-by-side refrigerator and a stand-up five-foot freezer. When either of them opened the door, I had to be there and breathe up a fog for them to see. But even if they saw it, what would they think? Well, I couldn't worry about that; I'd take it one step at a time and hope for the best. I went back to the booth they were sitting in and sat down. It was mostly talk about Jake, his studies, and his basketball, with an occasional reference to my missing self. They finished eating while I thought of the possibilities of when and how often they might open the freezer. Finally, the check was paid, and we were off again, hopefully home to open the freezer, see the fog, and figure it out. Oh, if it could only be that simple.

We headed back home. I planned to stay with either Jen or Jake, whoever was closest to the freezer. When we went into the house, Jen went straight for the phone to see if there were messages; there were none. I knew she had given the police her cell phone; they would use that number. *Is she losing it or just being very thorough?* I stayed close to Jake as he went to the kitchen. He headed for the fridge, and I went into the freezer side. He opened it. I breathed as long as I could, and the fog was thick. He seemed to look at it and then closed the door. I hoped he would say something about it to Jen, but he didn't. Damn!

Jen called the police to check in. "Yes, may I speak to Sergeant Blake, please? ... Oh, no. I'll call back another time. Good-bye."

She hung up with a few expletives under her breath.

"Mom, I'm going to Jordan's house, okay?"

"Sure, son. Got your cell phone with you?"

"Yeah. Call me when Dad gets home."

"Okay, will do." As soon as Jake was out the door, Jen started to cry again.

She spent the rest of the afternoon crying and doing housework. I felt she was trying very hard to stay busy and not think about me. What did she really think was the reason for my disappearance? She could *not* in her wildest dreams or nightmares get anywhere close to the truth, so what *did* she think? Was it that I was with another woman? I couldn't believe she could think that for long. Was I off with one of my buddies? Certainly she would know if that were the case; I would have called her. Yeah, that's right. Oops, that brings me back to another woman; I certainly would not call about that, but no. I could tell her something plausible about where I was and still be with some other chick. *Nah, she knows how much I love her, and she trusts me. I know that. Then maybe she thought I lost my mind or was kidnapped.* Oh, God, she would really be a mess then.

Oh, I was chasing myself in circles trying to figure out what she thought, so she must have been going crazy too. I threw myself down to my knees and prayed as I had never prayed before. In fact, I was begging God to help me so I could help my family. This had already hit Jen hard; for Jake, it would take another day or two, I thought.

Then, as though God had heard my prayers, Jen walked to the freezer, the big freezer, and opened it, apparently looking for something to thaw for dinner. I stood inside, my ghostly body filled with all kinds of frozen things, and I blew the fog. She jumped back, and her eyes got as big as silver dollars. I did it again; she cocked her head and just stared. Then I caught an idea. Jen and I had both been in the service, she in the navy, me in the Marine Corps. In fact, that was where we met. So I blew an SOS at her. She dropped the package of chops she had in her hand and fainted. She had never fainted in her life! I jumped out, tried to help, to pick her up, and then remembered I couldn't or even alert anyone to come to her aid.

It was ten minutes before Jake and Jordan came through the door, laughing and carrying on. Jordan spotted her first and yelled to Jake, who ran to her and closed the freezer door. That seemed odd to me, but it must have just been habit, like turning on a light switch when you know the power is off. I had never seen him move so fast.

"Mom, Mom, are you okay?" I was so proud. He took her pulse at her neck and then ran to the sink, grabbed a dishtowel, ran it under cool water, and swabbed her forehead. Meanwhile, Jordan ran across the street for his mom, Linda, who came running. By the time Linda and Jordan got there, she was coming around. Jen started babbling. "He's in the freezer, he's in the freezer!"

"Now, Jen, what are you talking about?" Linda asked.

"Stan is in the freezer—the freezer!"

Jake jerked open the freezer, and I jumped back in and let out a long breath. He quickly closed the door. At first I was disappointed, but then he said, "Come on, Mom. The stress is getting to you. Let's get you up to bed." I followed.

He started walking her to the staircase, and she tried to pull away from Jake. He tightened his grip and whispered, "I saw him. Play along."

I was crying I was so proud, but I had no tears.

"Jake, do you want me to do anything?" Linda asked.

"No, I'll get her to bed, and I'll call if I need help. Thanks."

"Come on, Jordan. Let's go home so Jake can deal with this."

"Okay, I'll text you later, Jake," Jordan said as they walked out the door.

As soon as they left, he said, "Mom, I didn't want anyone to think you were nuts, but I saw a fog that looked like someone exhaling in cold air when I opened the door, but what is it?"

"Oh, Jake, when I opened the door, I saw the fog, and I stood there and watched. Then the fog spelled out SOS in Morse code. Your dad and I both had to learn it in the military. I can't explain it, but I know it's him, and I'll prove it to you. Here is what your name looks like in Morse code. Morse code, as you may know, is a series of dots and dashes that can spell words. Look." She took a piece of paper and wrote his name in code. "So if it's a horn, it's a short blast and a long blast. In this case, it would be a short breath for the dot and a long breath for the dash."

"Let's go!"

They walked down to the freezer. I jumped through the door, and she then opened it. "Are you ready? Watch closely," Mom said. "Okay, Stan, if you're here, spell Jake's name."

I breathed out Jake in code. Jake's mouth dropped open. "But how can this be?"

"I don't know, I don't know, but I know it's Dad, someway, somehow. The air won't stay cold enough except for short blasts of code; only part of your name came out. So we have to ask questions where the answer will be short, preferably yes or no questions."

"Okay, okay."

I was so happy and relieved that they knew I was there and not dead somewhere, or that I had run off with someone. I had to answer the questions as best I could. But this would be like a guessing game, with no way to guide her queries and no way in the world for her to figure it out. I would have to find a way to move them in the right direction, but I didn't know where to begin. I could only trust the Lord would help us. Jen went over and asked the first question. I moved back into the freezer. "Stan, I will try to ask yes and no questions, one long blast for yes and two short blasts for no. Are you here but invisible?" Then I gave one long blast. "Yes."

"Did you drive home?"

"Yes."

"Did whatever happened to you happen on the way home?"

"Yes."

Jen asked the questions, and Jake opened the freezer door when it was time to answer. So far, the questions were good.

"Did it happen at the plant before you started driving?"

"No."

"Did it happen while you were driving?"

"Yes."

"In the parking lot?"

"No."

"On Plant Street?"

"No."

"On the highway past the power plant?"

"Yes."

"Did a person do it to you?"

"No."

"Did you hit something?"

"No."

"Did something in the car do it?"

"No." Then I blew truck in Morse code.

"Tru ... true? No, doesn't make sense." She thought for a minute and then looked up. "Truck?"

"Yes."

"Hazardous?"

"Yes."

"You stopped?"

"No."

"You were in contact with a vapor?"

"Yes."

"But you were able to drive home?"

"Yes."

"Can you write?"

"No."

"Can you eat or sleep?"

"No."

The questions went on for some time, most yes/no queries but some in short words. Yet we weren't getting any closer to a cure or knowing what in the vapor caused this. But bit by little bit, they came to the point where they knew almost as much as I did. I was finally able to get them to understand that I had been with them from the moment I arrived home until present. I was also finally able to get a message to them to drive back to the place where the truck was, but if by chance it was still there, *not* to go near it.

Since they wouldn't be able to communicate with me away from the freezer, I told them to wait one hour after we arrived at the scene before leaving. That way, they would be sure I was back in the car.

It was late afternoon by the time we reached the spot where it happened. The truck was still there. I approached the truck cautiously. No one was around it or near it. It was unlocked, and the keys were in the ignition, which was very strange. I climbed behind the wheel in hopes of some great wisdom coming to me. Then I looked over through the passenger-side window and saw a man sitting on the grass. He was wearing a power company uniform. I slid through the door, walked over to him, and stood there looking at him. He glanced up and then away. I started to walk away, and as I did, I said aloud, "Mister, I wish you could see me!"

"Me too. Huh?"

I snapped around, and he stood up, and we were both staring at each other with our mouths open.

"You can see me!" he said.

"Yes! Who are you, mister?"

"Bob Corley, the driver of that truck."

We talked for ten minutes or so, staying close to where Jen and Jake were, and pieced together what had happened.

It seems Bob was driving the truck loaded with a vapor by-product to a disposal plant when the vapor started to leak. He saw it in his mirror and pulled off to fix it. When he did, the pipe spewed the vapor on him and me passing by in my car. He was able to close and tighten down the gate valve that someone who had loaded the vapor hadn't done properly. After the truck started bouncing down the road, the vapor began to seep out. After being sprayed with the material, he started to lose feeling. Eventually, like me, he could not touch, feel, pick up, or do anything. Now I had an ally—or at least someone to talk to and someone who could see me. What could I learn from this driver?

I lost track of time, and the next thing I knew Jen and Jake drove away. I had forgotten my own plan. I asked Bob if he could show me where he loaded the vapor. We walked through the gates, passed the guards, and went into the building. There were huge tanks that held this vapor by-product. My office, where I worked as a mechanical engineer, was near this plant, and everyone had his or her own opinions about the dangers of it, but now I was painfully aware of a very real danger. Bob said that the vapor was created when the water that kept the reactors cool collected in its reservoir. This vapor came off like steam from boiling water, but unlike steam, it did not condense back into liquid form again. Therefore, it had to be siphoned off, or it would build up and spill over. But none of this information helped fix the problem of our invisibility. We came back out no wiser than when we went in.

Meanwhile, Jen must have discovered that I had not gone home with them, because I saw her return and park the car. Bob lived close by and had walked back from his house in hopes of discovering something there, just as I had done. We exchanged address info, but of course, we had to memorize it, as we could not write. I did tell him the discovery of the breath showing in cold air. Then I ran to get into the car before Jen left again.

I sat there with her for ten minutes, and then she started the car and headed for home. She talked a lot about her feelings and what she and Jake had discussed. She could not be sure that she was actually talking to me. I guess she was just hoping I was there.

It was about eight o'clock when we got home, and Jake was there waiting. We headed to the freezer, and they quickly knew I was now with them again. They learned what I had been doing and understood that they could not go to the police with this, as they would end up in rubber rooms.

Jake might have been only fourteen, but he was full of ideas. While his mom was returning to get me, he began searching the Internet for anything that might relate to my dilemma. His searching revealed the strange story of a man, Doctor William Huffington, a PhD in science and higher mathematics who had been a crusader against nuclear power. He was getting too much media exposure, so he was arrested and charged by the FBI and Justice Department with attempting to blow up several nuclear power plants. Acting on an alleged tip, the FBI got a search warrant and found all the evidence to arrest him. A federal judge ordered a physical evaluation and found him mentally unfit to stand trial. The judge ordered him to be confined to a mental institution for an undetermined length of time, until he was rehabilitated enough to stand trial. Even with a mountain of evidence against him, one extensive article made the claim that he had been framed by the government to silence his claims of the horrific dangers of nuclear power, both as weapons and as power-generating plants.

Originally he was committed to a military mental institution, but he was later released to the Rosemont Psychological Hospital that wasn't far away. By the time they released him to Rosemont, he had been fully discredited as another conspiracy theory kook by those news organizations that were friendly with the administration. He was virtually forgotten.

Jake then Googled him and found an old website with contact info. He e-mailed him and asked if he knew of any problems to humans caused by the vapor from the cooling water. When Jen returned with me later, Jake was so excited and told her about it. I didn't think that Jake would ever hear back from this man, but I was proud of his initiative.

Now it was late, and Jake said he was going to bed, and Jen agreed, so the house was adjusted for the night. When Jen crawled into bed, she said, "I hope you are here with me. I miss you so much. I want you to hold me." She was softly crying.

I wrapped my arms around her, but she could not feel it. She slowly drifted off to sleep, not knowing I was holding her—well, kind of. I walked the house all night, looking in on them to see they were all right, not that I could do anything about it if they weren't, but it made me feel good.

Day Three

The long night was finally over. The sun was just coming up over the horizon as the night fought to hold its reign. Jake was up, and this being Sunday, he would wake Jen in time for church. Jen wanted to skip it for obvious reasons, and Jake agreed, somewhat reluctantly.

"Did you check your e-mail for an answer from that guy?"

"No, but I'll do it now."

Sure enough, to everyone's surprise, he did respond, and he wanted Jake to come and see him. He made it sound important. He requested that Jake come at either eleven or two o'clock. Jake e-mailed back and said we would be there at eleven. Jen fixed breakfast for Jake and just some coffee for herself. I still had no hunger, and it was obviously not required to sustain me. I guess all things have some positives. It was quite nice not to feel hunger or thirst and especially not to need to relieve either bladder or bowel. But to not be able to hug my wife or my son was more than enough reason for me to find a way out of this, whatever this state was. I found it interesting that the man asked them to bring heavy coats and perhaps gloves.

After breakfast and some more querics from the freezer, they dressed and we headed out for Rosemount Hospital, which was about an hour's drive from our home. It was a beautiful day, and the sun was shining brightly. It would have made for a nice pleasure cruise, were it not for the present circumstances. We arrived a little before eleven and were given visitors' passes. Then we were escorted to the visitors' lounge and offered coffee or other drinks. Of course, my reference to *we* was really Jen and Jake; my presence there was unknown to anyone other than them, or so I thought.

Ten minutes later, a tall, thin gentleman about sixty years of age with black hair grayed at the temples came in. He was dressed as if he was going to church—perhaps he had come from there—and he walked with a slight limp. He had many wrinkles on his face, and his expression was a somber one without a hint of a smile, but he had kind eyes. He spoke with a voice that was reminiscent of Gregory Peck, a deep voice with similar inflections. I can't think of Peck without thinking of his starring role as Atticus Finch in *To Kill a Mockingbird*, one of my all-time favorites.

"I am Doctor William Huffington, but please just call me Bill."

Jen introduced Jake and herself, and they all sat down around the small conference table in the director's office.

He asked what had happened to cause Jake to write to him. "Well, sir, I read about you on the Internet, and as I said in my e-mail, I'm wondering what if any side effects to humans could be caused by exposure to vapor from any part of a nuclear reactor."

"I don't believe that is so, young man," he said, staring deep into Jake's eyes with his piercing, steely blue eyes. "The director of this facility was kind enough to allow us to use her office so that we could have complete privacy and talk freely. No one would be interested in meeting a kook like me unless they had experienced something having to do with my abhorrence of nuclear power plants and some of their many dangers. I suspect you or someone you know has had such an experience. Is that so?"

I watched Jake and Jen sit there dumfounded. Nothing about this man would cause me to think he was crazy; then again, what would I know about crazy? He just seemed like he was, if anything, perhaps too brilliant.

Then he asked a question that was like a bomb exploding. "Is there anyone else here with us?"

No one could speak. I was rocked to my core, and by Jen's expression, she was also. The silence was deafening, and then Jake said, "Yes."

I watched his reaction; it was as if he had known all along. Jen still could not speak. His following query was almost as shocking. "How did this person encounter the vapor?"

Jake again took the lead and explained it really well.

"You have found a way to communicate with this person?"

"Yes, we found that if he—my husband, Stan—went into our freezer and breathed out fog, he could answer the questions we asked in Morse code, but it couldn't stay cold enough except for mostly yes or no answers. Stan and I were both well versed in the code, and we used a long blast for yes and two short blasts for no. I wrote down our questions and answers." She handed him the annotated sheet, which he read quickly.

"Okay, I am satisfied. I can't be too careful with the FBI always snooping around. I'm actually not allowed visitors, but the director has studied me and knows that there is nothing mentally wrong with me, but they don't listen to her, and I've asked her not to continue to make a fuss, as I could end up back in the military hospital, and I never want to be there again. At least here they let me move around, work on the computer, and live a reasonable life as compared to what it would be like back in the military hospital. That was why I asked you to bring the coats and gloves. I will take you down to our meat locker, and we can talk with him. It's very cold in there and should sustain longer answers."

"Bill, is there a cure for him?" Jen asked.

"How many days has he been in this state?"

"It happened on Friday afternoon around four." Jen held her breath.

He cupped his chin with his thumb and middle finger, tapped his nose with his forefinger, looking down, and thought for a second. "Yes, yes, I believe we have time."

"There was one other man who suffered the same fate as Stan, the driver of the truck that was disposing of the vapor," Jen added.

"Was he exposed at the same time?"

"Yes."

"I am going to need your help to save these two men soon; after about ten days, there will be no way that I know of to reverse their conditions."

"What must we do? We will do anything," Jen responded.

"I have enough material at my home to prepare an antidote serum." I can't leave here, so I will have to instruct you as to how to do it. The FBI is always keeping tabs on me, and if they caught me outside, my goose would be cooked."

"Will they follow us?" Jake asked.

"No, not if you pay close attention to my plan. The staff here is very helpful to me, so they will cover for me. They all know the truth. When you leave, whoever is on stakeout will come in, as they do with every visitor, to be sure they weren't visiting me. The nurse on duty will say you were here to visit Mrs. Parker—a nice lady, but she suffers from dementia and agrees to everything. We will meet her before you leave."

"Okay, we can do that, no problem," Jen replied.

"Here is my home address, and there is someone there, but he is unfortunately in a permanent state like your husband. He is my younger brother and, to my knowledge, the first to suffer from exposure to the radioactive gas or vapor as you called it. I couldn't find the cure in time to save him from his fate. Take this fob and key. Enter the rear at night with the key and then hold up the fob as you walk through the house. You will be entering the kitchen. Straight ahead is a door that leads to the basement. Once you are in the basement, close the door behind you. You can then flip the switch on the left side; that will turn on all the lights, and they cannot be seen from the outside. You will be in a room that is set up like a small lab. In the corner there's a small, white refrigerator. Take two of the silver vials that are on the top shelf, put them into the small dry-ice carrier that is on the bench. The ice is marked. Then take four syringes from the cabinet over the left side of the bench. Lastly, there is a green container under the bench on the right side close to the refrigerator; bring it as well. Come back tomorrow after two with all these things. Be sure your husband and the other man are with you, and I will give them the antidote. Are you completely clear on all my instructions?"

"Yes, I've written of it all down exactly as you've prescribed it, and we will follow it to the letter. Are you sure that it will cure my husband and the other guy?"

"Nothing is for certain in this world, but it is the *only* chance he has, so pray that it works."

Then Bill took us to visit Mrs. Parker. We talked with her for a while, and she seemed nice but thought Jake was her son. That was good, as she would possibly remember him that way should it be needed. Jen took a current photo of Jake from her wallet and gave it to her to keep. She held it with reverence.

"Now, in the interest of time, we will forgo the meat locker and get you out of here before the spooks become suspicious. Jake, don't send me any more e-mails. It may draw focus on us as well."

"Yes, sir, no problem."

He was going back to his room as we left the hospital.

"Now, Mom, don't look around like you're trying to find someone. We don't want the spooks to get suspicious."

Jen chuckled a bit and then said in a serious voice, "Okay, son."

We drove about halfway home and then stopped for lunch at Burger King. From inside, we looked for any cars that stopped to possibly observe us, but we saw none. After lunch, we headed for home. Jake watched to see if any car pulled out when we did, but again no one did. We arrived home around two.

The rest of the afternoon, I listened as they walked through their plan for that evening; they didn't want to get caught.

Jake spent some time at Jordan's with strict instructions to be home at six for dinner because we would leave at seven. It would be another one-hour drive to the doctor's house. They would gather the supplies and get them home for safe transport the next day to the hospital at two, which meant leaving home a little before one.

Jake walked back in at five thirty, and we ate, or should I say they ate, and we left about quarter to seven. Twice on route, we made a left turn and went around the block to see if anyone followed. Again no one did. We reached Bill's house just after dark and parked down the street. Jen and Jake both wore dark clothes, and they slipped up the side driveway to the back door. She slid the key into the lock, and we quietly entered, held up the fob as instructed, and moved carefully toward the basement door. She and Jake stepped into the staircase, pulled the door shut, and flipped the switch. Voila, there was light. The place was exactly as Bill had described it. Jake went for the green container as Jen gathered the syringes. Then a tall, thin man walked into the room. He looked a little like Bill, so this had to be the brother Bill spoke of. He said, "Since you have the fob, I take it my brother sent you."

I looked to see if there was any reaction from Jake or Jen, but there was not. I said, "You're in the same condition as me, and only you and I can see and hear one another."

"Yes, but I am permanent. I surmise that you still have a chance to be cured, or else you wouldn't be here."

"Yes, I pray that it will work. I have a wife and child as you can see."

"I certainly hope it works for you; you are the first person I have been able to speak with in years. Can we talk awhile?"

"Of course. My son found your brother online, and he asked us to visit."

"I see. My name is Joe Huffington, and I stay here when I'm in town, but I travel a lot all over the world, all for free, my one big perk, but I so long for some company to talk to. So I'm so glad you're here." I asked him to come home with us, and we could sit all night and talk. He beamed at the idea. Jake and Jen had gathered all the supplies that Bill had asked for and were ready to leave.

"Stan, we're leaving now," Jen said.

"Come on, Joe, let's go," I said.

"Right with you, Stan." Our foursome headed out, two visible and two not. This was more like an adventure from the *Twilight Zone.*

When we reached home, as had become the custom over the last few days, we went to the freezer and checked in with one another.

I told them that Joe, Bill's brother, was with me so we could talk all night. Without the ability or need to sleep, company was a great way to spend the long hours until morning. Talk we did too. It was great for me, so I can only imagine how great it must have been for Joe. He told me about places he had been and the things he had seen, including walking through gunfire in Iraq and Afghanistan. He had seen every woman he ever wanted to see and sat in the Oval Office with Clinton and Bush. He told me things that would blow your mind, particularly about Clinton's women.

Day Four

We talked and talked, and then before we knew it, the sun was climbing up over the horizon. He was so grateful for my invitation, but I assured him it was selfishly motivated.

Soon enough, more time had passed, and then Jen was up. Shortly thereafter, Jake was also rumbling about. It would not be long before we would go back to the hospital. Joe said, "You cannot take me home; it would be too dangerous for your car to be seen there. The FBI watches the house occasionally. Don't worry. I have traveled all over the world; I can get home just fine."

"Gee, I didn't think of that when I invited you. I feel badly."

"I thought of it right away but didn't say anything for fear you would react just this way. You have given me a night to remember I am only sorry that when you are cured, we won't be able to do this again."

"Don't you mean *if* I am cured?"

"Oh, I have great faith in my brother. He is a brilliant man. You'll see."

"I already figured that out as well,"

"Stan, you are the first person that I've ever met that has shared my condition, but I am sure there are more. Where is the other man who was involved with you?"

"He lives close to the power plant, and I have to try to find him before we visit your brother."

"Oh, well, maybe I can go with you so I can meet him. Would you mind?" Joe asked.

"No, that would be fine. Happy to have you."

It was almost noon when it was time to go. We had a short freezer chat. I gave Jen the address for Bob, and away we went. Jen drove to his house and parked up the street a few houses.

"Stan, let's go get him." Jake and Jen had been told at the freezer that they could not approach the family, as they would just alarm them.

"Right, we will be right back."

"Ah, Stan, she can't hear you, remember?"

"Oh yeah, I forgot for a sec."

Joe and I went up and through the door. We searched the house from stem to stern, no Bob!

"Stan, time is almost up. We need to get back in the car before they leave."

We had to drive past the plant, so I would watch to see if Bob was back at the truck. As we rounded the bend, the truck was gone, and again, no Bob.

"Stan, do you know where else he might be?" Joe asked.

"No, I didn't know him until the accident. I have no clue."

"Well, if you are cured today, I will continue to watch for him," Joe added.

I was sad for Bob. He might have missed his only opportunity to be cured, as time was running out before the serum would no longer work. I wondered if he had gone traveling the way Joe did, or maybe he was just out walking around. Whatever it was, we were working on a timetable, as we had no way to communicate to change plans.

Joe and I were being transported to the hospital, and Jen did not know that Bob wasn't with us.

We arrived at the hospital, went inside, and signed in to see Mrs. Parker. Our sign-in from yesterday had already been fixed.

"I will take you to Mrs. Parker's room. Please wait there until the Doctor Bill comes for you. Those government people may come in and ask to see where you are," Nurse Brown said.

"We understand," Jen replied.

"I'll take those things you brought with you to the basement where Dr. Huffington said he needed them."

"Thank you, Nurse."

Nurse Brown then escorted us in to see Mrs. Parker while Joe and I stayed by the nurse's station to see who came in, if anyone. Sure enough, within minutes, two young men with short hair and wearing suits came in, flashed their FBI badges, and wanted to see who came in and whom they came to visit. They saw from the log that the visitors came to see one Mrs. Rose Parker. They asked to be shown her room. They looked through the glass and saw the two people whom they had observed entering the hospital only moments ago. Mrs. Parker was smiling and talking, so they seemed satisfied and left. I breathed a sigh of relief. Soon Bill came for them. He had already prepared everything, but nobody visible knew that Bob wasn't with us. We went down to the basement and over to the freezer.

Bill asked. "Are you here, Stan?"

"Yes," I breathed.

"Is the other man?"

"No."

"What happened?"

"Could not find him." Jen interpreted the code for Bill.

"Are you ready?" Bill asked.

"Yes. Joe is here." Joe asked me to tell Bill that he was looking good and that he was glad to see his brother. I did, and Bill's eyes welled up and spilled over.

He tried to cover up by being cute. "Wish I could say the same." They both laughed. Bill talked to him for a while, and I gave Jen his reply in Morse code. Bill thanked me for creating a way for them to communicate; it had been their only opportunity to talk since Joe's accident. It was a sad moment and one I had to look forward to if Bill's cure didn't work.

Bill then went on to explain what was about to happen. "Okay, Stan, listen carefully because when we walk out of the freezer, I won't know if you understand or not. When we go into the other room, I am going to pour some liquid out of the green container into an elongated pan. Then I want you to roll your hand and arm in it. It would be best to use the arm you do not write with. Your arm will become visible and corporeal for about two minutes. I will then be able to give you two injections. The first will feel like any normal shot that your physician might give you. The second will burn as if your arm is on fire. You may scream as loud as you wish; we won't hear you. The pain will dissipate in about one hour. It will take twelve to twenty-four hours before the chemical that is causing your malady will be flushed from your system. When you feel like you have to urinate, it is working, and you will be within an hour of being back to your normal self. Do you understand each and every thing I have told you?"

"Yes. Have you done this before?"

"Only with a chimp, but it worked fine. If I had only discovered the secret before Joe's time was up." He wiped his eyes, and his voice cracked toward the end of his statement. He choked back his tears and cleared his throat. "Okay then. Let's go into the other room."

I removed my long-sleeved shirt and waited until the putrid-smelling liquid was poured into the pan. I then laid my arm into it and sloshed it all over. At first, nothing, but then slowly it started to become visible, not to me or Joe—it already was to us—but judging by Bill's reaction it was becoming visible. Then Bill prepared the two hypodermics, and as promised, the first was easy. I was already for the burn, but I had no idea what burn meant until about five seconds after he hit me with the second shot. I did scream. I could not help it. I had never experienced such pain in my life, and worse yet, it would be an hour before it ended. Finally, I got to where I could stop yelling, but it still hurt like hell. I was sweating and felt slightly nauseas. Bill assured me it would pass relatively quickly now that the worst was over.

Nurse Brown came in with Jen and Jake saying that the FBI was no longer parked outside.

"Oh. Just in time," Bill stated.

Bill handed Jen a rubber glove and said, "You may touch the green area of his arm," which is the part she could see.

She put the glove on and touched it and said, "I love you, Stan, and soon you will be with us again completely."

"Stan, I am going to stay here with Bill. I may never see you again, I hope," Joe said with a smile and a wink that only I could see. "It has been great to know you and have your company. I will always be grateful for that."

"I feel exactly the same about you too, Joe. If I should make it back, is there anything that you want me to tell Bill for you?"

"Yes, tell him I love him and to never feel guilty that he could not bring me back. He has given so much to so many and to me as well. Please make sure he knows how much I mean that."

Bill said, "You all better go now. The spooks may return and start to wonder just how much time one can spend with Mrs. P."

"Thank you, Bill. Thank you so very much. I will be eternally grateful." Jen reached and kissed his cheek, and Jake said his thanks as well. We said our good-byes and made our exit. I had to walk close to Jen with her coat hung over our two arms, which were side by side.

As we rode home, I was euphoric, so sure that by morning I would be the old Stan again. I did kind of wonder what the hell I was going to tell the neighbors and everyone at work. I watched TV until I was tired enough to sleep, and I went up to lie down beside Jen. The night passed, and something wonderful happened. I fell asleep, and when I woke, I had to piss like a racehorse. I dashed to the toilet and pissed and pissed. Green piss, never heard about that; it had to be either from the shots or from the liquid that was on my arm.

"Wait a minute! I pissed. I pissed!" I said aloud.

That was the first time I had pissed since the incident started, and I had slept also. Maybe this was the beginning of my recovery.

Still, I had no reflection in the mirror. I went downstairs, but I still had no desire for food or coffee. With everyone still asleep, I went back up to our room and lay down again. I slept again. I don't know for how long, but it was a deep sleep. When I woke, I started jumping up and down and yelling, "I'm back! I'm back!" I was back, 100 percent back! I was hungry, and I could see myself in the flesh and in the mirror. I jumped back in bed with a startled Jen, who was now sitting straight up and looking at me like I was cuckoo. She was looking straight at me! "Baby, it's me! Aren't you happy to see me?"

"Stan, what the Sam Hill is wrong with you?"

"Mom, Dad, what's all the yelling about? How's a growing boy supposed to get his beauty sleep!"

The three of us just starred at each other with looks of bewilderment.

THE END ... HUH.

Deadly Red Planet

PROLOGUE

The year was 2030, and on January 15, NASA launched the last flight in a series known as Hercules. Its mission was to study Mars and determine if there is or was ever life on what appeared to be a cold, red, barren wasteland of a planet. Hercules 9 was to be the final flight of this NASA's series. When the final preparations were made for the historic final flight, the crew spent its last night in preparation in NASA's launch site at Cape Kennedy. All awaited the final famous "All systems are go" command from NASA. This flight to the red planet was a manned flight on board a newly designed ship, the first ship built to travel in space at warp speed. It was appropriately christened *Enterprise II*. Its five-person crew was made up of three Americans and two Russians.

The flight crew:

Flight Leader/Pilot: Russell J. Colt, Lt. Col. USMC, nickname Ace
Height: 6'3"; weight: 235 lbs.; eyes: brown; hair: brown

Flight paleontologist: Renee Black, Major USN
Height: 5'8"; weight: 150 lbs.; eyes: blue; hair: blonde

Flight Surgeon: Capt. Jason Quigley, USN, nickname Quig
Height: 6'1"; weight: 205 lbs.; eyes: gray; hair: black

Flight Engineer: Vladimir Chertoff, Capt. RA
Height: 6'4"; weight: 260 lbs.; eyes: brown; hair: brown

Flight Botanist: Nadia Navratilova, Lt. RA
Height: 5'5"; weight: 120 lbs.; eyes: black; hair: black

Lt. Coronial Colt, nicknamed Ace, was the most experienced of the five-member crew, and he had made two flights to the moon and one that circled Mars aboard the Hercules 4 craft. However, the other four astronauts were also very experienced in space flight and experts in their respective fields. One could say this was the cream of the current astronaut crop. Just as the Apollo series had placed man on the moon in the last century, man took his first steps on Mars. Hercules launched on time and successfully.

The crew was in constant contact with Mission Control, and they were all in good mental and physical shape. All appeared to be in good spirits from the recordings shown on TV.

Mission Control monitoring systems recorded a successful landing on Mars at 1800 hours on January 30, 2030. Traveling at sublight speed, the *Enterprise* landed at the exact location and time as planned. The duration on Mars was for seven days, and then the return to Earth. The schedule was laid out in advance, and the astronauts had their own areas and respective assignments. All was proceeding as planned until late afternoon on the fifth day when one of the crewmembers didn't return to base. She had gone out to do her research and never returned. A two-day search failed to find her or her remains. When the crew returned from that second day of searching, Ace had to report the bad news to Mission Control. The crew speculated that she must have gotten lost and ran out of oxygen. Mission Control ordered to abandon search and prepare to take off per preflight plans.

The liftoff was perfect, and two weeks later the *Enterprise* safely landed back on Earth. The flight had been deemed a success, with the one sad exception, the loss of Astronaut Lt. Nadia Navratilova. During the weeks that followed the return of the *Enterprise*, Nadia was awarded posthumous metals. She also was given a hero's parade and burial back in her hometown even though there was no body within the casket.

Upon touchdown, the four remaining crewmembers were whisked away to go through the usual decontamination, physicals, debriefing, and physiological evaluations. The first step was to go into the decontamination booth with all gear on. Then, while the process was happening, they stripped off all their clothing and were examined by two doctors wearing uniforms who searched for any insects, sores, rashes, or any other irregularity of the individuals. Furthermore, their suits and clothing were examined thoroughly for anything unusual.

A couple of small insects were found on the suits of one astronaut, and they were bottled and sent to the lab for analysis. The little insects were about the size of a common housefly. They looked more like a ladybug, although not as cute. They had wings under a hard shell that opened to allow the wings to be useable. These ugly, little guys seemed harmless enough, as there had been no ill effects on the astronauts. But what the scientists were most excited about was that there was life there, no matter how insignificant. That would extrapolate to perhaps more life, even more sophisticated life.

One of the little bugs was studied and proved to be definitely not of Earth. When it was cut open, the very small amount of acid that dripped out from the insect was enough to dissolve the instruments used—the glass, wood, metal, and everything else the acid-like liquid came in contact with. A second bug died within two weeks and was put in formaldehyde and stuck on a shelf. Everyone was trying to figure how to get more funding to extend the series and return to Mars in search of more life.

Florida, home of Cape Kennedy, is known for its many interesting creatures living in and around the Everglades. Most notable are the alligators, but many nonindigenous creatures like rock pythons, Burmese pythons, feral hogs, and a host of other creatures have found the Everglades and surrounding areas to be most fertile feeding grounds. Little did anyone know that a new, small alien creature was about to take up residency on planet Earth and specifically in the Everglades, at least at first. This little bug would be more deadly to mankind than all the other creatures combined.

While the world focused on the fact that there *was* life on Mars, no one seemed to care about what kind of life was there. The common thinking was that there was life; therefore, there had to be other life. Within a week of the flight's return, people started disappearing. First person reported missing was a schoolteacher, followed by a young guy who worked at the corner market, and then a lawyer. There were also reports from the homeless community that some of the homeless were missing. By the end of the first month, there were thirty-five people and numerous dogs and cats that couldn't be accounted for. They had simply vanished, seemingly into thin air, and the numbers doubled near the end of the second month.

CHAPTER 1
DEADLY TRUTH

This is where I came in. I am a detective with the Somerset Police Department. My name is Howard Miller, and I have been a cop for fifteen years. This would turn out to be the weirdest case of my career. I was assigned this missing person's case, and I was determined to solve it. This would take me down a road named Bizarre.

My first hint was when a 911 call came in from a frantic man who said that his wife was severally attacked in her sleep and that he needed an ambulance right away. The black and white (cruiser) first on the scene thought I should see this, and the dispatcher sent me in to investigate. The couple, Kim and Thomas Gibson, had decided to sleep outdoors the night before. The husband awoke to his wife's horrifying screams and called it in.

As the EMT opened the sleeping blanket on the now unconscious woman, they discovered that her right leg all the way up to her hip was gone. Well, it wasn't really gone; it was just that everything inside the skin was gone. The bone, muscle, and fat had been removed somehow. It looked like she had a flesh-colored stocking lying there on the ground where her leg should have been.

On closer examination, I noticed that blood was oozing out of a small wound above the knee on the inside of her thigh, and a hole about the size of a baseball higher up in the larger part of the thigh. There were no other outward marks anywhere on her body, and nobody on the scene had ever seen anything even close to this. The hole in the blanket looked like it was made by strong acid similar to that of a car's battery. Mrs. Gibson was rushed to Riverside Hospital with an escort of police cars. It seemed like they wanted to interview her at the first possible moment. I introduced myself to Mr. Gibson. "May I ask why you and your wife decided to sleep in the park last night?"

"It was such a nice night, with no rain predicted. We do that frequently when the weather is nice and warm enough. We both enjoy the outdoors and especially sleeping out so much."

He began to cry, so I gave him a few moments to compose himself. "Was your wife feeling well when you turned in for the night?"

"Yes, she was. In fact, we made love, drank some wine, and then fell asleep around two in the morning. That was all I remember until she woke me up screaming. She said her leg felt like it was on fire, and then she passed out. When I pulled back the blanket and saw her leg, I was horrified and called you guys right away from my cell."

"You didn't see anything or anyone—nothing unusual—before you slept?"

"No, I told you we made love out there. We would not have done that if anyone were around. The only thing I saw as I woke up was a dog about the size of a cocker spaniel just as it disappeared into the tree line."

"Are you sure it was a dog? Could it have been something else?"

"I can't be absolutely certain. As I said, I saw it for just a split second."

"All right, Mr. Gibson. That will be all for now. Thank you."

About that time, a man dressed in green walked toward us.

"Which of you is Mr. Gibson?"

"I am."

"Mr. Gibson, I am Dr. Wayne. Sir, we need your permission to remove the dead part of your wife's leg. It is nothing but the outer layer of dying flesh, and it will become infected if we don't. The good news is that the hip bone was not damaged, and we will be able to fit her with a prosthetic."

"Oh, Doc, that is good news. She would not do well in a wheelchair or on crutches. Where do I sign?"

"Here is the consent form. Sign at the bottom, please." He handed Gibson the metal chart.

"Is she going to be okay, Doc?"

"Yes, she should recover without any other physical problems. However, she may need a great deal of counseling when she becomes conscious and realizes she has lost her leg."

"Doctor, I'm Detective Miller. Do you have any information on what caused this?"

"Not really, but I suspect some form of acid powerful enough to dissolve flesh and bone was injected into the leg. How and why it was injected into her and why it didn't eat through the outer layer of flesh is a mystery. I have a friend at the university medical school, and I had a brief discussion with her about this. She is anxious to examine the remains of the leg for clues that might be found there."

"Who might she be, Doc.?"

"Dr. Janice Kelly, head of the science department at the university medical center. She is a pathologist and geneticist. She and I were in med school together. We have remained friends and have worked together in the past to solve other medical issues. When she heard about this situation, she was more than willing to help. Her training and her natural curiosity were key to her becoming head of the science department."

As the detective on this case, I had access to the lab, and I accompanied Dr. Wayne that evening. Around five, he brought the amputated remains of Kim Gibson's leg to the lab where Dr. Kelly was waiting.

"Hi, Rob. Bring it over here and let's take a look."

"Hi, Jan. Good of you to stay and check this out. Jan, this is Detective Miller who has been assigned to this case." We exchanged a few pleasantries, and Rob picked up the medical chest and placed it on the examining table. After slipping on a pair of medical latex gloves, he opened it, pulled the remains from the dry ice, and set it on the table.

"Well, Jan, what do you think? Ever seen anything like it before?"

"Can't say I have. Only in the insect world does anything even close to this exist."

"You think an insect did this?"

"Not sure yet, Detective, but it is very possible. Only I am not aware of any such insect that attacks prey of this size. Spiders and some other insects inject their prey with an acid-like substance that dissolves the innards of said prey and then allows them to suck out the fluid."

"Well, there went my appetite. That's quite disgusting!" I almost gagged.

"Rob, when you called me earlier and told me about this, I couldn't think of any other way to remove all the meat and bone and leave only the outer layer of flesh, with the only mark being a small puncture on the thigh. Lets open it up and see what we find, shall we?"

"Sure, Jan, do what ever you wish. I think I'll slip down to the cafeteria and get some coffee. Want some?"

"Yeah, sure, just black. Thanks."

"I think I'll join you!" I was happy to leave that sight behind.

"Ok. We'll be back in fifteen minutes or so. Come on Detective."

As Rob and I disappeared from sight, Jan began opening the leg sack. She recorded her findings for our review. By the time Rob and I returned, she had the leg opened, and she pointed out several things. First was a trace of a very strong, unknown type of acid in addition to a numbing agent, also unknown. That explained how the acid was injected without her waking from the pain. Evidently the numbing agent wore off, and she woke up screaming, which woke her husband up. "Doc, we examined the bag thoroughly and found only a hole on the underside, about where the wound was."

"Then, Detective, that leaves us with one only alternative. It had to have been something that crawled into the bag through the hole we discovered. Did anyone see anything that might have been able to enter the bag?"

"No, the husband said he saw only a dog run into the tree line, but it was about the size of a cocker spaniel, too big to get into the blanket."

"Have either one of you been able to talk with the victim?"

"No, she has been sedated since she arrived, and I have not been allowed in to see her. Not even her husband has been able to see her."

"We really need to talk with her."

"I agree, Doc," I said, looking directly at Rob.

"Well, gentlemen, at this point I am inclined to suspect an insect of some sort, and if I am right, I doubt it is of this world."

"Oh, come on! What we are dealing with—little, green Martians or what?"

"Jan, I get the distinct impression that the good detective does not go for your theory."

"No, and I can't blame him. Deducing things like this must be very hard for a man trained to deal only in facts that can be proven. I almost hope you're right, Detective, because if I am right, we will have a major problem of epidemic proportions on our hands."

Rob sighed and nodded as they cleaned up and headed for their respective homes. I was too restless to go home, so I did what I had said I would not do again. I drove over to my ex-wife, April's, place. She left me years ago because she couldn't deal with being a cop's wife. Nevertheless, for reasons unknown to me, she still loves me. She seems to be able to deal with me as a part-time lover but not as a husband. Women ... go figure. So I went by, and we drank some wine and went to bed. After wearing each other out to our mutual satisfaction, we talked awhile before we fell asleep. I told her about my case and the nutty Dr. Kelly who thought that we were in search of a bug from outer space. We had a good laugh and finally drifted off to sleep.

April had already left for work by the time I woke up the next morning. She was thoughtful enough to cook me breakfast, consisting of scrambled eggs, bacon, and a pot of coffee. They were still warm, and I enjoyed them before I returned to my home. She also left a little note telling me how much she had enjoyed her midnight delight. The term *delight* was from a song we both liked called "Afternoon Delight." We always referred to lovemaking as a delight and simply changed the time to correspond. She and the note she left for me were great for my ego.

During the next few weeks, I was able to interview Kim Gibson, but she could tell me nothing. More people were disappearing at an even faster rate. At last count, close to one hundred people were missing, and calls were pouring into the station about dozens of dogs and cats disappearing without a trace. The mayor was furious, and the press was speculating about some sort of mass murderer who disposed of the bodies without a trace. Some folks thought that the disappearances could be attributed to terrorists. Citizens were demanding that the person or persons be brought to justice. And just like crap, it all flowed downhill and to good ole me. Finally, a break!

I was sent out to investigate a local farmer who said he had shot and killed some kind of animal that was eating his cow. I called Dr. Kelly and asked if she wanted to go along, and she was, as I suspected, most anxious to see this thing. I picked her up, and we arrived at the farmhouse where we met Paul Dowd, the farmer who had called in the report. He showed us the animal he had shot still lying on top of the also dead cow. The dead animal had eight legs, a hairy, reddish body, and large fangs that were still imbedded in the cow's side. It was roundish in shape and was just under a meter in diameter. The cow was nothing but skin, still partially filled with its own dissolved fluids. The cow was like a cow costume half-filled with water. The eyes were gone, and fluid leaked onto the ground from every orifice. The fluid steamed like acid and was still dissolving everything it touched. Fortunately, it had lost a great deal of its potency after dissolving the cow's flesh. Dr. Kelly tried to get some of the fluid into a glass jar, but even in its diluted state, it dissolved the glass. Fortunately, none of it reached her hand. That was something no other known acid could do. "The acid will eventually neutralize after a bit. Perhaps I can capture some then," Dr. Kelly told us. "Detective, can you help me pull the creature away from the cow?"

"Sure." We grabbed it by the legs, so as not to get near the acid, and dragged it about five or six feet from the cow.

"Mr. Dowd, might you happen to have a fire extinguisher?"

"I've got one in my car," I said as I headed for my car. I knew exactly what she was going to do—spray the thing, whatever it was, with my fire extinguisher to neutralize the remaining acid. We then bagged it for transport to her lab.

"Mr. Dowd, when and how did you discover this thing?"

"Well, sir, I came out at daybreak and saw a cow on its side. Cows don't lie down like that unless they're sick or dying. From a distance, I could see something was on it, so I grabbed my shotgun and ran down to see what it was. When I saw the cow was dead and this thing was on top of it, I shot it twice, just to be sure it was dead."

"Have you seen any more of these things around?"

"No, sir, and I hope I never do."

"Mr. Dowd, please do not disturb the cow, as we will send someone back for it. Remember that cow still has that very corrosive fluid inside of it. So please keep everyone away from it. Perhaps you have a tarp or something to cover this animal with?"

"Yes, ma'am, I'll take care of it." We drove back to the lab, discussing what we had just discovered along the way.

I dropped off my new friend and her prize and headed back to headquarters. I told her I would drop by later to see what she discovered. I followed up on a few more sightings that had been phoned in, but they turned out to be false alarms, or if the thing had been there, it was long gone. Around 1600, I stopped back to check in with Dr. Kelly. "Hello, Dr. Kelly. Nice to get the red-carpet treatment from your security team."

"Well, I just figured you'd simply bully your way in anyway." Then she looked up and winked.

"So, any luck?"

"Not much. I made a photographic diary and then carefully sliced into this alien-looking creature, being very mindful of the deadly fluid and taking a bunch of pictures as I went. I found the acid-like substance is contained within sacs in the head and attached to the fangs. I carefully carved around these sacs and fangs, so as not to release any acid, then placed them carefully into a large glass container. Now I was free to dissect the remains." She went on to tell me that the description of this thing matched nothing her research could find. She scoured the Internet and talked with colleagues, the best in their fields, but to no avail. This was unlike any living organism on this planet, bringing her back to her original premise, not of this world.

"Dr. Kelly, you are a very smart woman. But really, how can you still believe this is some alien life form? Where is it from? How would it get here? What is it? This thing is the size of a large dog but heavier and stockier."

"Detective, I didn't say I had all the answers, but I will stake my reputation that this creature is not indigenous to our world. That's all I'm saying."

"And another thing," I said. "Didn't you say that whatever attacked Mrs. Gibson had to be small enough to crawl into her sleeping bag through that little hole? Well, there is no way that this thing could. So now I suppose you are going to tell me it comes in different sizes, huh?"

"Detective, you're a genius!"

"Huh?"

"Have you ever seen a tick after it has gorged itself?"

"Yes, but what ..."

"The tick swells up to four or five times its size, and then slowly as it digests its meal, it returns to normal size. But what if this thing starts life small and then grows as it feeds, but unlike the tick, never returns to its original size?"

"So you are saying each time it feeds, it increases in size? Then how large could it get?"

"That I don't know, but some animals on earth can continue to grow without anything to stop that growth unless controlled by lack of available food, life span, or death from disease or predation."

"Doc, I think that's about all my brain can accept at one sitting. I'll talk to you later. Good-bye."

"Good-bye, Detective. Oh, by the way, don't you have any other cases? You seem to spend all your time with me."

"Well, I'm not quite sure how to take that, but this is the biggest case I've seen since I joined the force, and the captain said to stay with this and only this case until it's solved—or I end up a beat cop. But don't you want me around?"

"I didn't mean it that way. I was just curious."

"Okay good. I'll see you soon." I waved as I walked away and headed for the station. My brain was whirling with too much information. I decided to stop along the way at Kelsey's for a quick drink. I consider myself a great detective, but I do like to bend an elbow and sometimes the rules. I always thought I was a Dirty Harry type of cop. I just wanted to cut through all the red tape and nail the bad guy. But how was I going to get the bad guy when more and more I was beginning to believe that the doc was on to something? My brain was fighting my instincts.

"Hey, Kelsey, give me a double bourbon neat, will ya?"

"Sure, Howard, comin' right up!"

"What's happening, Kelsey?"

"Same shit, different day. You?"

"Same."

Before I could continue what I was saying to Kelsey, I noticed some news footage of the Mars expedition.

"Hey, Kelsey, turn that up—will ya?" I shouted, pointing to the TV hanging behind the bar.

As Kelsey turned up the volume, they were discussing the proposed tenth flight of the Hercules series.

Interviewer: "Dr. Thurgood, do you feel Congress will go along with an additional flight due to your discovery from Hercules 9?"

Thurgood: "We are optimistic at this point. Any discovery of life from another world is extraordinary and requires further investigation. We really need to go back to Mars."

Interviewer: "Just to remind our audience, can you tell us about the discovery from the returning flight of the *Enterprise*?"

Thurgood: "Of course. When we were in the decontamination chamber with the astronauts, we discovered two dead insects and another that eventually died on one of the suits. They were small and rather insignificant, but they prove that life does exist on Mars, and if there is one life form, there must be others. That's why we feel strongly about going back."

"Oh no you don't!" I exclaimed as I slapped down the money for the drink, slugged it down, and ran out the door. I drove straight back to the doc's lab. The security guard refused to let me go in, so I pushed past him and took off running toward her lab. I didn't have time to explain. The security guard and nurses chased me, but I reached the lab before anyone caught me.

"Dr. Jan, you might be right!" I said as I burst through the lab door, one step ahead of the guard.

"That's okay, guys. I was expecting him. You may all go."

As the guard and the two nurses walked away, Jan asked, "Right about what, Detective?"

"I stopped at a bar—"

"Yes, I can tell that all right!"

"And I was watching a report about the Mars flight that returned a few months back. Did you know that they found some dead insects on the suit of one of the astronauts?"

"Yes, but what's that have to do with our mystery?" It seemed to click before I could get the words out. "I see where you're going, detective."

"Do you agree they could have been stowaways and that's how they got here?"

"Well, that would answer many questions, wouldn't it? Now we may be on to something. I need to see that bug they found."

"I'll get a search warrant tomorrow."

"No, that may not be necessary. I know Dr. Thurgood, who was director of the Hercules series."

"Yes, that's the man I saw being interviewed."

"I'll call him now."

Jan picked up her cell phone, pulled up his number, and called.

"Hello, Brad, how are you? Janice Kelly here."

"Well, hello, Jan! How are you? Long time no see!"

"Brad, listen, I'll get straight to the point. I need to see that bug you found on the astronaut's suit. We may have a situation here. Can I see you tomorrow?"

"I'm afraid that won't work, too much going on right now, but if you want to go to the base now, I can do it."

"I wouldn't normally put you to this inconvenience, but it is terribly important!"

"Okay, Jan, if it's that important."

"Brad, thank you!"

"I'll meet you at the front gate in forty-five minutes then."

"Thanks again, Brad. See you then."

"Well, Jan, you really know a lot of bigwigs!" I said.

"Not really, Brad and I just worked on a project together some years back, and we got on well. So we've stayed in touch."

"Old boyfriend, huh?"

"Certainly not. Get your mind out of wherever it is. Let's go, Detective, if you want me to help you solve your case."

"Okay, Doc, but will you please call me Howard? My car is out front."

She nodded, and we drove off. It was a long drive to the base, and we got to know each other a bit. I was in awe of this woman. I had never been around such a learned person. She told me of some of the things she had been involved with while she was with the lab—deadly pathogens, strange viruses, some even made, and insects and sea animals that had been newly discovered. For a guy who was used to solving most cases on his own, I was sure that without her, I might never find the answer. If the killer was some kind of bug, I might be off this case.

As I pulled up in front of the main gate, Dr. Thurgood was waiting. He shouted from his car, "Follow me, I'll get you through." The marine at the gate waved him through and then waved us through. I thought how great those young marines looked in their dress blues and how snappy the gesture was that they used to wave us through. It reminded me of my days in the corps. I had two years of embassy duty in China and two years with the parade unit at the Marine Corp Barracks in Washington, DC.

We pulled up to the main building entrance and headed to the lobby, where Dr. Kelly met us. We made the introductions, and then he led us straight to the lab. Then we all put on protective suits and went straight into the room where the remaining bug was stored. Dr. Kelly examined it and found that this little creature was a smaller version of what had killed the cow. However, this little guy had wings!

"This just keeps getting worse. Howard, this little version can fly, and that means its range is much greater than I had first thought."

"Jan, would you mind explaining what's going on here?"

"Sure, Brad."

She gave us a succinct version of what had transpired and what she suspected. They talked for a while, and then Thurgood said, "I think we must be dealing with a creature that goes through a metamorphosis where it eats, grows, and at some point sheds its wings. This is the way it evolved. When small, it needs flight for protection from predation and to increase its range. As it grows, it has fewer and fewer natural predators to fear, and it becomes too large to fly. Like the stork that eats the baby crocs, but with age comes size, and the hunter becomes the hunted."

"You mean Mars, right?" I said.

"No, I don't think so. We were studying Mars too closely during the Hercules series and even before that. We searched and searched for life there and could find none. In addition, this critter needs a prey animal. We frankly didn't pay much attention to this little guy because we were so intent on going back to find what else might exist there. We thought there might be some form of underground life forms we had somehow not detected. However, this thing is a surface dweller."

"How did it survive without a food source until we got there?"

"Well, Detective, it may be like a common flea in that it can lay dormant for a very long time. Then when a warm-blooded animal comes by, it hatches into the flea and jumps on its host. That would be my best guess at this point."

"I agree with you, Brad. That seems to be the only logical answer."

"Logical? There is nothing logical about any of this. I think I must be dreaming!"

"You must not send anyone back to Mars, Brad. We may have already sealed our fate. It's just too risky, and bringing back more of these would be disastrous."

"I agree with Jan, Dr. Thurgood."

"Yes, yes, you're right, at least for now. But I suspect that this guy somehow is from another planet and it was somehow transplanted to Mars."

"That brings up a whole lot to speculate on, but for now we need to find and wipe out this bug."

I began to laugh. "Now just who do you think we should share our little preposterous tale of warning with? Perhaps the media, the CDC, the FBI? Or should we just stay quiet and try to seek it out and kill it ourselves? But how many of these buggers are out there?"

Then a stroke of pure good fortune came our way. My ex-wife called me to tell me one of her students brought in a jar of very strange-looking bugs to her elementary school science class. She called to ask me if I thought it might have anything to do with my case.

I hurried to her school. She was on her lunch break, so I had a quick sandwich with her, and then she gave me the bugs. They were those little buggers all right! There must have been a dozen of them in that jar. They were evidently too stupid to know that if they excreted some of that acid, they would be free. Thank God that was the case, or we may have had many causalities. It reminded me of when I was a kid. I would catch wasps in a jar, turn it upside down, and the wasps were too stupid to fly out the opened bottom. They'd just kept flying up and banging against the glass bottom of the jar. Or maybe they had to bite into something to release this acid-like venom.

She brought me to her classroom and introduced me to Johnny and the rest of the class. I explained to everyone that these bugs could hurt them and make them very, very sick and to warn their friends to leave them be and certainly not to try to pick them up. If they found any more, they should tell the police exactly where they saw them. I said good-bye to the kids, and April walked me to the hallway. I carefully took the jar of critters. "You are a doll!" I exclaimed, and I kissed her and drove off to see Dr. Kelly.

This time the guard let me pass without a query.

"Doc, Doc, look what I've got!"

"Oh my God! Where did you get these?"

I told her, and she was amazed. We agreed that we had to find out where the student discovered them.

"I told April that we would need to talk with the student and his parents, and she gave me his name and address."

"Now, who's April?"

"She's the teacher of the student who brought them to school, and she's also my ex-wife."

"Perhaps we should try to see this student after three because he would be home from school by then."

"Okay, Doc, but what do we do now—with the bugs, I mean?"

"I want to try some experiments on them to see what will kill them. First I need to separate them into different containers. This could be tricky."

I watched her carefully lift them, one by one, with what looked like a long pair of tweezers. Again, they did not excrete the acid-like substance. Now there were sixteen jars, each with one of these nasty, little bugs in them. She pulled out some over-the-counter wasp spray and shot a blast into one jar and then recapped it. The bug seemed agitated by it, but after twenty minutes, it was still alive. She noted that in a journal along with all the ingredients in that spray. Next she tried to drown it in tap water but no dice. On another one, she tried fingernail-polish remover, still nothing. She ran through a series of different products that could be purchased over the counter. None worked. These little bastards seemed indestructible. It was now shortly after three.

"Doc, take a break and let's go interview the kid."

"Oh, yes, thank you for reminding me. Let's go."

I was glad to see that she was as interested in the solution to this case as I was. I had never had a partner before, but this gal would be a good one. When we arrived at the Simpson home, little Johnny was in the front yard.

"That's our little guy right there."

"Howard, we should not talk to him without one of his parents there."

"Yes, Mother!"

"Indeed!" Jan said with a straight face, but I saw the twinkle in her eye.

I walked to the front door as Doc stopped to ask Johnny to come and talk with us.

"Mrs. Simpson, I am Detective Howard Miller, and that is Dr. Janice Kelly from the University Medical Center. We have a few questions for you and Johnny."

She freaked. "What's wrong? What's wrong with my baby?"

Jan spoke up quickly. "Nothing, ma'am, nothing. He took some bugs to school today, and we just need to know where he got them. That's all."

By now little Johnny was coming up onto the porch. His mom opened the door and stepped back. "Come on in then."

"Hi, Mr. Policeman."

"Hi, Johnny."

Johnny's mom knelt down and held little Johnny's face in her two hands. "Son, these nice folks would like to know where you got the bugs you took to school today."

"Oh, they were down by the creek, Mommy."

"Johnny, would you show the policeman where exactly?"

"Sure, this way!" replied Johnny as he bolted to the back door. I ran right beside him to be sure he stayed away from them.

We ran out behind his house through a batch of trees and to the small creek that ran parallel to his home. He showed me where he had found the bugs, and there were approximately a dozen more.

I asked Johnny if he could run back to his house and get me another glass jar from his mom. Within a minute or so, he returned with the jar and his mom. "Excuse me, please. Can you tell me what this is all about? You're beginning to frighten me."

"Sorry, ma'am. This a police investigation."

My new partner quickly overruled me. "Forgive the detective. He's been a police officer too long, and you do need to know to keep Johnny and the rest of your family, including pets, out of these woods until we can be certain there are no more of them. I think I captured all that are here and in close proximately. However, a team of CDC folks will sweep the area in a few days. These bugs carry a virus hazardous to humans and animals. We will be making an announcement later today on television and radio to inform folks of the danger."

Then she turned to me. "I have the rest of them. Let's go, Howard." Looking at Johnny, she said, "Now remember—stay away from these bugs. Okay?"

"Okay, I will."

"Good-bye, ma'am, Johnny. Here's my card should you happen to see any more of them." I handed her my card, and we left.

As we drove back toward the lab, Jan said, "Well, tap water didn't work, and now we know one more thing that won't work, stream water. They were in it."

Doc got on her cell phone and called someone she knew on a first-name basis at CDC. She sure knew all the right people.

"Damn, woman, is there anyone you *don't* know?"

She just gave me a look as she continued her conversation.

When she was finished, I asked about it.

"Howard, the CDC will be here tomorrow with a full contingent of equipment and personnel. You might want to alert your boss and see how he and the mayor wish to handle the PR. Soon it will be all over the place. Even the military or National Guard may be called in, but the CDC will be in charge."

"Right, and I am taking you with me, as you are the one that has this raining down on us."

"Fine, let's go. I'll be happy to carry your water for you."

"You are something, Jan, you know it?"

I was really beginning to take a shine to this brassy woman.

"Oh, and, Howard, before you ask, yes, this guy was an old boyfriend from college. Thought I better mention it in case he acts a little familiar. I don't need any comments from the peanut gallery either. Got it?"

Yep, I really liked this brassy woman.

We arrived at the station about five and caught the captain as he was leaving.

"Cap, I need to talk with you!"

"Miller, can't it wait until tomorrow?"

"Captain, I think you really need to hear this now."

"And who are you?"

"My name is Dr. Janice Kelly, and I have been helping Howard … Detective Miller on this case."

The captain looked at me with a puzzled expression, and I simply smiled and nodded. He paused for a moment and then said, "All right. My office—and let's be quick about it."

"Cap, you better sit down 'cause you ain't gonna believe this one. Jan, be my guest!"

I sat back to watch the fun. Jan told him in vivid detail what we had discovered. I watched his lips part then his jaw drop lower and lower, and his eyes got as big as saucers. I could hardly contain myself. I had never seen the captain at such a loss for words.

"Well, Captain, that's about the sum of it."

He began to mumble and stutter. Finally, regaining his usual demeanor, he walked to his door, opened it, and then bellowed, "Someone get the mayor on the blower right now!"

"Young lady, you are going to get the privilege of telling our illustrious mayor that story."

"Guess you get to carry his water too!" I said, and then I just howled.

"Shut up, you damn fool, or I swear I'll suspend your ass!" he bellowed as he stormed out into the lobby. "Where in the hell is my call to the mayor?"

Finally, they reached the mayor's aide. "This is Captain Ickes. Where in the hell is the mayor!"

Ickes slammed down the phone and said, "He's over at city hall for the city council meeting. Let's go, you two! Miller, you drive to city hall—and make it code three!"

The captain was a good man and a super cop. He was also a former career marine who had won the congressional Metal of Honor and had retired after twenty-two years when he was wounded. He was next in line for chief of police. Somerset has been a very peaceful place ever since ol' Cap took the reigns. But damn, he knew only two ways to talk. It's what his cops called his mayor speak and cop speak. You can guess which one he had used since we got to the station. Jan would soon hear the other. We reached city hall, and he rolled right into the council meeting and interrupted the mayor's pontification.

"Captain Ickes, what is the meaning of this?"

"Sorry, Mayor. It's a matter of utmost importance, and you and the city council must hear it now or you will all be caught with your pants down."

"Well, come up here and tell us all about it."

"Actually, I think it best if Dr. Janice Kelly, head of the Science Department at our own university medical center, tells the story. Dr. Kelly, would you please come up and tell the mayor and the city council what you told me just a short while ago? Thank you."

"Mr. Mayor, ladies and gentlemen. What I am about to tell you is most unbelievable … but nonetheless true."

She went on just as before, getting the same reaction from the people in the room that she had gotten from the captain. Whatever was on the agenda was quickly whisked away, and this became the meeting that lasted until two in the morning. The mayor called the governor and asked for National Guard troops to be sent in to prevent anyone from coming into or going out of the town. It was feared that panic was sure to ensue and that people would try to leave. That would allow a stowaway of one of these critters, and the contagion would spread.

The governor had already begun getting the Guard mobilized, based on a call from Jan's old boyfriend, Roger Talent of the CDC. By dawn, the entire city limits would be barricaded with armed troops standing watch at every road, path, or highway out of town. By ten hundred hours, the CDC trucks rolled in. The city of Somerset was in a total lockdown.

The editor of the town's only newspaper and member of the city council put out an early addition of the paper, carrying the whole story, including photos of the alien in both bug form as well as what we thought was the adult form. Little did we know what was about to ensue. The town behaved rather well, I thought. There was no looting and no real panic or massive attempts to break out of town. This was a good thing. There were enough deaths from this damn bug. Soon the story was picked up by the wire services, and it was everywhere. The media nicknamed it the Nadia Bug when they heard it had come back on the Hercules flight and had killed one crewmember, or at least that was the speculation.

Jan and Dr. Talent worked night and day trying to find a poison that would kill the insects. Nothing worked except stomping them, but that would not completely eradicate them. Special soles made from materials used in NASA's space program seemed to resist the powerful acid, plus the little ones didn't contain enough acid to cause long-term problems. The larger ones could be shot and killed if you could hit them in the head or spine again just behind the neck. It was the fang sacs that contained large reserves of the acid; fortunately, after the bug died, the acid was slowly released and consumed the fallen creature. The National Guard was on the lookout for them and did manage to kill quite a few of them. Nature had done a good job of helping this bug survive. The wings helped it flee from danger while it was small. Then as it grew in proportion to its ability to feed, its sheer size and strength was its protection.

Then one came out of the woods about the size of a grizzly. This was the largest one seen, and it took a rocket launcher to bring it down. The rocket hit the area of the acid sacs, and it was almost completely dissolved by its own acid, along with anything within a ten-foot radius. That photo went around the world in less than a day.

I didn't see much of Jan during those days, and I had to spend most nights with April, because she was scared to death that one of those creatures would get in her house. It was strange that our relationship, which had become one of just using each other to relieve our sexual desires, was now being one of additional need. I talked with Jan for a few minutes each day to find out what didn't work to kill the creatures. The list became extensive.

It was Saturday night, and I had promised April that I would be there before it got dark. She had promised to have a nice dinner and a couple of bottles of wine. Bribery was a great thing—dinner, wine, and each other for dessert, as she always referred to it. It was a perfect evening with her. Since I had been there almost every night, it seemed almost like being married to her again. We turned in, feeling a bit playful, and we were really enjoying each other when she stopped and said, "Did you hear that?"

Of course I said no. What does the guy always say in a moment like that?

Then I heard it, a sound like breaking glass. I grabbed my weapon and ran down stairs, paying no mind to my naked condition. I stopped at the last step and looked around. Nothing. So with my weapon raised to the defensive position, I walked slowly through the house.

Suddenly something hit me from behind, knocking me to the ground. My instinct was to spin, and when I did, I knocked the creature to the ground. I jumped to my feet, not realizing blood was streaming down my back. The creature reared up like a spider, fangs showing and moving toward me.

I began to back up and then decided to take a shot at the head. I fired and hit it, but it didn't stop. It kept coming, so I shot it in its front leg. It buckled and wailed like a banshee. I shot the other front leg. Now it was facedown, still squealing and trying to push forward with the two front legs gone. I began to feel the pain in my back, reached around, and came back with a bloody hand. I was really pissed, so I shot each leg and listened to the creature's pitiful screeching. Unable to move, I stuck the barrel two inches from its spine and fired. It went instantly limp—game over! I win! April came down and took me to the couch and tended to my wounds. I had one of the guard patrols take the corpse to Jan at the lab.

A couple of weeks had gone by since all hell had broken loose and my run-in with one of them at April's. The CDC and Guard were sending men out to bug sightings and stomping the little ones to death since no other solution of any magnitude had been found. Then came the day the science fiction turned 180 degrees around, and the fiction part was dropped. Three weeks back, the news had reported that a man from our town had flown to Africa before the quarantine took place. The news reported that the man had asked for a blanket and went to sleep. When he arrived at the airport, they couldn't wake him. They pulled off the blanket and found that he was a sac from the stomach down.

Later they found a male lion and a giraffe in the same condition, except completely sucked dry. A week later, a large bull elephant was found in the same condition. Then yesterday a huge creature was witnessed running down another elephant. At first, no one believed that it could be that big, and no one had taken any photos of it. That had news people scrambling to get over to Africa to see and photograph it. A few got through before they shut the airport down. The photos came streaming across the wire service and onto the front page of every newspaper and in every TV newsroom. It was a much larger version of the creature than I had shot in April's house, mine being about the size of a Saint Bernard. The photos of the creature in Africa showed it to be approximately twenty feet high. That's the size of a two-story building! The press had dubbed him Mr. Big. It was comfortable staying in the plains of Africa. Therefore, only a few people were attacked by it. However, it would soon kill off the elephant population and then all the large animals. How big would it grow to by then? About the same time, a slight break came through from the lab. Jan called me right away.

"Howard, some slightly good news. It seems these creatures can only breed when they have fed and grown the first time. After that, they can no longer breed. The reproductive organs are gone in the several large creatures we have dissected, including the one you killed. So it is imperative that we find a way to keep them from reaching that second stage. That's where we must concentrate our efforts."

"Well, that's good news, Jan. How have you been? You must be exhausted."

"I am, Howard, but I have got to crack this. They were going to send me to Africa to check on Mr. Big, but now in light of this latest discovery, there is no need. So I will just keep plugging away. Oh, must go. Talk to you soon. Come by the lab some time. I miss you. Bye."

I don't know why, but that made my day! *I must be getting soft on her. Oh, don't be silly.*

I followed the reports of Mr. Big, and it seemed that nothing would bring it down. Gunfire, rocket launchers, and even bombs did not even faze it. At this size, it was almost indestructible. What was it going to take to stop these things? We were losing the battle. They were beginning to show up outside our town. We could not contain them any longer, so the quarantine was lifted. An answer had to be found. Furthermore, more bad news came from Africa. It seemed that the big ones did have a bigger role in the promulgation of the species. They protected the smaller ones, thus increasing their odds for survival. As they multiplied exponentially, our fate was being sealed. If a way to eradicate them in mass didn't happen very soon, all life on earth would disappear. Now they were hunting in packs with Mr. Big protecting the pack. We were beginning to see how their social structure worked, something heretofore not seen or known.

The photo that came in was Mr. Big with at least twenty creatures about the size of the one I had killed around him. This brought a whole new dimension to the problem. In this formation, they could attack the villages and slaughter whole tribes of indigenous people, as their primitive weapons would be of no use. There was a report of another Mr. Big in China, and then one was sighted in Wyoming. It was looking like our darkest hour had arrived.

Then more sightings came in of the big ones and the packs they hunted with. Northern Russia was the latest, which meant that they were not confined geographically by temperature. Three more big ones were seen in the rain forest of South America. In South America, the outbreak had now grown to epidemic proportions. It had been about three weeks since I had last talked to Jan, and I stopped by the lab to see her. This once very attractive woman had lost way too much weight. Her eyes were hollowed out, her skin was pasty looking, and she had a terrible cough.

"Jan, I'm taking you out of here. You are literally killing yourself! This is not your fight alone, and I won't allow this."

"Howard, I'm fine. I'm just a little tried."

"Don't believe her, Howard. She has been running on about two hours of sleep a day. She won't listen to me. Please, if you can get her out of here, do it. She will kill herself if she keeps going like this. She is no use to us dead."

"You must be Roger?" He was an odd duck. He was skinny, tall, about six foot six, bald except for sidewalls, with a hook nose.

"I am, and I care about her. Please get her out before it's too late."

"You got it!" And with that, I scooped her up in my arms and carried her out. She kicked and hit me, but I would not put her down. I put her in my car and drove straight to my house. I put her in bed and sat over her to make sure she stayed there. Maybe she subconsciously knew she was not in the lab anymore because she slept for twenty hours. When she woke up, she smiled at me and said,

"You are my white knight."

Then she collapsed again. I called Bob Wayne from Riverside Hospital and told him what had happened. He came with an RN, fed her intravenously, and had the nurse stay with her. Two days later, she woke up and sounded like my Jan. She was still way too thin, but she was eating like a horse. I almost could not keep up. A day later, the nurse said she was fine and left.

She kept begging me to let her see the news. I told her that when she was back to her normal weight, she could—and not until then. She fussed a little, but I knew that she knew that I was only protecting her from herself. I lied to her and said that I didn't know what was going on, though I did, and it was bleak. These insidious damn bugs were taking over, and we could only slow the tide that seemed inevitable.

The NATO forces were considering using nukes on the big ones, but that wouldn't help. We didn't know if it would work, and the big ones were now on every continent. We did know that they were impervious to radiation. Then NATO got the idea to airlift the ones that were ten to fifteen feet in height to the North Pole. The much bigger ones were far too heavy even for the largest of choppers. The big bugs would not freeze but would starve from lack of food. We knew that they slept standing, much like a cow. The plan was to get the world's most powerful helicopter to drop a heavy steel chain on both sides of a sleeping beast. Then a man would connect the special clamps together, and the chopper could lift it. If the chopper got the beast up off the ground, the plan was to take it above ten thousand feet to see if the lack of oxygen would kill it. If not, onto the North Pole to drop it from as high as possible to see if the fall would kill it. If that didn't work, just leave it there to starve and then drop more big ones, and perhaps they would cannibalize each other.

It seemed like a win-win plan. So the military tried it with the one in Wyoming first. The airlift worked! The chopper was able to lift it, but neither lack of oxygen nor the fall had any noticeable effect on it. Now the only thing was to monitor it and hope it couldn't somehow cross back to populated parts of the world. Fortunately, it did not. They picked up another from California and did another successful drop. However, they did not attack one another.

Nevertheless, all were optimistic that hunger would eventually drive them to cannibalism. This was likely a futile effort, and it might have only been a morale booster for the people of the world. But it was doomed to failure, as the creatures were becoming large faster than we could haul them away.

Jan had made a full recovery. April had become accustomed to living alone again, and I was wondering how it would all end. Africa was now overrun with these horrible creatures. It was estimated that these creatures in Africa had killed 20 percent of the population, and 25 percent in India. Other countries either weren't reporting or had much lower numbers. However, there were more and more sightings of these creatures everywhere. Jan's team estimated that, based on rate of growth and the sizes they could reach, life on earth as we knew it would last only another fifteen years. As life on each continent became extinct, the production of new eggs would cease until a new food source arrived. The existing ones would die off in time, and the continent would lie void of all but plant life, with no chance to repopulate it with any life form. The world united against a common foe. Muslims and Jews worked side by side, as did all races, nationalities, and colors. The old saying became the law of the land; *the enemy of my enemy is my friend.* Maybe this was God's way to destroy the world, as he had promised never to do it again with water, or perhaps it was a way to unite us and stop wars between the same species.

But was the earth to keep such horrible creatures to lie in waiting for another race or species to repopulate the world, only to be eaten up by these voracious creatures again? Shoot, why worry about that? God could do anything, so no need for me to try to outthink him. I had to protect Jan, April, and anyone else for as long as I could.

Jan went back to work at the lab. However, she was not going to make the same mistake of working herself to death or starving herself. She was appointed the head person to deal with this problem, and I resigned as a detective and worked side by side with her and her team. I would see that she took care of herself. She knew the end was near, and nothing they did in the lab was working. Every man, woman, and child was out there killing the creatures as fast as they could, but they were way too prolific for us to get ahead.

It was Thanksgiving, and Jan asked me over to her place for dinner. I thought she would have many friends there, so I dressed up as though I was going to a semiformal dinner. I bought a magnum of Dom Perignon champagne. I did not believe in that fashionably late crap, so I arrived right on time. She opened the door, and I couldn't believe how beautiful she looked. All her weight was back on, and

I swear in better places. I couldn't believe my eyes. Her place was decorated nicely, and there was a large one-hundred-gallon saltwater fish tank with the most beautifully colored fish I had ever seen. She invited me into the kitchen and handed me an extra-dry martini. How did she know?

"Well, here's to you, my dear, and thank you for saving my life, even if it may only be for a short while."

I noticed the nicely prepared dining table, and to my shock, there were only two settings.

"Oh, I thought it was going to be a grand affair, but only two of us?"

"Well, it is just the two of us, but nonetheless, it *will* be a grand affair."

I wasn't quite sure how to take that, but I hoped I had it right.

She smiled and said, "Let's sit down, shall we?"

"Sure, let's do."

I headed for the couch, and she followed. I sat down, and she sat close. I started to think about what that body beneath her fine clothes looked like, and I hoped that before dawn, I would know. Crash! The sudden sound caused me to drop my drink, and reflex caused me to pull my weapon. There before me was one of those horrid creatures, and I had had my fill of them. Then it reared up, fangs protruding. Jan panicked and ran toward the kitchen. It followed her, and as it passed by the fish tank, I shot. I missed the creature and hit the fish tank, shattering it and dousing the creature in saltwater. I readied to fire again when I saw it drop flat to the ground and literally dry up before our eyes. To my amazement, it was the saltwater that it couldn't take. That's why we hadn't discovered the antidote sooner. It was too simple and right under our noses all the time.

Jan heard me yell, "Yeah, baby!"

When she saw the creature dead on the floor, she thought I had shot it. Then I told her what really happened.

Again with the cell phone. This time she said, "Dad, it's me. It's plain, old saltwater that kills them almost instantly!" She hung up without another word. I looked at her, confused. She laughed and gave me the biggest and best kiss I'd ever had. She pulled away and took my hand and led me to the staircase.

"In case you're interested, it was General Kelly, commander of the joint chiefs of staff, I was just talking with."

"Hold it! You're that Kelly!"

"Yes dear, that Kelly. Now come along quietly."

I was babbling like Porky Pig as she led me up the staircase and into her room.

"By the time I finish with you, Mr. Detective, the Nadia Bug and all her relatives will be heading for the big meltdown."

While we made love, planes were fueling and loading their Bombays with bombs filled with God's wonderful oceanic saltwater. The water that covered three-quarters of the earth's surface would now serve up the deadly cocktail that would save the world from alien creatures. So simple that we damn near never found it. Only by the sheerest of accidents did we find the fix ... or was it by accident?

THE END ... ONLY FOR THE BUG.

CRYPTURE 4
What the Night Brings

CHAPTER 1
A WEEKEND TO REMEMBER

I was sitting in my library when Maria, my housekeeper, announced that Mr. Kevin Longstreet had arrived for our appointment. "Ask him to join me here, and bring us some tea, please."

When he came in, I said, "Mr. Longstreet, thank you for coming. Please have a seat on the couch. Pardon me for not getting up, but that is rather difficult."

"That's quite all right. Please, I was quite curious about why you invited me, ma'am?"

"As you know, many people have wanted to interview me or write an account of my crazy story, and I have declined all of them for nearly ten years since ... since that weekend. I have decided to tell my story to you."

"Why me, ma'am?"

"Several reasons. First, you're the only writer who writes books about weird, untold stories and presents them in an objective manner. Second, I believe that you will honor my terms. And finally, you are the only one who has respected my privacy." He nodded as if he understood. We had tea and made small talk. I wanted to get to know him a little and confirm that what I thought I knew of him was accurate. He certainly didn't look like what I expected. He looked like the picture on his book covers, but that was simply his face, and he was rather handsome, but he was way shorter and chubbier than I would have guessed. I think that photo on his covers is at least ten years old. But no matter; he wasn't there to become my lover.

"Kevin, I want you to warn the public, to stop the incessant calls asking me to tell this story, and to report it in a factual manner, not for sensationalism or to sound like some science-fiction story. I'm giving you the exclusive rights to my story. Do you agree to my terms?"

"Yes, ma'am, and I will have my publisher draft a contract to include all of those items. When did you wish to start?"

"Now, if that's agreeable with you?"

"Yes, ma'am. Let me retrieve my notebook and recording device from my car."

I nodded, and he scurried off. Meanwhile, I had Maria make more tea and some finger sandwiches. When he returned, I said, "Kevin, would you like me to just tell you the story, or would you prefer to ask me questions?"

"I think it works best when you just tell me the story and for me to ask questions when I need additional info. Would that be okay with you?"

"Fine, that's just fine." He turned on his tape recorder and took up his pad and paper. I began.

"My name is Abra Scott, and I once lived in Bonita Springs, Florida, near where what I am about to tell you took place. I don't and won't live there anymore. When I hailed from the suburbs of Columbus, Ohio, I wanted a warm climate.

"I moved to Florida after I graduated from the Ohio State University in 2006. I had a full scholarship there for gymnastics, but that's another story.

"I was five foot seven inches, weight 150 pounds, and had a typical gymnast's body with strong, muscular legs, and tiny waist. Then I met Jake, Barlow was my fiancé. We met about a year after I moved here, and we'd been together ever since. I was very fit, and many would-be suitors told me so. They said I was real easy on the eyes, and so there was never a shortage of men wanting to date me.

"Oh, I know you won't *want* to believe what I'm about to tell you, but it happened nonetheless. What happened did so within twenty-four hours. I will never forget what that night brought, for it left me as I am today.

"What is it about the night that conjures up so much fear in humans? Little children fear the night, yet they have not been taught that fear.

"Ever notice how the slightest noise causes you to twitch or jump or send a cold chill running up your spine? How the same sounds by day would not even register with your senses—the snap of a twig, the rustle of the wind, the crackle of dry leaves under the weight of a small animal, or the flap of a bird's wings. Well, after you spend this night with me, you may never venture out again in the dark for long.

"I was engaged to a wonderful man—smart, tall, handsome, well built, a college basketball star, and best of all, he loved me and me alone. I was one lucky gal—well, I was until that night.

"It was mid-July, and the weatherman was predicting a rather warm day. Jake and I decided to go horseback riding on a deserted stretch of beach. We set out early because it was cooler then. Jake met me at the stable just before dawn. His parents owned a ten-acre property with a stable, so Jake always had a horse to ride. He took me riding once shortly after we first met, and it has been a passion for me ever since. As an engagement present, his folks gave me my own horse. I named her Jolly. We loaded the horses into the trailer and headed to a place known as Deadman's Beach."

"Deadman's Beach? Can you elaborate?"

"Sure, at least what I know of it. Not sure why it's called that or when it got that name, but Deadman's Beach is a secluded stretch of beach that was part of the nearly two-thousand-acre estate of the Detwiller family. This property had been in that family for 150 years. Builders and developers have tried to buy this property for decades. When the last Detwiller inherited it, he planned to sell it. But before the final deal was inked, his wife, twelve-year-old daughter, and nine-year-old son were mysteriously and savagely killed on the beach. He broke off negotiations and remained there as a recluse until his death from natural causes at the age of ninety-two. The details of their deaths were hushed up, and little is known to this day about the exact cause of their deaths.

"The long, narrow property has a narrow private road that runs along its eastern border. This property is totally surrounded by state and national parks. How it was not taken by eminent domain is unknown, but the owners' great wealth probably had a lot to do with that. It is bordered to the south and west by the Gulf of Mexico, just west of Everglades City and the Everglades National Forest. To the north are Big Cypress National Park and Fakahatchee Strand Preserve State Park. The old mansion that was midway between the road and the gulf hasn't been lived in since Darren S. Detwiller III died more than ten years ago. Neither of us had never been on this beach before and had only the map Jake had gotten from somewhere to guide us to the area of entry near where the property met the Gulf of Mexico." I continued my story, starting with how Jake greeted me that morning ... "Hi, babe! Wow, you look great!"

"Good morning to you, kind sir, and you ain't so bad yourself."

He came over and kissed me, and that caused us to take our first twilight delight in the hay of the barn. What a great way to start this great day. After helping each other remove the unwanted hey from our bodies and composing ourselves, we saddled our horses for a ride along the stretch of beach known to the locals as Deadman's Beach. The sun was just an inch above the horizon, and the azure-blue sky was laced with high stratus clouds. The sea air was fresh, crisp, and clean.

Florida is known for beautiful beaches where legions of surfers, beach bums, and beach parties with ditzy, beautiful, and well-built blondes live and play all year-round. But nobody talks much about the aforementioned ten-mile stretch of beach with no houses, surf shops, or lifeguard stands. We drove down the blacktop road and came to a right turn, the last right turn before reaching the Detwiller property. Beyond that turn, the blacktop continued about fifty feet but looked as though it hadn't been driven. Then it ended abruptly at the edge of the Detwiller property. A metal sign read *End of state maintenance*. The road turned to the dirt road on the property. A mailbox was falling down just to the side of the dirt road, and the forest on either side of the road was dense. According to the map, the road continued to the end of the property. "Where will you park?"

Jake said we'd drive to the end of the road, park our vehicle, and unload the horses. When we reached the end of the road, there was a large turn-around and only the forest ahead.

With the horses unloaded, we walked then down a narrow path that led to the beach. Once there, the sand was an ugly shade of brown, and nobody had cleaned up the tree droppings or seaweed or anything that had washed ashore. Maybe it was because the land behind the beach has very rough terrain that is heavily forested with palm and pine and scrub brush.

We talked and walked, leading our horses. Jake's horse, Buttermilk, was a sixteen-hands-high Appaloosa stallion, mostly white with varying shades of gray patches all over. He even had a black spot around his left eye, which made him look as if he had a shiner. Jolly was my horse, a thirteen-hand Palomino gelding, solid bronze with four white stockings. The plan was to explore the entire ten-mile stretch, swim and have a picnic lunch, sunbathe, and maybe be a bit daring out in plain view of Mother Nature.

There could *not* have been a more perfect day! A few clouds were in the bright blue sky, and an occasional big, white, puffy cloud would drift by, taking the sun off us for as much as a minute. When it returned from hiding behind the clouds, the brown color of the beach looked closer to red, bloodred. We were the only people in sight, and it would remain that way until we were off this property. The thick, lush green forest was to our right and the beautiful, blue gulf to our left. After about half a mile, the sand was the shade of an old, red, clay brick house. We decided to have a little race, so we lined up, and I yelled, "One … two … go!" I knew that Buttermilk was faster than Jolly, but they both loved to run. We raced about a mile, and Jake pulled up to wait for me. Then we walked them another mile while we talked of our future, the date we would marry, how many children we wanted, and where we wanted to live. We each owned a home, but we had our sights set on selling both and buying a brand-new home. We had so many plans. I remember thinking that this was one of the many standout days of my life. Doing nothing very special but being with each other in a setting of sheer beauty, save the bloody red sand.

As it approached eleven o'clock, Jake announced that he was hungry. We parked our ponies, broke out some of our little lunch, spread a blanket, and opened the wine and settled in for more of whatever. We ate cheese and crackers, sipped wine, laughed, and talked. I swear I can't remember any other day that we were so talkative. We talked about our future and how we were both anxious to marry, but Jake wanted kids right away, and I wanted to wait until our careers were more established. He wanted a small, intimate wedding, but my folks were set on a big one. I really didn't care one way or the other. Jake and I were both athletic and were both sticklers about our weight and appearance. While we talked, I made Jake a tomato and mustard sandwich. I chuckled a bit as I made his sandwich, thinking back to the first time he'd made one and how awful it had sounded to me. He'd finally convinced me to try it, and it was actually quite good. When we finished our lunch, I asked him, "Where to now, big boy?"

He stood up and offered me his hand, but as I started up from the ground, he pulled me violently into his arms and began kissing me as if it was the first time. The kissing brought us back to the blanket, and soon pieces of clothing began to disappear. Afterward, I said something I'd always wanted to say. "Now that you've had your way with me"—I'd always wanted to say that—"what now?"

"Let's move on, pilgrim; we're burning daylight." Jake tried to imitate the voice of John Wayne.

We packed up and rode on some more. I hoped the last part of the day would be as sweet as the first. We found a nice stretch of beach that was mostly flat, just sloping slightly toward the water and the surf. The wind was calm, just a slight breeze, and the surf was relatively quiet. We decided to return to watch the sunset on this very spot. We rode on at a gallop because we wanted to reach the other end of Deadman's Beach and get back to our spot in time to watch the sunset.

Up ahead, I saw what appeared to be concrete jersey walls, so we slowed to a walk. When we reached them, we stopped, and farther up the beach we saw hotels and even people on the beach, but they were at least three hundred yards away. We figured the jersey walls must be where the property ended. There was a large sign fastened to the barrier, but it faced the other way. My curious Jake jumped off Buttermilk and over the wall. "What does it say?" He told me it read in large letters, *Private Beach—No Trespassing—Keep Out.*

We were now aware that we were trespassing, according to the sign. We had not seen a sign posted at the other end, and there was no practical way for us to go back except back the way we had come. That is exactly what we did.

"Jake, why do you suppose there was no sign at the other end?" I said.

"Perhaps this one was intended to keep hotel guests out; they can generate a lot of trash. The other property line abuts the Everglades; not too many folks vacationing in the Glades."

"Do you think we could be arrested or get in trouble for being here?"

Jake laughed at my query. "Don't fret, my dear. If anyone tries to run us off, well, I'll just shoot them." He laughed some more.

"Jake, be serious!"

"Yes, dear. No, I doubt anyone will hassle us. I don't even think anyone is patrolling or watching this stretch of beach. Let's head back to our spot and spend the night as we planned."

I didn't feel any worry or concern after that. We thought maybe it applied only to a small portion of that end of the beach, so we rode back until we reached our special place where we were going to watch the sunset and spend the night. Oh God, how I wish we had made a different decision.

CHAPTER 2
OUT OF THE SEA

We tied the horses to trees down the beach, a ways from where we would make camp, and removed their saddles. Jake gathered up large pieces of driftwood while I gathered tinder and smaller pieces. We got enough to keep a nice beach fire going through the night. This fire would keep away the chill of the evening as the temperature dropped. We would also use it to roast some corn on the cob and marshmallows and comfort me from the darkness after Jake fell asleep.

We ate and then lay on the blankets next to the fire and enjoyed all of nature's beauty. When you watch a sunset from a beach, the sun looks a thousand times bigger than usual, and it seems to just slowly slide right into the ocean. You almost expect to hear it sizzle and see the surf bubble up like boiling water. Now the giant red ball was about a foot above the water. We had already unpacked our supplies and were ready. We had just gotten the fire started and the blanket spread when the lower edge of the sun dropped below the horizon. I took pictures as it slowly sank into the ocean. The ocean breeze began to cool as the waves rolled easily, making a soothing rhythm, and the smell of the ocean added to the beauty of the night. The full moon reflected off the ocean and seemed to shimmer like crystals vibrating on a drum slightly tapped. At that moment, the world could not have been sweeter to us. Now, the moon was high and full. The sky was filled with stars—I swear, more stars than I had ever seen before in my life!

With no one around and all the natural ambiance surrounding us, we began kissing and soon made love under the heavens. It was wonderful to be so in love.

After a while, the fire died down slightly, and Jake threw some big, thick logs on the fire that he said should last the night. The sun would be up in about five hours. We crawled into our sleeping blankets, and it wasn't long before Jake, good ole Jake, stopped answering me, and I knew sleep had overtaken him.

I settled back, staring at the stars, and reminisced on this wonderful day. Soon my eyes started to blink longer and longer, and I too drifted into sleep.

For some reason, I woke suddenly and sat upright. I looked around, and there down the beach about fifty yards or so was a man walking out of the water. He was walking upright, so he didn't appear to be injured. At first I thought it was a man who had perhaps been night swimming and decided to get out of the water in a different location from where he had entered. As he got closer, I could see that it was too tall to be a man, so I crouched down and continued to watch it. A cloud that had partially blocked the moonlight drifted away. When the light from the full moon returned, it shone brightly on what I originally thought was a man; it was a creature so hideous that I couldn't believe what I saw. I rubbed my eyes quickly and looked again. Before I could really focus on it or wake up Jake, another large cloud drifted across the moon. Fortunately, he was walking parallel to us and not toward us. I could only see an outline now as he disappeared into the forest behind the beach. Whatever it was, it didn't seem to notice or care about the fire or us. My heart was beating hard in my chest, and I was frozen in silence and fear. How could I have seen such a thing? Was I dreaming? Did I overdo my wine consumption? Or was it just a young man and the night shadows were playing tricks on my mind?

I woke Jake and told him what I had seen.

"Honey, you were dreaming. Go back to sleep."

He moved closer to me and put his arm around me. He told me in that way, that condescending way he has when he thinks I'm being too emotional or silly, "If what you saw or think you saw was really there, if such a thing really happened, the horses would have gone crazy. So if you don't want to play some more, best get some sleep." That comment, though a bit condescending, was also comforting and made me feel a little bit better. I had asked Jake to tie the horses down the beach a ways so, well, so they couldn't watch us make love. Oh, I know now how silly that sounds, but damn it, that was my motivation at the time. Now I wanted them closer, much closer. I just kept pushing on Jake until he agreed, but when he started walking away, I got scared, so I jumped up and went with him, down to where the horses were tied, and we brought them back closer to us. Then, if that thing came back, the horses would sound an alarm. I could not go back to sleep, but my Jake didn't have any problem. Even the horses had no problem sleeping. Not me, oh no! Now every little sound had me jumping like a catfish on a pole.

It seemed like hours, but it was probably not that long when I finally settled down and started to drift off. I was startled awake when I heard the brush rustle. I stayed motionless and watched the tree line. I saw a dark form move fast, directly at the horses. Jake's horse, Buttermilk, reared up, broke free, and thundered down the beach. This thing swung its arm at my horse, Jolly, as she reared up. In the moonlight, I saw blood sprayed everywhere, and she dropped to the ground, kicking and whining. This creature dropped and bit into her neck until she fell silent and lay motionless. I could hear sounds like hogs slopping at the trough. The snorting sounds of it eating and of bones crunching made me gag and retch. I had to swallow my own puke for fear it would hear me or smell it. My mind raced for ideas of what to do, but fear blocked all rational thinking. I lay motionless and quiet. I had never known fear like this before. Somehow Jake slept through the whole event. I was afraid to wake him for fear he might try to do something. I just prayed silently that God would protect us and that it would eat and leave. I was too scared to cry over Jolly.

The option to ride away from this thing was now gone, leaving us with the option to walk or run! That was not much of an option at all; that was death for sure. I just knew it. It seemed like hours, but my watch said only one hour. The beast continued making disgusting slurping and crunching noises. My other fear was that Jake would make some noise or wake up before this creature was finished and left. I prayed for it to walk back into the ocean and disappear the way a nightmare does when you wake up.

Finally, it stood, looked up and down the beach, and held its head up as though tasting the wind. My fear spiked, and I stopped breathing. Then it ran back into the woods. I let out a sigh of relief. But then I realized that was not what I wanted at all. If it had returned to the ocean, it would most likely not return, and we could start moving quickly toward civilization. But in the woods, he could be anywhere, even a few yards away from us, stalking us, and we wouldn't know it. This was freaking me out. I feared it would jump out and attack us at any time.

I had to get Jake up quietly so we could work our way back to get help.

CHAPTER 3
ESCAPE NOW

"Jake, Jake, wake up, Jake," I whispered as quietly as I could, my heart beating so loudly I thought the thing could hear it.

I clasped my hand over his mouth as he woke to keep him quiet.

"Jake, be still for a second, and listen to me. That thing you didn't believe me about has killed and eaten my horse and run yours off." He took my hands to stop them from shaking. "We need to get moving quietly. I beg you to believe me and be silent. Look at the horse if you don't believe me, but do it slow and easy." I insisted in such a way that he seemed to believe me. Tears were now streaming down my face as I told him of Jolly.

Jake is a member of the NRA and has a concealed-carry permit. Fortunately, he had taken his .357 Magnum out of the saddlebag when we unsaddled the horses. He took the weapon, and we grabbed what we needed to hike the fifteen or so miles back, about halfway across this stretch of beach. When we started to move, we heard a scream like a banshee. It was that thing howling at the night. We stopped dead in our tracks. Jake grabbed me and put his hand over my mouth; he must have thought I would scream. Hell, I was too damn scared to scream. Was it about to attack us? We started moving again. We had hiked about five hundred yards when we heard branches cracking and the dried leaves and twigs snapping in a rhythm as though somebody was running through the brush. We hid beside a sand dune and prayed it would go on by, listening and waiting until there were no more sounds. Jake checked his weapon and said, "Let's go but slowly. Keep a close eye out."

Jake led the way, and we walked as quietly as we could down the beach. Since we were at the halfway point, Jake thought it best to move in the direction of the hotels. There was help there. At the other end was our vehicle but no one there to help us. If only we had the horses, we could outrun that damn thing. The moon gave us just enough light to see where we were walking. But each time a cloud passed between the moon and us, we stopped walking. We didn't want to take a chance of making a noise by falling and getting hurt. Each time we stopped, we had a chance to look carefully around and listen for something moving in the brush. We thought perhaps it was still back where it had killed Jolly, and we heard no more screams.

We walked and walked, Jake holding my hand tightly. It seemed like hours, but I checked my watch, and it had only been an hour and a half. That was discouraging for me, and I started to feel as if I couldn't walk much further. Walking in soft sand is hard, and my calves were beginning to cramp. Jake was having no trouble at all. Without him, I would have probably just given up.

Another cloud covered the moon. We stopped to rest, and then we heard it or something running through the brush. Jake kept trying to reassure me that he was a damn good shot and a .357 Magnum would stop it cold. When we had stopped, we sat on a large piece of driftwood; now we were huddled down behind it. We heard the beast scream just as it came at us from the woods. Jake waited until it was within range and fired. The beast fell. I hugged Jake; he had killed it. "I want to take a closer look at this thing." Jake walked toward it.

"No, Jake! It may not be dead, or it may carry some disease. Let's just get out of here." Of course he wouldn't listen; he had to get a closer look at it. I kept begging him to get us out of there. He took some close-up photos, and finally he agreed. We started moving away from it, and I began to relax slightly. Maybe we had walked a mile or two, but we still had a little more than that to go. Then we heard the scream and something running in the brush.

Jake whispered, "It must be a second one. Let's keep moving but move closer to the water. We can move faster on the sand hardened by the surf, and if it attacks us, we will have it out in the open."

I trusted him and did so without challenge. Now we could jog instead of slipping and sliding through the loose sand. I was just beginning to get a rhythm when suddenly we heard a noise, and it ran out onto the beach straight at us. Jake fired but missed, and it was on him. Jake kicked and fought, but this thing was too big and powerful. He threw the gun toward me, and I grabbed it, but I couldn't fire for fear of hitting Jake. Then things seemed to go into slow motion. Jake was on his back with this thing on top of him. Now I could shoot, but before I could pull the trigger, it opened its large mouth. The mouth looked like the jaw of a tiger or lion with large, pointed canine teeth. It sank them into Jake's face, and I heard the sound of crushing bone.

I screamed with rage and fired twice at it. I think I hit it at least once, and it ran into the woods. I looked at Jake. His face was gone; blood was gushing out onto the sand. I gagged again but forced myself to reach into the blood to feel for a pulse in his neck; there was none. I started to cry, and then I heard its cry. I started running as fast as I could, but my sight was blurred from the tears I could not control. Soon I could not run any further, so I stopped running but kept walking. My whole life had just been turned upside down; the love of my life was brutally killed by this damn beast. I wanted to hunt it, but in the dark, it had all the advantages. Finally, I gave up. I saw another large, hollow piece of driftwood, and I crawled up inside to rest and maybe wait for daylight. My thoughts rapidly changed from fear to anger to self-pity to giving up to just not caring. I just cried and cried.

Then I heard it again; the sound came from down the beach not from the woods. My first thought was Jake. Had it gone back to feed on his body? That's when I snapped. I jumped up and ran back to Jake. I was not going to allow this damn beast to eat him as he did my Jolly, as if he was just another piece of meat. I was screaming and running at it, and when I got within forty feet or so from Jake, I stopped. It stood up and let out that blood-curdling scream. I didn't remember being afraid anymore; I was full of rage, temporarily insane perhaps and definitely not thinking about myself. I had calculated that I had only two shots left. I had to make them count. The beast turned and faced me with vicious, red eyes. This was my first close-up look at this monster, it had the general shape of a man but much taller. It had dark green reptilian skin and a small fin about six inches in height that ran the entire length of the spine. It had long arms with five fingers just like a man but with partial webbing between those fingers and long, slightly curved claws on each finger. It screamed at me, revealing those large canine teeth, top and bottom, then ran toward me. "You fucking piece of shit. I'll kill you!" I quickly raised the weapon with both hands as Jake had shown me and fired. I couldn't miss from that range, but I did. It jumped to the left so fast I could not believe it, and the bullet missed completely. It swung its long, clawed arm at me and ripped through my arm like a hot knife through butter. The flesh on the outside of my arm was laid open. Fortunately, the main artery was somehow not severed, or I would have bled out in seconds. It swung again and caught me across the chest but only slightly. I somehow managed to hold on to the pistol with my other arm. I fired again and hit it square in the chest. It fell but was not dead, at least not yet.

I was out of ammo, so I ran toward the woods and found a rock. It was heavy, but my adrenalin was pumping. I picked it up and ran back to bash that ugly face in. When I got there, it was dragging itself back into the sea. When it saw me coming, it let out its horrific scream, but I was not afraid. I was determined to kill it. It was in the water almost where it could swim away. I was up to my knees in the surf. I raised the rock over my head to slam it into its head. It turned and slashed my leg, and then it buckled, and instantly my head was under water. Then it must have swum out into the ocean.

I dragged myself back onto the beach. I began to feel the sting of saltwater in my wounds. The sky was starting to lighten, and I knew the sun would be up within roughly forty-five minutes. From the woods, I found some cordage and tied a makeshift tourniquet around my arm, above the torn flesh. One of the bones in my arm was broken. I made a splint from a piece of driftwood and wrapped my arm with part of my shirt. The cuts to my chest were oozing blood, and I wrapped up my leg with some cloth I ripped up from my underwear. Bleeding to death was now my primary worry. I didn't know how much blood I'd lost, but it was leaking a lot, especially from my arm. The tourniquet greatly cut down the blood loss but not completely. Both my chest and leg were bleeding as well, but neither was losing that much blood, as both were much less severe than my arm.

Walking was very difficult due to the injuries, and my arm had to be tight against my chest to prevent it from swinging and perhaps causing the bleeding to become worse. I figured I was at least two or three miles from help. I was weak from thirst, not to mention the loss of blood. All I could think about was help. Where could I get help in time to save my life? I walked and walked, or maybe staggered is a better term. How much longer could I go on was the question that kept rolling through my head. Now the sun was up and bright and getting hot. Thirst was becoming more and more a problem. Could I make it the last mile and a half? I had to hang on. I wanted Jake to be picked up before the tide came in and took him out to sea. Now the tears started again. Just what I didn't need—more fluid loss. I hurt. My wounds hurt; my stomach hurt and my heart was in emotional shreds. Maybe I was supposed to die; maybe that was how I would be with Jake, in death rather than life. I decided to rest, so I walked to the edge of the woods and found a palm tree that gave enough shade for me to hide from the sun. I lay down and was instantly asleep or unconscious.

CHAPTER 4
AM I ALIVE?

When consciousness slowly began to creep in, I wondered if I was alive or in the arms of the Lord. When I realized where I was, I knew I was alive but didn't know how long I had slept. When I awoke fully, I was in a hospital bed, wrapped up like a mummy. When a nurse came in, I asked her, "How long have I been here?"

"You've been here asleep for five days," she said as she took my pulse.

"How did I get here?"

"Some fishermen saw you lying on the beach and brought you in."

"My fiancé, where is he?" I watched closely as her eyes dropped and her expression saddened. I began to sob, as I knew what she was about to say.

"They never found him. They scoured the beach but found the remains of a horse, some supplies, and another horse roaming around one of the neighborhoods. That was all; they were searching for another survivor, since two saddled horses must mean two people. There are two police detectives waiting to talk with you as soon as you are ready."

"Not now, please."

"Do you need anything?"

"I'm sore all over, especially my chest."

Then she told me that I had lost one of my breasts. I began to cry so hard that the nurse rang for the doctor to give me a sedative. When she told me that, my mind flashed to Jake. He always commented on how he thought I had beautiful breasts. I didn't give a damn about the loss of the breast, but knowing that I would never hear him remark about them again was what caused me to break down. I begged the doctor not to sedate me, just to give me ten minutes alone to compose myself. He agreed. "Nurse Pickett, check back in on her in ten to fifteen minutes, please."

"Yes, Doctor." They left the room.

As instructed, after a while Nurse Pickett returned. "Are you okay enough to speak with the? One detective has already gone, and the other is most insistent."

"Yes, I think so. I guess I'm ready now. Can you tell him to please come in?"

The nurse left the room, and a detective came in.

"Hello, Ms. Scott. You look much better than when I first saw you. I'm Detective Reynolds, Todd Reynolds, and I'm with the homicide division of the Everglades City Police Department. We are trying to piece together what happened out there on the beach. What can you tell me?"

"Homicide? Why homicide? No human did this horrible crime!"

"When someone is killed, homicide takes it until murder has been ruled out, so that is where we are now."

"Detective, I don't know where to start."

"Just start at the beginning and take your time."

"Well, Jake Barlow, my fiancé, and I went out early for a day and night of horseback riding."

I told him the story in vivid detail, and I was doing fine until I got to the creature part. Well, then the wheels came off. I saw his expression change. Oh, it was ever so slight, but it was there—that look of disbelief. However, I told him the entire story, at least up to the point where I fell asleep or passed out.

"Ms. Scott, here's what we know from what we found so far. We found a half-eaten horse on the beach. It looks more like the handiwork of a mountain lion, not some creature from the Black Lagoon. We found the .357 you mentioned, all rounds expended. We did not find Jake Barlow's body, but we did find blood in the sand where the weapon was found. We are having it checked for type and DNA. The weapon has two sets of prints on it; they too are now being checked for identification. When you were admitted, you had powder burns on your right hand. Tell me, Ms. Scott, are you right handed?"

"Yes, I am right handed."

"Is it possible that you were wakened suddenly? Saw Mr. Barlow standing and thought that he was some creature and shot him?"

"What? You think I couldn't tell the difference between my Jake and this creature, and you think I killed him?"

"I am not accusing you of anything yet, but you must admit a creature from the sea, that's a bit hard to swallow. Put yourself in my shoes. How was your relationship with Jake? Any problems?"

"Detective, our relationship was as good as it could be. We made love three times between the time we were at the barn until he died; that ought to tell you something about our relationship. And the only problem we had was trying to escape from that thing." I hated that prick for even suggesting that I could have killed Jake.

"Ms. Scott, I am only doing my job, so please try to stay calm. How do you account for the fact that we couldn't find your fiancé's body?"

"We were tiring trying to run on the loose sand, so Jake said we should run on the hard sand at the water's edge. He thought that would give us more time to react if the creature attacked, and he must have been taken out with the tide."

"Who owned the handgun?"

"That was Jake's; he had a carry permit. He always carried it for self-defense. It's the only thing that saved my life."

"Did you think …" Reynolds's cell phone began to ring. "Excuse me." He abruptly stood and walked from my room.

He was gone about a minute, and then he pushed open the door and stuck his head in. "They found your fiancé's body. I'll be back."

I tried to relax and rest, but his tone and questions were such that I felt as if I were on trial for the horrific events that happened. The nurse came back, saw my tears, and took my blood pressure. She told me it was elevated and gave me a sedative. I fell asleep very quickly after that.

It was morning when I awoke the first time, and now it was morning again. I had slept for another twenty-four hours. When the nurse came to check on me, I told her I was very hungry and wanted to eat.

"Ms. Scott, breakfast is over, but I'll go and see what I can find for you. That detective is outside again, waiting to see you."

"Can you tell him I'm still sleeping?"

She smiled at me, nodded, and winked. I decided to make that bastard wait as long as I could. Logically, I knew he was just doing his job, but that didn't allow me to think kindly of him. He was accusing me of killing the one good thing in my life, which was taken so brutally from me. I began to cry uncontrollably. About twenty minutes or so later, Nurse Pickett returned with some cereal, bananas, and best of all a small container of coffee.

"Sorry, Ms. Scott, this was all I could round up, but lunch will be in about an hour."

I ate and enjoyed every bit of it. I was just enjoying my last little bit of coffee when Detective Reynolds pushed into my room. Before he could start to ask me more questions, two doctors entered and ordered him out so they could examine me.

They had set my arm in a light fiberglass cast. When they opened my gown, I saw the three large cuts that required stitches to close the wounds. They ran from my right shoulder down across my breast to my hip. The remaining nipple had to be sown back on, and it was bruised and swollen. It looked disgusting! Then they took the bandages off my left leg where five very deep claw marks ran from my upper thigh to just below the knee, again with lots of stitches. Jake had always told me what beautiful legs I had; well, I had them no more, not that I gave a damn at that point. The doctors talked to each other as though I were a cadaver. It felt like I was dead and yet watching what was happening all around me. At that moment, I really didn't care if I was. Finally they were finished, and one doctor left without a word. The other stayed to answer my questions. He told me that it would take several years and many operations to remove all the scars once I was completely healed. The plastic surgery needed would most likely not be covered by insurance.

"What is your estimate of time for all these operations, Doc?"

"It would take three years at a bare minimum to get you back to what you looked like before the attack, but you may never be able to heal the emotional scars of what happened to you."

Later, the detective returned to tell me they had found the lower half of a body that had washed back up on shore, and he pulled out a picture of the shorts on the body to see if I recognized the trunks as the ones Jake was wearing. I wasn't sure at first that I could bring myself to look at it, but the detective assured me it was just the trunks, nothing else, so I looked and began to cry.

The detective, seeing my reaction, left the room. An hour later, he was back.

"I need to ask you some more questions, Ms. Scott."

I interrupted him before he could get started. "First I want to ask *you* a question, Detective. Do you think I did it, that I killed my Jake?"

He just looked at me with his cool, emotionless expression. His dark eyes seemed lifeless, and then in his nauseating, monotone voice, he said, "Ms. Scott, at this time we are very interested in you as a prime suspect."

Angered by his very presence and his stupid statement, I threw back the sheet, sat up, and with my good hand reached back, untied my gown, and pulled it off over my busted arm, exposing my totally naked body to him. His formerly lifeless eyes opened as wide as his mouth as he jumped from his chair and stumbled backward. I pointed to my breasts. "Then how do you explain this and this?" I pointed to my upper thigh. He left the room, and I heard later from Nurse Pickett that he was gagging as he ran for the men's room where he was overheard puking his guts up. I never heard from him or anyone else from the police department again.

A week later, they released me from the hospital. To date, I have not had any of the surgery necessary to restore me to the way I was before the attack. The word got out to the press about my story of the creature, and reporters hounded me for weeks. I refused to give any interviews, or even discuss it with anyone, as I would not be subject to being made a fool of. They finally gave up, as their persistence was no match for my stubbornness.

Only once before, have I told the story I am telling you now. That once was to Detective Reynolds. My story of what started out as two lovers on a super weekend that turned into that horrific, terrible night on Deadman's Beach.

I have many nights when I wake in a cold sweat from nightmares of that thing, whatever it was. I must confess that occasionally I search the Internet for clues, sightings, or any rumor of such a thing—all this to no avail. Those questions, those stinking, lousy questions continue to haunt me to this day. Is it something from outer space, some leftover creature from another age? Is it the only one left of its kind, or are there more of these breeding and walking out onto the land to feed on man and animals? Are they just in this one area or around the world? These questions will be with me to my grave. I don't socialize much anymore, and I certainly don't date. I won't let any man see this torn-up body, and I won't get it fixed. I will stay as I am until my death as a constant reminder to me of what happened; no amount of people scoffing or telling me I'm crazy will remove what happened from my reality. And as I said in the beginning, you may choose to believe me or not; I don't really give a damn. However, if you are ever thinking about going to that stretch of beach, you had better reconsider or you may find yourself realizing that it was, in fact, a true story. Only you probably won't be around to confirm my story or live to tell yours.

THE END ... WHO KNOWS?

CRYPTURE 5

I, Realtor

"Good morning, this is Vikki Jordan with breaking news at half past the hour. The news desk here at WJWG has just learned that a local Realtor has been taken into custody at the scene of a horrendous fire. He was arrested for setting fire to a property he had placed on the market for sale. Details are sketchy at this point, but we know that it was for sale for one million dollars, and preliminary reports say the owner died in the fire. Stay tuned to WJWG for updates on the hour. Now we return to our program still in progress."

Eighteen Months Earlier

My name is Jack Forrest, and I live here in Columbus, Ohio. This is my story. I was twenty-eight, working a decent nine-to-five-er with no future, second in command in my department of the largest architectural and engineering firm in the metro area, but no chance to advance without going back to school for another four years. That is not an enticing thought to a young man with bills to pay and no silver spoon to suck on. So that left me to figure out how and where I would make this vast improvement in my financial dealings.

First, I had to have employment of some kind to create cash flow, pay current debts, and of course have enough seed money for whatever new venture I decided to embark upon. I thought of many things, and each thing I thought either required a heavy influx of cash or starting out working for less than I was currently earning. Then it came to me as I drove to my boring job one morning. As I turned off my street and headed down Willow Lane, a young man was installing a post for a real-estate-for-sale sign, and a well-dressed middle-aged woman was removing from the trunk of her shiny, big Cadillac a sign panel that would hang from that post. Her car and her clothes were expensive. That's when it hit me; *I'll become a real estate salesperson!* I saw all those real estate people riding around in big, fancy automobiles while I drove a cheap foreign car. They were always dressed to the nines and could talk the shine off paint.

That's when I started making my plan to get a career selling real estate. I thought about all the money I could make. A Realtor friend of mine, Jeff, told me, "You are only limited by your own mind and willingness to work; no one can hold you down, except you."

That cinched it; I was on the phone signing up for a night course in preparation for taking the state-licensing exam. Two months later, I was ready for my lucrative, new venture. Next order of business was to find the right company to join. My friend Jeff who told me about it in the first place was a ten-year veteran of the business, and he was with a company called RE/MAX. Well, sure, I had heard of it. Who hasn't? It was the best-known brand in the real estate industry. The number-two brand was far behind, according to my friend. So I asked him to introduce me to whoever did the hiring at his company. He said, "Sorry, pal, no use. They won't hire you." I just wanted to punch him! He told me all the great things about RE/MAX, and now he tells me I can't join them. I asked him why.

"Well, you see, Jack, RE/MAX hires only experienced agents. That's a small part of why they're so well respected, trusted, and used by more buyers and sellers than any other company, and they're international."

"You sound like a walking commercial for them and … well, I have to be with the best. Can you tell me the name of your broker?"

"Sure, his name is Bob Davengale, and his number is 555-2000. If you can get him to hire you, you'll be the best salesperson on earth." Then he laughed.

Well, my friend was right, and I was not accepted at RE/MAX. I could see why they were the best in the business, so I vowed to get the knowledge and the experience to join them later. I joined Showcase

Realty, another firm. They were supposedly the second largest firm in the area, with a good training program. They did offer much training, so I set out to get all the training I needed. I put myself through some rigorous sales and marketing classes, the Realtor code of ethics, and real-estate law classes, and I queried my broker at every opportunity. By the end of six months, I had sold only two houses, but I was really starting to roll. My broker said if I wanted to make the big bucks, I had to be full-time. Enough said; I quit my other job. Then I flew high, real high. I started making more money than a person should have the right to. I have won award after award in my local board, and that, plus the money, makes life very sweet! Because I was riding the crest of my new career, I was receiving referrals left and right. I hoped that soon I could be good enough to move up to RE/MAX. That would be a gold-letter day for sure.

One night I was called to the home of a man who said he wanted to sell. "Jack, my name is Basil H. Helmeyer, the third. I'm told by friends that you are the new young gun in town and selling up a storm." Well, who was I to argue?

"Well, I try to do my best, sir." Basil no less. I had never met anyone named Basil. He sounded as strange as his name was unusual.

"Would you be willing to come by my home and discuss selling it for me?"

"Absolutely. Let me check my schedule." We set the appointment. He wanted $1.2 million for his home; that was a bargain. At least that is what the comparables showed and what my good judgment told me. I would find out later—too late, in fact—that all was not as it appeared.

We met, and he signed my exclusive right-to-sell agreement, paid me my retainer, and gave me a key to the side door. I took my interior and exterior photos, measured up the rooms, and wrote up my remarks. I called in the for-sale sign installation, bid him good day, and off I went. I had very specific instructions from ol' Basil that under no circumstances whatsoever was the property to be shown after five o'clock in the afternoon, and everyone had to be completely out of the house by six o'clock. If they were there after six, I would be fired on the spot. Oh, yes, he made me write that in the paperwork. The property was well priced, as I mentioned, but it was a bit on the dull side—dark colors, furniture, and so on. I wanted this one to sell but not too quickly, as I could get many buyers from a house like this. Plus, he was not in a tremendous hurry. I had it all figured out; this was my highest-priced listing to date. He didn't know it, but he was going to get much more marketing than was usually in my marketing budget. See, I knew that some real estate agents weren't as willing to walk the extra mile as I was. I wanted to continue to receive many referrals.

Anyway, the house had a lot of showings but no offers by the end of the first month on the market. So one weekend I decided that I would do an open house for the public, and I always wanted to benefit from spending my Sunday in someone else's home. In addition to the possibility of selling the home myself and doubling my fee, it also gave me a chance to meet other buyers that perhaps this home wasn't right for. Basil seemed a little reluctant about the open house, but I convinced him it was necessary. I was there early and got set up. I brewed coffee to serve piping hot and in the seller's china (they can't take it with them, thus I have more time to talk and get to know their needs). Suffice it to say, I was ready and waiting.

As I waited, I thought I heard someone walking around upstairs. Now I had told Basil that everyone who lived there, which I thought was just he, had to be out of the house during the open. I stormed upstairs, ready to lecture someone, but no one was there. I looked in every room, in every closet, in case someone was trying to hide from me, but I found no one. I shrugged my shoulders and went back to the kitchen, thinking I must be hearing things. The open house was to start at one o'clock, now fifteen minutes away. Then I heard it again and dismissed it as just an old-house noise. However, it got louder and more distinct. When I was about to run up there again, the door opened, and in walked a couple with their own agent. The agent and I exchanged cards and a bit of verbal pleasantries, and they began to look around. About the time they started upstairs, another couple came in, this time without an agent. I thought to myself, *Watch me work!* That was my little mental motivator to do my best. "Hello, Ma'am! Welcome to the first public open for this wonderful home, and please allow me show you around."

We did our introductions and handshakes and started through the house. "Welcome, Mrs. Jackson!"

She smiled and then stopped and said, "I can hear someone walking upstairs." I explained that with an older home, sometimes you needed to put rugs over the old hardwood floors to eliminate that noise, and it must be the other couple and their agent. As we returned to the main hall, we heard people running down the steps. I went to the foyer in time to see it was that agent. Her clients were already out the door. I called to her. When she turned her face toward me, it was flushed, and she was speechless. She paused for a second and then ran out. I made a joke out of it with the woman that I was with. But in my mind, I wondered if their hasty retreat was tied to the footsteps I had heard earlier.

The open-house traffic ended with only one more couple and an agent previewing. Both the couple and the agent commented on the footsteps. I gave them the same answer I had given Mrs. Jackson. I locked up the house after I had put things back in order and killed the lights. I had a date with my girl, Mai Le, so I stopped thinking about the spooks and concentrated on getting home, getting refreshed and dressed, and having dinner with my sweetie. Oh, yes, she was a most delicious gal, more so than I had been with in a long time. Mai Le was originally from Viet Nam. She was petite but with wonderful curves in *all* the right places. Her long, straight, pure black hair that hung to the top of her shapely rear outlined her deep, dark eyes. She was the real deal, every curve and that long hair. But hey, that's just a detail, and that detail was all mine. I was to pick her up at seven thirty for dinner at eight, and then we would go back to her place for a nightcap and perhaps some time alone together.

We had a great dinner. I had actually found, after much research, an Italian restaurant that could really make lobster fradiabalo. It was actually as good as my dear ole momma used to make. It goes great with a bottle of Dom Perignon and topped off with some cherries jubilee. We had a great conversation, which covered many subjects like when we would marry, more her idea than mine, my still wanting to join RE/MAX, and the results of my open house that day. That last topic of conversation took place after we enjoyed one more treat, each other.

After we were lying back in each other's arms, she said, "So you didn't tell me how your opening went today."

I decided to tell her the whole story, and when I finished, she sort of laughed slightly, rolled over, and went to sleep. I guessed from her reaction that it was not any big, spooky deal, so I cuddled up behind her and drifted away myself.

Monday arrived. Mai Le got up early and made coffee and then woke me up with a nibble. We had a shower together, to conserve water of course, then some coffee, and she hustled off to work. I had a walk-through inspection at ten thirty, so I took my time and then headed home to change.

After my walk-through, I had a call from Basil. He asked about the open house, and I gave him the head count. My turn. "Basil, I kept hearing people walking around upstairs as I conducted the opening. Can you explain?"

"No, lad. Maybe I have ghosts." Then he laughed in such a way that I felt stupid for bringing it up.

"Well, Basil, it was heard by every person who came in, and it chased away one agent with her clients. I mean, they ran from the house."

At that, he snapped and said, "If you are too damn afraid of my house, we can forget any more opens!" He hung up abruptly after his rant.

I dropped the issue and did *not* call him back. After Mai Le's reaction, coupled with Basil's comments, I decided to write the whole episode off as an overactive imagination and coincidence.

A week later, I received an e-mail from a party interested in seeing the Basil property. I set an appointment to show it to them at noon the next day. When we got there, all went well, but it was not the house for them, so I made another appointment to show them some other properties. We said our good-byes, they left, and I stayed to turn out the lights and lock up. I was almost to the door when I heard a young woman's voice. I couldn't make out all that she said, but what I did hear was, "Help me, help me." I suppose in hindsight I should have called the police, but I was too macho for that then. But not too macho to get the hell out of there PDQ.

That was it. I was out of there. I left as quickly as I could. As I drove back home, I decided to do some research. I had sold a house to a police officer and his wife, so I took a chance that he might be in. I stopped by his station and was lucky enough to catch him. I asked if anything strange had happened in that house recently.

Joe checked the reports and said, "Looks like two years ago, Basil's much younger wife died in the house. In fact, according to the report, she was violently murdered, and they never found the assailant. It seems that the husband was the most likely candidate, but we were never able to get enough evidence to convince the district attorney to issue a warrant for his arrest. Is that what you are looking for?"

"Yes, I think so, maybe. I have that house listed for sale, and strange things keep happening in there. So I thought it might be haunted," I said, sort of tongue and cheek.

Joe laughed. "Come by the house some time and see what my wife has done to it. It looks a whole lot different than when we bought it from you."

"Sure, Joe, you bet—and thanks for the info." We shook hands, and I left.

I didn't have another appointment until five, so I decided to grab a sandwich and drink, head home, and search the Internet for information about haunted houses and captured spirits and the like.

After I ate and fired up the computer, I read for two hours or more. I was fascinated by the information I found. For example, Wikipedia, the free dictionary, had this to say on the subject: *The concept of a vengeful ghost goes back to ancient times and is part of many cultures. According to these legends and beliefs, the ghosts roam the world of the living as restless spirits, seeking to have their grievances redressed, and return to the world of the dead after justice is done, but in some cases remain unappeased. In certain cultures vengeful ghosts are mostly female, said to be women that were unjustly treated and died in despair. Exorcisms and appeasement are among the religious and social customs practiced by various cultures in relation to the vengeful ghost. The northern Ache people group in Paraguay cremated old people thought to harbor dangerous vengeful spirits instead of giving them a customary burial. In cases where the person has been killed and the body disposed of unceremoniously, the cadaver may be exhumed and reburied according to the proper funerary rituals in order to appease the spirit. Others have been known to salt and burn their body, or where they were killed or what they were killed with.*

That and many other articles seemed to point to the idea that a spirit killed violently could stay where they were killed until their murderer had been brought to justice.

I needed to get to my next appointment and to call Mai Le on the way and give her an idea of what time I'd be by her place.

I met my clients. They loved one of the houses I showed them. As always, I was all prepared, and they had a loan in their hip pocket, so we wrote up the paperwork. I scanned it to the listing agent, said good-bye to my clients, and headed for Mai Le's place in time for some of her homemade food. After dinner, we watched a movie. As it was about to end, I got a call from the listing agent telling me my contract had been signed as written by her seller. She was sending me back a ratified copy. I then called my clients, the buyers, and gave them the good news. That was good news for me as well, and Mai Le was all smiles for me.

It was no secret that we would marry, but I wanted a number in the bank first. We popped a split of champagne and toasted another transaction that put me ahead of this same time last year. Mai Le raised her glass. "To you, my love, well done! Now if you can sell that big listing, you will be real close to your goal, and we can make plans."

"Oh! I talked to the police friend of mine, and he told me that Basil's wife was brutally murdered in that house two years ago."

"Really?"

"And this afternoon before I met the people I sold to tonight, I did a lot of research on the web. It seems that many believe that when a person dies a traumatic death, sometimes their spirit doesn't leave the place where they died until their death has been avenged."

"Yes, many people in Viet Nam believe that also."

"Do you remember that I told you I heard someone walking around that Sunday when I did the open house and that everyone commented about it, and one group ran from the house?"

"Yes, I remember, but I thought you were just messing with me; that's why I did not continue with it."

"Well, I think it's her, and she called to me today when I showed it."

"You should stay away from there. These ghosts can be violent. This is very serious and not to be treated lightly. Remember, this is your unlucky year. Getting involved in this will surely cause you great harm. Jack, promise me you will stay away from there!"

"Sure, darling, sure. Come here." *After ole Basil goes to work tomorrow, I am going back there to see if I still hear anyone. Mai Le's superstition is silly, but I don't want her to worry, so I'll just agree. Maybe find out what really happened there.*

She leaned over to kiss me. "Well, you do that, baby." End of discussion.

The next morning, I was up early. I headed home to do paperwork, make some calls, follow up on cases, and write my personal notes. Then around eleven, I headed over to Basil's house to see what I could learn from the spook that was living there, if anything. He never said I couldn't go to the house unless with a client, only that I had to be there for every showing. When I arrived, the house was dark. If I told Basil once, I told him every time we talked, "Leave some lights on and open the drapes!" He always said he will, and he never did. However, given the nature of my visit, I left the lights off and the shades closed. I climbed the stairs to the second floor. After my research, I wasn't afraid of this whatever it was anymore, and I began to softly call out, "Tess. Are you here, Tess?"

Then I heard footsteps, like someone sliding their feet across the wood floor.

"Tess, is that you? Can you speak to me?"

A raspy whispery voice answered, "Yes, I am Tess. You are Jack?" I felt her touch me.

"How can I feel your touch? Are you incorporeal or invisible? If invisible, then you are not dead?"

"I am neither, and I am both. I am dead, as you understand it, yet I still have form that can feel and be felt. I am, however, invisible and able to move at a speed no other form can move. I was married to Basil, but he ended my life."

"Can you tell the police, I mean since they can feel that you exist?" I asked.

"No, I am only able to be this way with you, but I do not know why. There is something different about you that allows my form to be as if I were alive, save only the ability for you to see me. Go to the bedroom and open the top drawer of the large dresser. Take out the album that is there, please."

I walked to the room, and in the top drawer was a large photo album. I opened it and began to turn the pages. She asked me to stop at a large photo of a woman.

"Is this you?"

"Yes, it is. That picture was taken two weeks before my death. I wanted you to see me so it would be easier perhaps to talk with me."

I could not take my eyes off the photo; she was the most beautiful woman I had ever seen in my life. I could feel my emotions drawn to her like water to a sponge. Now her voice had new meaning to me. It was as though I had known her all my life. I know, such a trite saying, but I felt it for the first time in my life.

"How are you able to speak to me?"

"I do not know. All I know is when you first entered the house, I felt something different, inexplicable." While I was still staring at the photo, it was as if the photo were speaking to me.

"You appear to be in your mid to late twenties, but Basil must be over sixty?"

"And you are wondering what did I see in a man so much older than myself?"

"Well, actually, yes, I am." We sat on the bed; I knew she sat, as I saw the impression of her rear on the bed.

"My father was from the old country, and I was given to him in order to pay a debt of one hundred thousand dollars that my father owed. My father said he would be killed unless the debt was paid. I was property that had value, so Basil would forgive the debt, and he would let my father live if I would marry him. At first I said no, but my mother begged and pleaded until I felt I was left without a choice. How could I let my father die and my mother be alone? I was a virgin when he married me, and he used me like his own private whore. I hated the touch of his cold, boney fingers on me and his noises when he pushed himself in me. I used to throw up after he was done, and I would run to the bathroom as he laughed.

"Oh, how horrible. I didn't like him from the minute I met him, but I am not required to like someone to work for them."

"I have a favor to ask of you, Jack, and please excuse me for asking, but would you mind holding me for a moment? I am so lonely."

"No, no, I guess that would be okay," I said. As I stood up, she also stood. I put my arms out and waited. Slowly she walked into my arms and I could feel her body tight against me. I was aroused quickly, and I felt her back away.

"Oh, I'm sorry, I didn't—"

I interrupted her. "No, no, it wasn't your fault. I am so embarrassed. I don't know why that happened." I felt my face and ears get hot. "Why did your body cause me to become erect so quickly? I have hugged women in that manner before and not had that reaction."

"It's okay. I felt it too. I just don't have a penis to give me away."

"I ... I better go now," I said, still embarrassed.

"I understand, but will you come back tomorrow? I am so lonely here without someone to talk with." I could not say no, so I agreed to come back at the same time. As I started to turn to the door, I suddenly felt her soft, warm lips on my cheek and then her hand as she wiped the kiss away.

I smiled slightly and walked out. All the way to my office, I could not get the picture of her and what happened out of my mind. It was as though she intoxicated me. Throughout my appointments, I was distracted and felt dazed. Mai Le called me, and I brushed her off, making an excuse that I wasn't feeling well and would not stop by that evening. Frankly, all I wanted was to be back in that house with Tess, yet I wasn't sure why. If my mind were a hard drive, she was the worm virus that was slowly consuming me, and I couldn't stop it, nor did I want to.

I am normally a very good sleeper; I can count on one hand the number of times I could not easily drift away once my head hit the pillow. But this night, I could not sleep a wink. I just tossed and turned throughout the long night. By morning, I was a wreck, and I was sleepy. Go figure. Anyway, I got up, poured down as much coffee as my gut could hold, and hoped it would get me through the day. I tried to put a couple of CMAs (comparative market analysis) together, and my concentration was zip, but I struggled through with the aid of more coffee. I made it until it was time to drive over and visit Tess. I hoped that Basil, the bastard, my new name for him, wouldn't be there.

As I was arriving, I saw him driving away in the opposite direction. That was pleasing to me; I would be able to spend some time with Tess. Soon I was in her arms and kissing her wildly!

What? I was daydreaming. Why did such thoughts enter my mind? And yet, truth be told, that is exactly what I wanted to happen. I was really losing it. I walked into the house and started up the stairs. I heard her call to me, and happiness filled me. I moved faster and went to the room where we looked at the photos.

"No, Jack, I am over here in the bedroom," she said as I heard her voice getting closer. Soon I felt the soft skin of her hand in mine, taking me back to where she was lying originally. When she stopped, I did as well.

She reached out her hands and picked up my hands and slowly pulled them toward her. Soon I felt the warm, soft flesh of her bare breasts and her hardened nipples.

She spoke softly. "I wanted to show you that I was aroused by you just as you were by me yesterday."

My heart was racing a thousand miles per hour, and I thought it would explode. She walked me to the bed, and I could see the impression of her butt as the mattress sank slightly under her weight. I was speechless and not planning to stop her from anything she wanted to do. I was wearing a tie and dress shirt but not for long. I was wearing navy blue slacks with a buckle belt but not for long. Oh, I helped too. I kicked off my loafers and socks without using my hands.

Soon she stood and wrapped her arms around me. What a strange sensation. I could feel her, every piece of her, her nipples still firm pressing into my chest, her lips on fire against mine. I was erect—oh, was I erect—pressing up against her stomach, our tongues playing and teasing each other. I moved slowly forward, forcing her to the bed; all this was happening without me seeing her. The thought flashed through my mind that if someone were watching me, it would look like I was having fake sex with myself. By the time that thought had run its course, I was deep inside her. I closed my eyes, and it was like making love. I would open them, and I felt as if I was hallucinating. But I had never made love like this before. Yes, mechanically it was like any other time, but it wasn't emotionally. I was in love ... or lust with her—there, I said it. Only to myself, of course. But I had to admit it to someone. Mai Le was as far from my mind as she could be. I could attempt to describe to you in the language of love all that was happening, but how could you relate? Here I was writhing about someone yet without someone ... at least in the sense that we are used too. She moaned in the softest, sweetest voice, and I felt exactly what she felt. It was as though we were two parts of the same entity, each feeling what the other felt. I know, for example, that she reached an orgasm three times. Then she conveyed to me the last one so that I could join in with her and climax during her orgasm. It was glorious, mind bending, and like nothing I had ever experienced before or ever would again. I knew that this could only happen with her. She was supposedly dead, but dead people are cold and stiff from rigor mortis. *She must be alive,* I reasoned. *But how could she be alive and invisible? She must be in some in-between state, some state known only to God but perhaps caused by Lucifer. Will this affair take me to hell, or is this something that God has allowed?* So many thoughts like that shot through my mind in a nanosecond.

"Jack, I love you," her trembling soft voice confessed.

Her putting into words what we were both feeling was like having another orgasm; it felt warm and soothing over me. I could do none other than to repeat the same words back to her. We celebrated the verbalizing of our feeling in another embrace that led to another joining of our bodies. You could have just let the world go by, and we wouldn't care. Hours drifted by as we lay with each other and talked of things that could never be.

Suddenly she sat up and said, "You must leave. Basil is returning now."

"How do you know? I hear nothing!"

"Trust me, I know. Please, how can you explain being in this bed naked and alone? Remember, he cannot see or hear me, even if I wanted him to."

I was not sure how she knew, but I wasn't taking any chances. I jumped into my clothes and ran out into my car and took off. I looked in my rearview mirror and saw him coming from the opposite direction again.

"How could she know that?" I said aloud.

That answer would have to wait for another day. I drove straight home, and as I did, I felt my body slowing down, way down. I was craving sleep for the first time, and that's exactly what I did. I turned off the ringers on the phones. I even put the car in the garage so anyone coming by would think I wasn't home since I usually leave it out.

I ate just enough to kill the hunger in my gut, and when my head hit the pillow, well, I have no memory after that.

Over the next two months, my world went to hell. I spent every moment with Tess that I could. I referred all my current clients to another agent for a referral fee. Mai Le and I broke up after a terrible argument. I stopped seeing my friends and family. I was for Tess, and Tess was for me. Some force that was all-consuming bound us; it was consuming both of us. After I learned that Basil would get drunk and beat her, humiliate her in front of his friends, and make her do sexual things of a most sick nature, I hated him. I mean, I wanted to kill him.

He called me one day on my cell phone. He would have freaked out if he knew where I was, whom I was with, and what we were doing. He wanted an appointment with me to meet at the house. I had to leave and come back later.

I arrived at five per his instructions, and when I sat down at the kitchen table with him across from me, I felt her nibble at my ear. I said, "Stop," without thinking, and to which Basil replied, "Excuse me!" He said it in that tone as if someone had just insulted him, and he wanted to see if they had nerve enough to repeat it.

I waffled it off, and she giggled. I looked at him quickly for any response, but there was none. She was right; he could not hear her at all. I wondered what would happen if she hit him.

"Jack, the reason I asked you to come by is that I wanted to do this face-to-face. Did you know that the listing expired in your multiple-listing service, and other agents have been calling me to list the house?"

I didn't know, and my mind scrambled to find an answer. "It must have been a computer glitch. I can fix it immediately."

"No, it wasn't. I checked my listing agreement. It expired yesterday." I knew he was right; the listing agreement had expired, and I didn't know it until now. The house was now fair game for any Realtor who could get it, and it was my fault. He told me he was going with another agent and firm. He told me that I had changed, was not marketing the home, that I had become harsh toward him, and he didn't appreciate it one bit. He was right. In the beginning before I knew Tess, I worked it hard, almost sold it once, but since then ... well, you know, I'd been preoccupied.

My first reaction was to tell him what he could do with his stupid house, but then I heard Tess crying. She had figured it out, and why hadn't I? Well, the savvy salesman here may have been preoccupied, but he hadn't lost his skills. I thought to myself, *Not on your life are you taking this listing from me.* "Listen, Basil, you're right, and I apologize. My girl left me recently, and I had some difficulty adjusting, and perhaps I took it out on you unintentionally. But you know how hard I worked in the past, and I'm ready to start again, work hard for you, and get it sold. All I ask is give me a two-week extension and see if I don't do a great job ... please."

He hesitated, and when he did, I knew I had him, but he had to win or at least think he did. "I'll give you a week. If you prove yourself again, I'll give you an additional sixty days."

"Oh, thank you, sir. You won't regret it." I quickly wrote up the amendment for the extension and passed it to him to sign.

He stood without offering me his hand. "You see that I don't." He stood there as if he were excusing me. His face had no expression. I left quickly with my small victory, knowing I would be able to come back tomorrow.

I had no longings for Mai Le, eating lobster fradiabalo, driving my street rod, hanging with my friends, seeing my family, playing basketball, or anything else that was once important in my life. It was Tess, Tess, Tess! I was obsessed with her. I worked hard enough over that next week to get my sixty-day extension from that bastard and, more importantly, to be able to continue to see and make love to Tess, my Tess.

Thirty days after signing the new listing, we got a contract on the house that satisfied old Basil. Antonio and Megan Crosswire were the purchasers, and in another thirty days, we would be at closing, and new people would move into the house. When Tess and I discussed what we were going to do, I put my arms around her and said, "No worries, mate. You can move in with me, no problemo!"

With that, Tess started to cry, something she hadn't done since we met and became involved with each other.

"I, I can't go with you, Jack!" She cried heavily now.

"Why? What's the problem? There is no one there but me. I don't even have a dog."

"You don't understand. If I leave this house, I will cease to exist as I am, and I will be dead, real-time dead. It's the house that somehow keeps me as I am, whatever I am. Why do you think we have never left here?"

"Damn, I never really thought about it. I just thought you didn't want people to stare at me. If people saw me talking to someone that wasn't there, I mean, really. But how do you know you can't leave?"

"Jack, I can see myself. One day after I became somewhat comfortable with my new life, I opened the door and reached my arm outside, and I could not see it anymore. I pulled back immediately, and my arm was still there, but in that split second that it was outside, I could feel it dying. I knew—I just knew that outside these walls I would cease to exist. I am doomed to live in this house until whatever force that put me here like this decides to change it." She began to cry again.

I did my best to comfort her, and after a while, she settled down, and slowly we got back to things we usually talked about, which excluded nothing. One subject was how we could get Basil convicted of murder. There were no witnesses, no body, and no murder weapon. She said she was a God-loving person and would not kill him, as it was a mortal sin to her. She hoped someday this state she was in would end and the Lord would bring her home. Oh, we used to talk about what I would do if one day she just wasn't there anymore, and I could not imagine being without her. I would look through the photo album over and over to see what I held in my arms every day. I would feel her face, much like a blind person would do in order to see someone. Oh, she was beautiful.

One day as we lay in bed after making love, I asked her, "Why did your husband kill you?"

Her response was shocking. "He came home one night, and I wasn't feeling well. I had fixed him dinner, and he fussed about it. Afterward, I wanted to go to bed early in hopes of shaking off the bug I had contracted. He would not let me. I kept asking if I could, and he just kept right on talking. Finally, I got mad and just stormed up to my room. He barged in after me and pushed me on the bed. Normally, if he wanted it, I would go somewhere in my mind, and he would just do it. He never took long, and then he would leave and go to his room. I would then go shower and cry, trying to wash him out of me and off me. That night I was already sick and mad, so I told him to get the fuck out of my room. He then informed me that it was *his* room and I was *his* wife, which meant he could do whatever, whenever and wherever he liked, and I could only agree or he would beat the snot out of me. I began screaming at him, and he picked up the poker from the fireplace and smashed it across my back as I ran from him. I remember falling and rolling over just as the poker came down into my head. I felt the pain of the blow. He then picked me up and carried me to the bed, got undressed, ripped off my clothes, and then began kissing my breasts. Then I felt him in me. When he finished, he got up and went into the shower. I cried until I fell asleep.

"I'm not sure how long I was asleep, but when he came back into the room, he was dressed in jeans and a hoody and dragging a large trunk, which woke me. He rarely dressed that way unless he was doing gardening or other work that may require such dress. I had a terrible headache and felt woozy from the blow. I got up, stumbled to my bathroom door, and grabbed my robe. I turned back to tell him I was going to leave him and screamed, dropping the robe. He looked up at the robe as it fell to the floor, looked around, and then turned back to what he was doing. I yelled at him. 'What are you doing?' But he acted as if he didn't hear me or even see me. I couldn't believe what I saw. Basil had the trunk open, and he was lifting me from the bed and putting me in it. I was looking at myself, but how could that be? I pinched myself to see if I was dreaming, and then I ran into the bathroom, and all I saw in the mirror was nothing, no reflection of myself, yet I could look down and see myself.

"I went back to the bedroom. He had finished with the trunk and locked the latch. He was dragging it to the staircase, so I followed him. He slid the trunk down the staircase and into the mudroom and then opened the door to the garage. The Suburban was backed into the garage, as usual. He opened the tailgate and struggled to get the trunk into the back of it. I watched in horror, not believing what I was witnessing. Then he pulled it out in the driveway, and I walked out also. I was instantly nauseated, and I ran back inside before he could close the garage door. That's when I first suspected that I couldn't leave the house. He drove off with me, yet without me, and didn't return until just before sunrise the next morning."

"He must have disposed of your physical body, and if we can find it, we can get him convicted."

"I have seen many movies like *Ghost*. I'm like Patrick Swayze, except you for some reason are able to hear me and feel me. I often think of that movie and wonder if I am stuck here until he is convicted. Oh, Jack, I do love you, but this half life is wearing on me." She began to cry again, and I just held her and let her cry as I tried to wrap my brain around all she had just said to me. By the time she had regained her composure, she told me it was time for me to leave before Basil, the bastard, came home. We hugged and kissed for a while, and then I got into my car and drove away.

That night would be a defining night in my life. I fixed some dinner and had a few beers. I tried to watch a ball game, but it didn't hold my interest. So I tried watching a lighthearted movie, *Chicago*, with two beauties, Renee and Catherine. This was a good musical with some nice jazz and dancing in it. Nope, that didn't help either. I couldn't stop thinking of how to get Basil to confess and avenge Tess or how I could find the body. I had mixed feelings about this. On one hand, if we got him convicted, perhaps Tess could leave the house, but what if she was gone forever after the conviction? But if he wasn't, how would I see her? I couldn't go into that house after the new owners moved in. What reason would I have? I suppose I could keep a key, but what if someone was home all day? Not only that but my money was beginning to run low. I was obsessed with a woman I could not see or take out of there. It was all just too impossible. Then I got an idea. What if I brought Joe, my cop friend, over to the house, told him the whole thing, and had him ask any question he wanted to convince himself that I wasn't ready for a straitjacket. Then maybe we could convict Basil. It seemed the only way. That was the best I could come up with. I would talk to Tess about it, and if she agreed, I would bring Joe there. That seemed good enough to let my brain shut down and get some sleep.

Next day, I called Joe. He was off for the next two days, so I asked if he would meet me for coffee. He said no but that Kathy had gone to work and I could come by his place. He'd buy the coffee if I bought some danish pastries from Maria's Sweet Stuff bakery shop. I had introduced Joe and Kathy to Maria's when I was showing them houses. She is also a client of mine. They loved it, and I am convinced they bought the house they bought because it's within walking distance of Maria's.

I agreed and headed for my car and then Maria's.

"Hey, Maria, how are you? Oh, how I love to walk in here; it always smells so delicious!" I said, taking in a deep breath.

Maria came running to give me a hug. "Hello, Jack! How have you been? You haven't been by in a while. I thought you had abandoned me."

"Never, never abandon my favorite girl, but you know, Maria, if I came here too often, I would blow up like the balloon."

"Okay, okay, come sit down."

I sat at the counter, and Maria poured me a coffee and cut the first slice of a deep-dish cherry pie. She knows my taste buds as well as she knows me. We spent twenty minutes talking, and I was really enjoying that pie. The thought crossed my mind that I hadn't been in there since I started seeing Tess, and I missed going there and just realized it. Not to mention how nice it was talking to my friend and client, Maria.

"Okay, Maria, I need a dozen danish pastries to go. Just mix them up; you choose."

"You got it, sweetie. Be right back."

"Thanks, Maria." As I reached for my wallet, she stopped me.

"No, Jack, here you are. It's on me."

"No way, Maria, I don't want you to do that. Next you'll ask me to sell one of your houses and want me to do it free," I said, laughing.

"All right, then maybe I charge you double, like you do me." She was also now laughing.

"Touché, Maria. Touché."

I thanked her, kissed her cheek, and left for Joe's house. He had the door open waiting. He wasn't looking at me. He was looking at the box of danish, and it made me laugh. That was something else I had not done in a while.

We shook hands, and he invited me in. "Bring that box of goodies to the table. Coffee is ready."

I sat and watched him inhale two of those pastries. Then he leaned back, took a big pull on the mug of coffee, and said, "Okay, what's on your mind, and *no*, I don't want to sell my house."

"I want you to hear me out with an open mind. What I am going to tell you is both real and bizarre. It's also unbelievable, but I want you to believe it because it is as true as I am sitting here," I said in as serious a manner as I could muster.

"All right, let's hear it."

I told him the entire story, and he listened intently. "Joe, what I want to do is find a way to prove that this is not the ramblings of some deranged madman. I want this man to go down for his crime."

There was a long silence, and then Joe started to laugh like crazy.

"Joe, please, I am telling you the truth. I know how it must sound, but I have never told you anything that was not true, have I?"

"Not till now." He stopped laughing and leaned forward. "Even if I did believe you ... which I don't. What would you have me do? Go tell my superior and lose my job or be sent to see the shrink every other day?"

"Look, come to the house with me, ask me any questions. She will tell me the answer, and if when we're done you don't believe me, I'll drop the whole thing. Fair enough?"

"But I can't go in there without probable cause or a warrant. I could lose my job."

"Joe, not everything relates to police work. I am asking my friend and client Joe to look at my listing and see if he thinks it might work for someone he knows or at least be able to talk about it if the opportunity arises."

"But I thought you said it was sold?"

"No, I said it was under contract, and I am required to continue to bring more offers until it does close."

"All right, but when I say it's time to go, I want to go. Agreed?"

"Sure, Joe, whatever you say. Let's do it!"

"Ah, I want another danish first," Joe said, already reaching into the box.

"Okay, I'll have one, also." Joe refilled our mugs, and we ate danish and drank more coffee.

Finally, we were on our way to the house, and as I pulled up, Basil was just getting into his car. I told him I was surprised he was still there and that I was showing the property for a possible backup contract. He nodded and drove away.

We went inside, and Tess told me she was sitting on the right side of the couch. I had Joe sit in the chair, and I sat on the other side of the couch.

"Okay, Joe, you promised to keep an open mind. Remember?" He nodded and rolled his eyes at the same time. "Tess, this is my friend Joe, the cop I mentioned to you. Joe, meet Tess. Tess is sitting to my right, and she is ready to answer any questions."

"I can't believe I'm doing this."

Tess said hello, but evidently only I heard it.

Then I got an idea and said, "Joe, I want you to pay close attention. There is no mirror or anything that could serve as a mirror on the wall behind me, is there?"

"No."

"Then I am going to stand up and turn around. I want you to drop your pants for a moment, and Tess will tell me the color and type of underwear you have on."

I expected an argument from him, but he said, "You're on!"

I turned around and heard him unbuckle his belt, laughing at the same time.

"Tess told me you have dark blue briefs on and your belt buckle came off the belt."

"Okay, what's the trick?"

"No trick, Joe, really!"

"Okay, you may have gotten a glimpse of them if I bent down at the house, but you're on to something. Turn back around again and put your hands over your eyes. Have her tell you everything I am doing."

I did as he said and repeated whatever Tess said.

"You just pulled a red and white handkerchief out of your right rear pocket and you are waving it around."

"Oh my God! How the hell are you doing that?"

"Tess is telling me."

"Okay, I want to tie it over your eyes, because there must still be a trick here. I just can't believe this," Joe walked up to me from behind and tied the handkerchief around my head, covering my eyes. Then he returned to where he was standing before.

"Jack, I want you to tell me what I am doing."

"You are standing on your left foot with your right hand on your head." I was simply repeating what Tess said. "You placed your left foot on top of your right. Now you are sticking out your tongue and rolling your hand on your stomach with your right and your head with your left."

"My God, you got all three right. How are you doing it?"

"I am *not*! It's Tess; she is sitting there watching you and telling me, just like I told you."

Joe walked over to where I pointed and touched her but felt nothing there. "There's nobody here."

"You can't see, hear, or feel her. I can hear and feel her but not see her. And I still don't know why it's different for me than anyone else."

"Okay, I believe you. You've convinced me."

"Then you can ask her questions you wish to prove Basil murdered her." I was excited that he was beginning to believe me.

"I would have to get answers that would lead us to some hard evidence that would convince the DA to file an arrest warrant."

"Well, where do we go from here, Joe?"

"Look, I am a uniformed police officer. I don't do murders; those are turned over to the detectives to solve, and I don't know where to start. Remember, when you stopped in the precinct, I had to get that case from the cold-case storage room. Is there anything she can tell me that she thinks might help?"

I could hear Tess sigh. "Jack, I told you everything that happened that night. Did you tell him?"

"Yes, I told him."

Then I said, "Joe, I told you the story this morning that is all she knows."

"Then the only thing I can think of is to go to the station and read the entire file and see if that raises any questions that I can ask. Maybe ask one of the detectives, causally, where they start when there are no real clues."

I could tell that Joe was getting into this a bit, and I hoped he would glean something from the file that would help to ask the right questions.

"Listen, my friend, in three weeks this house goes to closing, and that will end my ability to enter this house and see Tess. She will die if she tries to leave the house. Please find something."

"It's my day off, as you know, but drop me at my house, and I'll run down to the station and pull the file again. I'll go through it for unanswered questions or ideas that might help us."

I did as he asked and then came back to spend time with Tess. We spent the remainder of the day in bed, which was where we spent most of our time together. When we finished making love, she began to tell me that Basil had only one living relative, and that was a younger cousin who lived in Panama.

"If Basil dies, he has already left the house to him in his will, but he would not ever live here due to his job in Panama. He has also provided for the real estate taxes to be paid directly from his bank for the next twenty years. If this house was not sold and something happened to Basil, we could be here forever."

Jokingly, I responded, "Okay, you scare off the buyers, and I'll kill Basil, and we'll live happily ever after, right?"

"Oh, Jack, that's a wonderful idea!" she said that in a serious tone that shook me to my core.

"You are joking, right?"

"No, I'm not. Look, Basil is a murderer. Don't you execute most murderers? Don't you feel he should die? If we could get him arrested for my murder, as brutal as it was, he would get life without parole or even the death penalty."

She worked on that idea for a while until she could sense me becoming upset, and then she dropped it. Joe called later that evening and told me that he had been all through the file, even talked to the detective in charge of the case when it was a fresh disappearance or kidnapping and nothing. Without something new from Tess, we were done. That was not what I wanted to hear.

That night I lay in bed at home thinking about what Tess and I talked about earlier. I was just fantasizing, or so I thought. She did have a very good point. Basil was a murderer, and he did deserve to be punished, but all evidence pointed to a run away or kidnapping, so how would he ever get caught? There was absolutely nothing to cause anyone to suspect anyone of murder. No body, no eyewitnesses, no bloody murder weapon—nothing, nothing, and more nothing! I fell asleep and dreamed in way too vivid details that I did just as she had suggested. It was easier than I thought, and my dream told me exactly how it could be done. I woke in a sweat, breathing hard but somehow enamored with the idea, yet disturbed at the clarity of how I could do such a thing. For the first time since I've known her, I began to wonder if maybe I was being used. But I shook off that notion quickly. I loved her.

If killing Basil was the Ying, than the Yang started the next morning at Maria's, when I felt that first twinge of how Tess was taking all of me. The fact that I was not working and spending every possible moment with her should have been a wake-up call to me, but it wasn't, and I would go to her today as I did every day and fall back under her spell. Spell? Curious. I had never used that word with Tess before. *I am in love with her, aren't I? Well, of course I am.* But now, a very small seed of doubt was beginning to slowly germinate in my consciousness. I ordered myself to stop thinking and go to Tess. With the exception of Basil's closing later that week, it was my last closing, and since I had not been working, there was nothing in the pipeline. I was already subsidizing my life with Tess. I guess I was still financially afloat because we could never go anywhere or spend any money.

When I entered the house, I thought I heard voices; I called out to her, and when she responded, I ask to whom she was talking, but she said she was talking out loud and watching because she felt scared.

"What are you afraid of?"

"If I can't see you anymore, I will walk out of the house and die. I can't live without you." Then she started crying again.

"We aren't going to let that happen. We'll figure it out, but you still didn't answer my question. What are you afraid of?"

"I don't know, Jack. I just am."

I took her to the couch and sat her down. I told her about my dream and about how easy it seemed to me to kill him. "I would make an appointment to come by one evening, on the guise of discussing the upcoming closing. I would ask him to show me something in the basement. When he opened the door, I would shove him hard, down those narrow steep old steps. If that didn't kill him, I would hit him so it would look like that was from the fall. I would leave and come back the next day to discover the body. I would have someone with me for verification."

"Oh, Jack, it's perfect. Will you do it for us?"

"I don't know if I could really kill another person, though." I wanted and waited for her reaction.

She began crying heavily, and it was heartbreaking to hear. I tried to comfort her, but I knew that only my agreement was going to stop the sobbing. Finally, I blurted out, "I'll do it!"

She slowly calmed down, continually confirming that I meant what I said, and I did. She took me by the hand and walked me to the bed, the bed where we spent many hours and enjoyed her over and over. She made me feel like a king and now her protector and caregiver. My fate was sealed and my soul cast to hell. I still couldn't believe I could actually go through with it. For what I was about to do, I knew I would burn in hell for eternity.

As I drove home that afternoon, it was my turn to cry, and I did. What I didn't do that I should have done was to get on my knees and beg Jesus for help and to save me from this terrible deed I was about to do.

Later I began to rationalize again that he was a killer and I was taking the law into my hands. Again, I was talking myself into it. I could not sleep that night. By morning, I was going to go to Tess and tell her there had to be another way.

I was like a freshly caught fish on the deck of a boat, flipping and flopping for my life, but unlike the fish, I had a soul to think about as well.

My heart demanded I do it, but my mind said don't. On my way to see Tess, I drove by Maria's. I made a quick U-turn, pulled into her parking lot, and ran inside. I got her usual warm greeting and sat at the counter. I ordered a cherry danish and a mug of coffee. I wasn't exactly sure way I did that, but best guess, I was reaching out for the feeling I had the other day when I was in to get Joe his bribe. Maybe the influence of a friend could help. I enjoyed the lighthearted conversation with Maria so much that I ordered another round and stayed until her lunch crowd started wandering in. I paid my bill and my respects to Maria and left. Part of me wanted to go home, and part of me didn't. I have never been so screwed up and wishy-washy in my life. I didn't know which end was up. You guessed it. I finally went to Tess and took of her sweet love and body again and again.

We were lying there, talking after we had just exhausted each other, when I heard a man's voice whisper, "Tess, where are you?"

"Who is that?" I asked.

"Ah, I, ah, don't know."

That was a lie. I knew it immediately. But who was it? I felt her leave me, and I went to the hallway that overlooked the foyer. There before my eyes was a sight I could not believe. I sank to my knees as I saw what was like a scene from a movie. It lasted thirty seconds or so, but it seemed to be in slow motion.

There, right there in the foyer before my very eyes, was a man, a man who seemed familiar to me. He was standing there with his hands up like he was holding someone by the upper arms, his head bowed slightly as though he were listening to someone. Then his head snapped toward me. At first, I thought he was looking at me, but I was naked on the floor, behind the banister. He looked back as quickly as he looked up. Then he bolted for the door and was gone. He was so familiar. Who was he? I knew him, but I couldn't place him. As I dressed to leave, it hit me like a ton of bricks. It was the man who bought the house, but not with his agent or wife. Then I realized what I had been looking at. He was holding Tess, and she must have told him I was upstairs. He looked and then ran out the door. I sat there in silence, my jaw on the floor. I could not believe what I had just witnessed. She had something going on with him, also. How many others had there been? Her words were lies, all lies. She didn't love me; she was using me.

Then I felt her touch me, and she told me, "Jack, it's not what you think; please let me explain."

She helped me up and back to the bed. My legs were weak and wobbly, and I felt cold, really cold. I got back in the bed and pulled the covers over me. She lay beside me, her soft body warming me.

"Jack, please hear me out. They came by one day—that man, his wife, the agent, and the home inspector. I was bored, so I followed them around and listened to all they had to say. At one point along the way, I hit my toe on the coffee table and yelled out. Nobody heard me except him. He turned toward me and asked if anyone else heard that; of course they all said no. Everyone continued what they were doing, but he kept looking around as if he was still not convinced. You know, I am almost always naked. Why should I dress when no one can see me? It's just an unnecessary chore. Well, he excused himself to use the facilities, and I followed him. I don't know why, maybe just being naughty. I sneezed as I stood next to him, watching him piss. He reached up and got my breast. Then he felt me all over, and I said stop. He heard me and asked who and what I was. He was holding me tight, and I told him. He didn't want to believe it, but as with you, he knew it was true. Somehow, he managed to get a key, and he comes back from time to time to find me. He says he wants to make love to me, so I stay far from him and stay quiet. I had to tell him you were here to get him to leave. I could not risk you being hurt or drawing attention to us from any more people. Do you understand, Jack?"

I was still stunned, but I agreed and told her I had to leave and get my head straight. I said I would be back tomorrow.

She said she understood, so I quickly dressed and left. I drove around and around trying to buy the tale I had just heard. I just could not make it wash, even though I wanted to believe it. I tried and tried to clear my head and tell her all was okay, but I had more questions. I decided to return and have her convince me some more.

When I arrived, something told me to park around the corner and walk up to the house. When I got there, another car was in the driveway. It was the red Jag. The same red Jag she told me the buyers rode up in on the day of the inspection. Now I am no fool; it's possible that he had come back to bother her, but I didn't believe it. I was beginning to understand but had to be absolutely sure. So I slipped into the house with my spare key, took off my shoes, and crept up the stairs, walking close to the wall to avoid any stair squeaking. I looked into the room and saw what I must have looked like, a naked man moving up and down. It looked real stupid, but I knew, I knew she was under him, and I could hear her making love talk with him. The last straw was when she moaned that she loved him. I ran down to the foyer, put on my shoes, and went to my car. I drove two blocks to the Shell station and pulled from my trunk a five-gallon gasoline can. As soon as the can was full, I drove back to the house and parked away from the house again. I took the gasoline and poured it around the foundation. I knew this old-style frame Victorian would burn good, real good. I was so enraged I wasn't thinking straight. I wanted her dead. She had cost me everything, and it was all a big, fat lie. I struck a match to the wet fuel, and the flames shot up the walls of the house. Neighbors were already out, screaming and watching the fire as it grew. The flames exceeded my expectation. They shot up the exterior walls and were licking at the roof. My first instinct was to run, but it was no use because the neighbors all knew me. I was the big Realtor known by all, thanks to all the money I had made. I had built my reputation as a neighborhood expert.

I moved back away from the heat and sat on the grass and watched it burn. I could hear the sirens and knew it wouldn't be long. Soon the police would be here to take me away. I looked back and wished I could see Mai Le one more time. I realized what a fool I had been, and my dreams of being a successful RE/MAX associate and a pillar in my community were disappearing as fast as my most expensive listing.

Firemen were running around like crazy, fighting a losing battle against a raging inferno. A female police officer approached me, asking me if I knew how the fire started. I told her my name and said that I had started it. She then asked, "Do you know if anyone was still in the house at the time you started the fire?"

I told her one of the new owners were still in there. She ran to the fire chief and told him, but the house was engulfed now, and they couldn't send anyone in. Besides, anyone inside that inferno would have most likely already succumbed to smoke inhalation before the fire trucks ever got there. The chief knew this fire was too hot to squelch; he was simply trying to contain it until it burned itself out.

The officer returned to me and said, "Mr. Forrest, please stand up." When I did, she put handcuffs on me and said, "You are under arrest for arson and possible murder. If bodies are found inside, the charge will likely be revised to first-degree murder. You have the right to remain silent, and anything you say can be used against you in a court of law. You have the right to an attorney. If you cannot afford one, one will be provided for you. Do you understand these rights as I have explained them to you?"

With my hands cuffed behind my back, she walked me to her car and put me in the black and white. She told me she would transport me to the precinct, and the detectives would take my statement. At the station, the detectives interviewed me, booked me, and put me in the lockup. I found out the next day that Tony, the buyer, had jumped out the window and broken both legs and one arm. I am told that when they asked him why he happened to be in there, he was quite red faced and never did provide a satisfactory answer.

My trial came quickly. I made a deal with the DA that I would plead in exchange for a lesser sentence, and since no one died, he reduced it by dropping the attempted murder charge. It was now strictly an arson charge. Once again, my negotiation skills covered my needs. I wanted time to repent and to set myself right. They gave me twenty years with the possibility of parole in fifteen, maybe less for good behavior.

It is amazing how fast you can get from the county jail to the prison when you plead guilty. You can visit me anytime you like. I'll be here, no appointment necessary.

Oh, by the way, a side note for my fellow Realtors. It was my third or fourth day in county lockup as I awaited my trial. I was sitting on the side of my bunk when I felt a hand touch my shoulder, but there was no one there … well that's not exactly true. I guess that *"I can't leave the house"* nonsense was exactly that … nonsense.

So if you list a house for sale, and you hear a voice, the voice of a sultry, young woman with no one in sight, run, don't walk, to the nearest exit—and do not return!

THE END … DOUBTFUL.

CRYPTURE 6
Bitten

Thursday, October 21, 2010

The summer of fun and sun had now melted into fall. The school year was well under way, and football season was half-over. Bobby Gentry was cocaptain of our football team, and we were enjoying a winning season. He had the right build at six foot three in his senior year, wiry and strong. He was a wide receiver and small forward for the varsity football and basketball teams, respectively. He was my favorite player on the teams, and I wondered how we would fare without him next year.

My wife, Janet, the school superintendent, and I watched him play along with the rest of the team from our local high school. In a small town like ours, the folks really get into the rivalries of the high-school sports. On most Friday nights, you will find damn near the whole town sitting on the bleachers in the den, our nickname for our football stadium. This was where all home football games as well as track-and-field events took place. Our town is Eagle Creek, Nevada, our team is the Wolverines, and I'm Dan Duggan, sheriff for Eagle Creek.

It was a typical fall evening, perhaps a little drier than usual. The first snow had yet to arrive. The weather this night was clear but cold, and a full moon lit up the near cloudless sky. Janet called me at the office. "Hi, honey. I left some fried chicken and mashed potatoes wrapped up on the stove that you can heat up in the microwave when you get home. I have to stay late at the high school to help Beth Dorn and a bunch of students decorate the gym for the homecoming dance Saturday night."

"All right, dear. How late do you think you'll be?"

"I hope not too late, around ten maybe. See you then, love, and I trust you'll wait up?"

"Yes, dear." I chuckled as I said good-bye and hung up. When my wife suggests I wait up, I always do.

The homecoming game would be played Friday, the night before the dance. I remembered how Janet and I celebrated our senior homecoming dance; she must have been thinking of that also, and that must have been why she wanted me to wait up for her. Those thoughts had me smiling when Sally, my dispatcher and office clerk, walked in. "Something funny, Chief?"

"Huh ... ah, no—nothing. What do you need?"

"Just thought you'd want the mail."

"Sure, just leave it."

I went back to thinking about Janet. I hoped she wouldn't be too late, but I knew Beth. She could talk incessantly, where my wife was straight to the point, no wasted words. Those two were so different in many ways. My wife was tall, naturally blonde, and very shapely in addition to having been a high-school and college athlete, while Beth was short with black hair and built like a bowling ball. She had never played a sport in her life and was a bookworm. However, they were close friends, and Beth was a good teacher.

I picked up the mail and resumed my duties.

Bobby and Jeanie were the textbook high-school sweethearts, popular and well liked. Jeanie was a tall blonde with a great smile that would light up a room. She was homecoming attendant her freshman year, and rumor had it that she would be this year's senior homecoming queen. The announcement would be made next Monday at the pep rally. In addition, she was head majorette for the school band her sophomore through senior years, and a cheerleader for the basketball team all four years. The two seniors had gone together since freshman year, and they were definitely an item. They were even planning to go to the same college in the fall. Bobby and Jeanie are the focus of a bizarre investigation I had to solve.

I got home that night about 1800, heated up my dinner, and ate it in front of the TV with a cold longneck. I had a few more and watched more TV while I waited for Janet to get home. I was afraid to go to bed and wait because if she came home and I was asleep, well, it would be the cold shoulder for a few days after. Plus, I didn't want to miss whatever she had on her mind. So at about 2230 when she walked in, I greeted her at the door. "Sheriff, what are you doing up? Now you march yourself straight to bed at once." The twinkle in her eye was all I needed to dash up the stairs to our room. By the time she came through the door, she was wearing only panties and a bra.

The peacefulness of waking up and holding my beautiful naked wife in my arms while she slept was something I knew I could happily grow old doing. The phone by the bed caused me to jump, waking Sleeping Beauty. "This better be important!" I grumbled as I reached for the phone.

"Sheriff, you better get down to the hospital quick. Jeanie Blackburn has been hurt bad." I knew Janet loved that girl, and I thought best not to tell her until I knew what was going on.

"What is it, dear?" she said.

"Oh, there's been an accident, and Briggs needs me right away. You go back to sleep, and I'll see you shortly." I dashed to the bathroom before she could clear her head and start asking questions. When I came out, she had fallen asleep again, so I slipped out quietly and raced to the hospital.

I slammed my patrol car into a parking space near the hospital entrance and ran to the nurse's station. "What room is Jeanie Blackburn in?"

"Room 303, Sheriff. Doc's up there now." I jumped in the elevator, hopped off on the third floor, and made a beeline to Jeanie's room. I saw Doc standing over her. Hell, he was her mom's doctor when Jeanie was born. Dr. Ben Charles was the most trusted doctor at the hospital. To the folks around town, he was simply known as Doc. In his late fifties, he was a spry fellow who kept abreast of all the latest treatments and medical discoveries. He was tall and thin with thick white hair that he still wore in a flattop. He had a thin mustache and always spoke with authority but never condescendingly. People always felt they were in good hands with him as their doctor. I called him over to find out what had happened.

"She is still unconscious. I hope she doesn't lapse into a coma. She is badly beaten up and has some kind of animal bite in her thigh."

"What kind of bite?"

"Not sure—large dog, cougar, bear, wolf. Won't know until I get the saliva from skin samples around the bite, but it's a bad one." We walked over to look at her. She had stitches, butterfly bandages, and bruises all over her. She had a glucose bag hanging next to her with an IV in her arm.

"Her parents have been here almost since they brought her in, but I just sent them home to get some sleep since she was still unconscious." As we talked, she seemed to move a little and then started to moan a bit. Her eyes opened slowly and then closed, so Doc quickly shined a small flashlight into her eyes. "Looks like she's coming to, thank goodness." Within a few minutes, her eyes opened.

"Doc, where am I?"

"You're in the hospital, dear, and you're gonna be fine."

"I remember waking up, thinking I had a nightmare, but then I realized that I wasn't in my bed."

"Can you answer a few questions for the sheriff?"

"Hi, Jeanie. Do you feel up to it?"

"I guess so, Sheriff."

"Okay, just take your time, and start from the beginning."

"Okay, Sheriff. Well, Bobby and I joined some other kids to decorate the gym ... where is Bobby?" she screamed. "Is he okay? Please tell me."

"I don't know, Jeanie. We haven't found him yet, but we have an APB out for him, and we're doing everything we can to locate him. Please continue telling me, and it may help me to find Bobby."

"Well, after your wife thanked us for helping, she asked for two volunteers to stay a little longer to sweep up and take out the trash. Bobby said we would do it, and she let the other kids and Ms. Dorn leave. After we finished, we walked her to her car and started to walk home. We took the shortcut through the woods as we always do." She paused and began to cry as though she were reliving what happened all over. Doc came over and gave her a sedative and told me that was all for now.

Jeanie had been found staggering around the streets by some early-morning garbage collectors who called it in. Briggs was on duty. He went to the hospital, and that was when he called me. But now we knew where the attack took place. Briggs had gone home, as his shift was over, to get some shut-eye. I drove over to the school and took the path that Jeanie said that she and Bobby had taken. I walked about halfway down the path that ran through the woods from the school to the subdivision where Bobby and Jeanie both lived. I came upon the crime scene. There was blood everywhere and part of what must have been the shirt Bobby was wearing. Most disturbing was Bobby's right hand and part of his arm below the elbow. I grabbed a roll of yellow crime-scene tape and roped off the area. I marked the spot where the arm and hand were with a numbered crime-scene stake, bagged the arm, called the coroner, and drove back to Doc at the hospital with sirens blaring. I didn't want to leave it for the coroner, as some animal could take it before he got there. More importantly, I didn't know if it could be saved if Bobby were found alive. When I got there, Doc told me it was too decomposed to save, but I asked him to freeze it for evidence. "Doc, I guess this eliminates Bobby as the suspect for what happened to Jeanie."

"You actually considered him a suspect? He loved that girl."

"Just SOP for police work, my friend, but don't tell Janet I said that. I'll be in the doghouse for weeks."

"You're right about that."

"Oh, speaking of Janet, I better run by the house and talk with her before she hears about this from someone else."

I drove back to the house. I heard her in the shower and went into the bathroom. "I'm home, babe."

"Well, why don't you come in and join me, big boy?"

"I think you better come out when you're finished. There's been a problem concerning a couple of kids from the high school."

She was out in seconds, putting on her robe and demanding details.

I told her what I knew so far, and she began to cry. I just held her until she regained her composure. "Babe, what time did the kids actually leave the school?"

"Well, it was about ten when we finished, and I thanked everyone for their help and then asked for two people to help me sweep up and remove trash. Didn't see the need to keep everyone for that. Bobby and Jeanie said they would, and everyone else, including Beth, left. It took about fifteen minutes to finish and lock up. They walked me to my car and ... Oh God, Dan, I offered them a ride, but they said they wanted to walk. I should have insisted!"

"It's not your fault. Don't even go there. It was their decision. Don't you remember how we used to always try to be alone? You couldn't have forced them."

"As I drove off, I saw them take the shortcut through the woods walking hand in hand. Oh, Dan, they had their whole lives ahead of them." She began to cry again and then got angry, demanding I do something to catch whoever did this. That's my girl.

"I'm going back to the hospital in a few hours to see if I can get Jeanie to finish telling me what happened."

"I'm going with you." Then she stuck her index finger in my face and said, "And don't you dare say no!"

"Yes, dear."

She then walked off to the kitchen for coffee and a sandwich for me—cold leftover meatloaf with lettuce and ketchup. Tasted pretty good with a mug of hot coffee. About 1400, we headed for the hospital to speak with Jeanie some more. I hoped she could give me a description of the attacker. When we walked into her room, Janet ran to her, and they cried together. I looked at Doc, who was checking on her, and rolled my eyes. "Women!" Doc laughed and walked out, shaking his head. As I gave the ladies a chance to talk their women talk, I reminisced about Doc.

He and I had both been born here in Eagle Creek. He was about ten years older than me, and we didn't know each other well before he graduated high school. Then he went to college and then medical school. Young Dr. Ben Charles pursued his dream of becoming a doctor at a big-city hospital while I went straight into the Marine

Corps. I never thought I would return to Eagle Creek, and yet we both did.

Ben Charles was working in a large hospital near Washington, DC, when he got word of his dad's illness. He returned to Eagle Creek to tend to him and just stayed on after his father died.

After doing twenty years in the Marine Corps out of high school, where I worked my way through the enlisted rank, became a warrant officer, and was ultimately promoted to major, I retired. I spent a great deal of my enlisted rank time in the shore patrol. I surprised myself when I found I enjoyed police work, and when I retired, I returned to Eagle Creek, became a deputy sheriff, and, a little over a year later, was elected sheriff. Besides both of us returning home, we shared one other thing: we married our high-school sweethearts.

I had to interview now, so I walked over and once again asked if she felt okay enough to tell me the rest. She said she was all right but asked if Janet could stay while we talked. I nodded, and Janet held her hand as I asked her to continue. She confirmed what Janet had told me about when they left the building. "We were holding hands and walking slowly to my house. We took the shortcut through the woods, old Palmer property. It was a beautiful night, and the moon was really bright and lit up the woods, so we walked slowly and talked about our future. I remember how the leaves and twigs crackled under our feet as we walked along. We stopped under a big tree, and Bobby and I were kissing when I pulled back suddenly and asked Bobby if he heard a noise, a noise like someone running. He said he hadn't. Then I heard it a second time, and that time Bobby heard it too. He was sure it was George, one of his buddies, playing a joke on us. Bobby thought we should teach him a lesson. He told me to hide behind a big tree, and he would hide behind another. 'When he gets between us, we'll jump out screaming.' I agreed, and we hid like Bobby said, and the running footsteps got closer and closer. I saw something huge; it looked like a wolf running fast. I couldn't believe it, so I rubbed my eyes, and about that time, Bobby jumped out screaming. I followed his lead, and I was closest, and I felt a sharp pain in my upper right thigh. It hurt so bad I screamed and fell down. After it bit me, it stood on its hind legs. I saw Bobby move toward the sound, but he was immediately knocked to the ground. It must have knocked him out, as he didn't move. All I could see was an outline of some large man, but it didn't really look like a man; it looked more like a bear. The rest must have been a dream as this man, this whatever, began to devour his flesh. The sound it made as it ate caused me to throw up. I crawled away, hearing it eat like a starved animal. I went unnoticed as I crawled away in the direction of my home. I was terrified; my only instinct was to get as far as I could from whatever it was that had attacked us. I looked back once and saw it, whatever it was, stand on its hind legs and begin to drag Bobby by the ankle with one hand. I got up and tried to run, but my leg hurt so bad I kept falling. I remember falling a second time, and that was all until I woke up here a short time ago.

"As I woke, I was afraid to move or even open my eyes. I thought that thing was standing over me. I fought not to scream, and then I heard him walk away, and that was when I peeked and saw you talking to a doctor."

"Jeanie, we have all been very worried."

"Oh my God, Bobby's out there hurt. You must find him, Sheriff! You must!"

"What is George's last name, and do you know where he lives?"

"George Johnson, and he lives on Maple Lane, but I don't know the house number."

"Okay, Jeanie, thank you. That will be all for now. Try and get some rest now."

As I was finishing my notes, her parents came back in. I pulled them aside and asked them for any info they had, but they knew less than I did, so Janet and I left them to have their visit. They were good people and really shook up about what happened. Janet and I went to the car and started home.

"I don't sense that Jeanie is that concerned about Bobby. What do you think?" She disagreed strongly. "Your too damn much a cop! Do you think she could have hurt Bobby?"

"Well, no, but ..."

"But nothing. That poor girl isn't able to show all her feelings at this time. She's still scared to death." I dropped the subject.

As sheriff, I now had a big job ahead of me. What could have done this, and where was Bobby, and was my whole town at risk? The next morning, I returned to the hospital. I wanted to ask Doc more about the injuries Jeanie suffered. I went to the nurse's station, and they said he was with a patient, so I went to the lounge and asked if he could meet me there. I shoved the coins into the machine and retrieved a large black coffee. As I sat there sipping the hot liquid, I thought about Bobby. I was certain he was dead, but I wasn't going to say that aloud for anyone to hear.

About that time, Doc walked in and went straight for the coffee machine. "Good morning, Dan. What brings you slumming so early on a fine morning?"

"Good morning to you too. Doc, tell me more about Jeanie and her wounds."

Doc brought his coffee and sat at the table. "Dan, all I can tell you at this point is that she was mauled by what appears to be a large predator. The bite on her thigh was the bite of a large animal. It could have been a bear, a very large dog, or perhaps a cougar or even a wolf. We will know more when the DNA tests are back in about a week or two."

"Why will it take so long, Doc?"

"We have to send it to the labs at the FBI, and they don't move with the greatest of speed."

"All right, Doc. Let me know, will you, please?"

"Sure will, the minute I know something."

I headed for my car and drove back to my office. I grabbed some more coffee and stared out my window at the large expanse of woods leading up the mountainside. It was a beautiful sight, and looking at that view seemed to help me think through things. I had a lot to ponder, the physical evidence and the things I had been told. I couldn't remember the last time I saw a mountain lion, although they were supposedly making a rapid comeback from near extinction. I had to notify the newspaper to warn people about being in the woods after dark.

When I came back into the office the next day, the newspaper reporters were waiting for me, and they were full of questions. I had no answers to their questions. They left still hungry for details. I wasn't the least bit happy that they were all gathered at my office, and I let the editors know it in no uncertain terms.

"Sally, I'm going back to the hospital to see Jeanie again. I'll be on the radio if you need me."

"Okay, Sheriff. Don't forget your meeting with the mayor at noon."

"Got it. I'll be there."

As I drove to the hospital, I thought about all that I had seen and heard since this strange case started. I just didn't buy the mountain or wolf part.

When I arrived at the hospital, I ran into the doctor.

"What's new, Doc—with Jeanie, I mean?"

"Well, not much—oh, one thing that I found this morning when I changed the dressing on her wound was that she had dark, straight hair growing around the wound, very coarse hair at that, so I cut some of it and sent it to the lab for analysis. Her wound is almost healed."

"Doesn't hair tend to grow under bandages?"

"Yes, but nothing like this," he said as he walked on to do his rounds.

I stood there for a second, deep in thought. The nurse shook me back to the present as she offered to escort me to Jeanie. I thanked her upon our reaching the door and went in. "Good morning, Jeanie. How are you feeling today?"

"I feel really good. Look," she said as she whipped back the covers to show me her leg. I stared at it in amazement. I could not believe my eyes. Her leg, which I had been told when I first saw her would require four or five surgeries to replace the missing flesh and remove all the scars, was completely healed. It was not even red, bruised, or swollen. Only the large hair follicles around the wound still existed.

"Doc had to shave off the black hair around the wound. It was so gross, but now my leg looks almost like nothing ever happened to it!" Jeanie seemed filled with great joy. As the head cheerleader and majorette, her legs were important to her; a huge, ugly scar would not work under the short-skirted outfits they wore.

"I'll be right back, Jeanie!" I raced out to find Doc. I found him at the nurses' station.

"Doc, what the hell is going on? Jeanie just showed me her leg, and it's all healed?"

"I know. I told you that when you first came in, and I have no answer, but I'm keeping her here a few more days to run some tests. I put a rush on the lab for the answers to the hair and skin samples for DNA analysis. Dan, let's get some coffee. Nurse, will you look in on Mrs. Robinson for me? This way, Dan, please."

The doctor and I walked toward the cafeteria, got coffee from the vending machine, and sat down.

"In all my years of practicing medicine, I have never seen anything like this. It defies all logic and medical knowledge. I have seen my share of quick recoveries, but this is beyond imagination. How that wound, so deep and with so much flesh missing, could totally rebuild itself is beyond me."

"Based on what you have seen so far, what would you guess did this?"

"When I first examined the bite mark, it most resembled the jaw print of a large cougar. I don't need to tell you, but they usually stay up in the hills, rarely venturing down here into the town, unless it was old or injured in a way that it couldn't hunt."

"True, although I did shoot one about five years ago near town, actually about this time of year."

"Oh, yes, I do remember you telling me about that. So do you think we may have another?"

"Doc, I'm not sure what to make of it. From what Jeanie told me, it stood upright and dragged Bobby away like a man might do. Do you think she was so terrified that her mind was playing tricks on her?"

"Well, it is possible, but I've known Jeanie since she was born—shoot, I delivered her. Her folks are very good people, and Jeanie is as honest a young girl as you would hope to find, so I'm sure she believes what she's saying."

I sipped my coffee, deep in thought. What could have bitten her like a cougar and walked upright? "Doc, could it have been a bear?"

"Oh, I suppose, but while bears can stand, even walk on their hind legs, I've never seen one drag prey, except on all fours."

"Jeanie must have been in shock or something, and her mind must have played tricks on her. I think my report will show that Bobby was attacked by a cougar and carried off. What do you think, Doc?"

"Dan, I just don't have any other explanation at this point, but if we could just find Bobby, it would be of great assistance in figuring out what this is all about."

"You're right, Doc. I don't have any good answers, and the mayor is up my butt over this. We plan to scour the entire woods between the high school and where Jeanie lives. I will just list Bobby as missing for now. Thanks, Doc. I'd better get going."

"Okay, Dan. I'll see you later."

I felt we were extremely knowledgeable in our respective fields, yet this case had us both scratching our heads and unable to come up with reasonable answers. I had signs posted making the wooded area where Bobby and Jeanie were attached off limits and had the local radio and TV station, WJWG, reminding everyone to stay indoors as much as possible after dark and to be sure to lock doors and windows, especially at night.

A week later, Doc called me and requested I get over to the hospital ASAP. I rushed over to the hospital and straight into Doc's office.

"What is it?"

Doc put down the report he was reading, pulled off his half-rimmed glasses, leaned back in his chair, and said, "I was wrong. It was not a cougar that bit Jeanie. It was a wolf. Both the hair that grew on her thigh and the saliva found on pieces of tissue at the wound site confirm wolf or wolves! What I can't wrap my head around is why did wolf hair actually grow at the wound?"

"What the hell are you saying?"

Doc stood up and began to pace back and forth.

"I don't know what I'm saying. There is no reason why a bite from any animal would cause hair like the hair of that animal to grow there. It just does not fit any known science. I have done two things since I found out about this and before I called you. First, I called Jeanie and asked her to let the hair grow."

"Wait—you released her?"

"Yes, yesterday afternoon."

"But why?"

"I had no reason not to; she was healed. I don't understand how, but she was. Anyway, I told her to let it grow, and when it gets about an inch long, come in so I can see it and harvest some of it for another test. I'll also draw some blood and urine for analysis. Second, I called an old friend who is a Native American and a doctor. I want his take on this. He will be here the day after tomorrow."

"What are you telling me? You're going to have a witch doctor solve this?"

"I have no preformed ideas, but if you can give me a more reasonable explanation, I'm all ears." I just sat there dumbfounded. "Dan, have you found Bobby yet?"

"Funny you should ask that. My deputy was on his way this morning to Buffalo Pass. A hiker phoned in this morning and said he found a skeleton up there."

"But that's twenty miles away," Doc mumbled under his breath. "Can you take me there ... now?"

"Well, I guess so. Why?"

Doc grabbed his hat and started out the door, telling his nurse he would be gone a few hours, and I followed.

"Doc, what's up?"

"Can you call your deputy and tell him not to disturb the site or the remains and get us there ASAP?"

I grabbed the radio and contacted my deputy, who had just reached the scene.

"Briggs, Doc and I are on the way. Tape off the area but do *not* disturb that site."

"Roger that, Sheriff."

I hit the lights and siren and punched it.

"Hold on, Doc. We'll be there in no time!"

"Just get us there in one piece, thank you!"

By the time we got to the crime scene, I found Briggs waiting and the scene taped off. Doc put on his rubber gloves and took a close look at the remains. Unfortunately, vultures and other scavengers had picked the carcass clean of every scrap of meat, but a portion of the shirt that the victim was wearing was still on the underside of the skeleton.

I told Briggs to get the shirt for ID purposes. "The county coroner is standing by to take the remains as soon as I authorize it."

Briggs said, "Sheriff, you'd better take a look at this."

When I looked and then Doc looked, we couldn't believe what we saw.

"Briggs, get several photos and a casting of this."

"Right away, Sheriff."

"What does that look like to you, Doc?"

"It looks like the front part of a wolf's paw and the back half of a person's foot but much larger."

We looked for other prints but to no avail. The remaining footprints must have been lost due to wind and/or other animals around the carcass. After Doc, Briggs, and I were done with the investigation, I turned it over to the coroner's personnel.

As Doc and I drove back to the hospital, neither of us said a word. It was as though we were afraid to say what we thought, for fear that talking about it would somehow make it real. When we reached the hospital and Doc got out, he turned and leaned down to say, "I will wait for a copy of the autopsy report, and I'll let you know what happens with Jeanie's tests."

"Thanks, Doc. See ya later," I said as I drove away.

The homecoming game had to be canceled, as did the dance. The league gave us a forfeit, but Janet had no choice. The entire town was in shock.

Two weeks went by quickly without further incident, but we didn't know anything more than we had in the beginning.

Doc showed up at my office with another man. By his appearance, I knew he must be the Indian doctor, and frankly, I had mixed emotions about meeting him. I was afraid the doctor would confirm my deepest, unspoken suspicions.

"Dan, I'd like you to meet my friend, Dr. Timothy Sky. Tim, Sheriff Dan Duggan."

We shook hands and exchanged a few of the usual introductory pleasantries.

"Gentlemen, have a seat, and tell me what we are dealing with here."

"Dan, I've explained to Tim some of what we know so far, and he has examined the physical evidence. But first, let me tell you of Jeanie's latest test results. The hair that grew around the wound site is now gone without a trace—no coarse hair, no large hair follicles. Second, blood and urine are as they should be. In other words, she is a perfectly normal teenage girl. It's as though her body never experienced this episode."

I asked where we should go from here.

"Tim has told me ... well, let him explain it. Tim."

"Okay, I believe what we are dealing with is the wolf spirit, which has been brought back for some reason we have not yet discovered. It has invaded a human host to give it a physical presence and an ability to kill as it thirsts for blood and flesh. I am—"

"Wait just a minute. Are you for real? You can't be serious!" I had to interrupt.

"Hold on. Hear him out. I know it sounds crazy, but we are seeing the proof, and we don't want to admit its existence. I don't understand it either," Doc retorted, so I shut up and leaned back with my arms folded across my chest.

Tim continued. "As I was saying, I am convinced this is what has happened. If the wolf spirit has completed its reason for being here, you have seen the end of it. If not, when the next full moon appears, it will take control of its host again and attempt to finish what it must do. You cannot stop it; it will not be stopped until it has completed its purpose."

Trying not to be sarcastic, I said, "If it appears again at the next full moon, what can we do to protect the citizens?"

"If it is a person it is after, it will hunt, kill, and eat that person. However, if in its pursuit for the intended, he can't locate or get to that person, it must consume human flesh to survive. During the time of the full moon, keep everyone off the streets. It must eat each time it appears or die. Someone will die at each appearance until the one he was sent for is devoured," Tim said.

Doc, Tim, and I checked the calendar. The next full moon would be November 22, and Tim told us we must be ready.

"Oh my God! This is absurd!" I exclaimed.

"You must keep folks in and armed. Bullets will not kill it but will stun it temporarily. It will try to avoid the pain if it can—that is, unless you are its intended; it will stop at nothing to reach the throat of that poor soul," Tim added.

I looked at the calendar again. "We have approximately two weeks until the next full moon!"

"Yes, Sheriff, and you best pray that its business is finished here in Eagle Creek or you must deal with it, and it is unstoppable."

"Dr. Sky, have these spirits ever come before?"

"Yes, many times. The white people have another name for him, and they totally misunderstand him. You call him ... werewolf!"

"Oh, well, I'll just go home and cast some silver bullets. Won't they kill it?" I asked.

Dr. Sky began to laugh and then stated, "I'm sorry, Sheriff. I'm not laughing at you, but you must have seen too many horror flicks. It works in Hollywood, but that is not reality. If its job is done, it will abandon the body and become incorporeal until he is summoned again and returns."

Doc sat there shaking his head. "Okay, so we take all the precautions and still have to just hope his mission is complete so it will not return. I still hope you are wrong about this whole thing."

I had to ask Tim. "How do you account for the hair and the wound healing so quickly?"

"Legend says that anyone bitten by the spirit wolf may be turned into a werewolf but only if the spirit wishes it before the bite. In other words, a strictly defensive bite will not cause the victim to change. Believe me, guys, I hope I'm wrong about all of this!"

"All right, Tim and I are going back to the hospital, and we will keep you posted,"

Doc and Tim left. I turned to the dispatcher, Sally. "I'm going home. Call me if anything happens. Briggs is on patrol."

"Sure, Chief. I'll be leaving at four today. Okay?"

"That's okay as long as all is quiet, and stay indoors, especially at dusk and beyond."

I was about halfway home when Sally hit me on the radio. "Chief, the coroner just called for you, said that dental records confirmed that the body was in fact Bobby Gentry. No need to run DNA tests."

The rest of the week went by with nothing new to the case. I knew that the good citizens of Eagle Creek would soon be beating down my door, expecting answers. How could I tell them this tale from Dr. Tim Sky?

I left for the office early again, like I had since Monday after I met with Dr. Sky. Everything seemed back to normal, and not much was happening. I spent a couple of hours on paperwork, and then I relieved Briggs at 0900 for the rest of the afternoon. I felt it necessary to activate our one reserve deputy. Bill Stallings was that deputy. I had him take the three-to-midnight shift, and then Briggs would be back at midnight. At 1500, I told my dispatcher I was heading home and Stallings would be on patrol. I pulled into my driveway and walked into the house. I took off my gun belt and hung it on the tree stand behind the door. I went to the kitchen to grab a beer from the fridge, then headed for the master bedroom and changed out of my uniform. I grabbed another beer and stoked up the fire still burning in the fireplace. I threw on another log and settled into the old lounge chair in the family room. The house was as quiet as a tomb, save for the crackling of the fire. I relived the whole episode in my mind, from the first time I saw the wound on Jeanie's leg to the wild, bizarre story of Dr. Sky's and everything else I had heard and learned. It was hard to comprehend. All my training had taught me to deal with cold, hard facts. How could I believe all that I had been told? Yet what other explanation was there?

The door suddenly burst open. I jumped up, startled to see Janet walking in with her arms loaded with groceries.

"Well, if you're home, how about a hand?"

"Sure, dear."

"Why are you home so early? You didn't get into a fight with the mayor again, did you?"

Janet was my high-school sweetheart and the only true love in my life. She is a beautiful woman and a great wife and partner. We were unable to have children, so we focused all our love on each other. She was shocked at what had happened, and in her role as superintendent of schools, she had postponed the dance one week due to the situation.

"Is there anything new about Bobby and Jeanie?"

"Yeah, a werewolf did it," I said with a strong sense of sarcasm.

"What! This is not a joking matter, dear. I have been visiting with Jeanie and have been to Bobby's home and spent time with both families, as you well know. This has been very traumatic to all my kids at school."

"That's why I'm home. I can't believe it either, and you have been wonderful in your care for those two families."

I told her of my entire morning and what Doc's friend said on Monday when they had their big meeting. I had been reluctant to tell her of that until now. But I couldn't keep it from her any longer.

Janet expressed her shock and disbelief. I cautioned her not to say a word about it to anyone for fear of starting a panic. She agreed. "No, sir, don't worry. I don't want to be committed to the funny farm."

"I feel better now that I have shared this with you, even if you don't believe it. However, it will be important to me that you treat this info as if it were true. I want you as safe as humanly possible."

"Maybe I'm the one it's after," she said as she pushed me up against the wall and started biting my neck and growling. That started something that took half an hour to conclude. As I lay there beside her, staring at the ceiling, I wondered if it was better to leave her in a state of disbelief as long as she was cautious. Hell, I couldn't believe it either. I decided to leave it alone for now and turned on my side to face her. "Why, Mrs. D., that was too good to be legal!" I said as we lay there in each other's arms.

"Well then, Sheriff, are you going to handcuff me to the bed so I can't escape?"

"I might just have to do that, Mrs. D. However, I think I'll let you cook dinner first."

"Au contraire, Sheriff man. We are invited to the mayor's house for dinner tonight. Did you forget?"

"Oh, no, Janet! I did forget. Must we go? I hate those parties. Maybe you have a sudden case of a stomach virus or something."

"No, babe, you need to be there for the sake of your career. Besides, I like going, and I bought a new dress for the occasion."

"Oh, now I see why the afternoon playtime. I should have known you were up to something," I said as I ran naked to the foyer and back.

"What was that all about? Oh no you don't, Dan. You stop this right now!" she said as I handcuffed her to the bed, laughing.

"Dan Duggan, you get these cuffs off me this instant!"

"No, I won't, at least not until the dinner party is over." I walked into the master bath, turned on the shower, and stepped in. By the time I returned, the bed was a wreck, and her Irish was showing.

"You know, dear, when you get mad, your red hair actually seems to glow." I couldn't contain my laughter.

"If you don't get these cuffs off me real damn fast, you'll be glowing!"

I realized that I had taken this gag about as far as I dared, so I walked to the foyer again, got the key, and released her. She jumped up, stomped off to the bath, and climbed into the shower.

"Good idea. I can hear the water sizzle as it hits your body. That should cool you off."

She kicked open the shower stall door, stared at me for a moment, and then demanded, "Get in here this second!"

"Yes, ma'am! Seems there will be more playtime today."

Regrettably, by 1800 we were on our way to the mayor's house for cocktails at 1800 and dinner at 1900. I couldn't wait for it to be over. Even though the mayor's dinner only happened once a year, that was once too many for me. I hated the way the women doted over me, especially the mayor's wife. Janet would tease me that the mayor's wife wanted to have an affair with me. I failed to see any humor in that.

But tonight would be different. Tonight I would be given the third degree about the killing of Bobby Gentry, now that the coroner's office had confirmed that the skeleton found by the hiker was Bobby's. He had died of massive trauma inflicted by a large animal, and all we had to go on were large scrape marks on the skeleton, which we concluded could only have been made by a large carnivore. The town was enraged, and everyone wanted to know what the sheriff's department was doing about it. Janet would rescue me, and so would Doc. In this relatively small town of approximately twenty thousand people, anyone who was important enough or had a major hand in running the town was invited to the mayor's invitation-only, black-tie dinner. His formal party was given every year on October 25. This was an important date for the mayor, as that was the day he was sworn in as the town's mayor.

Finally, the dinner portion was over, and the mayor asked Doc and I to join him in the parlor.

"Listen, boys, we have to get this mess cleaned up! As you could tell from most of the conversation here tonight, the town's folk are really upset over the Gentry boy killing. Their fear of this being the beginning of a rash of killings is foremost in their minds, and they want this animal or whatever hunted down and killed. Now, Dan, where are we really with this situation?"

"We have activated reserve deputy Stallings to help, and we are keeping a good surveillance on that area where the boy was killed. Doc, do you wish to share your friend's theory?"

"No I hadn't planned to, but now that you brought it up, thank you very much. I guess if the mayor wishes?"

"Yes, by all means, please fill me in."

"Well, here goes." Doc began to tell the mayor the theory of Tim Sky. By the end of the story, the mayor was sitting in his lounge chair with his mouth open and his eyes as big as saucers. "Well, gentlemen, that is quite a theory, I must say! Now I trust we have not told this to anyone else?"

"No. Only Tim, Doc, my wife, and I know—to the best of my knowledge, Mr. Mayor," I said, with Doc nodding in confirmation.

"Can we count on your wife keeping this information to herself?"

"Oh, yes, sir. She said that she would be afraid to tell for fear of being committed!"

The mayor laughed. "Yes, I see her point."

"In the off chance that Tim Sky is right, I will have every deputy on duty on the night of the full moon, and I've asked and received confirmation from Sheriff Morgan from Mountain Forge. He has promised he will give us three deputies from dusk until dawn for that night as well. A curfew for all minors will also be from dusk until dawn. I have asked my wife to make certain that there are no after-school activities on that night nor any late classes or adult education classes. I am also sending out a bulletin asking all store and shop owners to close promptly at 5:00 p.m. on Friday, November 22. Mr. Mayor, I need your help in enforcing these rules. We are going to be flooded with calls about why that night and that night only when we are searching for an animal. I need a plausible answer for that. Any suggestions?"

"Wow, you are on top of it, and you are right. We do need a good, reasonable answer for the public," Doc agreed.

The mayor suggested, "Well, what about telling them we have reliable Intel that a terrorist may come our way that night? What about that?"

"No, I think that would run even a greater risk of panic."

"Plus, wouldn't people be expected to evacuate in that instance?" Doc asked.

"Yes, yes, you're right. That won't do."

"Wait, what about if a deer hunter out in the woods that morning in the hills nearby has seen a very large wolf. This would be our plan to see no one else dies. My top deputy, Al Briggs, is an avid deer hunter; he needs to be brought into this anyway. We'll see that he goes hunting that morning but is back by 9:00 a.m. with the news, which will give us time to get things in place and still look spontaneous. Thoughts?"

"I like it. Do it," the mayor commented.

Doc thought for a moment and then concurred.

"Okay, we have our plan. Remember, *only* key personnel must know of this. Mayor, may I respectfully request that you refrain from telling your wife about any of this?"

"Well ..."

Doc cut him off and said, "I agree with Dan on that."

"Oh, all right, I suppose you are right. She does tend to go on a bit, doesn't she?" The mayor laughed.

Doc and I tried hard to keep a straight face.

Our work went on as usual, but behind closed doors, the people in the know were planning the notification and implementation of Operation Wolf. Dr. Sky stayed in town, planning to stay until the Wolf Spirit had gone. In his mind, there was no doubt that the spirit would kill its intended or continue killing until it did. Al Briggs was now part of the plan and set for deer hunting the morning of the full moon. Janet's part would be a bit easier, as the full moon would fall on a Friday. She could more easily get everyone out of the school and off the grounds. The mayor and those in his key staff who were trustworthy were in place. Everything was in readiness, waiting for the day when Briggs would tell the tale of the wolf.

The town had begun to forget about the danger, as nothing had happened that could be linked to a wolf for several weeks, and most were probably thinking the wolf had simply moved on. I felt that this supported Tim's theory all the more. If Bobby was the one the wolf spirit had been sent for, then, according to Tim, it would not return. The day was nearing, and soon we would know.

It was 9:00 a.m., Friday, November 22, 2010, and as planned, we had Briggs drive into town in his personal pickup. We wanted anyone about at that time to see him quickly driving toward the sheriff's office. Later, we had reports that he had been seen. He met with me and told his story. The plan was unleashed; I called the mayor's home, and the mayor contacted his lead team. They went to the newspaper editor and arranged an early printing of the morning paper. The radio station WJWG was notified, as was WJWG television station. PSAs (public service announcements) were broadcast all day long.

"Good morning. We are interrupting our regularly scheduled morning broadcast to bring you an urgent message from the mayor's office. There has been a sighting of a large wolf in the hills just outside of town by Deputy Sheriff Al Briggs. Early reports are that while deer hunting near Buffalo pass, a large wolf was spotted. Fearing another episode like the one that happened a month ago, when a high-school senior was brutally killed and another student severely bitten, the sheriff's office has issued a curfew for five o'clock this evening. All residents are advised that they should remain indoors tonight. Shops and other businesses will close at five as well. The sheriff, his deputy, and several deputies from Mountain Forge will be patrolling tonight, especially near the wooded areas. An air raid siren will sound at five o'clock to alert and remind people to be off the streets. The sheriff warns that anyone trying to play hero and goes out in an attempt to kill this creature will be arrested on sight. Anyone without a place to go may go to the hospital were extra beds will be provided. We will rebroadcast this message every hour on the radio, and a streaming message will run all day on our sister TV station. If you should see or hear this animal, please call the sheriff's office immediately. *Do not attempt* to deal with this animal yourself. The sheriff has several volunteers who will be taking calls and relaying them to the authorities. Stay tuned to WJWG radio for any updates on the subject.

"Once again, the sheriff's office has put out a curfew for five o'clock this evening because of the sighting of a large wolf near Buffalo Pass, suspected of being the animal that killed Bobby Gentry. Now back to the *John Williams Show, Your Money Matters*."

Every deputy was given a shotgun and twenty rounds of ammunition in addition to his sidearm. The town had only two sheriff's vehicles, so some deputies would be driving their own vehicles, marked with red flagging.

Spotters were posted all around town to report any sightings back to the sheriff's office. Now, it was just a matter of the wait, waiting for something so different and strange. How many would die if he returned? Would he get the one he was sent to kill on this night? So many questions, so few answers.

Back at the command post, all was ready. I was there to get things going, and then I would be on patrol as well as the deputies. Doc and Tim were there but ready to go if needed to administer care. The dispatchers were in place to take reports of sightings and forward them to the men in the field. The waiting game began.

Doc and Tim kept me updated as I drove around looking for anything out of the ordinary. By 2000 hours, only one sighting was reported, and it turned out to be a black German shepherd. Between 2100 and 2200, nothing strange was reported, and at 2300, there were two more sightings, but both turned out to be false alarms. From midnight to 0300, there was one more false alarm. Doc and Tim sat waiting, drinking coffee by the quart, it seemed.

Around 0400, I was cruising the commercial district off Market Street when I spotted a large shadow. I couldn't believe my eyes. The head of a wolf was on a body that looked like an NFL lineman by its size and shape. I doused my headlights and drove as quietly as possible toward the shadow reflecting against the wall of a building in an alley off Fifth Street in the commercial section of town. When I got close enough, I got out with my shotgun at the ready and crept up alongside the alley. I peered around the corner of the building and saw the beast. Now it was on all fours and seemed to be eating something. Then it stood and sniffed the air. It was huge, must have been seven feet standing on its hind legs. I continued to watch for a while, a sight I could hardly believe. I even pinched myself to be sure I wasn't dreaming. It had dropped back down and continued to eat when I felt the wind shift. I knew what that meant. This thing raised up again, but I didn't wait to see what happened next. I ran back to the cruiser and headed in the opposite direction. I saw it coming after me, and it appeared to be gaining on me. I glanced at the speedometer. I was doing eighty! I felt a cold chill run down my back, and I couldn't remember a time that I was so scared. I grabbed the microphone and radioed, "This is Sheriff Duggan. I am being pursued by a large wolf; it's chasing me south down Market Street toward the river."

I heard the dispatcher start to laugh and say to someone, "Can you believe what the crazy sheriff is calling in now?" She kept laughing.

Doc must have been there. I heard Doc's voice. "Sheriff needs immediate assistance. Last reported southbound on Market. All cars converge on Market and Randolph Streets. Suspect sighted there." Soon I heard the sirens wailing in the night from all directions. I looked over my shoulder, saw no sign of my purser, and then plowed my car into the sign in front of the Taylor building at Market and Randolph. I was dazed but conscious. I turned to see if the beast was near. I saw something or someone running toward me. I grabbed the shotgun that was on the floor. I couldn't get my door open. Then I saw Briggs's car arrive. What a relief.

"I got you, Dan. Hold on!" I heard him call from his shoulder mic for ambulance or for Doc as he ran toward me, shotgun at the ready.

The beast had disappeared, perhaps from all the sirens. Briggs stood outside the car, keeping watch for that beast, his shotgun ready. Then we heard the loud howl of a wolf, but I couldn't tell from where it emanated. Briggs put his back to me and readied the shotgun while I watched out the other side. The siren from the ambulance was near us, and Doc and Tim took over attending to me. By now Stallings had also arrived. He and Briggs kept a sharp eye out for the beast.

I heard Stallings ask, "Doc, how is he?"

"Appears to be okay. Just shaken up a bit, but his pulse is weak, and he appears to be going into shock. We need to get him to the hospital ASAP."

Tim already had the gurney out, ready to load. "Al, we need a hand." Briggs took a quick look around, laid the shotgun on the roof of the car, and the three men gently pulled me out of the car onto the gurney from the passenger side. I was loaded into the ambulance. Before we drove away, I told Briggs and the other deputies now on the scene to go back to their patrolling. As the ambulance went screaming toward the hospital, the sky was beginning to lighten. Soon the sun would be up. This was what everyone was anxiously awaiting.

Briggs showed up at the hospital shortly after sunup. When he came in, Janet, Doc, and Tim were all there talking with me. I had a huge bandage on my head and a pair of shiners that caused him to laugh. "Gee, boss, you look like a raccoon." In addition, I had a fat lip and a few scrapes, but all told, I was not in bad shape. I told them I was watching the wolf chasing me when I slammed into the decorative wall in front of the Taylor building.

The other good news was that I was the evening's worst injury, and Tim thought that might mean the spirit had left its host. Later that day, we would discover that we were both wrong.

Janet found out that I would be released later that day, after the results of the CAT scan were back and if there was no problem. She told everyone, "With a head as hard as Dan's, there was not much chance of any injury; he's got more skull than brain."

Surprisingly, that drew a laugh from everyone, except me of course. Janet drove me home around 1500, sat me in my easy chair, got me a cold beer, and told me to stay put and rest. I was really enjoying life, but it was about to be abruptly interrupted.

"Dan, it's Briggs. Over," came the call on the radio.

"Yeah, Al. What's up? Over."

"If you're able, you better get over to the Blackford residence. We've got bodies. Over."

"Roger that. Call Doc and have him meet us there. I'm on my way. Over."

"Roger that, boss. Out."

"Honey, I need you to drive me over to the Blackford residence."

"When?" Janet called back from upstairs.

"Immediately. Somebody's dead."

Janet came racing down the stairs. "Oh my God. Who is it?"

"I don't know yet. Let's roll."

Janet was no stranger to fast driving; she had scared the hell out of me on many occasions.

The Blackford house was only ten minutes from our place, and Janet made it in five.

"You wait here until I see what the scene is like."

"The hell I will. Let's go!" she replied as she pulled her .38 from her purse.

"All right, but do not touch or move anything. This is a crime scene."

The first person I ran into was Briggs. He was tossing up lunch in the toilet off the hall, and he pointed toward the bedroom. I hit the door first, quickly turned, and said, "Honey, you don't want to go in there!"

She could already smell it, and she nodded in agreement.

The only person in the room was the coroner, and he seemed immune to the sights and smell.

"God, Richard, how can you do this work?" I was gagging as I spoke.

"Appears they have been dead since about midnight. The cause is the same as the Gentry boy. As you can see, most of the flesh has

155

been removed from Mr. Blackford, save the organs, and about half of it from his wife."

"Where is Jeanie?"

"She isn't anywhere in the house or on the property. Your deputies searched it top to bottom," Richard said as he looked up for the first time.

"What the hell happened to you? You look like you've been shot at and missed, shit at and hit." He chuckled and went back to bagging evidence.

I let out a big sigh and not one of relief—as a matter of fact, just the opposite. "So our werewolf is still with us. Damn."

Richard stopped what he was doing and looked up at me again. "What did you say, Dan?"

"Oh, nothing, nothing at all." I walked back to the living room, trying not to step in all the blood.

Doc and Tim rolled up and took a look.

Tim stood up from looking at the bodies. "Bad news, boys. Unless the Blackfords were the intended, he may still with us, and he's meaner than ever. So that means we'll wait another month to know for certain. To top things off, Jeanie's missing. She is probably already dead as well."

"Al get an APB out for Jeanie, will you, please?"

"Already done, boss."

"Good work!"

"Try to keep the press out of here. I'm going home. My head is killing me. Keep me posted on any new developments. Al, you're in charge."

"Got it, boss. You get better. I'll keep you up to date. Oh, I already notified the mayor, so hopefully he won't bother you."

"Al, if I didn't know better, I'd think you're after my job," I said with a wink.

"If I were, I'd have it!" he said as he returned my wink.

Janet drove us home, and I went to sleep. Doc awakened me shortly after dark, telling him they found Jeanie in a drainage ditch alongside the road. She was naked, covered with scratches, and filthy dirty. She was back in the hospital for observation and some tests.

"Dan, I have not told her about her parents yet. I am not sure if she could take it right now. She seems to be suffering from amnesia, but it may be just the shock from whatever she has been through. I am hoping some rest and warm food will help her regain her memory. Stop by tomorrow if you are up to it."

"Okay, I will be by in the morning as soon as I can get a cruiser under me. Good night and thanks for the call."

Next morning, I was up early and hitched a ride with Janet to work. I walked into the office, where reporters were waiting.

"Sally, call down to the city garage to see if they have a car for me and have them get it here on the double."

As I attempted to make my way to my office, the throng of reporters with questions stopped me just outside my door.

"Sheriff, what is the latest on the Blackford murders?"

"Look, folks, all we know so far is that they were killed by a wolf or wolves much in the same fashion as the Gentry boy. We are scouring the area for any sign of it or them. Meanwhile, that is all we have."

"Sheriff, we hear that Jeanie Blackford is in the hospital again. Can you tell us about that?"

"Yes, she is back in the hospital. She was found yesterday in a drainage ditch and is suffering from temporary amnesia. She may have witnessed what happened to her parents, and that might be what is causing her loss of memory. She has been fortunate to escape from the wolf or wolves twice."

As the words came out of my mouth, an idea hit me. Could she be the host?

"That's all for now. We will contact you through the mayor's office when there is more to report. You'll have to excuse me now." I turned and closed myself into my office.

As soon as the reporters left, I buzzed Sally. "Is that car here yet?"

"No, sir, not yet."

"Call them again and tell them if I don't have that car in ten minutes, I am coming down there and kicking ass! I want that car *now*!"

"Yes, sir!"

Ten minutes later, Sally buzzed back and said, "Sheriff, your car is here, but it is a plain one."

"About time! I don't care if it has feathers as long as it runs!"

"Tommy, if I were you I'd get the hell out of here!" Sally said over the intercom to the mechanic that had delivered the sheriff's car.

"Yes, ma'am. I'm gone," replied Tommy.

I flew out of my office, slamming the door. I grabbed the keys from Sally and stormed out the door. I hit the lights and siren to relieve my anger and drove straight to the hospital like a bat out of hell. I parked in a "reserved for hospital use only" space. Then I walked casually to the nurse's station to see if Doc was available. There's something about speeding with lights and sirens that just calms me right down. They told me Doc was with Jeanie in room 132. I made a beeline for that room.

"Doc, how is she?"

"She remembers everything except from about eight o'clock the night of the attack until she woke this morning."

"Doc, is Tim about?"

"Yes, I believe he's in my office. Why?"

"I have an idea I'd like to run by him."

"Okay, I'm just about finished here. Jeanie was given a sedative a little while ago, so she will be out for a while."

As we walked to Doc's office, I explained my crazy thought, and Doc seemed to indicate that he thought it a possibility. When we saw Tim, I went over it again.

"There is only one problem with that theory, and that is that she wouldn't have bitten herself. A human can think in the abstract and think that a wound would cover their trail, but not an animal, not even a spirit animal."

"Damn, I was hoping we had something here," I said, letting my frustration show. "Now we're back to square one again."

Tim thought for a second and then asked, "Doc, didn't you tell me the girl was bitten by the animal that attacked her and the dead boy?"

"Yes, yes she was. Why?"

"Can you show me the wound site?" Tim asked.

"I can, but there's nothing there. It healed completely in a couple of days, not even a trace. I still can't figure that one out."

"I don't know why I didn't think of this before. Was there anything else strange about the wound?"

"Well, yes, actually there was. The day after the attack, when I changed the bandage for the first time, there was long, course black hair growing around the puncture," Doc stated.

"That's it. By golly, that is it!"

"What's it?" I shouted.

"The spirit transferred to her. You see, when she was bitten, the wound was like a radio beacon that would guide the spirit to her, like a pheromone does for an ant or bee. If the host is not as strong or agile or something else the spirit beast wants, it can transfer by biting the new host. Yet it can make the actual transfer later as long as the moon is full before it does. Since the wound healed so fast, he must have transferred sometime before the sun came up on the night of the attack on her and Bobby. That meant it hadn't fulfilled its purpose. It would remain dormant inside the host until the next full moon. Then it would take over her body on the night of the full moon and become the beast and search for its intended victim. Yet it would kill and eat for strength. The beast within her took over as the full moon reached it's full intensity, and she ... it feasted upon them before it began its search—unless, as I said before, they were the intended. There is only one thing out of place, and that is the previous host body. You see, once he abandons a body, it dies within days as it can no longer eat human food. Did you find another body days after the first attack?"

I responded, "No, but that does not mean anything certain, as people set out into the desert, underestimate its danger, and die or fall victim to a predator and are never found. We have many animals that will scavenge that may not usually be scavengers if an opportunity presents itself."

"Oh, one more thing. The longer it takes to find its intended one, the hungrier the spirit gets, so the number of bodies will increase the longer it is here. I mean, each time he appears, he will need more flesh," Tim said.

159

"Great, just fucking great. We would be better off to help it find that person and give them to it!" I said sarcastically.

"Dan, Doc, if you want to stop this spirit, you will need to do the following exactly as I lay it out. It may seem cruel to you, but it is the only way. You must keep her under surveillance at all times until the next moon. I am convinced that, based on what I have learned here today, she is the host of the wolf spirit. If I should be wrong, then Jeanie would be safe, but we will still have a problem."

"What would you say the odds are that you're right?" I asked.

"I would say that they are about ninety-nine to one that I'm right," Tim said with certainty. "If Jeanie is the host, then the only way to save her life is to kill the spirit within her. If it transfers or leaves as a result of completing its work, she will die, and that is certain."

"How can you be so sure you are right about this, Tim?"

"I am right, but I don't think I can give you a satisfactory answer. I may be able to convince you with a question. How do you know that God and Jesus Christ exist?"

"I see what you mean. Tim, please continue."

"If we can kill the spirit while it is inside her, she will live."

"But you said it could not be killed," Doc said.

"It can't in the usual sense, but it can be starved to death within the host. It must be prevented from transferring to another host. The only way to do that is to lock the host up and deny it the ability to feed. If it can't feed and it can't transfer, it will die."

"Will a cell in my jail work?"

"Too risky. This spirit is too strong; if it breaks free, more people will die. The only place certain to be safe enough is the vault in your bank. Does it have air in it for breathing?"

"Yes, that was a safety requirement ordered by the town council when the bank wanted its permit to build," I answered.

"Great. Then on the day of the full moon, Jeanie must be sealed in the vault before dusk, and that vault cannot opened for any reason whatsoever until sunup the next day. I hope you can get the bank to cooperate. If the timers need to be recalibrated, you must see that it is done. If the door can in any way be opened from inside, that must be dismantled so it cannot escape. It must consume blood and flesh on each full moon. If not, it will starve to death within the host body, yet the host will not starve. Now the hard part is yours; you must find a way to keep her here in the hospital until she is transferred to the vault. That is almost a month away."

"I will need to talk with the judge and get permission for this, as Jeanie is now a ward of the court. There may be legal and ethical considerations. Yes, the judge will have to approve this for certain. If I can get the judge's agreement, then I'll also have to make the arrangements with the bank," I said.

"If Jeanie should remember that her parents are dead, she may need to be put under the care of Thomas Longstreet, the hospital's psychiatrist. I am sure he will need to keep her for observation after we tell her, which we would not do until she was physically okay. Why, he could even get a court order if she became difficult. On the afternoon of the fifth, we could sedate her and then transport her via an armored car to the bank for her time in the vault. Dan, I'll bet you can arrange that part. What do you think of that idea?" Doc asked.

"Wow, Doc, I always thought there was a bit of larceny in that heart of yours. I love it! I must tell you though that Janet is going to be against this whole idea. She'll think we're putting Jeanie at risk for great psychological danger."

Tim said, "I think you have no choice, but if we're wrong, Janet would likely be correct in her assessment. However, you're the sheriff and are the one to make the final call. I once heard a statement that the good of the many outweigh the good of the few … or the one. Now, I'll leave it to you guys to involve only those people who have an absolute need to know or are needed to accomplish the mission. If we are successful, we will have saved countless lives."

Each member of the team went to work on a part of the plan. Doc worked out the details with his friend and colleague, Dr. Longstreet. I worked out the transport with a buddy of mine who owned an armored car business. Tim got the mayor on the team to make the arrangements with the bank president, Danika Owen, and guaranteed the repair of any damage that came from the use of the bank's facility. The president of the bank wanted to open two additional branches, and the mayor let her know, in no uncertain terms, that her cooperation in this matter would not be forgotten. The vault company had a team ready to dismantle the inside vault-opening mechanism after the bank closed at noon on Saturday.

Since at the time of the full moon the town would be in the depths of the Christmas season, the bank put out an announcement that on December 22 the bank would be closed to make emergency repairs to the vault. All was in readiness, and now the last item was dealing with Jeanie on a day-to-day basis and waiting for Tuesday, December 21 to come.

About a week later, after Jeanie's constant query about where her parents were, she was finally told. She broke down and became hysterical and had to be sedated. Dr. Longstreet was brought in to try to help her with the emotional trauma. She did not want to go home and be alone, so she was transferred to the psychiatric ward in a private section where she could receive visits from friends and teachers who would help her with her studies. Janet took off her administration hat and returned every day to help her and tutor her. It seemed to help, and yet it brought out all the emotions of not being with her mom and dad on that day. The thought of the Christmas holiday season near at hand was also troubling. Jeanie was a delightful girl, so polite and kind; it was hard to believe that a beast so cunning and cruel lurked within her. A beast that had killed without mercy and that could eat the flesh of a loved one without remorse. These facts were hard to bring together.

Janet began coaxing me to take Jeanie into our home and raise her as a foster child or perhaps even adopt her. I fought it at first but slowly began to come around a little.

I told her, "Don't vest yourself in this child until we see if she will even survive the upcoming ordeal. It is possible that she will be dead in less than a week."

"There are times when I could just pop you!" was her response. I decided to leave the room before she did just that.

The weeks leading up to the next full moon seemed to drag on. Finally, it was the morning of December 21, and the bank vault was ready. The money had been moved to another location, and the walls of the vault were lined with rubber. The timing mechanism was checked and double-checked. The armored car driver was waiting, and the truck was ready. Doc and Tim were ready with the sedative; it was time to proceed. Two vault company trucks would be parked in front of the bank all day and removed after 2100. By then Jeanie would be sedated and locked inside.

At 1700, the sedative was administered in a dose that would last at least five hours.

At 1707, the truck and driver pulled into the emergency room entrance, and Jeanie was wheeled out on a gurney. Once loaded, the driver—with Jeanie, Doc, and I on board—drove to the bank.

At 1718, the armored car pulled into the back-street delivery entrance where the gurney was unloaded and wheeled up to the large steel door. Danika Owen, the president of the bank, was waiting to open the door and the vault. Now all the tellers' cash drawers were balanced and the cash moved to the new location.

At 1722, the gurney, once it was placed inside the vault, was lowered to prevent her from falling when she awoke. The ventilation system was checked and in good working order.

At 1731, the vault door was closed and locked, and it was unable to be opened until 0800 when the timing lock mechanism would unlock itself. A battery backup system would prevent any power outage from interfering with the opening.

At 1745, the entourage left the bank. The doors were locked and the alarm armed. Some thought we should leave some men posted there with high-powered weapons. Tim vetoed that idea saying the wolf spirit was too cunning and his senses too keen, and it would know, and if it wasn't Jeanie, it wouldn't be there anyway. Meanwhile, everyone followed the same procedure as last month.

There was nothing to do now but wait and see what the morning brought. The night was the longest of my life.

At 0700, the armored car was loaded with the money that was removed from the vault the day before and scheduled to be brought back for the bank's regular operation.

At 0730, all parties involved in the mission met at the rear of the bank and were let in again by Danika Owen. The three additional deputies borrowed last month were back again and were there with the Briggs, Stallings, and myself, all carrying shotguns, just in case. Coffee had been provided to all as we waited out the last remaining minutes. What would we find when the vault door opened? The speculation filled the room as the last minutes ticked down. It was like waiting and counting down to a new year, but with no idea whether we would be celebrating or shooting or crying at the last tick.

With a loud click, the vault door unlocked itself. I moved everyone back, and the deputies and I moved forward with shotguns at the ready. I walked up to the door and swung it open. What I saw was unbelievable.

There was dead silence in the bank; some even held their breath, awaiting my findings. But I just stood there. Finally, Doc walked over and looked in.

"Oh my God!" He had his medical bag in hand and ran inside the vault. Now everyone else ran to the vault door.

There inside was Jeanie, totally naked, bruised, and bloodied. Her clothes were torn to shreds and strewn about the vault floor. Her young body was wedged between the cage doors inside the vault. There was no telling how she got so contorted and mangled, much less how she wedged herself in between the bars five feet off the floor. The cage doors, made of high-tempered steel, were twisted as if they were made of tin. There was blood on the floor as well as fur. She was unconscious and had a dislocated arm. Doc and Tim carefully separated her from the bars and Doc popped the arm back in place and a put a brace to hold her head still. Doc discovered that she had several broken teeth as well. An ambulance had been standing by across the street in case it was needed, and it certainly was.

They rushed Jeanie to the hospital and began working on her. Doc knew she was in a comatose state. They set about closing and bandaging up all the wounds. They gave her blood and glucose, cleaned her up, and made her look halfway human again. They worked feverishly on her, and by the time she was back in her room, she looked dramatically better than when they found her. She had huge a bandage wrapped around her head, two black eyes, twenty-five stitches in her face, and another hundred or so over the rest of her body. The coma was actually a blessing for the short run, as she would not have to endure the sight and pain associated with all her injuries. The beast within her did not feed, and according to Tim, she was free from its grasp.

The full moon of early December came, and we trusted Tim's assessment. He had been right about everything and didn't fear her being with us. She was still in a coma and didn't recover until the Sunday before Christmas.

Janet took her vacation time and spent every day with Jeanie, talking to and reading to her. I had to visit Jeanie in order to see much of my wife. Janet provided a substitute teacher and lost her pay while she was out, but she didn't care. Jeanie was her most important consideration.

Jeanie would make a full recovery, and the spirit was no longer within her. It took quite a bit of counseling and time to get used to the fact that her boyfriend and parents were dead. She was never told that her parents died at her hand. After all, what purpose would it serve? Janet and I did all we could to make her feel at home. Jeanie seemed to respond well with us, and we were pleased with that.

However, a new year was approaching and with its first full moon. What would it bring? There were still some unanswered questions. Most importantly, since the spirit didn't claim its intended, would another spirit come to finish the job? Would Jeanie be the host? Was she susceptible to being the host of the wolf spirit again? Was she perhaps not a host but cursed by the bite to roam the earth forever, not sent for someone but just to feed in the light of the full moon as a savage beast? These questions and more would await that which only a full moon could answer.

THE END ... NOT.

CRYPTURE 7
She

CHAPTER 1
HE SAID

Out of the corner of my eye, I spotted her. I watched her walk down
the main street of town, appropriately called … Main Street. She
was long-legged, shorted-skirted, and walked with authority. What
a gorgeous pair of legs they were. As a self-pronounced leg man, she
was an eleven on a scale to ten. To say she was beautiful would be a
gross understatement. I was mesmerized and couldn't take my eyes
off her. She was tall, approximately five foot eight, and her tight red
skirt came short of her knees by a good four inches, revealing those
perfect, slightly tanned legs. Those legs that carried her with grace
and poise as she strolled down the boulevard. I couldn't help but
think that with all that beauty there must be a man in her life—or
perhaps many men. I had to know, so I quickly looked both ways and
crossed the street. I followed her into the Librarian's Bookstore. It was
a small nonfranchised bookstore that looked new and inviting. They
got quite a few authors in for book signings, and some I had gone to
see. Inside, the dark green carpet felt rich and went well with the dark
wood, stained bookshelves and the light beige walls. There were a fair
number of browsers there for this time of day.

I felt like a stalker but knew I meant no harm. I just had to see …
see if the third finger of her left hand was naked as I hoped. I had
only seen her profile until now and noticed a large pair of really dark

sunglasses hid her eyes. Once inside, they came off, and I casually moved around to clearly see her face. Oh, what a beautiful face and large chestnut eyes. *Isn't there any flaw to this woman?* I chuckled out loud as I thought, *I'm like a dog chasing a fire truck. What would I do if I caught it?* Fortunately, she didn't appear to have heard me.

We both moved to the shelves of books and looked like two regular people searching for something to read for self-improvement or entertainment. There were a few other folks doing likewise. I was close enough to see her hand, but the way she was holding a book, I couldn't find the object that I was seeking ... or should I say, the object I was not seeking. She seemed intent on finding just the right book. She would study each book she pulled from the shelf and stand with her weight on one foot then in a few minutes shift the weight to the other, bending slightly the relaxed leg. I noticed that she was well put together topside. Her thin, white blouse transmitted that info to me. Quickly, I grabbed a book, any book, from the shelf in front of me and waited and watched out of the corner of my eye. I caught a whiff of the perfume she wore. I noticed a slight trace of honeysuckle, and it was just as captivating as she was. She shook her long, blonde hair from her face as she reached up to return a book to the shelf. I wondered how one woman could look so gorgeous. As she retrieved another book, she glanced my way and smiled politely, slightly revealing her nice pearly whites. I was thankful she didn't have a mouth full of crooked or broken teeth. Wouldn't that have been a kicker? But this was a woman who took great pride in looking nice, and she would likely be the last person to allow bad teeth to spoil that beauty. I hoped she didn't notice me eyeballing her. It could really make things uncomfortable, but it was hard to keep my eyes away from her. I returned the smile and tried not to leer. As she quickly returned her next selection to the shelf, she revealed the answer to my lingering query. I saw the finger that I was so desperate to see, and it was as bare as mine! I looked intently to see if there was a white ring indicating that perhaps her ring was at the jeweler's for a repair or cleaning, or perhaps she had forgotten to slip it on. But again I was pleased, for her entire finger was as tanned as the rest of her. Now what? How could I start a conversation with her and not come off like a pickup artist or worse?

As she moved about the store, her attention seemed to focus on her quest for the right book. When she moved to another row, I waited a bit and then followed, staying as far as I could from her so as to hopefully not attract attention. My brain searched feverously for the right phrase or way to begin a conversation. I hoped she would drop something or perhaps smile at me again. Finally she found the book she desired and headed for the counter. I took the book that was in my hand. I didn't even think about what it was. I just strolled to the counter behind her. Oh my God, she was lovely from every angle! Her skin seemed to have the texture of silk. She turned her head and looked at me, flashed a very slight smile, and quickly turned back. I tried to speak, but the words locked up in my throat. I felt like a teenage boy trying to muster up the courage to speak and ask the most popular girl in school to go with me to the prom. Damn, that was frustrating! She waited, and within minutes the clerk came to assist her. "May I help you?"

The words that came next were like those of an angel or how one might expect an angel to sound, soft and pleasant almost like a melody. I know what you're thinking, and you're right. I was hooked.

"Yes, I'd like this book, please," she said as she opened her wallet.

She couldn't have been more perfect, and I wanted to know her almost to the point of obsession. I had been in love before and in lust before, and always they started the same, like a raging fire. They ended like a smoldering pile of ashes. That was the way all my past relationships started and ended, but I was certain she would be different, if only I could meet her. The clerk rang up the book and asked if she needed anything else.

"No, thank you. That will be all."

He smiled and then closed out the sale.

When she passed him her credit card, I tried to see the name, but her thumb covered too much of it, and I couldn't make it out. He ran the card, handed it back, and said, "Thank you, ma'am."

She sidestepped to allow me access to the clerk while she put her card back into her wallet and then the wallet back into her purse. Then it happened. I laid the book in my hand on the counter, and as I did, she glanced over and saw the title and began to laugh softly. I looked at the book and immediately felt my face getting warm. I was so embarrassed! The title of the book was *How to Spice up the Bedroom*. Even the clerk was barely able to contain himself. I was mortified, to say the least. My mind raced for something to say. If there had been a glimmer of hope of meeting her, this would spoil it unless I came up with something fast. My mind whirled and twirled but came up with nothing. Her purse now closed and her book tucked up under her arm, she silently turned and walked out the door, with me just standing there, mouth agape and red-faced.

"Sir, how would you like to pay for this?"

His words snapped me back to reality as she walked away. The reason for my red face quickly turned from embarrassment to anger. I glared at him and then turned and walked out, leaving the book right where it was.

Now what would I do? *I can't just let her walk out the door and presumably out of my life.* I followed her again, hoping I would think of something clever to say or perhaps find out where she lived or worked. I stayed a safe distance, for now she would become suspicious if she saw me. My mind wasn't cooperating; I couldn't come up with anything. I kept following and then stopped suddenly and ducked into a store. She had stopped to talk with a slightly older woman right there in front of me. I pretended to browse in the store and occasionally looked out the shop window. She was still talking. The third time I looked, she was gone. I quickly walked in the direction we had originally started, but I couldn't find any sign of her. Certainly there was nothing that would or could come of it. I tried to put the sour grapes to it by telling myself perhaps she was as nasty as she was beautiful. But I just couldn't get her out of my mind. And I tried—man, how I tried. I went straight to a bar and pickled myself. That didn't work, and as I walked—or should I say stumbled—home, even my inebriated brain was still focused on her. Of course, by now I had thought of plenty of things I could have and should have said to her, and I vowed if I should ever run into her again, I would!

I reached my front door and finally got the key into the latch. I stumbled into bed, and when I woke the next morning, not only was I hung over, but I had dreamt about her as well, and in my dream, I saw all of her, kissed all of her, and made love to all of her. In short, I was more captivated by her now than ever before, and she was still in control of my thinking. Thank goodness it was Saturday and I didn't have to go to work. I brushed my teeth and did something I had never done before. I drank a beer. I had heard the old saying, *a little hair off the dog that bit you,* but had never tried it. To my amazement, it seemed to work!

I have always kept a journal of things that happened to me in my life that I wanted to recall, just as my mentor taught me to do. So after my head cleared a tad, I decided to write down the experience. My hope was that once written down, my mind would consider her case closed, so to speak, and I could forget about it. So I did that, slammed the journal shut, and considered the episode closed. Next, I decided to wash my car, which thankfully I wasn't driving last night, and begin anew without the fragments of her beauty and the sting of her laughter buzzing in my brain. Well, it didn't work, at least not completely. I did sort of forget about that dumb book I had grabbed in hast, but her beauty just would *not* go out of my head. *How long will she stay firmly embossed on my mind?*

The weekend came to an end, and another workweek started and then ended. Two weeks since that fateful day, and still she was as fresh in my mind as if it were just yesterday. I wondered if it would help for me to talk it out with someone. But who? I felt I had to get help, and so I thought, *What the hell. I'll go see the company shrink.* I had met Dr. Dirkus at a company picnic when we just happened to sit at the same picnic table. He struck me as a nice guy. He didn't try to psychoanalyze me, and he didn't speak with a German accent or wear a monocle. He was just a normal kind of guy, so I decided I would see him. After all, that was what he was there for. Right? So I made the appointment for the next day and then went to the office on the tenth floor, wondering if the shrink could really help. I didn't really feel confident, but anything was worth a try.

I walked in feeling a little strange about being there, but I was still trying to remain hopeful there was a way to forget this obsession that should be gone and forgotten.

"Good morning. My name is Sam Whitley. I have a ten o'clock with Dr. Dirkus."

"Yes, Mr. Whitley. Dr. Dirkus was called away on an emergency, but his partner is in for him today and will see you. Please have a seat, and someone will be right with you."

Damn! Just my luck. Now I had to tell my tale to someone I hadn't met before. *That will be even more embarrassing. Maybe I should go.* I started to get up ... *On the other hand, maybe he'll give me good advice.* I sat back down, and within ten minutes, the door opened, and a woman walked out. I thought, *See? She looks normal enough, but she's here seeking help. So it's cool for me to be here too.* She walked straight past me and out the door with just a quick smile as she walked by. No sooner had the door closed behind her than the receptionist informed me that I could go in.

As I entered, the room was decorated nicely with a comfortable, homey feel. Lots of certificates hung on the wall behind his desk, two chairs sat on the visitor's side of the desk, and behind that in the corner was a chair and, yes, even the proverbial couch. They really have those in a shrink's office! Amazing. There were two other doors in the room. One was slightly ajar, and I could see it was a restroom. The other was closed, and I presumed it was the rabbit-hole exit, the kind all doctors and lawyers have so if they don't want to see someone who might be in the lobby, or if they're coming in late for your appointment, they can slip in undetected. Since he was out of the room, I just couldn't resist. I had to try out the couch. I lay down, folded my arms across my chest, took a deep breath, and closed my eyes. Lying there, the top of my head was facing that rabbit-hole door, so I couldn't see it open. As soon as I was relaxed, the door opened. I quickly started to get up when a soft voice said, "No, Mr. Whitley, you may stay right there." It was a woman! Oh, maybe it was just another nurse or clerical person.

I put my head back down. I could hear her heels on the hardwood floor coming closer. As she got closer, I turned my head to the right as she passed by it. Then I freaked out. Sheer panic set in, and I could immediately feel a cold sweat break out on my forehead. I was looking at a long pair of legs and a short black skirt. I knew those legs instantly from the bookstore and intimately from my dreams! There were none like them in the world, or at least my world. Oh my God, what to do now? Surely she would recognize me!

"Good Morning, Mr. Whitley. I am Natalie Barnes, Dr. Dirkus's partner. How can we help you today?" she said as she sat down.

I can't believe my eyes! I immediately thought of that Humphrey Bogart line from the classic movie *Casablanca*: "Of all the gin joints in all the towns in all the world, she walks into mine." Sitting there in all her radiant beauty was the object of my affection … or obsession. How could this be? I had heard of and experienced coincidences, but this was too much? Much too much!

She looked slightly different, her blonde hair that was loose when we I first saw her was now pinned up, she wore glasses with black rims, her skirt was longer and the colors she wore more sedate and conservative. But she was still the most beautiful woman I'd ever seen.

"Mr. …"—she paused as she looked at her notes—"Whitley, you seem suddenly agitated. What's troubling you?"

"Ah, I just remembered I have to leave." I started to get up.

"No, Mr. Whitley. You are not leaving in the state you're in," she ordered.

I did as she said but looked at her like … *How dare you!*

"Mr. Whitley, you are obviously very troubled. You're sweating and acting very nervous. We take very seriously the mental state of the employees working here, and because you are on company time, you must comply. Do you understand?" I nodded my agreement. Her voice relaxed a bit, and she continued, "Now, please relax, and tell me what is troubling you. You may lie back down if you wish."

What a predicament. I come to see the shrink to help me forget about … the shrink! I took her advice and settled back down on the couch. Then I took a huge deep breath and tried to, as she put it, relax. Again my brain was on fire trying to gather my thoughts to paint a coherent picture to her about what was troubling me. *She* was troubling me! Are you kidding? This could only happen in the movies.

"Well, it's like this, Doc—"

She interrupted me. "Mr. Whitley, I am not a doctor. I am a psychologist. Psychiatrists are medical doctors, like Dr. Dirkus. I just want you to be clear. You may continue, please."

It was apparent that she didn't recognize me, "Well, Ms. Barnes, I am fearful that I am becoming obsessed over a woman."

The idea had come to me, and because she didn't seem to recognize me from the incident at the bookstore, I thought it might just work.

"Tell me about her and the situation."

"Well, I saw her walking down the street and was immediately captivated by her beauty. I wanted desperately to meet her, not in a pickup, sleazy way but in a respectful and nice way. Do you understand?"

"Of course, I understand."

"Because I felt it was a million-to-one shot, I couldn't bring myself to just walk up to her and start a conversation with her, but I was so strongly attracted to her and wondered if she were married, so I walked up close to her and saw she didn't have a wedding ring. But I felt funny doing that because I still didn't know how to approach her without making the wrong impression. So I went home and decided it was probably best to just forget her. However, that was easier said than done. I didn't want her to become some kind of obsession, yet I'm not even sure if that is what it is, so I came here.

"So, Mr. Whitley—"

Now I interrupted her. "If you are going to help me with this problem, couldn't you please call me Sam? The other makes me feel uncomfortable and too formal for me to be telling you these intimate things about myself."

"Certainly ... Sam, if it makes you feel more at ease. Have you seen this woman again?"

"No, but again, the reason I am here is that I simply cannot get her out of my mind. It has been over two weeks now, and nothing I do erases her from my mind for any length of time at all."

"How would you feel about going out with a girlfriend? Perhaps someone that you see occasionally to see if that helps."

"I already thought of that but can't bring myself to do it. I just want to see her. Do you think I'm in love with her?"

"Well, love is a complicated issue. What do you think?"

"All right. Do you think there is such a thing as love at first sight?"

"I believe all relationships start with some form of physical attraction. It sort of starts the ball rolling, and then time together sifts out whether it is love, lust, like, or even an obsession."

"That's great because that is what I think as well. But how can I have time with her to see if we can get on well or not if I can't meet her? As I said earlier, she is the most beautiful woman I have ever seen, but I want more than that. I want to know if she is as beautiful on the inside. Would she be interested in me? Could we build a relationship based on love, trust, respect, be good to one another, etc.? Do we have the same things in common? I want to know her, that woman that lies beneath that beautiful face and body. What could I do or say that wouldn't come off wrong?" I was really laying it on thick; even I didn't believe all of that.

"Whoa, slow down. Lets save that for our next session, as our time is up for today. And since you have calmed down, I can excuse you until then."

"Will I see you next time or Dr. Dirkus?"

"Normally we stay with the patient through the resolution, but if you would prefer—"

I cut her off again. "No. No, I feel comfortable with you. I would rather see you."

"Okay. See Ms. Squires up front and tell her to schedule another time with me."

With that, she stood and extended her hand, and I took it. Her handshake was firm, and her skin felt as velvety as it looked. I could feel my heart beating faster, and I now had a way to see her again. Perhaps my plan could work. I was excited and couldn't wait to come back again soon! I made my next appointment on her next available day, which was same day of the following week, only at nine in the morning. I went back to my office, and now it was worse than before. Now I knew her name, she knew mine, we had talked together, and my brain had more data to digest over and over. Plus, now I had a plan in place to make her like me and then trust me. And eventually I would tell her of the day in the bookstore, and hopefully she would remember the incident. I would clear up the book part and then ask her out. *When she laughs about that book, this time it will be with me and not at me.*

The next seven days were filled with work and some play. I had my usual Tuesday poker night. It was at Bob's, a buddy of mine from basketball days, and Bob's sister was visiting. She didn't live that far away but came to stay with him for a few days to help him with some work project. She was a real cute and shapely strawberry-blonde. He tried real hard to set me up with her, but I played dumb to his very obvious hints and suggestions. I knew I was in deep trouble with Natalie because otherwise I would have been happy to take his sister out. I was hopeful for the ultimate success of my plan. Plus, I didn't want to start something I might not ever finish. After all, Bob was a friend.

Through that entire long week, I thought mostly of Natalie. Fortunately, like Christmas to a kid, that special day came, and when the allotted time arrived, I walked into her office with my best suit on, shoes nicely shined, a three-day-old haircut, and a light spritz of my best cologne. I was greeted by the receptionist and told to go right in, as I was the first appointment of the day. When I opened the door, there she was in all her splendor, sitting behind her desk. This day, once again, she had her long blonde hair pinned up, and when she stood, I saw she had on a pants suit. She removed that same pair of black-rimmed glasses, picked up her notepad, and gestured for me to take the couch. I complied. She looked fabulous, but I was disappointed that she wasn't wearing her short skirt. I was so looking forward to seeing those perfect legs of hers.

"Good morning, Mr. ... Sam. How was your week? Did you see that woman again?"

"Good morning, and no, I haven't seen her, but she has not been out of my mind. I must be in love with her."

"Why do you feel it's love and not just a sexual or physical attraction?"

"I think because I don't see us in that context. I see us walking on a beach, sitting in a nice restaurant, laughing and talking. Going to visit my folks with her and going with her to visit her parents. Do I also see us making love? Yes, but I believe it is in proper perspective with our relationship. It is part of our relationship but only part. I know that when I am with her in my mind, we have a happy, healthy, but not solely a consuming sexual relationship. I even turned down an opportunity to go out with the sister of a friend last week, and she was a good-looking woman. I know if it weren't for this woman I'm in love with, I most likely would have gone out with her."

"Sam, I believe you may be in love with the *idea* of being in love with this woman, but since you've never met, remember you have created her in your mind, with the exception of her outward physical appearance. She may be a totally different person in reality, and you may have no common interests."

"I'm listening, but I believe the major things that I think about her are very close to reality."

"For your sake, I hope you are correct. Have you done anything in attempt to find her again?"

"Yes, a few things. I've gone back to the bookstore in hopes she would return. I look at every woman I see that might be her. If I had been able to get her name, I could search the Internet. It seems my only chance is to run into her again. What I want to know is if I should see her, how do I meet her? As I said to you before, I don't want her to get the wrong impression of me. I'm sure she probably gets hit on a lot, and I surely don't want her to think that or get the wrong impression."

"That can be a problem, as women do often recoil when approached by a man on the street. Since you do feel you know her a bit, can you think of a way that you would want to be approached if you were her?"

"And that is my greatest fear. Can you tell me, from a woman's point of view, not that of my shrink—oops. Sorry, I mean my psychologist ..."

She laughed, and it was a very nice laugh. "Sam, I've heard the term before. It doesn't offend me. However, it's not my place to tell how to meet a woman but rather how to deal with your feelings."

She wasn't helping me in the way I wanted help. I had seen her in line one day at the deli on the first floor of our office building; I had been on my way to a meeting. And that gave me an idea.

"Okay, let's say for instance I found myself standing behind her in a line at a restaurant. While we were both waiting to be seated, could I ask her to join me?"

"Not right off. That would seem like a pickup line. Perhaps you ask politely if the food is good there. If she responds pleasantly, ask another nonthreatening question, nothing personal. Most importantly, stay away from the obvious pickup lines like 'Do you come here often?' or 'What's your sign?' Those things reek of the pickup artist. Be real, and speak softly with a sincere smile on your face. Don't act like you are romantically interested. If all of that goes well, you might say, 'You know, I hate to eat alone. Would you care to join me?' If she declines, accept it graciously as if it is no big deal."

"Would that work with you, for example, Ms. Barnes?"

"Yes, I believe it would, as long as I felt safe and not pressured."

"Do you think I could ask her out again if the lunch went well?"

"What do you think? I think I've made enough suggestions." Her watch gave a slight buzz. "Oh, my next appointment is now waiting. We'll discuss that at our next meeting." She stood, closed her notebook, and extended her hand.

"Oh, time's up already! That seemed very quick." I looked at my watch and nodded that yes, in fact, my half hour was up. So I accepted her handshake. "Okay, I'll just go and set up next week's appointment. Good-bye, Janet, and thank you." I watched her face, and she seemed comfortable when I called her by her first name, but she said nothing and turned back toward her desk. I left, set up an appointment, and returned to work.

Same problem still existed. I couldn't get her out of my mind for any appreciable amount of time. The rest of the week dragged on, just as the prior week had, all in anticipation of my next meeting with Her Loveliness. Secretly, I hoped she would go back to her short skirt.

Friday rolled around, and I walked down the hall to the deli for a sandwich. I'd been going there whenever possible in hopes of seeing her there again. There was always a line there at noon, so I usually waited until one. But it was noon the day I saw her there, and so I'd been going at noon. I turned the corner, and the line was a bit long but not terrible. I looked for her in front of me, but no luck, so I decided I didn't need this line and started to walk out. As I reached the door, there she was. I opened the door for her. "Well, hello, Sam. How are you?"

"Fine. Yourself?"

"Very well, thank you."

"I haven't seen you here before. Do you eat lunch here often?"

She looked at me funny and then said, "Remember, don't use that one with your lady friend."

I laughed and nodded, and then with an obvious fake clearing of my throat, I said, "Is the food good here?"

She laughed. "Yes, quite good."

"That's a lovely dress you're wearing."

She thanked me through her laughter.

"Gee, I really hate to eat alone. Would you care to join me?"

She laughed and said, "Better. Much better. Don't forget that."

"No, I mean, would you mind if I did join you?"

She got that same funny look like when I addressed her by her first name. She hesitated, and I feared she would say no, so with a smile I said, "After all, it would help the person behind us get to a table more quickly." Once again, that sweet laugh of hers.

"Sure. Why not."

We worked our way though the line, gathered our food, and sat down in the corner of the crowed deli. Now we were able to talk as man and woman, not as patient and shrink. She was wrong about one thing she had warned me about. She cautioned me that the person I had imagined based on her physical beauty might not be who she was inside and that her personality might be different. In fact, she was exactly as I had envisioned her. Our lunch had gone on for over an hour when suddenly she looked at her watch and said, "Oh my goodness. I have to go. I'm late for an appointment."

"Go then, and I'll take care of your tray."

"Thank you!" she said as she smiled and scurried off.

I sat back down, leaned back in my chair, and sighed like a contented man. I was so happy that I actually seemed to be making progress—or at least so I thought. I leisurely returned to my office and awaited five o'clock. I couldn't wait to get out of there and go home to daydream about her and relive our lunch together. It was grand, and I was higher than a kite. I wondered how our lunch together would affect our next visit.

Then I got an idea. Saturday morning, I walked over to the bookstore where I had first met her and searched for the book I had accidentally picked up that was so embarrassing at the time. I was a little embarrassed buying it, but my idea was priceless, or so I thought. I took it home and wrapped it up in some nice wrapping paper with a large red bow. No card though. I put the package in my briefcase. I would take it to my office the next Monday and leave it in my desk until the time was right. I returned home with my prize and struggled through the rest of the weekend.

I ate at the deli every day from then on in hopes of dining with her again, but no luck. When Wednesday rolled around, I prepared to see her again at my nine o'clock time slot. I couldn't wait. I walked in and headed straight for the couch. Once again, she stood up and greeted me. Yes, she was wearing a skirt, just not as short as the other one, but wow—what legs. I wondered if she had been in gymnastics, as her calf muscles were so toned. I would save that query for our next luncheon.

"Well, Sam, what progress have we made?"

"Good, very good."

"Oh, so did you meet up with her?"

Oh no! She just boxed me in. Now, what do I say? I can't say yes. That would mean another woman or that she is the one. I couldn't give her either answer.

"No, it's just that I feel you are getting me prepared for when I do, and you have helped me clarify my feelings about her." I knew that was a BS answer, but it was all I could come up with quickly.

"Thank you, Sam, but you're doing it, and I think with one or two more sessions you'll be back to your old self and you will no longer need to come here."

Now that would be music too most people's ears ... not mine. I now knew I had only two more times to get my mission accomplished.

"Oh, I'm not as sure of that as you are, Janet. You have been a great help in getting me settled down. I doubt if anyone else in the world could have accomplished what you have for me."

"Nonsense, Sam. Any decent psychologist or psychiatrist could have helped you with this, but thank you for saying so."

This was the first time she had a real smile when we were in her office. Was I beginning to make a connection? I hoped so. I was falling in love with her more and more.

She was even getting used to me calling her by her first name. "Janet, what happens if my love for her is rejected when I finally meet her?"

"Sam, you know that we can't always have what we want just because we want it. You're a smart man. You know that is true. Sometimes it's the old story of the unrequited love. However, as you know, time heals it. You'll meet someone else, and life goes on. Does that make sense to you?"

"Yes, of course it does. I guess I was hoping somehow for a different answer."

"You mean some kind of miracle answer like in the movies?"

"Yes, I guess. It does sound silly when you put it that way."

"Sam, you may have an opportunity to meet her, and even though she wasn't wearing a wedding ring, she could still be married or engaged or in a serious relationship ... For that matter, she might even be gay. You may find that she is nothing but a figment of your imagination built on her looks and demeanor. After all, that is really all you know of her. Isn't it?"

"Yes, yes, you're right. But what if all that isn't true and she is, in fact, an unattached, single heterosexual woman? How can I have my best chance with her? If I never see her again, well then I guess your time-cures-all theory will eventually happen, but what if I know where she is? I can't and won't stalk her or hire a detective to give me all her stats. I almost wish I could practice in a real scenario."

"That's a good idea. Why don't you do that with a female friend?"

I put on a sad look and said, "No. Unfortunately, I don't know many women around here. I transferred here about a year ago. Yes, I've had a few dates, but nothing came of them. Besides, how would I be able to tell if it was bringing the right results?"

"How about the woman you met a week or so ago? Your friend's sister."

I shook my head and said, "No, I can't risk leading her on."

"Sam, I can't solve—"

I cut her off in midsentence. "I've got it. How about you?"

"No, Sam, that isn't possible."

"Why not? You're single, aren't you?"

"Yes, but—"

"Unattached, right?"

"Yes, but—"

"Not gay, right?"

"Yes, I mean no ... I mean I'm not gay. Now you stop it! I cannot date a patient."

"But it's not a date. It's ... ah ... a scientific experiment. For the good of mankind or at least this mankind."

She was ready to fire back another rejection when my words must've tickled her and she began to laugh, which started me laughing, which made her laugh more until we were both laughing so hard that we had tears rolling down our cheeks. When we finally got it under control, I got to my knees in front of her, took her hand, looked longingly into her eyes, and said, "Please go out with me?"

"All right, all right, now get off your knees."

As I got up and sat on the edge of the couch, she gave me all the restrictions.

"Now this is for treatment purposes, not a date in any sense of the word. I am going to record it in my journal and post it as just that, an experiment. When and where? I will meet you there."

"How about this Friday at seven o'clock at Stringfellows Steak and Seafood house?"

"That will be fine. I will meet you there, and that about concludes our session," she said as her wristwatch did its annoying little buzz.

"I will ask your receptionist for a Monday appointment next week, and you can tell me how well I did. Okay?"

"That will be fine, Sam. I believe I have a ten o'clock available Monday."

"Good-bye, fair lady. Until Friday." I then folded my arm across my waist and bowed to her. I got another laugh from her.

"Sam, you may be crazy after all." She continued to laugh.

I smiled at her and walked out. I set my appointment and floated back to my office. The remainder of Wednesday, Thursday, and Friday moved like a fat tortoise going up a steep hill, dragging a forty-pound bag. But when five o'clock Friday finally came, I headed for home as quickly as I could, stopping along the way to buy six yellow roses. I also had my car washed and vacuumed, just in case I could sweet-talk her into going dancing. Once home, I showered, shaved, and brushed my teeth. Next I put on my best suit and shiniest shoes. At six thirty, out the door I went, driving straight to Stringfellows and my date with destiny. Beside me on the seat were the roses and the book I had wrapped to present to her at the opportune moment. At 6:55 p.m., I was walking into the lobby of the restaurant.

"May I help you, sir?" asked the hostess.

"Yes, ma'am, I have reservations for two for seven o'clock. The name is Whitley."

"Yes, sir, I see it here. Would you like to be seated now or wait for your guest?"

"We can be seated now, as here she comes."

"Sam, good evening."

"Good evening, Janet. You look lovely. I hope you like these," I said as I handed her the roses.

"Yes, Sam, they're beautiful! Thank you so much. How thoughtful."

"Perhaps we could get some water for them while we are here?" I said, looking directly at the hostess.

"Yes, sir. Let me get you seated, and I'll have a vase with water brought to the table."

"Thank you," we both said at the same time. Then we chuckled. So far so good. She took my arm as the hostess led us to our table. I pulled her chair out as my dear mother had taught me. I planned to be the perfect gentleman. Tonight might be the one and only chance to make my dreams with her come true. The conversation was supposed to stay away from our professional relationship and be the case study of a date. This was supposed to help me achieve my goal of how to win the hand of the lady I loved. Our conversation started out a bit tense, but soon we were able to laugh a little, and by the end of our meal, it felt like a real date. We learned a lot about each other, like where we were from, that neither of us had been married before or had any children, and we both had parents still living. We were really getting on well. The meal was finished; we had declined dessert but had coffee. Now the timing seemed right.

"Janet, I think this has gone well, at least for me, but it's not where a real date would end. So I suggest we go dancing to make this as real as possible. What do you say?"

She was quiet for a moment and then surprisingly agreed without even token resistance. I was on cloud nine. So we leisurely finished our coffee, I paid the tab, and off we went to Casey's, a local night club. She asked if we could take her car, as the lock on the passenger side was broken and she was concerned about someone stealing it. I agreed.

As she drove over, I couldn't help but sneak peaks at those lovely legs of hers, her short skirt now resting at midthigh. It kept moving up a little more each time she shifted gears. For the first time that night, I wondered what it would be like to make love to her. Those legs, those exquisite legs, caused me to get an erection, which I tried to fight off. All I needed to wreck everything was for her to notice it, and I'd be sunk. So I glued my eyes to the road ahead and tried to think of other things. By the time we reached Casey's, my other brain had stopped dominating my big brain, and I was able to exit the car without a lump in my trousers. Once inside, we found a nice table in the corner farthest from the band and ordered a drink. We talked some more, and then a great song came on, and *she* asked *me* to dance. She was a great dancer, but then in my eyes, she could do no wrong. We danced two or three fast songs, and then a slow one started. She started to walk off, but I gently took her hand and pulled her into my arms. I felt the initial resistance and then surrender. My cheek next to hers, I could smell the sweet, light scent of her perfume. As we danced, our bodies moved closer and closer, and our arms tightened to take up the slack. I didn't realize it, but I was dancing with my eyes closed. I noticed she was too when I pulled away at song's end. The song was long, thank goodness, but when it ended, we pulled about a foot apart and paused. I lost all my senses and kissed her. To my utter amazement, she kissed back. As another slow song started, and our arms were now wrapped up like lovers, not dance partners. This was the greatest night of my life. We closed the place down, and I felt like we were sure to become an item. As we drove home, she became quiet, and I was concerned.

"What's wrong, Janet? You seem pensive all of a sudden."

"Oh, nothing. I'm just tired."

I was hoping that was all it was, but my brain kept telling me it was more. I didn't push it. I decided to take her at her word and just say something nice to her without bringing up the romance we discovered on the dance floor.

She pulled into the parking lot of Stringfellows where my car was parked and pulled alongside as the lot was now abandoned. I looked into her eyes, and she gave me a halfhearted smile. I asked again if everything was all right. And again she assured me that she was just tired. I started to lean toward her for a good-night kiss, but she jumped out of her car, ran around, opened my door, playing as though she were the gentleman. We laughed, and she bounced back to her side of the car. "Good night, Sam, and thank you."

"Good night, Janet. Thank you for the great company. I'll see you Monday morning at ten."

She nodded and quickly disappeared inside her car and drove away. I saw the book, the one I planned to give her, but now was not the time. I followed as far as our route was the same, and then she turned right and disappeared from sight. I felt the greatest letdown at that moment. I started to imagine all that might have gone wrong. I found myself quickly home and depressed, so I had one final drink and went to bed. I worried through Sunday and Monday. I hurried to work, which started with my going upstairs for my ten o'clock appointment. I was told to go in, but she wasn't in yet, so I stretched out on the couch. When I heard the door open, I decided to say something to make her laugh.

"Would you like to dance, lovely lady?"

"Well, I must admit I have never been called that before."

It wasn't so much that response as it was the deep masculine voice that caused me to sit straight up. My eyes were probably as big as silver dollars as the shock ran through my entire body. I then turned my head and stood up abruptly. There before me was a short portly man in a brown suit with half-rimmed glasses perched on the lower bridge of his nose and bald as a billiard ball. I stood there in shock, and I must have had a puzzled look upon my face.

"Mr. Whitley, I am Dr. Dirkus. Please sit back down and let me explain."

I sat down ... actually it was more like just collapsing on the couch, but I did not lie down. What the hell was going on?

He sat down and then said, "My colleague was unable to come this morning, as she had a conflict in her schedule."

I immediately stood back up and responded, "Well, that's okay. I will simply reschedule for another day with her."

"Mr. Whitley, I am afraid that won't be possible. She has resigned from our practice and moved from the area."

I sat down again in shock, my mind racing. A million questions shot through my mind at warp speed. The only word I could muster was, "Why?"

"Mr. Whitley, Janet called me Saturday morning in tears and offered her resignation. She told me that she had violated her ethical responsibility with a patient and that she had become romantically involved with you. She told me that she was ashamed of her action in her role with our business. Unfortunately, I had to agree and reluctantly accepted her resignation."

"But you don't understand! It was an experiment, a case study—that's all. It was my fault, not hers. I begged her to help me. Please bring her back. I will not see her here again. Please, she did nothing wrong."

I wish I could, but she told me that she allowed you to kiss her, and she admitted she kissed you back. She consented, and that was where it crossed the line and violated all that we believe in. I simply had to agree with her. There is nothing I can do."

"Listen, Doctor, I am in love with her. In fact, I came to see you on my first day here. You had been called away, and she of all people was here to help me. She was the reason I came to this office, but I couldn't tell her, so I told her my dilemma except left out the fact that *she* was the reason for my visit. I know it sounds bizarre, but it is true. Please, I'll do whatever it takes ... I'll not come back to this office. I'll quit the firm. Anything to make it right. I was unaware of your ethics. It was all my fault!"

He just sat there shaking his head and telling me I didn't understand, until finally I lost it. I stood up and yelled at him and reiterated my points. He remained calm and restated his points.

"Then tell me where I can find her. I must see her."

"I'm afraid that's impossible."

"Did she say she had feelings for me?"

"That, Mr. Whitley, is not my concern. However, she is not accustomed to allowing men she has no interest in to kiss her and resigning her job over it. Frankly, she would have never allowed herself to be talked into this so-called case study. Furthermore, I will tell you it's unlikely she will be able to work in this field again."

"You, Doctor, are a king-sized jackass of the first order!"

With that, I stormed out, but by the time I reached the receptionist's desk, I was all smiles. "Hi, Ms. McGuire. Could you please give me an address or phone number for Ms. Barnes?"

"No, sir, I'm sorry. I am not permitted to give out such information." Then she looked both ways and slipped a piece of paper to me. She smiled as she held a finger to her lips as if to say *Mum's the word*. I smiled back and mimed the words *Thank you* and walked out. When I got back to my office, I looked at the note: *1231 Shady Lane, Apt. 1101*. I knew that building. I walked out to our receptionist and told her I was taking a long lunch. I then raced to the parking lot to retrieve my car and drove straight there. I slipped past the front desk of the apartment building and went straight for the elevators.

As I took the long ride to the eleventh floor, I tried to compose myself and think about what I would say. I had the wrapped-up book in my hand. Finally, the elevator door opened, and I hurried to her door. I knocked and knocked, but there was no answer. Back to the front desk to have them call her. The older, stiff-lipped lady there was not much help, but I did finally convince her to call her apartment. She answered.

"Ms. Barnes, there is a gentleman here who wishes to see you. His name is Mr. Whitley."

The lady paused as though she were receiving instructions and then said, "Yes, I understand. Good day." Then she hung up.

"It seems that Ms. Barnes does not wish to see you and requests that you not contact her again."

The old bitty seemed almost happy to deliver that message to me.

"Might I speak with her over the phone?"

"Good day, sir."

"Please! It is most urgent!"

"I said good day. Now leave before I call security," she stated sternly.

"Please, ma'am, it really is important."

She glared back at me and without a word reached for the phone. I thought she had relented, but no. She just said, "Security?"

"Never mind. I'm leaving."

I quickly headed for the door. I headed for the security garage door and waited. Within a few minutes, a car entered, and I followed the car inside and hid until it was out of sight. Then I walked around the parking garage until I found space 1101, same as her apartment. There was her car, the same red Pontiac Solstice she drove the night we met at Stringfellows. I remembered that the passenger door lock was broken, so I got inside and decided to wait for her no matter how long it took. I waited and waited until I finally drifted off to sleep. I don't know how long it was before I heard the door open. But when she saw me, she began to cry, so I jumped out and held her. She didn't resist; she just cried. I begged her to go back to her apartment and let me explain everything to her. She finally agreed.

When we got inside, I saw that her place was packed, and suitcases were sitting by the door. She was moving out for good and leaving first thing in the morning, she told me.

"Janet, you can't leave."

"Sam, I must leave. There is nothing here for me now. I quit my job and am heading home."

"But I need you! Don't you understand?"

"Dr. Dirkus can help you with your girlfriend problem, obviously better than I can. I let my guard down, and I made a mistake. We both know it. We got caught up in the heat of the moment, and there is no way I can help you now."

"But you don't understand. You are that girl."

"Sam, I know you feel as bad … as do I about Friday night, but please don't make it worse by trying to make me feel better. You came to me for help with another woman, not me." My mind raced for a way to prove to her that it was in fact her. That she was the person that I fell in love with at first sight and that I now knew that it was love, not just some made-up fantasy.

"Please leave now, Sam, and forget about this and let Dr. Dirkus help you with the woman of your dreams."

Then I remembered the book, that damn book, but it was in her car.

"Listen, Janet, I have something to give you. Come with me. I left it in your car."

She refused to accompany me. "Then may I get it and bring it to you? Will you let me back in?"

She nodded, and I walked down the long hall, took the elevator to the parking garage, and walked to her car. I grabbed the book. The wrapping paper was slightly torn and badly wrinkled, but it was the proof I needed for her.

Oh, I'm so freaking stupid. The door between the garage locked behind me, and I, of course, had no key. I banged and banged on the door, but no one opened it. I thought, *Should I run up the eleven flights of stairs to gain access back into the building?* I was just about to do that when I heard a car door close and saw a man walking toward me. I ran back to her car before he saw me, slammed the door so he would hear it, and then timed my walk to the door so he would get there first. As he reached the door, he opened it with his key, and I thanked him and followed him into the building. It worked; he assumed I lived there. I walked slowly behind him until he reached his door and disappeared inside. Then I ran to the elevator door and took it to the eleventh floor. Her door was unlocked, and I ran inside. However, once inside, I saw her suitcases were gone. There was a note taped to the first packing box in plain sight. I approached it cautiously, as

I feared I already knew what it said, and I knew it was the last thing that I wanted to hear. I picked it off the box and read the following,

> *Dearest Sam,*
>
> *I am sorry to have tricked you, but you have a way of convincing me of things that I otherwise might not do. It was so nice knowing you for the brief time that we did, and I sincerely hope you find your mystery lady and have the life you want.*
>
> *Please don't try and find me. It is time for me to let time heal my mistakes and to forget what happened between us. Good-bye and God bless you.*
>
>

Sincerely,

Janet
>

I ran to the elevator and out the front door in hopes of catching her. I was too late, and I wanted to just cry. I had found her, held her, kissed her, and loved her, and now I had lost her ... again. I was sick in the pit of my stomach. Then I stiffened. I would make her wish come true. I *would* find my mystery lady, and I *would* have the life I wanted ... with her!

I went home to make a plan, no matter what the cost, no matter how long it took. I had only one picture of her that I copied from the company website, and I made many copies of it. I put one on my fridge, one on my bathroom mirror, and one on my nightstand. I would not let time steal her from me. I would hire a private detective to find her, and I would go to her no matter where she was. The book would stay wrapped just as it was, and I would give it to her the minute I saw her.

The next day, I called in sick and put my plan into action. Every time I got something from the fridge, I was reenergized. The same in the bathroom—she was the first thing I saw when I woke and the last thing I looked at before I slept. Every time I looked at her, I was more determined than ever. This was not an obsession, as I had thought in the beginning. I was deeply in love with her and would track her to the ends of the earth!

Three months went by, and finally a call with some solid information about her from Bill, the private investigator that I had hired to locate her. She was found working in a small clinic in the posh part of London. She had gone home, as she had told me, but when the detective got there, she had gone, perhaps for good, and no one who knew would tell where she had gone.

Finally a story surfaced in a local paper. A family told how a young American woman had saved their young son from committing suicide. Seems she had moved to another small clinic, this one in a less affluent section of London. The story was picked up by the wire services and ran in her hometown newspaper's front page with her picture. Thank God for small towns. Bill confirmed she was still there and tracked down her work and home address. I took my two weeks' vacation, bought a ticket to London, and was on my way.

I landed at Heathrow Airport and immediately took a cab to a hotel near where she worked. It was late, but the next day, I would find her. I felt like a young kid on Christmas Eve. I couldn't wait for morning to see what awaited me. Finally I drifted off to sleep, and my wake-up call brought me back to the excitement of what lay ahead for me.

Quickly I groomed and readied myself to see her again. I got a cab to take me to her residence. With nothing but the book in hand, I raced to the door and knocked. A little old British lady answered and informed me that she was not working today but was asleep and that I would have to come back later. I sweet-talked her a bit and told her I was her brother. I also told her that I was with the military and was en route to the Middle East and had only a twenty-four layover in London. I explained that we hadn't seen each other in three years and I wanted so desperately to surprise her. I must have hit a nerve with her, as a tear ran down her cheek, and she opened the door to her apartment. I walked into the room, my heart beating so fast and hard that I was sure it would wake her. I stared at her sound asleep, her long hair going in every direction, the sheet lying across her waist, and her breasts showing through her thin, white sleeping garment. Her face was angelic, no makeup or lipstick, and her expression was one of calm and peacefulness. It made me wonder if she had forgotten me. Had time so quickly removed whatever feelings she might have had for me? I quietly went to her kitchenette and sat at the small table. I placed the book in its worn, torn, and very abused wrapping paper in the middle of the small table. I wasn't sure what to do next. Should I wake her? Let her sleep and be there when she came into the kitchen? Should I leave, with just the book to explain? I couldn't decide, so my indecision was my decision, as no action is an action, and soon I heard water running in her bathroom, I heard the toilet flush, and then I heard her slippers shuffling down the hard wood floors and getting closer. I froze, and panic set in. What would her reaction be? I hoped that I wouldn't startle her too badly. Then there she was before me, frozen in place, staring at me in disbelief. Neither of us could speak; we just stared at each other. It seemed like forever.

Finally, I cleared my throat and said, "Janet, I love you!"

She turned her back to me, and I could hear her softly crying. I rushed to her and just held her from behind. After a few minutes, she turned and hugged my neck.

"I am so glad to see you. My heart wanted you so badly, but my head told me no. What happened with your mystery lady?"

I gestured toward the table. "I can tell you, but it would be better to show you."

She looked at me with a puzzled look as she walked toward the table and slowly sat down. I sat across from her and gently pushed the wrapped book toward her. "I bought this for you the day after our first appointment. Still she looked at me with this cute, puzzled expression. She slowly removed the string and the tattered wrapping paper. When the paper was fully removed, she looked at the back of the book and then quickly looked up at me with a strange expression. With my finger, I made a circling gesture as if to say, *Turn it over.* She turned it over and laid it on the table and just stared at it. I watched her facial expressions go through a series of changes as she tried to get the significance of it. She looked up at me, puzzled. I pointed back to the book, and she read the title out loud with a question mark in her tone.

I said, "Six months ago, you walked into the Librarian's Bookstore on Main Street, and a man stepped up beside you with this book, and you and the clerk laughed."

A look of recognition seemed to slowly come across her face, and she looked at me and pointed at me, but all she said was, "You?"

I nodded, and she went back to that look like she was studying and remembering. I watched her with amazement as she slowly figured it out.

"You were there because you followed me into the bookstore?"

"Yes."

"Why?"

"As I told you at the office, I wanted to see if you were wearing a wedding or engagement ring."

"Why?"

"Because I saw you from across the street and needed to know."

"Why did you buy this book?"

We worked through the details from each other's point of view until we were back to the here and now.

"Now it's your turn to answer a question. Do you love me or have any positive feelings toward me?"

"Wow. You come straight to the point, don't you?"

"Yes, I do. I no longer have the luxury of time for you to see that I'm a good guy who is very much in love with you, so do you care for me in any way?"

She smiled and winked. "You figure it out. You're so freaking smart."

We stepped tentatively into each other's arms.

CHAPTER 2
SHE SAID

We locked our bodies and lips together. It took all of about a minute of kissing and pressing for him to scoop me up into his strong arms and return me to the bed where he had found me mere moments ago.

I didn't want it to happen. I truly did love him, but I guess it's like that old fable about the frog and the scorpion. I'm sure you remember it. The scorpion couldn't swim but wanted to reach the other side of the river, so he approached a bullfrog sitting on a lily pad just out of his reach. The scorpion beckoned to the frog, "Mr. Frog, would you please carry me upon your back to the other side of river?"

The frog was a savvy old frog, and he replied, "No, I dare not, as you are a scorpion, and you will sting me, and I will surely die!"

But the scorpion replied, "I would not. If I did, we would both drown. I cannot swim."

The good-natured frog thought that made sense, so he jumped from the safety of his lily pad to the shore and allowed the scorpion to climb upon his back. When the frog reached the safety of the opposite riverbank, the scorpion stung him as he crawled off the frog's back onto the shore. In utter disbelief, the frog said, "Why ... why did you do that? I did as you asked, and now you have stung me, and I am going to die!"

The scorpion calmly replied, "Because I am a scorpion. That's what I do."

Sam and I peeled off each other's clothes, pausing to kiss newly exposed body parts as soon as they were revealed. Our passion for each other was unstoppable. I was now completely exposed to him, save very brief panties, and he was down to his jockey shorts. I was on my back, and he was on his hands and knees above me, and I felt his soft lips. They felt so good as he tenderly suckled my now exposed breasts, moving from one then to the other. As he did, I slid my hands into his shorts. I was desperate to know his size and power. I was pleased, to say the least, as he was large, hard, and almost hot to the touch. So I pushed his shorts down as far as my arms would reach, then used my left foot to slide them to his knees, where he lifted one and then the other in order to free them from his now naked body. I lifted my head to see what I was about to receive, and his manhood was a beautiful sight to see. I lifted my buttocks as his big hands gently removed my panties. A slight chill ran down my spine in anticipation of the pleasure I was about to receive. The expression on his face and his deep moaning told me he felt the same. I slowly raised my left leg to feel him, sliding along his inner thigh, teasing him and daring him to take me. He smiled slyly and pulled his right leg to the inside of mine. Now he had both my legs to the outside of his and my hands gently but firmly pinned over my head by his. I was completely vulnerable to him, and I loved that feeling. It was now totally up to him to decide when he would penetrate me. Oh, how I wanted it. My breath was short and rapid. I yearned for him to enjoin with me. "Please, Sam, take me now," I softly begged. I pushed my hips upward to try to touch him, to lure him into me. Finally I felt the pressure of him trying to enter, and he slid easily to his target. We were both wet with anticipation from all the foreplay. I arched my back from the pleasure and moaned softly in his ear. He took long, slow movements within me, and the pleasure was unbelievable. He shoveled his nose into my armpit and breathed deeply, as though the slight musky odor that bypassed my deodorant in our sexual excitement was like some kind of aphrodisiac that turned him on and caused him to drive himself deeper into me. I had never felt such exhilaration before, and I was no stranger to sex. We made love over and over; it seemed we couldn't get enough of each other.

Finally I had the opportunity to be on top, my favorite position. Now I set the pace, speed, and intensity of our actions. My knees were straddled alongside his hips, and I was sitting on him while he was inside me. I was in total control of our sexual experience. The downside is that when I get this excited, I cannot control the lust that lurks within me. Sexual lust, yes, but more, and I was peaked. The feel of him completely inside of me caused me to climax several times, and with each climax, the intensity grew. I could see by his facial expression he was trying to control his release, but I knew it wouldn't be long before I felt the rush of his fiery hot liquid bust forth inside me. I always had to feel it; I wouldn't allow any man to cheat me from that experience. No man was permitted to wear a condom with me or withdraw before every ounce of his bodily fluid was within me. But the feeling was the most intense when I was on top. I was at a fever pitch waiting his release, but he held back. I could see the veins in his neck protruding. I knew he was enjoying it and didn't want it to end. Then when he could no longer control his body, he grabbed a handful of the bed sheets in both hands and held his breath. Finally he released his breath and his fluid in one explosion of what had to have been exultation. After his initial scream, he just whimpered and moaned, but I kept up the pace, causing the pulsing warmth within me. His body finally went limp, and so did his ability to remain firm.

I fell into his arms, but as my face nuzzled his neck, I could smell it, and I could feel it pulsating like his penis did moments ago. I wanted to wear him a few more times, but I couldn't pull away. The smell was intoxicating, just as the sex had been. I kept inhaling deeper and deeper until Sam exclaimed that I was tickling him, but then finally I could no longer control my urge and my lust, so I began licking and nibbling at his neck. It wasn't long before he became erect again, and I mounted him again, this time with a different outcome. I worked him fast, and when he started to swell inside me again, I knew it was time. I slid off him, and as I lowered my face to take him into my mouth, he must have seen the elongated canine teeth now protruding past my lips. "Ouch, be careful," he moaned, but he was too aroused to stop, and his hot liquid began to fill my mouth, along with his blood. He must have figured it out quickly. In a questioning tone, he said, "But I've seen you in the daylight … you eat regular food and are warm to the touch."

I finished and whispered softly in his ear, "Yes, my love. You shouldn't believe all that you have read about us. It may not be true." He tried to fight me, but his strength had been sapped, both from all the sex and his loss of blood, not to mention how strong we become when we are feeding. I went back to his neck and bit into it, drinking blood, gulping it down as fast as his rapidly beating heart pumped it into my mouth. He felt no pain as my saliva from licking his neck numbed his ability to feel my teeth sink into his artery. I now had his arms pinned above his heart, and he was as weak as a kitten. I stopped to save some of him for later but not too much later. His pulse had slowed due to lack of blood, and I wanted to finish him from his neck. My insatiable appetite only allowed me to cuddle him, kiss him, and talk with him for a short time. My need to feed was my strongest emotion. I held him in my arms to keep him warm and then whispered in his ear that I loved him.

He seemed calm, as if he knew there was no escape and this was his fate, and he gave into it. His voice was barely more than a whisper when he uttered, "I love you too." He then turned his neck to me as if to say it was okay. I kissed it, gently pushed my teeth into his soft flesh, and drank the rest of his hot fresh blood. I loved him, but ultimately, I am what I am. You can't fault me any more than you could the scorpion; I was doing what nature had designed me to do. Tomorrow would be for tears; I would cry then.

Sam chased me until I caught him, but that was not what I wanted. I really did love him. I tried to run from him, even left the country to avoid him, but he persisted to his own detriment, and now his chase had ended. As he slipped into unconsciousness and then death, a smile came across his face, and he seemed to have a look of contentment. We never know which ones will join us and which simply die as man was expected to do. Maybe I'll see him again, maybe not. He did look happy though, and the smile is still on his face. Will your death be as sweet?

THE END ... WELL, THAT DEPENDS ON YOU!

CRYPTURE 8

Time

PROLOGUE

As dawn approached, two Warbirds flew high above the skies of northern China in search of enemy aircraft. This was the Dawn Patrol, as it came to be known. Each patrol consisted of two planes in tight formation until it was time to engage the enemy. Their daily mission and many others like it was to deny the Chinese the ability to supply their allies with beans and bullets by downing their cargo planes, bombers, and fighters. Anything flying or floating was fair game for the Warbirds. They flew in almost all kinds of weather, although today was perfect. The early-morning rain clouds gave way to a sun-filled sky that was as blue as the ocean below.

Captain Leslie Carson piloted Raider Two, call sign Chick, twenty-nine years of age, had flown all sorts of aircraft since she was a teenager. Her profession before the war started was that of a popular movie actor who played sexy chicks and women who flew planes. Her most famous role was as Maverick in the 2042 remake of the movie *Top Gun*. She learned to fly the Warbird for the movie and rarely used a stunt double. The military wouldn't train her unless she enlisted, so Hollywood paid handsomely to have the plane's manufacturer train her.

"Raider One, this is Raider Two. Two Chinese bombers at twelve o'clock low."

"Roger that. Let's put them on the deck!"

The two Warbirds dropped down on the bombers like falcons after pigeons. Their talons were their laser-guided missiles that sent the huge bombers into thousands of burning pieces of scrap.

"Raider Two, bandits at three o'clock!"

"Got them."

Four MiG-22 fighters were flying straight for the Warbirds. As Red One broke left and Red Two broke right, the MiGs also broke to intercept. It was two on one, the kind of odds that flight leader Major Jake Hendricks, call sign Ice, loved. He quickly evened the odds as he took his bird into a steep dive, and when the MiGs pursued, he pulled his faster, lighter plane into an inside roll and came out of it behind the last MiG and with a burst of laser-guided bullets that sent that plane spiraling into the sea. Raider Two had been hit and lost partial rudder control, making her a sitting duck for the next pass by one of the MiGs.

Ice heard the call for help, downed the other MiG he was dealing with, and swung around to help his wingman. Ice dropped down on one of the MiGs and ripped it in half with a spray of rounds from his wing-mounted cannons. The last MiG bugged out and was heading home.

"Return to base, Raider Two. I want this turkey."

"Roger that, Raider One. Out."

Ice eased the throttle to the max, and the fleeing MiG tried every evasive maneuver he knew but to know avail. The sound of the locked-on warning of his instruments must have been the last sound he heard as his plane was eviscerated by a heat-seeking missile, courtesy of the US of A.

"Take that, you bastard!" exclaimed Ice as he turned sharply and raced to catch up with his wingman to provide cover and escort her back to base.

"Raider Two, I got your six."

"Roger that, Raider One."

These dogfights were commonplace, and the Allies lost many men. If there was any consolation, the other side lost more.

During the second year of the war, the United States shocked the world when it sent a brigade of heavily armed marines into occupied territory. At first, the enemy retaliated with a division of troops, mostly Chinese and Russian. Although heavily outnumbered, the American Marines seemed invincible. They were pushing back the opposing troops. It wasn't learned for several weeks that the enemy captured one of these marines and discovered one of our most top-secret weapons. These marines weren't American men but a newly built, highly sophisticated android. No one else had anything even close to it. This helped bring the war to an earlier end then was originally predicted.

The year was 2049, the end of World War III. It had started when North Korea sent a small nuke into the heart of Seoul Korea, which brought the Yanks and Brits in, which brought the Chinese in, and so on and so on until every free country was united against every Communist country. This war raged on for almost five years. It was to be the final conflict between those who believed that all men should be free and those who wished to rule by tyranny, the Communist philosophy, and those who hated America.

Once Cuba first declared war on the United States, the CIA was able to intercept their plans. As once tried by the USSR, China wanted to use Cuba as a base to strike deep in the heart of America. Chinese and Cuban troops would plan an invasion at the appropriate time. The United States got word of this plan and put in the countermeasure and set up a submarine blockade. The nuclear-powered subs sunk their ships, and American soil was never invaded by troops, although unfortunately a few nuclear missiles carrying cerium gas did penetrate America's defense systems, enough to poison the soil.

Since Cuba was deemed a danger too close to America to be tolerated, they sent in marines and in three days took out the Communist-controlled government. A vote was taken, and the vast majority of Cubans favored American control. So Cuba became a territory of the United States.

The Russian citizens took up arms against their own government, as did the peoples of South Vietnam. Victory came to both with the aid of American Marines. The South Koreans defeated their brethren to the north with aid from Britain and the United States. Most of the Muslim countries aligned themselves with the Communists as they thought they could win against the American-led forces. This would ultimately turn out to be a bad miscalculation on their part. They underestimated the determination of free people to remain so. They failed to realize that all men desire to be free, and they didn't realize that the peoples of the Communist countries would rise up against their own governments. It was the spark of a chance to be free that ignited them to action. It took WWIII to shake Americans out of the political wars starting with Korea and seen most vividly in Viet Nam. Some gutless leaders took the United States down a path that weakened them both economically and militarily, but, as during the revolution, a few good people held fast to the beliefs that made the United States great, and the United State and its allies finally prevailed.

Continuing to patrol the skies over China until the war ended was this American fighter pilot, a man who became as famous an ace of the skies as was the Red Barron during the First World War. He would earn the nickname of Ice because people that knew him said that he was so cool under pressure that he must have ice water in his veins. He flew the F-62, the latest and greatest fighter plane the marines had to date. A plane that had a nickname Warbird. Warbird got its name from the feathers painted on the underside of the wings and fuselage, which created a camouflage to the ground. Radar was always taken out quickly, and spotters had to be used from the ground. However, his enemies would call him by a different name, "the wolf of the skies." It seemed no one could make the Warbird perform like Ice. He was decorated over and over for his accomplishments with that plane. It was Americans like Ace, multiplied by the thousands, who turned the tide of the war.

Finally the Communists surrendered so that peace and rebuilding could begin. The people of every Communist nation were allowed to vote for the type of government they wanted, one of the conditions of the treaty. Not one nation voted to retain their Communist way of life. They finally realized that a form of government that was contrary to human nature couldn't endure and that political promises of a government that would protect everyone from everything was doomed for failure, as it could not sustain itself.

Ice received several accommodations and an honorable discharge and then returned to civilian life and resumed his racing career.

CHAPTER 1
WAR'S OVER

My name is Jake Hendricks, and I was now back home. The war was over, and it was time to get back to life as it was before.

As the sun rose, I watched the long shadows of the mountains as they moved across the salt flats. The cold night air slowly began to warm under the radiant heat of the sun. Once the sun had cleared the mountaintops, the flats became drenched in sunlight. Now the roar of screaming engines could be heard for miles. There were final tunings and adjustments as many hopefuls decided to risk fortune, life, and limb to set a new land-speed record at the Bonneville Salt Flats. Records had been set every year and then broken the next as man pushed the envelope further and further. Some records had stood longer, but eventually all fell. New designs, lighter but stronger materials, better technologies, and new fuel types continue to be developed, and the hopefuls forge on in their quests.

The year was 2050, and I was one of those men that had already hit a land-speed record of Mach one twenty years ago. It had never been done except in aircraft. Once that was accomplished, Mach two was only a matter of time. By 2040, that goal had been accomplished. Now the goal for the extreme categories was Mach three. That proved to be a difficult task, but my team and I felt we were ready to reclaim that world record on that fateful day. At ten hundred hours, a team of devoted speedsters backed by a man with unlimited resources would make the attempt. The computer models told us that the materials used to build our speedster would sustain that speed. The engines were capable, and the design would hold it to the ground. The variable was man. Could a man handle himself at Mach three? Today, here at the Bonneville Salt Flats, that query would be answered. The man at the helm would be me, but most who know me will call me Ice. That was my nickname when I used to race here before and after I became a marine pilot. I used it as my call sign. Could I set a new land-speed record today, and could I hit Mach three? I knew the car was capable, but was I?

At twenty-seven years of age, I had done it all. I had raced cars since I was eleven. I drove cars here at Bonneville and flew the marine F-62 fighter jet during World War III. The F-62 could achieve the speed of Mach three, and I knew the extremes it put on the human body. As a test pilot for the first plane to achieve Mach three, I wrote reports of these effects, which led to me being on the team that designed the pressurized suit men needed to wear to control the damage to the body at such speeds. That was why they chose me to regain my world record. Later, another claimed the record at Mach two. They even had to elongate the body to accommodate my height. The biggest question was could the vehicle remain grounded at speeds in excess of Mach two. In the sky, there is room for slight error. On land, however, there could not be the slightest miscue, or it would spell disaster. I knew that, and I tried not to show any concern. To add to my chances, the weather was picture perfect for this run, unusually cool and bone dry. There was also almost zero breeze; the windsock hung motionless. It was another advantage for me.

When the time came, all was in readiness, all except for me. As I climbed into my suit, I reflected on my life to that point, including the many accolades, being a leader of my high-school and college basketball and football teams, my days as a speed racer at Bonneville, and setting the land-speed record. The need to push myself for more, those days as a test pilot, and then entering the war almost as soon as it broke out. I rose quickly through the ranks, with many metals to pin to my chest. I though of all these accomplishments and my military service, again leading men and women into combat in the skies. Now here I was about to risk it all on a shot at regaining my position at the top by breaking a record at Mach three. All this, and I still felt empty inside, missing the thing I wanted most ... to love and be loved by a good woman. Oh, sure, I'd known my share of women, but nothing ever lasted. How could I have done so much and never found my soul mate?

The team calling me out broke my thoughts, and I had to shake them off and concentrate on what was about to happen. The team helped me into the cockpit of the Falcon, the name of the pencil-shaped land rocket that I hoped to pilot across the Bonneville Salt flats to a new land-speed record, without killing myself in the process. The canopy was securely buttoned down. The two powerful engines were fired. I slowly pushed the throttle forward. The mighty machine slowly began to move forward and then quickly began to accelerate. Within seconds, the machine hit Mach one, and the explosion of that feat was deafening. Then Mach two. Then, without warning, somewhere just under Mach three, there was a strange rumble that reverberated through the craft and me. I had never experienced anything like that in the planes I flew at that speed.

~

Meanwhile, inside the cockpit, all seemed normal. The speed indicator hit Mach three, and I began to slowly pull back on the throttle. My excitement was overwhelming. I had just done what no man had done before. I had set the ultimate record for a land vehicle. I knew this record would stand for at least fifty years or more. I would be an old man or gone from this earth before anyone beat it. As my vehicle finally rolled to a stop, I blew the canopy off the Falcon, the same type of canopy my Warbird had. I could see vehicles off in the distance coming closer and closer. I must admit I was looking forward to the accolades that would befall me very soon; my team would be ecstatic. I tried to stand, but my legs gave out. I was anxious for help to get me out of this uniform when the first vehicle showed up. I began to laugh, and then shock took over as more vehicles began to surround me. There would be no accolades, no congratulations. In fact, I didn't know what I was in for.

My team wasn't there. Actually, I didn't see so much as one familiar face. The salt flats, the vehicle I was in, what I was wearing, and the mountains off in the distance all were as they should be. Nothing else looked like anything I knew as reality, nor did the people. Yet they looked familiar somehow. Then I heard the sound of a rifle cocking, an old sound from a Winchester rifle. I had an antique like that one and knew that sound well. *I must be hallucinating ... maybe from the Mach three? What the hell is all this?*

As I looked at the people standing around me talking to themselves, I noticed their cars. I deduced what could be the only logical reason for what I was seeing. I had warped time and had somehow gone back in time about a hundred years. My God, how could that be? I had studied the theories, but could it actually happen? I was stunned at the possibility. There was speculation that if enough speed was reached, it could warp time. But it was just a theory. *Have I just proven that theory? What would they think back in my day? Did the vehicle just disintegrate before their eyes?* I stood again, and this time I stayed up, using the windshield to steady me. I was slowly regaining use of my body, but my fingers still didn't work. The people jumped back and made noises like they were afraid. Right in front of me was a 1947 Ford Club coupe, and it looked like it was brand-spanking-new. As a collector of antiques, I knew this car; my collection had many cars, including one of these—even the same color, black. I could imagine what these people must be thinking, that I must be from outer space. Their faces were ashen from fear as they murmured amongst themselves. After all, what else could they think, with my vehicle and my suit? If I was right and had somehow transported back in time, I must have appeared out of nowhere and perhaps looked as though I had just landed. I pressed the button on my suit that would allow them to hear me speak.

"Hello, everyone. My name is Jake Hendricks. I am from Dallas, Texas. How are you?"

"How did you get here, and what is this thing you are flying?" one man asked.

"If someone could help me out of this vehicle and out of my suit, I would be most grateful and happy to answer your questions."

I was not surprised that no one stepped forward to help me. In fact, I couldn't blame them. What a sight I must have been.

"Please, folks. If you could just lend a hand, I'll be happy to answer all your questions. Just lift the handle straight up, please."

Still they stood there. They were obviously afraid of this strange man in a suit that resembled the type of suit space aliens wore in comic books. One man jumped into his car and said he would go call the police. I was very happy to hear that. I had to get out of this uniform before my oxygen ran out. I could literally suffocate inside the damn suit. Funny, something that had saved my life during the ride could now be the instrument of my death.

"Good idea and thank you for getting the police here. However, if I don't get out of this suit soon, I will die in it, perhaps before your police get here. Would someone please help me?"

At first no one moved. Then, from the back of the crowd, a woman wearing overalls and a T-shirt, grease on her face and a baseball cap turned backward on her head, moved slowly toward me.

"What do you want me to do, Mister?"

"If you could pull up that long silver handle at the side of my vehicle, just pull it straight up until it stops." I had tried the electronic release, but it had failed.

As she grabbed the handle, the crowd pulled back, continuing to mutter among themselves. She opened the latch, and the side dropped down, and I was able to step out.

Pointing to the faceplate of my helmet, I said, "Now can you please just twist off the wing nuts that hold the mask in place?"

She nodded and slowly reached out for the first of fifteen wing nuts and slowly began to spin them off. Then my oxygen started to sputter.

"Please hurry, Miss. My air is now extinguished."

She began spinning them more quickly as I dropped to my knees. I felt someone else spinning the ones on my backside.

That was the last thing I remembered until I opened my eyes and saw an angel standing over me dressed in all white. For just a second, I thought I had died and this had to be heaven—until I heard this nasty voice say, "Nurse, move out of the way!"

When I looked up, there before me stood a fat, loud-mouthed country sheriff and two deputies, carrying, in addition to their service revolvers, one a shotgun and a submachine gun. I must have been a pretty scary fellow to rate all this firepower.

The beautiful young nurse responded in a voice as soft as a feather, "Yes, sir."

Now standing over me was this arrogant SOB. I just wanted to bust him right in the chops. But I quickly discovered that I was strapped onto the bed, both hands and feet.

"Where are you from?"

Having been in the military and flown several different types of Marine Corps aircraft, and also being pretty much a clown at times, I decided to give this prick a hard time since they didn't believe my real story.

"My name is Captain James T. Kirk of the *Starship Enterprise*," remembering the classic old *Star Trek* TV series, one of my favorites. That original series sprung a whole series of sequels, several movies, and a cultlike following from those who would call themselves Trekkies.

"I asked you where you were from, not your name or rank, so let me ask you again. Where are you from?"

Now he was really beginning to piss me off, so I replied, "I am from the planet Vulcan in the O'Ryan Star System, fourteen light-years from this planet. I am seeking out new life and new civilizations, boldly going where no man has gone before."

I could hardly keep a straight face as I continued to dish out names and lines from that old *Star Trek* series. If only I had Spock's ears and eyebrows.

"What is your purpose here? Why have you come?"

"Asked and answered. However, as an emissary from Vulcan, you should treat me with more respect. Vulcan is a member of the United Federation of Planets, as is Earth. I am being monitored, as I have traveled here from the future, although it was an accident that I landed this far back. Why just a little further back, and I may have been looking up at another ugly beast, a Tyrannosaurus Rex. You do not wish to give them reason to send troops forward, do you? Trust me when I say you would be no match for the power and technology of our time, any more than the weapons of your early caveman would be against yours."

With that, the sheriff ordered one of his men to release the restraints, but they stayed close. I tried to stand but collapsed back down. Quickly the nurse was back tending to me and ordering the sheriff and his men out of the room. He left, however reluctantly. This soft-spoken woman could get real feisty when she needed to.

"What is your name nurse?"

"My name is Rachel, sir."

"You don't have to sir me. Call me Ice. All my friends do."

I guess she was in her mid to late twenties, and she had it all—beautiful face, hot body, wonderful smile, and the voice of an angel. Best of all, the third finger of her left wasn't adorned with any rings or any marks of anything having been there.

I knew the sheriff would be back, so I decided to play hurt longer than I actually was. I also needed time to get to know Rachel. I needed a friend or many friends if I were to ever have the opportunity to return to my time. Oh, yes, I thought about the fact that I might never get back to my time. I had to get back to my vehicle and make another run and hope it would take me back to my time. It was my only chance. It would be a million-to-one shot, not to mention that the fuel I needed wouldn't be discovered for another seventy-five years or so. But maybe some scientist could help. "Rachel, do you suppose I could have some coffee and a newspaper?"

"Yes, I'll get them for you, sir … I mean … Ice.

She smiled and blushed slightly and spun around and left the room. She returned within a few minutes with the items I had asked for.

"Do you require cream or sugar for your coffee?"

"No, dear, thank you. Is this today's paper?"

"Yes, it is this morning's edition."

There it was, exactly what I wanted to see—the date. It was June 21, 1947! I had warped back in time 103 years, over a century! Having been a sci-fi junkie in my youth, I was fascinated with time warps and time travel, so I knew a little about it or at least the theories. The thing that most came to mind was that any change in the past could alter the future. Now I had to figure out how to get out of the sheriff's grasp and try to find a way home.

Bright and early the next day, old loud mouth was back with more of his questions, so I decided to come clean. Obviously, my other tact didn't work.

"Look, Sheriff, I must apologize for yesterday. I was just messing with you. All that stuff about Vulcan and time travel was just baloney. The truth is I was trying out a new car for the Bonneville Salt Flats, to try and set a new land-speed record. I must have blacked out and ran out of fuel when everyone came up to me. I guess my silly suit was causing everyone to think I was a Martian or something, so I played along. I am sorry for my behavior."

"Then how do you explain that car? There is nothing like it anywhere. My team has been all over it."

"Sheriff, I will make you a deal. I will loan you the car, and you forget I even exist. Your team can study it, and you can get credit for all you learn from it. How about it?"

"I'll get back to you." He abruptly left the room, but the deputies were still there.

Days turned into almost two full weeks, and I was about to be released. So tomorrow, sometime in the afternoon, they would set me free.

"Here's your coffee and danish, Ice."

"Thank you, Rachel. You sure look beautiful this morning."

She blushed a little. "Why thank you."

"When I get out of here, will you have dinner with me?"

"You ask me that every day, and my answer is still the same, maybe."

"I just like to hear it; as an optimist, it gives me something to smile about and look forward to."

"Oh, by the way, I saw the sheriff talking to Dr. Smith as I came down the hall. I'm sure he will be here next. I really don't like that man."

"Yeah, me too. I fear he wants to dissect me or something."

"Maybe you should escape from here and hide until he forgets about you?"

"I've given that some thought, but I made him a proposition, and he has yet to answer me. If he comes to see me this morning, I'll ask him for his answer. Wrong answer, and I'm gone tonight."

"Here is my address and phone number. You may hide at my place if you need to."

I no sooner hid the piece of paper Rachel had given me than the ol' loud mouth burst in and informed me that they were releasing me tomorrow afternoon. "I'm going to take you up on your proposal, and you are free to go. However, one slight change. You will not leave town, and you will tell me where you are staying at all times. Agreed?"

"Sure, Sheriff. You're the boss." Rachel had been pretending to be busy working around the room and me. She was awaiting his answer as well and left the room once she heard it.

"One of my men will drive you to wherever you are staying, and you will be under constant surveillance. Do you know where you will be staying?"

"Sheriff, I will have to let you know."

"You do that." With that, he left.

Rachel returned with my meal and told me that he had removed one of the two deputies posted outside my room. He was beginning to mellow just slightly; he must have deemed me no threat to the country.

Rachel returned with my dinner at 1800 hours. "The deputy outside was just replaced with a new one. Do you want me to help you slip out of here tonight? I can send him coffee with something to make him sleep."

"No, Rachel, that won't be necessary. He will release me once I have a place to stay. Can you loan me some money so I can get a hotel? I have none with me. I can get a job and pay you back."

"No, I won't lend you money. However, you can stay with me. I own a three-bedroom home, and you can use one until you find a way back to your time."

"But won't that look bad for you? I don't want people to get the wrong idea."

She laughed. "First, I couldn't care less what people think. Second, I'll tell my neighbors you're my brother who has come to live with me. Will that ease your conscience?"

I nodded and thanked her for her generosity.

The next morning, I sent word to the sheriff that I would be staying at 1101 Shady Lane. He had a car drop me there after the doctor signed my release. I figured we'd let him figure out to whom the house belonged.

"There are clothes in the closet of the bedroom. They belong to my brother. I hope they fit. You're about the same size, I believe.

"Rachel, you are a life saver!"

"When I get off duty, I'll fix dinner for us. Until then, just make yourself at home."

People of this time must have spent countless hours listening to the radio. It was an AM station, as that was all they had in those days. Some rich people had a relatively new thing called a television. In my day, almost everyone had a set in every room! It all seemed so strange yet comfortable.

Doc released me, and Rachel pushed me in a wheelchair to the outside entrance where the deputy was waiting. After a short ride, he pulled up in front of this little house with a huge front porch, with white square posts at the corners and on each side of the wide front steps that led to the large porch. It had two wooden swings that hung from chains in the roof of the porch; they were big enough for two or three people. I thanked the deputy for the ride, and he said he would be right here, following the sheriff's orders. At least he had the sense to be in an unmarked car so as not to concern the neighbors.

She had told me earlier that the style of her house was called a bungalow. As I walked up the sidewalk to the front porch, there were flowers of various colors that filled the flowerbed in front of the latticework from the front porch to the ground. I thought what a cool place she had. I retrieved the key she had given me and entered the house.

I went inside and was amazed at the size of the house on the inside since it looked small and cute from the street. She told me she lived alone, but her brother occasionally visited and left a large portion of his clothes there. He was working in London as a news correspondent and wasn't expected back in the States for a couple of years. I found the bedroom with his clothes and tried some on. Luckily, they fit pretty well. Then I lay on the bed, and it was so much more comfortable than the bed I'd been stuck with at the hospital. I stretched out on it and fell sound asleep.

I awakened when I heard the door close. "Jake, where are you?"

"I'm upstairs. Be right there."

I splashed some water on my face and headed downstairs for the kitchen. "Hi, darling. Glad you're home."

"What's this darling stuff?"

"Oh, just wanted to see how it sounded."

"Remember, this is a helping hand, not an invitation to any romance."

We were both talking a little tongue in cheek, but she made it clear this was not some kind of back-door seduction. I respected that and decided I better limit my comments in that area.

"Now, would you like something to drink?"

"Would you happen to have a beer by chance?"

"I do. I'll get it for you. Sit down. Make yourself at home."

I sat on this big overstuffed couch and took a deep breath and a long sigh of relief. She returned with a bottle, a glass bottle no less. The beer was called Stroh's Bohemian, and I took a big pull on it. Man, it was good! She had one as well and sat at the other end of the couch. We talked for hours.

"Would you like another beer while I fix dinner?"

"Sounds good. Can I help?"

"Sure, by staying here, enjoying your beer, and staying out from underfoot." With that, she headed off and returned with another cold Stroh's.

"I love your style, Rachel."

I sat there contemplating how the hell I was going to get home. My only chance was to see if there was a way to get a fuel that would run this thing. Then steal it from the sheriff and blast off out of there. Sounded easy enough, but those were two of the hardest things to make happen. This was a real pickle I was in. Soon Rachel returned and said dinner was ready. As we walked to the kitchen table, she stated, "Now it's nothing fancy, just soup and salad, but it should fill you up."

"Oh, I'm not fussy when it comes to food, and the soup smells great."

"Well, good. I hope you like it."

The dinner was great. She was beautiful, and the conversation was nice until she asked how I was planning to get back to my time. I steered the conversation back to her, her time, and how long she thought she could put up with me. That brought slight laughter from her. She had an early call the next morning, so after we washed and dried the dishes, she went to bed. I couldn't sleep, so I helped myself to another beer and sat in the living room and listened to the radio and big-band music by Dorsey and Miller. I fell asleep there.

I heard movement in the kitchen and went to investigate. There was the lovely Rachel dressed in her white nurse's uniform having coffee and toast. I looked at the clock on the wall; it was just a little before 0500. I joined her with coffee, and we talked briefly until it was time for her to leave.

A month went by, and Rachel and I were becoming great friends. On her days off, we went to local attractions like the zoo, a large park, and the local swimming pool.

She introduced me to the neighbors as a cousin instead of her brother, since they might actually meet him someday.

If we ran into strangers that we happened to talk to, she introduced me as her boyfriend. She had a bit of a mischievous streak in her, which was great, as I did as well. Sometimes we'd make up high-profile jobs we had, such as writers, actors, political figures, and such. We always got a kick out of people's reaction. Still, in my time alone, all I could think about was getting home.

Another month went by, and I was awakened most mornings by birds singing near my open window. It was so strange to hear such a pleasant sound. In my world, one would have to go far from the city to hear anything like that. I wondered how mankind had come so far to give up such simple God-given treats to become slaves to computers and gadgets. This was a very simple time relative to my world, and it felt nice to be there. This time in history was a pleasant time, with the exception of the sheriff's men always following me wherever I went. I wondered what life would be like there for me if I could never return. After all, in two months I hadn't gotten any closer than the first day I arrived. There I would be able to drive cars that I had once only seen in museums and in the hands of collectors.

I was enjoying my daydream when the door suddenly burst open. Rachel stood there with a small table with food and coffee on it. It was breakfast in bed, just like in the old movies. Wow. I had never done this before. I laughed with happiness. This had to be the most wonderful person I had ever met. If I couldn't return, she made being there as wonderful as it could be. I had known many women from all walks of life but never anyone like Rachel.

"Here you are, Mr. Iceman. Hope you like your eggs, bacon, and toast."

"Oh, yes, this looks and smells fantastic!"

I tasted everything. I could not believe the taste. Sure, I had eaten these foods before, but they were all processed and artificially colored and flavored.

"I think I'll marry you!"

With a twinkle in her eye and a sweet smile on her lips, she replied, "Why don't we start with spending more time together and we'll see how it goes?"

"Sure. Just kidding." I had once again opened mouth and stuck my big foot in it.

"I'll be downstairs when you finish. Enjoy."

I did enjoy the meal, and I really enjoyed her company. Funny, I had never really felt like this about a girl before, even when I thought I was in love a few times in the past. All these strange new sensations— birds singing, old-fashioned values, great-tasting food, and a gal that was as beautiful and smart as I had ever met. I hoped I wasn't dreaming—or if I was, that I wouldn't wake up. Oh, and somewhere along the way, she stopped calling me Ice and started calling me Jake. I figured that had to be a good thing ... or maybe that was what I wanted to think.

I finished my wonderful breakfast and headed down the hall to the bathroom. Even that was different. Back home, every bedroom had its own bath. This house had a central bath off the hallway to serve three bedrooms, which I found quite fascinating.

I went downstairs, no Rachel. I walked to the front and saw her talking over the fence with the neighbor woman—again, something that just didn't happen in my time. I picked up a newspaper from the front porch and returned to the kitchen table. I poured another cup of coffee from the old percolator-type pot on the stove. One thing that I missed was my flavored coffee. But hey, there had to be some things that I wished I could bring back from the future. I looked around the kitchen at the old-fashioned appliances and wallpaper. Shoot, they didn't even make that stuff in my time. The linoleum on the floor reminded me of the old TV reruns of *All in the Family* when Archie Bunker would call it *nalowlium.* About the time I opened the newspaper, she returned. "Well, glad to see you all up and about."

"Yes, I am having the best time learning about your time."

She grabbed a coffee for herself and sat down.

"Jake, tell me of the future."

"Don't you mean my past?"

"No, I mean tell me of *the* future."

"I don't know what you mean." I tried my best puzzled face.

"Come on, Jake. I'm not stupid. The things you said to the sheriff in the hospital, the suit you had on when they brought you in, the things you say, and on and on. Oh, and you talk in your sleep, loud enough to wake me and have me open your door and listen. The first time I looked in on you like that, I was worried, but from then on just curious."

"So wow. Well, I'm glad you know. I would have told you before but thought you wouldn't believe me and I'd lose my roommate."

"So will you tell me?"

"I am not sure where to start. It's all so different."

"Well, what do you do there—for a living, I mean?"

"When I graduated high school, I attended a virtual college prepared by the Ohio State University, then six years in the Marine Corps, flying several different types of aircraft, most significantly the F-62 fighter. I had just returned from my service at the end of the war when this scientific group contacted me. Seems they were trying to set a new land-speed record, and they knew of my racing experience and my ability to withstand the pressure of flying at Mach three. It was to test two things: a new fuel and a new suit for the safety of a person at speeds of Mach three or greater. This was a chance to be part of this great opportunity, setting a new land-speed record and driving again at Bonneville."

"Wow, that's fascinating. Tell me more!"

"No, no, it's your turn."

"You know what I do and where I do it. I also went off to college right out of high school, but halfway through, I dropped out and went off to become a nurse. It seemed that most of the girls I knew in college were just there to get an MRS degree."

"Wait," I interrupted, "What is an MRS degree?"

She looked at me strangely and said, "You know, MRS." And she pointed to the third finger of her left hand.

I thought for a second. "Oh, I get it. Duh!"

We both laughed, and she said, "I was bothered by that and decided that a career in nursing was about at the top of the ladder for a woman, short of a doctor, and well, I didn't have the money for all that."

We talked about so many things, each from our own time. For me it was like taking a walk through history, and it was awe inspiring to her, she told me. Suddenly she began to laugh out loud. I looked at her, and she finally pointed to the window, which was behind me. Then I also began to laugh. It was dark! We had apparently talked completely through the day, without so much as needing to use the restroom or want of food and/or drink. Once we realized that, we both needed to relieve ourselves.

"Ladies first!" I said, still chuckling about our combined complete loss of time.

When she returned, I excused myself and went to the restroom. Upon my return, she was starting to fix some dinner.

"No. I am taking you out for dinner. You can't cook tonight. Besides, I want to talk and learn more."

"Big boy, you got a deal!" she replied as she turned off the water she had started to boil.

After we dressed and were ready to leave, I asked, "May I drive your car?"

"Do you know how to drive such a relic as this?"

I informed her that I had driven many and owned a few old relics, as she put it.

She handed me the keys, and away we went. I really enjoyed driving her car. It was a really old car, yet it was like brand-new. It only had eleven thousand miles on it. This old but new Pontiac was a super nice car, and it still had a little of the new-car smell to it. She was red with red leather interior and a black convertible top. It had a big black plastic steering wheel to make this non-power-steering car easier to turn. It must have been eighteen inches in diameter. Huge!

"This is really great. I love this car. But I am afraid you will have to tell me how to get to the restaurant."

"Just go straight and turn left at the third light. Jack's Diner will be on the right in the middle of the block."

We arrived at Jack's Diner. I selected the booth in the far corner so we could continue to exchange information. I was enthralled by her mannerisms, including the way she placed her napkin across her lap, the way she rearranged the silverware to put each item in its proper place, and the dainty way she dabbed the corners of her mouth with her napkin after taking a sip of water. And her insights, how she sometimes seemed to know what I was going to say before I said it, how she seemed to understand easily what I told her of the future, like she had been there, and how she seemed to understand my slang, words or phrases that wouldn't have been known in her time. When she spoke, I listened intently. Her words and her tone of voice were to my ears as a good massage is to a tired back. I let her select the meal for us. I wanted to eat what she ate. She chose something that I guess was common in her time but never eaten in mine. She called it liver and onions with mashed potatoes and gravy. When I looked at her after the waitress walked away, Rachel laughed and said, "Now didn't you tell me to order for you and get what I was having?"

"Yes, but I have never had organ meat to eat. It is very high in cholesterol. The government recommends that it be used only to feed animals because they don't have a problem with cholesterol."

Now it was her turn to seem puzzled. "What is cholesterol?"

When I explained it, she seemed to understand but wasn't alarmed. I found that very curious. Finally, the serving of the food saved me. I thanked the waitress and looked skeptically at the piece of reddish brown meat and potatoes soaking in gravy, covered in cooked onions. She chuckled as she cut into the meat and took a dainty bite. I watched closely, and she seemed to really enjoy it. So I picked up my fork and knife. Next thing I knew, my mouth was going crazy with the pleasure of the taste. To hell with the cholesterol. I was eating good-tasting food.

We enjoyed our food, dessert, coffee, and most of all our conversation. After a second cup of coffee, she said, "It's getting late, Jake. We better go home. I have to work a double shift tomorrow."

"Oh, sure. Sure thing."

I motioned for the waitress and asked for the check. From my wallet, I handed her a Visa card. She just stood there. As I looked up, both she and Rachel were looking at me like I had two heads.

"Sir, what is this?"

"Why, it's my Visa ... oh my goodness, you don't have credit cards!"

I felt my face turn red, as I had never been confronted with a situation like this before. My mind raced quickly, and then remembering a line from an old classic movie, I said, "Where do I go to wash dishes?"

I was waiting for laughter to break the tension, but no, she called to her boss. "Jack, we got another deadbeat here!"

That brought a big man, I assumed to be Jack, on the run. However, by the time he got there, Rachel had laid money on the table.

"What are you some kind of moocher, buddy?" the man said.

"Let's just go, Jake." She wanted out of there before Jack and I tangled.

I drove home, apologizing all the way. She only laughed at me and said, "I want to live in your world where you can pay for a meal with a plastic business card!"

I explained to her about credit cards, debit cards, ATMs, and computers. This was not an easy task. I told her of the newest thing in banking; you could enter an ATM, place your hand on the screen, and a voice would say, "Thank you, Mr. Hendricks. How much do you wish to withdraw?"

"You tell it, and it spits out the money. Cool, huh?"

The next morning I discovered she had the day off, so we worked around the house. I helped her wherever she needed me, cutting grass, weeding the flower garden, and pruning some bushes. By the time the sun was setting in the west, she suggested we go out to dinner and maybe a movie. That sounded like a great idea. "You want to shower first or should I?"

She said, "Age before beauty," and we laughed, and in I went. As I came out of the bathroom, she went in. I sat on the edge of my bed, and a strange feeling came over me, a feeling I had kept in check until now. Something in my mind focused on her being naked in the shower. It had me aroused. I found myself walking into the bathroom naked. It seemed I couldn't stop myself in spite of the likely consequences. She had just stepped into the shower. "Jake, is that you?" I saw her towel being pulled into the shower from the curtain rod. As I stepped in, she put it up in front of her. "Jake, what are you doing?" I just stood there, looking in her eyes. She looked down at my erect penis and quickly back to my eyes. Her towel was getting soaked and likely heavy until it slipped from her hands. I stepped forward and took her gently into my arms. It was the moment of truth. She would either slap me or fall into my arms. I hoped for the latter. She surprised me and quickly slid open the shower curtain and made a dash for her room. I followed right behind, expressing my sorrow for what I had done. She jumped onto her bed and to my amazement said, "Close the door." I did and then fell into her arms. Needless to say, we didn't make dinner or the movie. She later confessed that if I hadn't made a move soon, she was going to. By morning, I forgot all about my time, my past, and thoughts of getting home ... unless I could take her with me.

Over the past two months, she seemed more and more at ease and accepting of where I came from and who I was. Now our relationship had taken a 180-degree turn. I wasn't a roommate anymore, and we no longer would use two bedrooms, or so I thought.

For the next two weeks, we were the happiest couple in the world. And then it happened.

Rachel had gone off to work this one morning, and probably an hour after she left, I heard a loud knock at the door. I rushed to open it, and there was my ol' buddy the sheriff. "Hendricks, we believe we have a fuel that will run your machine, and we want you to check it out and see if you agree."

"Sorry, Sheriff, I'm not the least bit interested."

"Hendricks, I wasn't asking you. I'm ordering you."

"And if I don't follow your orders?"

"Then you will be arrested and turned over to the feds. And your days of playing house with little Nurse Rachel will be over."

I wanted to slug him for that comment, but this was a battle that I couldn't win. "All right, Sheriff. Where and when?"

"At the salt flats. Where else? And I'll bring your funny little uniform. Be ready to leave here at seven forty-five in the morning. My deputy will be out front to deliver you. Oh, and don't get any bright ideas."

When Rachel got home that evening, she saw it in my face. "You have a way back?"

I went to her and tried to hold her, but she pulled away. "No. If you're leaving, it's over. The tears overflowed, but she stood there. "I often feared this day might come; that's why I wasn't in your arms sooner. But over time it seemed more unlikely, and you wore me down. The day you stepped into the shower, I knew it was over for me. I couldn't push you away again."

"Darling, wait. It isn't what you think. The sheriff just thinks they have come up with a fuel that will propel the craft. I doubt seriously that they have."

"And what if they have? What then?"

"Then I ... I, well they won't let me take it from them, so what's the difference?"

"You've answered my question." She ran to her room, and I heard it lock. *Now look what I've done.* I understood though. Yes, I loved her, and yet I couldn't take her with me. There was no room in the craft. *Everything I am is back there in my time, except her.* I hadn't missed home since I fell for her, but it had always been out of reach. And now ... now there was a chance. I took a cold shower and tried to sleep but couldn't. I tossed and turned all night. By morning I was exhausted, mentally and physically. I knew there'd be a knock on the door within an hour. What decision would I make? I really didn't know. My heart said one thing, my head another.

The sheriff didn't know it, but if that fuel worked and I hit Mach three again, who knew where I'd end up. The likelihood was back where I started. I could escape him this time and maybe get back home. But then what kind of life would I have just reliving the past in the future? When the knock on the door finally came, I was no closer to a decision than I was last night when I sent Rachel to bed in tears. Rachel never came out of her room, and off I went, future unknown.

When we reached the salt flats, my craft was there and covered with guys in white coats. The sheriff was also there. He took me aside and asked, "At what speed did you break the barrier and end up here?"

"At a little over Mach three. Why?"

"I don't want you to try to take it that fast. Just to slightly under, and if you don't want something bad to happen to your lover, you best not disappear. You understand?"

"Sheriff, you have my word. I'm done with that time, and there is no guarantee if I warped time that I would get back home." The sheriff had just helped me reach my decision. "Sheriff, if I get home, why would I care about what goes on here in a past that has already passed?"

They fired the craft, and I was told to quickly get suited up and ready to go. I did it quickly. I checked the craft for anything not right. I asked the chief engineer if the canopy was in working order, and he confirmed it was. Everything was in order. I climbed on board, strapped myself in, and closed the canopy. I revived the engine to fifteen thousand rpms and eased her back to an idle. I gave the engineer a thumbs-up, and the crew pushed me to the launch position. The windsock said the wind was at my back, and we were a go. I held the brake until I once again brought the rpms back to fifteen thousand. I released the brake and pushed the accelerator slowly forward to full throttle. I began moving faster and faster. Soon as I broke Mach one, breaking the sound barrier, I climbed to Mach two. The rush was exhilarating. I wanted to take her all the way, but I thought of Rachel and reached for and pulled the canopy release. It malfunctioned. I hit it hard with the side of my fist and pulled it again—nothing. I hit it again, and it blew. I shot skyward, and the parachute brought me down safely. As I floated down, I saw the craft begin to roll and explode into a huge ball of flames. The wind was taking me right toward it. I made it this far only to burn to death in the fiery aftermath? I tugged at the straps to turn myself away from the fire. It worked, but I was very close. The heat melted part of the chute, and I fell nearly one hundred feet, fortunately into a sand dune at the edge of the salt flat. I heard something break. It was my arm and my leg. As the ambulance pulled up beside me, I was laughing. I would soon be back in the hospital right where this whole episode started, and the lovely nurse was going to get an invitation to a wedding, her own. And she would have as her husband the handsome and broken Jake Hendricks.

When the doctors finished with me, they had instructions to bring Nurse Rachel in to look after me. The doctor liked the idea and played along. Of course there had to be a spoiler; my friend the sheriff was pissed and waiting. He forced his way in and began accusing me of deliberately sabotaging the trial and destroying the craft. When he was done bellowing and before I could say a word, a loud but familiar voice told the good sheriff in no uncertain terms to get his fat ass out of this room or the two orderlies that looked like King Kong and mighty Joe Young would help him find his way. The sheriff left so fast it seemed he had a tail wind. "Thanks, guys. I can handle it from here." Rachel ran to me and kissed my bruised and scratched-up face till you couldn't tell lipstick from blood.

Rachel and I went from friends to lovers to husband and wife. We were married, surrounded by our friends and neighbors. It was a fabulous day, and we were so happy. Now if you love happy endings, then stop here.

I'd like to tell you that Rachel and I lived happily ever after, but I can't tell you that. It's like reading a book or watching a movie, and it ends on a happy note, but you want more. You want to see the real ending play out, the next scene. Well, for you brave souls who left contentment behind in search of the real, the untouched, the unfiltered, here it is. You see, there is always more to the story, so venture on, if you dare, and see what happened.

CHAPTER 2
CONTINUE OR NOT

Over the course of the next year, Rachel and I tried to get pregnant, but it was to no avail. I ask if we should see a doctor about it, but she said, "Darling, it will all work out in time, or it may be God's will."

I loved her so much. Whatever she wanted was fine. "Okay, babe, but I thought you wanted kids?"

"I want your kids, but I won't take drugs to make it happen. I see the results of that type of experimentation at the hospital every day. I also don't want to know if you or I are deficient."

I didn't quite understand her thinking but chalked it up to the times. I had to remember that while I loved living in the past, being from the future had to have some effect on the thoughts of this time versus mine. I went along with what she was comfortable doing.

I even found a job as a mechanic at a local gas station. My life was about as perfect as it could be, and then it happened. I was driving to work one morning when I watched a small boy dash out from between two parked cars and directly into the path of the car in front of me. I watched in horror as the small lad was thrown high into the air and across the road. Oh, how I wished Rachel had been with me. I stopped as fast as I could and wheeled to the curb. I jumped out and ran to his aid. That's when I saw it, and I do mean *it*. The right arm was ripped off, and the body was in two pieces, separated at the waistline. The head was now twisted 180 degrees on the upper torso. A horrible sight to behold, but there was no blood, only a small amount of a brown liquid and wires. Wires were like veins hanging out of all the places where the body had separated. It was some kind of android, not a real boy. I breathed a sigh of relief knowing that some young boy wasn't dead. Yet everyone was scrambling around as though it were a real kid. An ambulance came, and the boy was taken away. Police were questioning the man that hit him. I walked over to them.

"Officer, I was right behind this gentleman when it happened, and I saw the whole thing. The thing ran out from between those two cars directly into his path. There was no way he could have stopped. No one could have prevented it from happening."

"Thank you, sir, for your information. Mr. Brown, looks like you are free to go. Now as for you, sir, let me get your information in case we need to contact you."

I gave them what they wanted and then went on to work. The first person I saw upon entering the shop was my friend Joey.

"Hey, Joey, you will never believe what I just witnessed. I saw a boy get hit by a car by the guy in front of me, and I ran to the boy only to find that it was an android. Everyone on the scene acted like it was a live person. How strange is that?"

Joey looked at me like I was crazy and walked away without a word. *Well, he thinks I'm nuts or lying*, I thought and went back to work.

This was almost as weird as when I found that I had traveled back in time! I couldn't wait to tell Rachel about this. I worked through the rest of the day, and when I left, I said good-bye to Joey and the boss, but they both just stared at me and said nothing.

I jumped in my car and sped home. Maybe Rachel could help me make sense of this crazy day! I slid into the driveway and ran in through the side door. Rachel was standing at the kitchen sink when I went running to her. I grabbed her and hugged her tightly, almost as if I was afraid that she too was a figment of my imagination.

She kissed me deeply and pushed her body into mine. That sent us scrambling for the bedroom. We both tore of our clothes and jumped into bed. Our lovemaking seemed more intense than ever before, and I kept her there, nibbling at and kissing her body until I was rested enough to go again. Finally we collapsed in each other's arms from sheer delight and exhaustion.

We lay there in silence for a while, just softly talking and touching each other, until she asked, "Well, dear, how was your day?" She had taken me to a place where I had almost forgotten the events of the day.

"Wow, wait until I tell you. It was so weird."

"What! Why! What happened?"

"That's just it. I don't know!" I then told her that I witnessed a boy being hit by a car and the reaction I got from Joey and the boss.

"That is very strange."

"But here's the weird part. The boy wasn't a boy; it was an android"

She sat straight up with a sad expression on her face. She sat in silence for what seemed eternity and then said, "Jake, did you tell Joey and the boss that part ... the android part?"

"Let me think. Well, I told the police officer on the scene that I didn't understand all the fuss over a machine. Oh, then I told Joey about it, but I haven't really had a chance to talk to anyone else. Why?"

She started to cry softly.

"What! Has this whole town gone nuts? Rachel, what the hell is going on?"

Five minutes it took until she finally stopped crying and started explaining.

"The reason that Joey and the boss and likely the police officer acted so weird when you discussed the boy is because how could you *not* know of this? The world knows of this. It is the biggest thing this world has ever experienced. They must think you are mental or malfunctioning."

"What the hell are you talking about?"

"Jake, you are going to find what I am about to tell you unbelievable. You believe that the year is 1947 and that you somehow warped time and ended up here in the past."

"You mean it's not 1947?" I scoffed.

"No, darling. No, it isn't. It is 2075."

"Come on, Rachel. It's been a long, crazy day. Please don't mess with me."

"Let me tell you. I read of the war you fought in, and it was a bad one. History tells that it came close to destroying all life as we know it. It was the cryleon gases invented by the Japanese and used by both sides during World War III."

"Yes, I remember that gas. We had it, and in fact I dropped many bombs containing that gas. It was very effective in killing many enemy combatants."

"Jake, what they didn't know at the time was these gases left a residual poison in the ground and in the water. The contamination spread everywhere. People were sick, and by 2055, people started dying, and all the scientists said it was irreversible. It would take at least twenty to thirty years before the ground again would be safe to grow anything fit for human consumption. Because of that war, most of the world started to become void of all life, plant and animal. The plants first absorbed the poison. The livestock ate the plants and either died or became poison themselves. It didn't take long before the answer became clear. It would take ten years, and the earth would be void of life. Fortunately, we had done much with robotics, mainly to use as soldiers during the war. Since everything was affected, even the oceans and the fish, those that didn't die were also tainted and deadly to eat." I didn't find what she was saying so incredible. After all, I had warped time. I knew of the gas, and what she said about robotics was true. Then it hit me.

"I didn't see it because I was here. I literally jumped over that time! Oh my God!"

"That is correct. We already had the technology to build droids that were so real, and so the scientists came up with an outrageous idea" transplant the brain of a living person into the droid. Then we could survive. It was to be the only way we could. This whole idea was very controversial; many thought it was wrong to play God. Yet others argued God had given us the knowledge to save ourselves from extinction. A scientific team was commissioned to figure out how to do it, and as it turned out, it was rather simple. The doctors were trained how to do it, the governments of the world approved it, and then it was simply a matter of how to determine the order in which the people would be selected. Here in the US, the president proposed a state-by-state lottery to make the selection of who went first. Every person's social security number was entered into the lottery, and television cameras watched the drawing. From 9:00 a.m. until 5:00 p.m. Mondays through Fridays, the numbers were pulled, and each state kept going until every person was identified.

"The operations began immediately with the first group of people whose numbers were pulled. Some people refused to have the operations. Some said it was wrong, some said they were too old, and some gave their place in line to another loved one. The government didn't interfere with their decisions, and the doctors worked long and hard.

"It took ten years to complete the operations, and many with larger lottery numbers died. Infants were placed into the bodies that resembled a five-year-old, changed every five years until age eighteen, and then placed into an adult body. A person had to be at least one and a half years old before the operation could be done. Fifteen different body styles were developed, and a person was given a body that was similar to his or her existing bodies. Anyone who wanted a different body had to go to the end of the line. That stopped the problem of everyone wanting to look like models. These bodies are indestructible, and in the rare case that one malfunctions, you are simply removed and placed in another. In fact, today it is a huge business."

"You said most of the world. Are there any real people left to bring back the human race?"

"Yes, the continent of Australia was the only one where no part of the war was fought. The continent was cleared and irrigated for growing crops and raising the animals that are eaten. Huge desalination plants were built that could remove the salt as well as any poisons. Fleets from every nation came to fill their cargo bays with food and water to the deliver to the rest of the world. That is how we were prevented from playing God!"

"Rachel, what about … I mean, are you …"

"Would it really matter if I were, Jake? I am still the Rachel you fell in love with, aren't I?"

"But you're from Australia, so you must be human."

I slid away from her a bit. I was repulsed by the thought that she might be a droid. Had I been making love to a machine? I just wanted to leave, run away somewhere. But I had to know for sure.

"Jake, suppose I am human, and we were in an automobile accident, and I lost a leg and an arm and had to wear prostheses. My face was scared badly, and I had to have plastic surgery. Would you no longer love me?"

I thought for a minute and then answered, "Of course I would still love you."

"Would you no longer want to hold me or make love to me?"

And again I responded in the affirmative.

"Then wouldn't I still be the Rachel you fell in love with?

"Well, yes, I think so ... no, I know so."

"Now suppose I am a droid. Wouldn't my body just be one giant prosthetic? Am I not warm to your touch? And yes, I do feel the same sensations I would when we make love as a flesh-and-bones body would. Yet I won't age, and I won't ever stop loving you, because I *am* real. I would still have my own brain, and since the soul is within the brain, I even have a soul, just as you do."

I sat there pondering the whole premise, my mind wanting to believe it made no difference, wanting to accept her. It was the emotional side of my brain wrestling with the logical side. Then my mind jumped the track.

"Why does it appear to be 1949?"

She laughed at the way my mind jumped.

"Our technology had become so sophisticated that it created two classes of people, those who could deal with it and those who couldn't. The governments of the world were now at peace. The Federation, as it became known, felt that the sophistication was becoming too great for us to handle. It was decided that we needed to relive and rethink what we had done. So a more peaceful time was chosen. We locked away all of our advanced technology where it is only used if absolutely needed. The hope is that we will live and grow into the new world as it actually happened on earth during that time. We think some day we will find another world that God has built, and then ... well, who knows."

Rachel never told me the answer to the question, and at times I was convinced she was definitely human, but sometimes I felt the opposite. For a while, I tried and tried to figure it out. There was no way, short of hurting her, to know. She felt, tasted, smelled, and functioned in every way as did a human being. Finally I decided that if I could find no evidence to the contrary, she was human, and I settled for that, although I knew all to well that in a few years it would become obvious!

If she were human, that would be one explanation for her wanting to be with me, and we were trying to get pregnant. However, that wasn't working, leading to the conclusion that she was a droid. But I was deeply in love with her. There was no denying that. And what would I do without her?

I chose to believe she was human and from that day forward would never discuss this subject again ... until.

THE END ... "OH NO," YOU SAY.

CRYPTURE 9
King of the Blacktop

The sun had set approximately an hour ago on what had been a glorious, sunny summer day in June. The birds and insects were all singing their sunset songs when suddenly the quiet of the evening was broken by the sound of screaming tires breaking loose from the pavement beneath them. The smell of exhaust permeated the warm night air as three highly horse-powered beasts launched to escape one another and be the victor of the race. The goal was to be the first to cross the white line illegally painted perpendicularly across the road one quarter of a mile away. To the victor went the bragging rights of the night and the starting or continuation of a reputation of being the fastest car in town.

Just as a gunslinger of the Old West had to be ready to be called out into the street for a showdown and risk his life against all challengers, so did the fastest car. The owner must prove over and over that he is and remains king of the blacktop.

An era has passed, the era of street drag racing, which was the sport of any red-blooded teen or young adult male who had ever owned or built a car from post wartime until the late sixties.

My name is Jake Grant, but most of my friends and acquaintances knew me as Butch, and I was definitely a part of the scene. Now fifty years later, as I look back on this time and my entry into it, I see what was never even in my thoughts as I looked to the future. The drive-in movies and the drive-in restaurants were also an important part of the scene and my life then. The fifties and early sixties were probably the best of these times. In my opinion, this was the best time in American history. That was a time when America led the world in the production of goods and services. They were great eras where almost anybody that wanted a job need only apply. A time before massive dependence on the federal government, rampant drug use, high inflation, politically lost wars, powerful unions that no longer served their membership, massive national debt, terrorism, leaders who spit on the Constitution and weren't held accountable for it, a time when a vocal minority demanded we turn our backs on God, and a host of other issues weakened the fabric of a nation from its once proud posture.

In towns large and small all across the American landscape, young guys like me and my friends were stacking their prized steed up against other like-minded young males, and even some females, all to determine who would be king (or queen) of the blacktop. Being king didn't get us any trophies, cash awards, or even mention on the daily news. However, in the circle of street racers, everyone knew the pecking order. In the "Ohio Valley," as it was referred, the same events were taking place. The Valley's main industry at that time was the steel mills. They ran three shifts a day to meet the need for their products. Small bars and grilles sat on street corners close to the plants and served each shift of workers. It was very common to see some guys sitting there clean and having breakfast or coffee while others with dirty clothes and faces would be having a beer or drink to wind down as their shift had just ended and before heading home. The mills provided good wages and a lot of jobs that cleared the way for many other businesses to grow up around them and prosper. Today, many of these mills have been torn down or sit rotting as a sad reminder of our more prosperous times.

I grew up in one of these small mill towns. Up and down the Ohio River, we loved our high-school sports, and the rivalries were intense. Football and basketball led the way, with wrestling and track and field as well. However, no matter what sport you played or didn't play, I and every cat and chick dreamed of his or her first car. We counted the days until we became the ripe old age of sixteen and could apply for and receive a license to drive a motor vehicle. Some wanted to drive, and others just wanted to be able to sit up close to their boyfriends and enjoy their newfound freedom. Bench seats were far more desirable than buckets, as it allowed her to sit right next to you with her arm around your neck. Like me, are you fortunate enough to remember those times?

Several elements helped to bring the drag-racing era to life. First was a large surplus of old cars that could be bought cheap by teens. These old cars would be souped up and customized by their new and proud, young owners, making them unique. American car companies were mostly headquartered in Detroit and built these now individualized cars in cities large and small around the country. They were built by American workers with pride. With very few exceptions, cars for the public were not manufactured during the years 1942 through 1945, due to the war effort of WWII. Therefore, people kept their cars longer, and kids needed to find cars from the twenties and mostly the thirties. That created the hot rods: strip off the fenders and running boards, the hood and side curtains, and drop in a bigger motor. Those cars still exist and are now known as street rods. They are being built again, mostly of fiberglass. Today I own or have owned quite a few of these cars, trying to relive those magical days gone by.

The second thing that was needed was a place to meet to hang out and size up the competition. A fast car was the ticket of admission, along with a willingness to put your pride up against another's. Beat the fastest gun and become the fastest gun. The drive-in restaurant was made to order as just such a place. One such place was located on old US Route 40, a.k.a. National Road between the towns of Wheeling and Elm Grove, West Virginia. That place was made to order for the place to hang. This drive-in restaurant was one of a chain of nice family restaurants with great food at reasonable prices where businessmen would have lunch and families could have weekend lunches and dinners. They had nice inside dining facilities as well as ample parking around the perimeter of the parking lot and directly in front of the restaurant. In between were the stalls—the rows of covered stations with a speaker and menu board at each parking spot that were used for ordering food and drink. Thus the term drive-in restaurant was coined. I ate lunch there almost every working day.

This created another time you didn't have to leave your car, that symbol of independence and adulthood.

A waitress in a uniform on roller skates would bring your order right to your car, prop the tray on your side window, collect the money, and return later when you blew your horn to remove the tray and trash.

Another wonderful place that a guy and his gal could be alone was the outdoor drive-in movie theaters. It was a great place where I could go to be alone with my girlfriend. Not sure if I ever saw a complete movie. The term was necking; that was what we called kissing. That went on until you were able to see how far you could go. It started at dusk with reminders to stock up on snacks and pop. A short bit of world news, and then a cartoon, and the first feature. Intermission followed that with more reminders to visit the concession stand and reload on goodies like popcorn, burgers, dogs, candy, and pop. The evening concluded with a second feature. There are only a few drive-in theaters left in America today, another victim of runaway inflation and the high cost of land. Many a kid of the next generation would be conceived in the backseat of a car during the double feature.

Friday and Saturday nights were the big times for us, but after school let out for summer break, every night could bring the teens with their rods. We would congregate, and the challenges for dominance would begin. The proving grounds would be an unfinished stretch of road that would eventually become part of Interstate 70 highway system, but for now it was just a bypass that took you from old Route 40 to Elm Grove. This would become one of the most popular proving grounds, the court where the winners would be adjudicated and reps would be earned. There was a pad already built, which was designed to eventually be a trucker's weigh station, but for now it provided a flat, straight stretch of road. A wild and crazy guy named Bill marked off in paint the starting line and a finish line, exactly one quarter of a mile apart. The pad provided a place where the bystanders and the next set of combatants could park and watch or wait their turn. Now the police weren't stupid, and they soon got the word about goings-on, and they would occasionally sit at the far end of the pad for such events so they could nab the perpetrators.

After the first racers got caught (fortunately, I wasn't one of them), word quickly spread throughout the drag-racing community like a Southern California wild fire. To counteract this problem, spotters were sent out to check and see if there were any unwanted visitors at the pad. Since the unmarked police cruisers weren't used much in those times, a black and white was easy to spot. Of course, without the aid of cell phones, the spotter would have to run the stretch and return with the word.

This constant surveillance curtailed the number of incidents of racing. Complaints subsided, and the police were satisfied and slowly dropped off the number of times they spent much time at the pad. This had us find new suitable stretches of blacktop. The police would usually return when one of those anti-fun-loving persons—we called them fogies or squares—witnessed such an event and called in to report it. Now I'm one of those fogies.

You probably figured out how I know so much about that place and time. I lived it, and this is my story. I remember one summer in particular. It was the second summer immediately following my high-school graduation. It would be my last summer before leaving the valley for good. It was a warm summer night in early June. It was early, around six at night. First on the scene was a '60 red-and-white Corvette that pulled into a stall—Tommy Wilson, nicknamed Slick, with his girlfriend, Sally. In the next stall was a '62 triple-black Vette owned by Jack Mills, and his girl Sharon was by his side. Jack and Slick were good friends who met when Jack bought his Vette. On the other corner was a black premiered '50 Chevy Fleetline, sporting a 327-ci small-block Chevy motor and a 4-speed tranny. Just rolling in was a '59 Pontiac Catalina belonging to Butch Grant; that's me. Seated next to me was my not quite steady girl, Sherry Hale. I was hot for that girl, but I was always number two with her, and when Bob Sampson was around, she would go out with him, not me. But the real love of my life was Mary Beth Smith, ever since I met her at her birthday party in eighth grade, kissed her in the closet of her house while playing post office, but I digress.

My Pontiac was a sleeper. Beneath its sleek, metallic desert-sand finish lurked a beast of an engine, a factory stock 389 with a triple carburetor setup Pontiac called Tri-Power. As time progressed, more and more cars belonging to the drag-racing set began to filter in, and soon the tooling began. "Tooling" was a local term of the day meaning to drive into the parking lot and just circle rather than park. You could not park for long without ordering, so tooling was the antidote. Also, it let others hear your mill (engine), which might lead to a drag.

If someone wanted to challenge you, they would pull out of their parking space and get right behind you and circle with you. If you didn't want to drag, you pulled into a parking space, but if you did, you would head out the back entrance and up the ramp to the unfinished portion of the interstate.

It wasn't long before the action started. A black-and-yellow 1956 Chevy Bel Air two-door hardtop cruised in and began to tool. This was a great-looking car with a nice rake. After the second pass, Sally and Jack traded places, and Slick pulled his '60 Vette out and jumped in up on the Bel Air's tail. The Bel Air pulled out on the ramp with Slick right behind him. Immediately, other cars, me included, headed for the weigh-station lot. The Vette and the Bel Air pulled up to the line. Someone always volunteered to be the starter and drop the flashlight. Tires squealed, and the Vette took a jump on the Bel Air, but soon the Bel Air screamed passed the Vette. At the end, the Bel Air took him by two lengths. Several spotters were at the finish line to give testimony of the victor. The two participants continued to the end of the freeway, off the ramp, and back to the Big Boy, as did the spectators.

When everyone returned, they were out of their cars and talking to the participants, and everyone had something to say about it. Like with any competition, there were some bad sports who couldn't abide losing, and once in a great while, a fight would ensue. But for the most part, it was like a club. If you got beat, you worked on your car to make it faster and tried again.

More cars came and went as the evening wore on, but most regulars knew that sometime around midnight a certain '55 Chevy two-door sedan adorned in flat-black primer would roll in, and some action would really get going. Al and Bill were two longtime friends that loved to build and race cars. This '55 was their current masterpiece.

As the story goes, Al bought this '55, two-door sedan from a little old lady. It was a solid car sporting a 265-ci V-8 motor and a power glide tranny. Well, that was to quickly change, because Al's girlfriend had a '60 Chevy Impala, a.k.a. Kathy's Clown, packing a 348-ci motor and a 4-speed tranny. So our boys had a plan. Pull the combo out of the Impala and swap it with the '55 drive train. They did it, and while they were rebuilding the engine, they installed a posi-trac rear end with 3:56 gears, tubbed the rear wheel wells to fit the widest set of tires that could be found, and fitted the front to fit the narrowest. The engine was bored sixty over and then equipped with racing pistons, a full race cam, solid lifters, and three-twos before it was put into the light '55 sedan body. Engine numbers like 348, 389, and 327 didn't signify horsepower but referred to size based on cubic inches of displacement. Al's '55 was ready to rock and roll! Within a week or so, the swap was done, and both cars were back on the road. You'd think they could have stopped there, but no way. Seems the Kathy's Clown mysteriously caught fire out on a lonely country road and was totally destroyed. Kathy was paid off by the insurance, and she bought another, a '61 Chevy Impala two-door hardtop, referred to as a "bubbletop." It was a sweet-looking white car with a red stripe between the side, bright metal strips. It was a very late build and almost at the end of the model year and somehow ended up with an early 409-ci motor, a motor that wasn't available until the '62 model. Since the car was technically a used car, no one really knew exactly how that happened, but we suspected it was a dealer order. Al would occasionally bring Kathy's car to Elby's and match it up with a few brave souls. However even the 409 was no match for the '55, christened the Black Marauder, he and Bill had built. In fact, I raced the 409 and beat it badly with my '59 Catalina.

I got to know Al and Bill after a while, and they had a garage they rented in Elm Grove, big enough to hold about seven or eight cars. I was able to put my '57 white-and-coral Pontiac Star Chief there. The plan was to swap out the motor from my '59 Catalina, a plan that never materialized. The summer all too quickly came to an end. I wasn't sure where my life would take me. I had a job working for my dad, who built houses and pools. I had lots of friends from high school, but they were beginning to move away, going to college, the military, and seeking employment. My secret love had married someone else, and my semisteady moved away to Columbus, Ohio. There were a few other girls I went out with from time to time but no one special. My two faves were out of circulation and GUD, a term of the day meaning geographically undesirable. So I decided to leave town. My plan was to seek my fame and fortune, as it were. I had no idea how I would do that, but I figured I had a much better chance in a bigger city. It was a plan I almost didn't make, due to being involved in a terrible automobile accident. Fortunately, I walked away from it. The choices were Columbus, Ohio, or the suburbs of DC. I had good buddies in those two towns that I could room with. In the beginning, I chose the latter.

Time does things to people, like change their goals and ideas. I did move with a high-school classmate, Nick, to the suburbs of Washington, DC. Several people that I knew had moved there, and I had two different buddies there that we could room with. I was able to secure work in the DC area rather quickly, but Nick had a little more trouble. Then when he severely broke his ankle playing touch football in the parking lot one Sunday, he went back home, never to return. To this day, he still lives back home. Even though it was a six- to seven-hour drive, I was highly motivated in order to have a girl to go out with. I drove home as often as I could afford it. It was hard to make many new friends in DC in the beginning.

I heard through the grapevine that Kathy got pregnant and she and Al got married. Bill and Al, who were almost inseparable, saw less and less of each other. A few months later, Al was drag racing his infamous '55 Chevy when almost at the end of the quarter mile a tire blew and the car went over the hill. Al died that night in a ball of flames inside the car. They said when they finally put the fire out it had burned so completely that all that was left of Al was a skeleton and that his skeleton hands were still on the remains of the steering wheel.

As for Bill, he went on building cars and racing them; he was trying to hang on to a dying era. It wasn't long after Al's death that Bill was building a car to race, replacing the freshly built engine and replacing the automatic tranny with a four-speed. Upon completion, he was revving up the engine when the clutch plate blew, shattering and ripping through the bell housing and floorboards, taking off the better part of his right foot.

This is where this story both ends and begins. The following June, I was back in town with my new girl, Susan, and we were sitting at Elby's Big Boy having something to eat and drink, and I was telling her stories from the glory days of street racing. A guy with a '62 Ford Fairlane started to tool. Well, since I hadn't raced my big pony in some time, I looked over at Susan for her approval. She must have been caught up in the stories, as I was surprised when she nodded. So out I went, pulled up behind the Fairlane, and off we went.

Now the starting line had worn a little thin but was still visible. The Fairlane took the right lane, so I pulled up beside him in the center lane. A male spectator ran out between us to start us when there. But before he could, from out of nowhere came the Black Marauder of Al's. It pulled up and stopped in the outside lane. The windows were shaded so you couldn't see inside. But how could this be Al's old Marauder? It had been totally destroyed by the crash and fire that killed Al. I was now sandwiched between the Fairlane and this ... this clone of Al's car. Out of the corner of my eye, I saw what appeared to be a flicker from within the car. I turned my head quickly, but whatever it was disappeared in an instant. At that moment, the starter jumped up and dropped the flashlight, and we were off. The Fairlane was no match for my swift Catalina, but all we saw of that '55 were its taillights as it beat both of us off the line and pulled farther and farther away from us. At the end of the race, the '55 just kept going until it was out of sight. The guy in the Fairlane and all the spectators, including me, returned to Elby's Big Boy. Upon our return, everyone parked and jumped out to discuss the '55, nothing about my victory. "Butch, who do you think was driving that car? It looked exactly like the Black Marauder."

"I don't know unless it was Bill. Is it possible that perhaps Bill built a duplicate of the car and he's been out of the hospital for some time now?"

We all sat around and speculated about it when some clown said, "Maybe it's Al's ghost driving it."

Everyone scoffed and laughed. That broke up the powwow, and all returned to their respective cars. However, everyone was back the next night. I rode out with John, a friend of mine with a pretty fast '57 Chevy Bel-Air. Word had spread like wildfire, and the place was packed. Some guy with a hopped-up '32 Ford three-window coupe rumbled through, and John jumped on him, and off we went. Again just like the night before, the '55 pulled up in the third lane. Once again a starter stepped out of the crowd with his flashlight. Just as we were about to launch, the dim glow of a cigarette lighter being lit revealed someone in a black hood but didn't reveal the face. Before I could say anything to John, we launched. Again the Black Marauder was way out in front of both of us until his taillights disappeared into the darkness. Once again we all returned to Elby's and compared notes. Several people saw the light from within the car, but no one saw his face, only the hood over his head. One of my friends that knew Bill ran into him one day and was told flatly that he did not have a car like the Black Marauder nor did he know anyone who did. He also said the friendship he and Al once enjoyed became very strained after Al's marriage to Kathy. Bill had only one real friend, Al, and he resented Kathy for breaking up their time together. Bill became a real recluse and was generally only seen when Al had a chance to go out with him. Once the baby came, they saw each other one last time. He told Al that Kathy had tricked him into marriage by deliberately getting pregnant and trying to break up their friendship. They got into a fistfight and never spoke or saw each other again. I was also told Bill refused to go to Al's funeral. He blamed Kathy for that as well, said Al needed him when they raced and Al was alone that fateful night.

The next day being Sunday, Susan and I had an early breakfast and then headed back to DC. I told my friends from back home that now lived in the DC area about the big mystery. Everyone had a thought about it, but nobody deemed it that newsworthy to keep the conversation going.

The next couple of weeks went by, and stories were relayed to me from back home that the mysterious '55 Chevy was always there in that third lane whenever a race was to happen. Yet no one ever saw the car anywhere else or ever saw the face of the driver. It always ended the same. The '55 would win the race and disappear into the darkness. Rumors started to fly, and everyone was on the lookout to solve the mystery.

It had been about a month since that fateful weekend when I was home and the Marauder was first spotted. The following weekend was a holiday, so I had Friday off and decided to go home. That Thursday night right after work, I picked up Susan and pointed my car home, and off we went. I hoped that leaving then would let us avoid the logjam at the tunnel on the Pennsylvania Turnpike. If so, I could make it in about five hours; if not, it could add three to four hours to the trip. Luck was with me, and we sailed through. It was the wee hours of the morning when I pulled into the driveway of my house. I knew the key would still be hidden on the molding above the door. Susan slept in my sister's old room next to mine, as she had moved to Columbus to pursue a nursing career. Also I remembered from my high-school days how to step down the hallway to avoid the squeaks in the old floors to avoid waking anyone. Susan literally followed in my footsteps and ducked into her room, and I headed for mine. Mom would tell me many years later that she never went to sleep until she heard me sneaking down that hallway. I always wondered why she slept so late. Now I knew. Dad, on the other hand, could sleep through an earthquake and would be up at five every day. I would always find him at the kitchen table reading the paper, drinking coffee, and smoking a Pall Mall cigarette. The latter killed him at the ripe old age of sixty-two. A habit I fortunately never took to. But I did so enjoy those moments with Dad, a chance for us to talk man to man. He certainly was without a doubt the man I respected most in the entire world. I was awed by his knowledge and common sense. I thought he was smarter than any teacher I ever had. But there was one other man I had a great deal of respect for. He was the man who taught me a skill for two years. In fact he reminded me a lot of my dad. His name was Bud Kessler, and he was the vocational drafting teacher in my high school for my junior and senior years. He was very much like my dad in that he spoke softly, but you always knew he was in control, and he truly cared about you and your future. Both men are gone now, but they live on in all the people they touched.

My mother really hoped I would marry Susan, so my first night in town, I went to Elby's with some buddies, and she stayed and spent time with Mom. I waited for someone to race, not because I really wanted to race but to see if that '55 was still roaming around looking for another drag race. I didn't have to wait long before a black '49 Merc came through. *Boom, I'm on him.* He accepted the challenge by heading for the exit. The Merc was ahead of me and pulled into the right lane. Everyone thought the right was the fastest lane and tried to get it if possible. We lined up, and before the start of the race when another car pulled up, it was him. Well, actually, I couldn't see him or whoever was driving, but it was Al's car or a lookalike to the former king of the hill. It was like déjà vu, but what was his game? Why didn't he join up at the end of a race like everyone else did? It really stirred the imagination. I looked over just as he lit a cigarette and glanced my way. The light from his cigarette lighter for an instant allowed me to get a look at him.

The starter started the cars, and the other two launched. I started driving but not trying to catch them; it was too late. The taillights of the Black Marauder got smaller and smaller until they were no longer visible. I returned to Elby's and sat there staring out into space.

John said, "Butch, what's the matter? You look like you've seen a ghost!"

"I think I did, kinda."

"Yeah right. Again, what's the matter?"

"John, I know you're gonna think I'm loony tunes, but when we were about to start, the driver of the '55 lit a cigarette, which he always did, right? But everyone who ever saw him only saw the light from the lighter and the glowing end of his cigarette. His hood always covered his face. Tonight he glanced my way, and I saw his face!"

"Well, go on! Who was it?"

I hesitated to say it. "It was a skull grinning at me!"

"You mean he was wearing a mask?"

"I don't know … I didn't think it was then, but what else could it have been, right?"

"Sometimes you can be such a nut!"

But something nagged at me. Something didn't seem to fit. "Why would someone put on a mask, duplicate Al's car, come out to race, always win, and never come back to claim his accolades?"

"Hell, I don't know. Maybe just to get the reaction he's getting."

"Well, tomorrow night, I will find out for sure." We ordered a couple of Big Boys with fries and Cokes and talked about other things but always came back to that subject when one of us had a thought. When I got home, I snuck into Susan's bed for a little fun and then headed for my room before someone caught me. I stared at the ceiling and made my plan. Once I thought I had it, I rolled over and went to sleep.

The next morning, I reviewed my plan in my mind. Tonight I would ride with John. I knew that he was planning to race, and when the Black Marauder appeared, I would slip out of his car and jump in on the passenger side. If he was still wearing that mask, I'd rip it off and see who was playing this elaborate trick. I told Susan I had something to do the next night and I would be back home around ten o'clock.

The day was spent with Mom, Dad, and Susan. It went by quickly, and there I was sitting in Elby's when John pulled in. I got into his car to verify that he was going to race that night. "Yeah, man, I just added a four-barrel intake and a big 750 holly carb. I'm going after Alex tonight."

"Can I ride with you? I'll get out while you line up, before you take off."

"You'd have to get out 'cause I don't need any extra weight!"

"I will 'cause I'm going to jump into that black '55 before the starter drops the flashlight. Be sure to take the middle lane; that '55 is always in the left. I might not have enough time to cross two lanes to get in that car."

"Man, are you goofy?"

"Maybe, but I have to know who's driving that car."

"Okay, man, it's your funeral."

"Cool, so we just need Alex to show."

It wasn't but about half an hour when Alex pulled in and John jumped all over him. So we headed for the spot. I knew I had to be fast. I would have seconds to get out of John's car and into Al's.

We pulled up to the line, and again the Black Marauder appeared out of the darkness. He must have been driving up with his headlights off, making it appear as if he was coming out of nowhere. It was an old trick of Al's and of Bill's to turn off their lights and slip up behind you, then blast their horn or slightly bump you in the rear. They had scared the crap out of me many a time with that stunt.

I jumped out of John's car, crouched low, and ran around behind it. I slipped up to the passenger door of the Black Marauder and jerked it open. But before I could jump in, they launched, tossing me to the ground. I jumped up and ran to the side of the road where the onlookers were parked. I stood there and watched as the three cars disappeared into the night, and I caught a ride back to Elby's with an onlooker. I didn't say a word as we drove back to Elby's. What I had seen as I opened the door were skeleton hands on the steering wheel, skeleton feet on the petals, and a skull that looked at me and said in a gravelly voice, "Hey, kiddo!"

The only person that ever called me kiddo was Al! To say I was in shock was a gross understatement. I know what I saw, I know what I heard, and no, I had not been drinking. But how could I tell anyone of this? I would be on my way to Saint E's for sure! Saint E's was short for Saint Elizabeth's, the local mental institution. I sure didn't want that, so I buried the secret inside myself. Every time anyone raced there, the Black Marauder was in the third lane. Now I—and probably only I—knew it *was* the Black Marauder. Many more weekends found me back in my old hometown.

But time was marching on, and I had a date with some guys at Parris Island at the end of summer. I found the time between those trips became longer and longer. It was June of the last summer that I would have for drag racing. I was determined to get into Al's car if it killed me. I had to know the how and why of this, and if I could never tell anyone, at least I would know how this could happen on God's great earth. I would soon find it had more to do with hell than heaven.

The last Friday night in July, I was back home talking to all my friends at Elby's. I hitched a ride with Jake, a guy who was waiting for a certain black '55 Chevy. Seems he had a notion his new 409 Chevy was going to be enough to put this shoebox in its place. I didn't have the heart to tell him that 409 would not cut it against a car that had beaten every contender that ever came his way. "Jake, you know that he never appears until you line up with another car."

"Yes, I know. A friend is bringing a '62 Doge Dart with a max-wedge motor." We'll line up, and hopefully that Marauder will show up."

"Jake, let me ride out with you, and I'll get out as you line up, okay?"

"Sure, but you gotta get out."

"Yeah, I know—weight."

We no sooner finished our burgers than the Dart pulled in and began to tool. We gulped down our Cokes and blew the horn to have the tray removed. Once removed, we blasted out behind the Dart, and away we went. I asked him to take the middle lane in case the Black Marauder happened to show up. He agreed when I told him my plan. We finally reached the stretch were the action would take place. Jake took the center lane as planned. Sure enough, just as we staged, the black '55 appeared in the third lane, as it did whenever two dueling chariots would show up to test their metal, out of nowhere. I had to be quicker this time. I jerked the door open and jumped in just as the three cars launched. "Welcome aboard, kiddo," the deep, gravely voice said. A cold chill ran up my back as I realized what I had done. Being there was not what I expected. Frankly I don't know what I expected. He laughed in that spine-chilling voice, and the bones that once were hands gripped the steering wheel. He wore only a black-hooded, full-length coat that was open in front, and he was literally nothing but a skeleton. He smoked his cigarette, and the smoke just swirled around his chest bones when he inhaled. He held it hanging low between his teeth, just as he did when he was alive. I sat there in fear, sweating from fear. "I can smell your fear, kiddo." Again he laughed. I was half sick to my stomach now, wondering if I was about to die by his boney hands. Or had I crossed a plane into some kind of twilight zone? I could almost hear Rod Sterling telling the tease at the beginning of the show. They say that when you are about to die, your whole life flashes before you. It did. I was certain I was doomed. I just didn't know how the end would come. So I started to ask the questions that had put me in this precarious position.

"Al … it is you … isn't it?"

"Yes! It's me, kiddo, or what has become of me"

"But how, how did all this happen to you?"

"I don't know exactly, but I heard the tire blow, and the car began to fishtail, and I could not control it. I was going so fast the car finally flipped and rolled over and over down the hill. As it burst into flames, I thought I saw a man in a black cape with a walking stick. He asked if I wanted to live. I screamed, 'Yes!' 'Will you give me your soul?' And I again yelled, 'Yes!' That was the last thing I remembered until I was driving the Marauder again … and again and again. I found myself pulling up to stage and race. When the quarter-mile line passed, I let off the gas, but she kept going, and then I was pulling up to the staging line again. Over and over again, it's always the same." His gravely voice began to break up. "Satan sure has a sick sense of humor, and I would hardly call this living!"

Then I saw him, for just a second. The devil himself—black cap, cane, and all—right in front of the car but *staying* right in front of it, and I seemed to hear him say, "Do you want to live, Butch?"

"Yes, but no, I won't give you my soul. I would die first!"

The next thing I knew, I was rolling on the ground back at the starting point, as though I never made it into the Marauder. Was I really in the car talking to Al, or did I simply fall, hit my head, and imagine it? I believe the former. I thanked God I was free from the hell that Al was enduring. As I sat up quickly. I saw the brake lights of my friend's car come on, followed quickly by the car in the right lane, and I watched the Marauder's taillights continuing off until they where out of sight. I felt sorry for Al and his never-ending hell on earth and wondered if God would ever intercede and free him. What would happen when the end to drag racing was brought about by the completion of Interstate 70?

I don't go back there much anymore; life requires moving on. But I often think of Al and those days. All in all, they were good days, the likes of which we will never see again.

THE END ... SURE 'BOUT THAT?

CRYPTURE 10
The Rae

PROLOGUE

As the sun was just lifting up out of the sea, the thirty-two-foot pleasure yacht, *Rae of Love*, weighed anchor, and we cast off the bow and stern lines. This magnificent navy blue yacht was free to roam the sea. She motored slowly out of port and then hoisted her sails and pointed her bow westward toward our destination, Hawaii. The wind filled her sails, and the sleek bow of the yacht sliced through the calm sea like a knife through hot butter. Our four-person crew was off on a great adventure to sail the seas, and now under full sail, we would choose the next port of call. My husband, Dale, was the captain, a forty-year-old retired navy commander. Our best friends, Bill and Priscilla Gordon, and I completed the crew. We did almost everything together, and this trip that had been planned for some time was no exception. Little did anyone on board know what perils awaited us as we sailed into our future.

Dale and Bill were college buddies and attended the Naval Academy in Annapolis, Maryland. Bill played football, and Dale excelled at basketball. They graduated together, enlisted together, had one tour together, and then were separated and assigned to different ships. Both Dale and Bill ended their careers with their own command. They joined together, but Bill got out fifteen days earlier, as Dale was still not back in port, due to Dale being at sea when his twenty was up. Dale liked to tease Bill that he was senior because of obtaining the rank first, but two better friends you would not find.

Pris and I became friends out of our marriages to these two men. We became very close friends and shopped together incessantly. We were very different though in almost every detail. I was a tall, natural blonde, and my features were light, including very white skin and blue eyes. Pris, on the other hand, was about the same height but with dark hair and eyes and light golden skin.

When Dale retired, my present to him was the yacht. He had no idea of the rather elaborate surprise I had planned for him. My family was quite wealthy, but Dale would never accept any large gifts or money from them. I, on the other hand, was quite used to receiving gifts from my parents. Dale sailed almost from the time he could walk and currently had a fifteen-footer docked at Miller's Pier. I decided I wanted to get him a new boat, but that would require Daddy's help. So my father and I researched and found the best sailboat builder in the country. We commissioned the building of the yacht, and I worked out every detail of our little surprise. So the Saturday after his retirement, I asked Dale if we could go out sailing for the day. Of course Dale never needed much of an excuse, so we drove down to the pier, and as we reached the dock, Dale jammed on the brakes.

"My God, my boat is missing, and some big yacht is anchored there!"

I played along and tried to act shocked while at the same time trying to keep a straight face. I had already sold Dale's old boat, with Dad and the harbormaster's help. We walked down beside this strange yacht moored where Dale's boat should be. He was furious and was about to head off to see the harbormaster when I said in a fake surprised voice, "Dale, look! Up in the sky! It's a bird, it's Superman— no, it's a plane!"

Dale looked skyward, and holding his hand above his eyes to shield the sun, he saw a biplane pulling a banner. He focused on the banner that read, *Happy retirement, Dale.* About the time he looked back at me, Bill, Pris, and all our friends jumped up from the boat, yelling, "Surprise! Surprise!" I threw my arms around his neck and kissed him full on the mouth, then whispered in his ear, "Dale, I love you. Happy retirement, sweetheart!"

He stuttered and stammered for a while until one of his navy buddies pulled out a naval pipe and piped him aboard, most ceremoniously. Dale enjoyed the surprise, and then I introduced him to the owner of the company who had built this beautiful yacht.

"There is one thing not yet finished on your new command, Dale, but I will have it done within a week. I just need from you what you will name her. Then I will have the wooden nameplate made and attached."

Dale looked at me and seemed to be thinking for a moment. Then he turned to the crowd of friends and, after getting their attention, said, "I hereby christen this ship *Rae of Love*, as she is almost as beautiful a ship as my wife is a woman!"

CHAPTER 1
AN IDEA WAS BORN

Later that night after all the celebrating and glad-handing was over, I invited Pris and Bill over to our house for a nightcap. That was when we came up with the idea of a sailing trip to Hawaii and back. The idea would develop into a real plan for adventure. This would be the maiden voyage of the *Rae*. Over the following two weeks, we thoroughly planned our trip and set the date to set sail. The nameplate was attached, and we took the weekends to give the *Rae* a couple of good shakedown runs. On the first night, I whispered to Dale, "I can't wait to make love on the deck tonight." He looked at me with devilment in his eyes and smiled. It was our secret tradition on the first outing of the season or a new boat to make love topside under the stars. So that first night we anchored about ten miles out, cooked some sea bass, and drank wine with our friends, Bill and Pris. Afterward, we went below, and when Dale and I felt that they were asleep, we snuck topside and fulfilled our tradition. I couldn't have been happier, and Dale seemed to be feeling the same. Our lovemaking was spectacular. Maybe it was the night air, maybe the new boat, or maybe a combination, but for me I think it was knowing that I wouldn't spend any more nights alone like I did when Dale was at sea.

The next morning, we sailed down the coast and then back home by nightfall. The following weekend, we went out again, and once again the ship preformed wonderfully. Now it was just a matter of getting the right weather conditions, and we were off.

Pris was the only one still working, and she had a month of vacation time accrued and the type of job, supervisor at the main motor vehicle department, that would allow her to take it all at one time. Dale and Bill had both earned their real-estate licenses before retiring and planned to work for another navy buddy who had retired five years earlier and now owned a RE/MAX real estate franchise in the San Diego suburbs, the most successful real-estate firm in the area. The boys planned to team up and work with military families only. It was not that we necessarily needed the money, but I knew Dale would get bored with nothing to do. Bill likely felt the same.

Finally the time came. All the plans had been made, and all the provisions were stowed. Every detail was worked out and every contingency planned for. The boat's motor was finely tuned, and her tanks were full. We had more than enough provisions to reach our destination. This was to be a trip of pure pleasure, and we were not going to have it ruined by some stupid miscalculation. This was to be the trip of a lifetime, and we allocated a month for it, but we were opened to extending it if all were in agreement. Pris said that if her employer wouldn't grant her extra time off, she'd quit.

We cast off at dawn on Friday and sailed off with the sun chasing us. The excitement on board was like we were kids on Christmas morning. We enjoyed the sun, the wind, and the surf lapping against the side of the hull as she sliced her way through the relatively calm ocean. The sun rose behind us, caught up to us, and then passed us and as it began to sink into the ocean. We lowered and secured the sails and dropped anchor. We cast out a few lines to see if we could catch some fresh fish to cook for dinner. We ended up with two sea bass and a decent-sized grouper. Pris and I fixed the side dishes while Dale and Bill cleaned the main course. We ate dinner topside, drank some wine, and then went to sleep. Dale and I decided to sleep topside, and the cool night air required us to use a two person-sleeping bag, which I didn't mind at all. We slipped out of our clothes and into the sleeping bag. The clear night and the reflection of the moon allowed just enough light to let us enjoy the sight of each other's bodies. The repetitive slapping of the waves against the hull caused a slight rolling motion of the *Rae,* and the smell of the salt air set a euphoria that was like an aphrodisiac. Dale always said how he loved to look at and feel my soft, beautiful skin—his words, not mine. I nibbled at his neck as he fondled my body. Finally the foreplay had reached the point that neither of us could withstand anymore, and our bodies melted together in pure exotica. It was familiar yet almost as exciting as the very first time. Dale and I always enjoyed being out on the ocean, but this was the beginning of the longest trip ever, save his tours on the big naval vessels.

The next day began at sunrise. Watches were of no use and were stowed for the duration of the cruise. We would live by the movement of the sun. One of the guys was usually first up, and coffee was always ready by the time I was up. As I poured myself some coffee, Dale remarked, "I saw a red sky this morning, so we may get some rain today."

"You still buying into that old theory? This will be a good day to test it. Now the saying goes, *Red sky at night, sailor's delight; red sky by morning, sailors take warning.*"

"Yes, Bill, and I have been right much more often than not, and you know that."

"Rae, do you believe your husband's theory about the color of the sky and the weather it predicts?"

"I don't know, Bill. He seems to get it right. What are we in for, dear?"

"Oh, I was telling ol' Bill here that we might get some rain today."

"Hey, how is one supposed to get their beauty sleep with all this noise up here?" Pris said, yawning as she came up the ladder from the sleeping quarters below.

"Here, dear. Have some coffee," Bill said as he kissed her cheek.

"Ouch. Wow, dear, you need a shave. Your whiskers are like sandpaper!"

"Aye, aye, boss lady."

"See that, Rae? He's well trained, isn't he?"

"Why, yes he is, Pris. And just how did you do that?"

"Just say no a few times, and they fall right into line."

Pris and I laughed while the fake laughs from our counterparts were purely sarcastic.

I then suggested we eat and get under way. Bill came back with that "Aye, aye, boss lady" and a silly salute.

Dale slapped him on the back. "Bill, you gotta knock off that aye, aye boss lady shit before they start to believe it!"

Breakfast had already been started, so we ate, talked, and joked around until the boys disappeared to topside, leaving Pris and me to clean up. Shortly after they went topside, we could feel the ship beginning to move, so Pris and I finished our chores and joined them.

It was a gorgeous morning, and with a strong breeze at our backs, we sailed on. However, as morning turned to midafternoon, the seas became a bit choppy, and we could smell the rain that was coming. Within an hour, we were in a heavy downpour. It only lasted about an hour, and the squall passed on. The wind quieted down a bit, and the mainsail was then raised again.

"Well, Bill, once again the old adage about the red sky comes true. You'd think by now you'd have learned."

"Dumb luck, ole buddy. Just dumb luck."

At sunset, we dropped anchor and brought in all sails.

While the gals fixed dinner, Bill slipped below deck, and when he returned, everyone began to laugh. Bill had gone below to shave, and his aftershave hit the air like an aerosol spray that had just been released. Bill raised his hands palms up and shrugged his shoulders.

"What!" he barked.

Everyone laughed even harder.

"Guess you're looking for a yes tonight, right?" I said, laughing still.

"Hey, my mamma didn't raise no fool!"

Pris apparently wanted to get him off the hook, so she kissed his cheek and said, "It was I who wanted a yes, so I asked him to do it for me. Isn't he just the sweetest?"

So far, the trip had been spectacular. We ate, drank, and talked until the night sky was full of stars. The *Rae* swayed from side to side in the gentle waves and smacked in rhythm against the sides of her. The soft warm breezes made this a most wonderful night at sea. Tonight it was Bill and Pris's turn to sleep topside. The entire scene was cause for romance and a night where the entire crew enjoyed the romantic pleasures of marriage.

Day three started off like the day before. But by late afternoon, we ran into another squall. This one came up quickly, and the rain and wind pounded the smallish yacht. The boys likely wished they were in something bigger, like what they commanded in the navy. But Dale stayed topside after they had dropped all sails and lashed them securely. The main thing now was to keep the *Rae* pointed into the waves. It was times like this that a seasoned sailor was worth his weight in gold. If this boat got parallel to the waves, she could capsize and sink. Finally we could see the sun again sinking slowly in the west as the wind and rain disappeared. We decided that since it would be dark in an hour or so, we'd anchor for the night.

Suddenly Bill yelled, "Land ho!"

We started to laugh, and I said, "What was that, Captain Kid?"

Bill pointed to a small island, and we all agreed to anchor near it and explore it the next morning. This island wasn't expected, as it didn't show on our map, presumably because it was so small. Dale dropped anchor about three hundred yards from shore; he didn't want to risk running aground. The sunset was beautiful, and the palm trees on this tiny island added a touch of scenery and a distraction from the vast open ocean. That dinner was great and the conversation with good friends even better. We were so happy about this little island that it took up a lot of our conversation. We speculated on what we might find there, hoping like most folks to find some buried treasure. This would give us an opportunity to try out the new metal detectors we had on board. A slightly stronger breeze came up, and a squall was heading our way, so we cleared the deck, tied down loose items, and headed below.

CHAPTER 2
VISITORS

The sound of the rain and the gentle rolling of the boat had me asleep in short order, only to be awakened by some unfamiliar noises. It sounded like people walking on deck and at least two men talking. I quickly woke Dale. A moment after Dale had just finished saying it was nothing, the door came flying open, and the bright light of a flashlight blinded us. This unknown person then turned on the lights in the room, revealing a large grotesque-looking man standing before us with a shotgun. He demanded that Dale stand and walk toward him. Then he ordered him to turn around, and he tied his wrists with a large plastic strap. I could hear a loud male voice coming from the cabin next to us where Pris and Bill were, and I assumed the same thing was happening in there. The man told me to stay put as he took Dale out of the cabin. The other man must have been taking Bill out as well, as I heard Bill say something to Dale before one of the men told them to shut up.

I heard them going up the ladder, and I quickly dressed before he returned. I'm not naïve; I was fairly sure what was to follow. I ran to Pris's room, and she was sobbing uncontrollably. I told her to dress quickly and settle down. We needed a plan. Pris was shaking so badly I wasn't sure how much help she could be, but she quieted down and dressed. I searched her cabin for any kind of weapon but found none. "Now stay here and try to be quiet. I'm going to my cabin to find something we can use to defend ourselves." She didn't want me to leave, so I slapped her and told her to try to get a grip. We needed to protect ourselves. I didn't tell her what I thought they would do with us when she asked, as I knew she would really lose it. I told her they were likely sea pirates here to rob us.

I looked around our cabin but found nothing to use. I knew there was a flare gun, but it was topside where the men were. I could hear them rummaging around, and I figured they were stealing everything of value they could lay their hands on. I went back to Pris when my search revealed nothing useful. It wasn't long before they were below deck, and I could see them occasionally as they passed by the cabin door. At one point, the other man, who was equally as grotesque, came into my room, smiled at me with his mouth of missing teeth, and then bagged all our small valuables, including our jewelry and watches. He even demanded my wedding and engagement rings and then said, "See ya soon." He grinned and walked out.

I wondered what they had done to Dale. Things seemed to get quiet, and I wondered what was next. It wasn't long before I had my answer. I head a cabin door slam and then Pris screaming at the top of her lungs. I ran and locked my door. The screaming was replaced my moaning. I knew what was happening and was certain it would be my fate as well. Finally I heard someone try the door. Then it was quiet, followed by a crashing sound as this huge ugly man kicked in the door. He stood there grinning; it was the man who had initially stormed in on Dale and me. He undressed completely in front of me; he was hairy like an ape and fat with a big belly. The sight almost made me puke. He walked toward me with his penis beginning to become erect. He ripped off the sheet I had covered myself with and seemed disappointed that I was dressed; perhaps he noticed that I wasn't when he barged in. He began to growl like an animal as he came toward me. He grabbed the front of my shirt and literally ripped it off my body. He went back to wear his clothes lay in a pile on the floor and retrieved a knife. I was sure he would kill me. He put the flat of the blade against my throat and just grinned. I couldn't stop the tears that I felt running down my cheeks. Then he stuck the blade under my bra and cut it off. I was so scared I could hardly get my breath. Next came the removing of my shorts and panties. There I was, stark naked in front of an ugly stranger who was about to take from me something that I had given to only one other man besides Dale. I wondered what the right thing to do was. Just lay still and let him do whatever he wanted, or should I fight with every ounce of strength within me? If he did what I knew he would, should I want to die, and should I fight until he kills me? Maybe having him do it to me dead was better. But no, I didn't have the courage to die. I rationalized that letting him do me was better than dying. So as he kneeled on the bed, I closed my eyes as tightly as I could and opened my legs. He smelled like dead fish; it made me gag. I felt him push himself inside me; he was big and rough. His weight was almost unbearable, his stench was unbelievable, and his coarse beard rubbing against my neck and face felt like someone was sandpapering it. He huffed, and the sounds were disgusting.

Strangely, after a while I didn't care anymore. He was finally making sounds as if he were ready to ejaculate, and I could tell he was trying to hold it back as long as possible. Finally when he did, snot flew from his nose all over my face, and when he finished, he just let his dead weight collapse on me. I couldn't support his weight. "I can't breathe! I can't breathe!" I was shouting as loudly as I could but could hardly make a sound. It seemed he didn't care. I went limp and was just about to black out when the pig finally rolled off me. I felt like someone held under water until the absolute last second. I almost wished I had died right there, right then. I didn't know it at that moment, but there was more, lots more to come.

After a while, the man got out of my bed and dressed. He walked to the door and turned back, wagging his fat finger at me. "Stay here and behave, or I tie and gag ya." When I couldn't hear the two of them talking, I ran to Pris in spite of his warning, and we cried together. The guy with her had cut her cheek, and I had to clean and dress the wound. The fact they didn't tie us up surprised me. Guess they figured two women wouldn't be a threat, especially after they had their way with us. I could hear them talking, but what they were saying was not clear. After a while, I didn't hear them talking, and I hoped at that moment, feeling a lift in my spirits as I though they had left. After all, they had taken all they wanted.

I lost track of time, but suddenly I felt the boat moving. Perhaps we were free and heading away from them. I ran topside and saw we were under way, but it was the man who raped Pris that was piloting the *Rae*, and I could see a slightly larger yacht following. We sailed out into open water far from the island; in fact it wasn't long before land was out of sight. The man turn into the wind to stop the boat, and the other boat pulled alongside. I ran to the bow and found Dale and Bill tied to the rails of the bow with their hands and feet still bound. They were both bloody, as they had been beaten severely. "I demand you tell me what the hell you are going to do with us!"

He laughed. "Just watch, dearie." He continued to laugh as the other man disappeared below deck of the *Rae*. Within ten minutes or so, he was back on deck and demanded Pris and I go aboard their ship. We protested, but he just snatched me up and literally tossed me into the arms of the other man on board their ship. Pris then came over voluntarily.

They began to eat and drink as we sat there wondering what the hell they were up to. Pris and I hugged each other for comfort while watching our husbands. After a while, I noticed that the *Rae* seemed to be setting lower in the water and the bow seemed higher than the stern. "What the hell?" They must have heard my utterance, as they began to laugh again.

"What's the matter, dearie?"

"You bastards! You scuttled her? Our husbands are on board! You can't just let them drown!"

"You want to save them? Go save them." Again they laughed. Pris dropped to her knees sobbing, but I was mad. I didn't hesitate. I dove into the water and swam for the *Rae* as fast as I could. There was no ladder over the side of her, but by now the stern was in the water. I climbed on board and ran to the guys. They were chained to the rail and padlocked. I frantically scurried about, looking for something with which to break open the lock or bust the railing. I found a small piece of pipe and began trying to break the lock, first Dale's and then Bill's. If I could just get one of them free, he could help free the other. Pris came on board, but she was little help. Bill said, "Pris, go to the radio, and send out an SOS!" She disappeared below deck and quickly returned, saying the radio was gone. She did find a larger pipe, and we both kept prying on the locks and rails, each being instructed by our husbands on how to best do it. Water was now pouring into the lower deck; she couldn't stay afloat much longer. Dale began imploring us to get off before we got caught and drowned. "You can't die because we do. Go! Go now! Go!" Those were the last words Dale spoke as the bow slipped under the sea, pulling Pris and me with it, but she let go. I decided that I would rather die than allow that fat bastard to wallow on me again. Dale kept shaking his head violently. I kissed him on the lips and let go. My lungs felt like they would burst as I fought to reach the surface, but I was deeper than I thought. I swam upward with all my might, and when I couldn't hold my breath any longer, I broke the surface, gasping and sucking in as much air as I could. Pris grabbed me and held me; we both cried violently as our men were now dead.

CHAPTER 3
DECISION TIME

The *Rae* and our husbands were gone. The other boat motored toward us. One man yelled, "Were you able to save them?" And again they laughed. I don't know which I wanted more, to die or kill him. To kill him, I would have to have sex with him. How else could I get close enough? The thought of enduring that again made my stomach retch. But the more my mind raced, the more it seemed like what I had to do. The boat stopped near us, and they threw a ladder over the side.

There was nothing more that could be done for our husbands except extract revenge or die trying. Pris was a great gal, but I couldn't chance her knowing what I wanted to do. However, I had to get us back aboard that boat. "Come on, Pris. Let's get on board."

"No way. I would rather die first."

"There is nothing more we can do for the guys, but unless we get aboard, we are nothing but shark bait." I knew how deathly afraid of sharks she was.

"I don't see any sharks."

"It's more likely you will feel them before you see them."

She swam to the ladder, and I was right behind her. My anger blocked out their disgusting appearances, and I focused on my revenge.

Back on board, we quickly discovered there were two other men aboard her, a mate and a cook. These were definitely all birds of a feather. The mate showed us to a cabin below and told us to stay there until told otherwise. I now knew this was most likely a suicide mission, but I didn't care. I wanted my hatred for these lowlife scums to remain peaked. If somehow I could kill the two men who did all this, I could die happy, and frankly, I couldn't see life without Dale anyway.

Pris was a mess. She lay on the bed and cried herself to sleep. I couldn't sleep. I had to find a weapon and figure out how to get these two men. We sailed for hours, and then I felt the boat stop and begin to rock with the waves. I looked out and saw the sun was setting. Shortly after we anchored, the mate brought us food and drink. Approximately an hour later, the door burst open, and there they were, my two targets. "Hope you ladies enjoyed your meals?" Everything they said seemed to be followed by mocking laughter. "Oh, what's this? Someone didn't eat their meal?"

"Pris wasn't feeling well, but I ate mine."

"Well, maybe a good romp in the sack will help." With that, the man who had taken her before grabbed her arm. "See you later, brother." Again with the laughter, and he dragged her crying and fighting out of the room.

The other bastard started my way and began peeling clothes again. When he reached the side of the bed, now naked, I held up my hand in a stop motion. "You don't have to ruin my clothes again." And I stripped and lay back down. I wanted him to drop his guard, so I just let him do his thing. When he finished and rolled his blubber off me, he fell asleep. Oh, I wished I had a weapon. I rolled my back to him and cried softly. Somewhere in the middle of the night, the other man coming in the room awakened me. "Hey, bro, time to trade."

"Okay, sounds good." But before he could get up, I rolled over and wrapped my arm around him and whispered in his ear that I wanted to stay with him. I promised to be real good to him if he kept me.

"Sorry, George. Seems the little lady wants only me. I'm sure you can understand that."

"Paul, you're a real prick. We always share."

"Not this time, little brother. Not this time." George stormed out, slamming the door behind him. I obviously had the man in charge, and he would be my first victim.

I played up to him, even voluntarily gave him oral sex. It was the most fowl deed I had ever done, but I had to get free run of the ship as quickly as possible. The next morning, I kissed him passionately, and he took me again. My body no longer mattered. I used it like a tool to get what I had to have, my revenge. I would most likely die anyway, so I was nothing unless I killed him. That was all that mattered to me now.

After he left, I went to find Pris and took her back to our room. She was near catatonic. She didn't cry, she didn't talk, and she just stared out into space. I put her in the bed and, after a shower, began to roam the ship. The mate made a fuss, but Paul was captain and ordered him to leave me alone. I wandered around, subtly looking for a good weapon. Finally I found it—an ice pick, and a big one at that. I smuggled it back to my room and hid it under my side of the bunk. I knew he'd come for me again tonight, and I would be ready for him. I stayed out of the men's way as much as possible and slept when I could. Finally the boat stopped, waking me. I knew dinner would be here soon, and then he would come in expecting his nightly session. This time I'd give him an unexpected surprise.

I was only able to get a little soup into Pris, and then they came. George made a last-ditch effort to trade partners, but Paul held his ground. After George dragged Pris away, I began to strip in a seductive manor. He quickly undressed and was all over me again with his stinking, smelly body, penetrating me violently. I didn't care. I even pretended to enjoy the sex, but inside deep inside me, I knew what would soon happen. I would have my revenge. He climaxed and rolled over on his back and was soon asleep. It wasn't long before he rolled onto his side and away from me. Perfect. I quietly reached for the pick and panicked when I couldn't find it. I eased myself out of bed and looked under the bunk. It had moved somehow. I secured it and eased back into bed. I had seen this in a movie and hoped it would work. I put the point of the pick behind his ear and with all my strength jammed it upward, hoping to hit his brain and kill him without a sound. A slight moan, and he was gone. He rolled slightly forward, apparently relieving any muscle tension. I didn't know exactly how it worked; I just hoped it had. I thought about the movies—when you think the bad guy is dead and then he jumps up behind you. I decided to play it safe, so I walked around and pushed him to his back. Then I raised the pick above my head with both hands and slammed it into his heart. I must admit it felt good. Then I thought about George and instantly knew what to do. I slipped down the hall to the cabin where I'd found Pris that morning. George was asleep. I reached quietly into my robe pocket for the pick. As soon as I wrapped my fingers around it, he opened his eyes. I didn't panic. "Your brother is asleep. Now is your chance, if you want it." He looked at me strangely, like he wasn't interested. I panicked. What if he wouldn't take me? What if he was too afraid of his brother and got up to tell him and discovered what I had done? I quickly pulled open my robe and showed him my body in the dim cabin light. Still he didn't respond like I expected, but he didn't stop me either. So I let my opened robe slip slowly to the floor, slid in beside him, and began to massage his penis. He quickly became erect. I kissed him and pushed my breasts into his chest, and he began to moan softly. He was strong like his brother and rolled on top of me to penetrate me. Like his brother, he smelled bad, he was heavy, and he was not at all gentle. But soon the moment came, and he did likewise. He pushed me onto the floor and whispered, "Happy now? Take your whoring ass back to my brother before he wakes up, and if you breathe a word of this to him, I'll kill you slowly."

I reached for my robe, slipped it on, and with my back to him retrieved the ice pick from the pocket. I then turned with my hand behind my back. "Sure you don't want a little more before I go?" He was lying there with his hands folded behind his head. He never got a chance to respond as once again I quickly raised the pick above my head with both hands and drove it into his heart. He lunged for me with the pick still in his chest and missed, falling to the floor. He then pulled the pick from his chest and tried to stand. I backed into the wall. I was sure I was dead, but before he could get to his feet, he collapsed. I dropped to my knees and sobbed. I had done it. I had endured all the humiliation and abuse but ultimately killed my husband's killers. The job wasn't finished; there were two more men, each capable of putting Pris and me through the same torture or just killing us. I had to do it—and quickly, before they woke. I pried the pick from his fat fingers and went to find them. The first mate was asleep on deck, and I was getting good with the ice pick. I jammed it into his heart area and pulled away quickly with the pick in my hand. He stood, took a step toward me, and then fell to his knees and then on his face. I kicked his head. No reaction. He was dead.

Only one man left on board, the cook. He was an older man and didn't seem all that strong. I heard him; he was up early and in the galley. I was on a killing high; I guess that's why I went for him with reckless abandon. I walked into the galley. He must have heard me. I was behind him with the pick raised high in the ready-to-kill position.

"No! No, don't! I'm a captive here just like you!" I stopped and stared at him as he fell to his knees sobbing. I lowered the ice pick. The nightmare was over, but I'd lost the love of my life.

THE END ... I REALLY THINK IT IS ... FOR NOW.

Printed in the United States
By Bookmasters